ARCH'S FLAPJACKS

¼ cup small-curd cottage cheese

2 tablespoons vegetable oil
(preferably safflower or canola)

1 ½ cups all-purpose flour

2 teaspoons baking powder

½ teaspoon baking soda

½ teaspoon salt

1 tablespoon granulated sugar (optional)

Additional vegetable oil or clarified butter

Butter, maple syrup, and/or fruit preserves

Whirl cottage cheese in blender. In a large bowl, beat together the eggs, buttermilk, and oil. Stir in the cottage cheese and set aside.

Sift together the flour, baking powder, baking soda, salt, and sugar, if using. Add to egg mixture and stir with a large wooden spoon just until combined. If mixture is too thick, add 2 to 3 tablespoons more buttermilk.

Heat a tablespoon of oil or clarified butter on a griddle or in a skillet over medium heat until the oil ripples. For each flapjack, pour in a bit less than ¼ cup batter. Cook flapjack until it is covered with bubbles and dry around the edges. Turn and cook the other side until it is golden brown.

Serve immediately with butter and toppings.

Makes 9 four-inch flapjacks

A banquet of praise for
DIANE MOTT DAVIDSON
and her latest *New York Times* bestseller
FATALLY FLAKY

"Master of the culinary whodunit."
Houston Chronicle

"[A] great cozy mystery writer."
Green Bay Press-Gazette

"Davidson is one of the few authors who have been able to seamlessly stir in culinary scenes without losing the focus of the mystery. . . . [She] has made the culinary mystery more than just a passing phase."
Ft. Lauderdale Sun-Sentinel

"Most readers scarf up every course she serves up and keep asking for more. . . . It's like sitting down with a hot cup of tea; always welcome."
Denver Post

"One can't ignore the irresistible pull of her recipes."
Lincoln Journal Star (Ne.)

FATALLY FLAKY

DIANE MOTT DAVIDSON

AVON
An Imprint of HarperCollinsPublishers

This book is a work of fiction. The characters, incidents, and dialogue are drawn from the author's imagination and are not to be construed as real. Any resemblance to actual events or persons, living or dead, is entirely coincidental.

AVON BOOKS
An Imprint of HarperCollins*Publishers*
10 East 53rd Street
New York, New York 10022-5299

Copyright © 2009 by Diane Mott Davidson
ISBN 978-0-06-134814-3
www.avonbooks.com

First Avon Books paperback printing: April 2010
First William Morrow hardcover printing: April 2009

Avon Trademark Reg. U.S. Pat. Off. and in Other Countries, Marca Registrada, Hecho en U.S.A.
HarperCollins® is a registered trademark of HarperCollins Publishers.

Printed in the U.S.A.

10 9 8 7 6 5 4 3 2 1

To Carolyn Marino

with deep gratitude for excellent editing
and for possessing a kind heart and a light touch

Life does not cease to be funny when people die any more than it ceases to be serious when people laugh.

—George Bernard Shaw

BRIDEZILLA BILLIE'S
WEDDING RECEPTION MENU

Aspen Meadow, Colorado
For her wedding on June 8, no, July 15,
no, August 22

Grilled Artichoke Skewers with Rémoulade

Deviled Eggs with Caviar

Crab Cakes with Sauce Gribiche

New-Potato Salad with Fresh Dill and Crème

Fraîche

Chilled Haricots Verts Vinaigrette

Baguettes and Butter

Chocolate and Vanilla Ice Creams

Wedding Cake

Chapter 1

Cynics say getting married is a death wish.

Now, I'm no Pollyanna, but I try to ignore cynics. Anyway, what I usually say is that *catering* weddings is a death wish. My assistant, twenty-two-year-old Julian Teller, and I laugh at that. Yucking it up provides a bit of comic relief within the stress of serving trays of appetizers with drinks, then lunch or dinner with wine, followed by cake with champagne or Asti Spumante—and doing it all quickly—to a hundred guests. Trust me: if there's one thing caterers need at weddings, it's comic relief.

Unfortunately, the events surrounding Bridezilla Billie Attenborough's wedding proved the truth of the original axiom. Still, it wasn't a death wish that proved troublesome. It was death itself. And as the bodies piled up around the Attenborough nuptials, I began to think someone was gunning for me, too.

Turned out, I was right.

* * *

I'm always telling my husband, Tom, an investigator with the Furman County Sheriff's Department, that I should adore weddings. The reason? I love being married—to him, that is. With his mountain-man build, handsome face, jauntily parted cider-colored hair, and eyes as green as a faraway sea, he's not only kind and loving—he's gorgeous.

"You're prejudiced," he says.

"So what?" I reply. "You're still the greatest."

"There are any number of criminals in our state penal system who would take issue with that assessment."

"I'm not married to one of them."

"Uh-huh."

Actually, having Tom for a husband means I can watch brides and grooms kiss, laugh, and embrace, and I can smile to myself, knowing I'm going home to a great man. So when there are wedding glitches, I remind myself: I'm helping people get married. And by and large, this is a good thing.

Here in Aspen Meadow, Colorado, if someone is going to have a hundred or fewer guests at their ceremony and reception, I'm the caterer of choice, by which I mean, I'm the only caterer you can choose. Our town also has but one florist, one photographer, one printing press—for invitations and the like—and a few bands. But these days, most couples choose a DJ.

Aspen Meadow has one of those, too.

If the bride, groom, or either family wants a bigger celebration, she, he, or they usually do all their own arrangements, and have their wedding down in Denver, forty miles to the east. There, you can hire a wedding planner, book a fancy venue, and have your pick of caterers, stationers, florists, even chocolatiers. If you go that route, though, you're going to pay. What with the gown, limos, and all the rest, you're probably looking at about a hundred grand.

I can remember when a hundred grand used to buy a house. And a nice one, too.

But for a hundred or fewer guests, I can do all the arranging. Once I'm given a budget and specifics as to menu, flowers, photographer, music, you name it, I draw up a detailed contract, then get signatures, along with a down payment. After that, I call the vendors, set the schedule, and arrange deliveries. Any changes to the contract mean big bucks, so, generally, people are content to leave well enough alone.

But Bridezilla Billie, as I'd come to call her, was never content. Billie's long-suffering mother, Charlotte, was footing the bill—Attenborough *père* having died of a bleeding ulcer long ago—and Billie seemed not to care that every single new arrangement she was demanding was costing hundreds, if not thousands, of dollars.

"It won't be a problem," Billie would say breezily, each time she called in April, then May, then June, to say we absolutely had to have lunch so she could talk about new things she wanted. "We can just put all this on my tab."

And then I would arrive at the appointed time, at whatever place she'd said she wanted to have lunch.

And she would be late, usually more than an hour late. The reason? She'd say she'd gotten lost, never mind that she'd lived in Aspen Meadow all her life. Or her Mercedes wouldn't start. Or she'd thought we were meeting an hour after when she'd originally said. One time, when she didn't show up at all and I called her house, she said she thought we were meeting the following week.

Billie was, in short, a flake.

Like most of the weddings I cater, Billie's ceremony was taking place in the summer. *Let the weather cheer you up,* I told myself as I typed up contract change after contract change and faxed them through to Charlotte Attenborough.

And so I planned and ordered food, and waited for spring, which at eight thousand feet above sea level, generally doesn't arrive until June. By then, the thick crust of ice on our town's lake has melted. The fresh scent of pollinating pines and newly leafy aspens fills the air. With snow still blanketing the Continental Divide—visible in the distance—the setting is particularly idyllic.

But this summer was different.

"Maybe I should quit doing weddings," I told Tom when Bridezilla Billie stopped insisting we have lunch, and instead started phoning me an average of seventeen times a day. She'd already moved her wedding date twice. The reason? She said she wanted to lose twenty pounds to fit into a new dress she'd just bought. She claimed she was working with Victor Lane out at Gold Gulch Spa to get into tip-top shape.

Getting into tip-top shape was the euphemism Billie used for trying to sweat off some of her rolls, the kind that had nothing to do with Parker House.

Did I know Victor Lane? Billie asked. Yes, I began, but she tossed her highlighted blond hair over her shoulder, helped herself to the Key Lime Pie I'd left on the counter, and cut me off just as she placed an enormous piece of pie on a plate in front of herself. Once she'd forked up a mouthful, she was eager to provide me with an update on embroidery that was being added to the waist of the new dress. Then I heard about the seed pearls that were being sewn into the train, and the lace now edging the veil.

Aside from myself, I'll tell you who I had sympathy for: her dressmaker.

"Why do you put up with her?" asked Jack Carmichael, my godfather, who had moved to Aspen Meadow from New Jersey in February. "I mean, I'm going out with Charlotte, and I can barely stand to listen to Billie for a New York minute."

"I feel sorry for Billie," I said.

Jack raised his gray eyebrows and did one of his energetic little waltzes around my kitchen. "You want to feel sorry for someone, make it her poor mother. You're too kind, Gertie Girl."

Gertie Girl was the nickname Jack had always used for me. It was short for Gertrude, my real name. Jack didn't like the name Goldy, he'd told me when I was very small. It had been one of the times he'd shown up without warning at our house, laden with gift bags full of books, puzzles, and games. He always loved to pose riddles to me, too. "What word appeared when So met Imes?" he asked when I was five. After a moment, I shrieked, "Sometimes!" which had caused him to erupt in gales of laughter.

"I learned kindness from you," I replied, when he stopped dancing around my kitchen. In addition to all the goodies Jack had always bestowed on me, he'd written me letters when I was away at school. And he'd sympathized with me when I was trying to get out of my first marriage, to an abusive doctor, now deceased, thank God.

To me, Jack was the model of the perfect godfather, which I told him often.

In my kitchen now, he hugged me, and I handed him a batch of the salty fried pecans I'd made for him and his new drinking buddy, a recently retired, much-loved local physician named Harold Finn. They relished the pecans with their scotch. I invited them over often, but they seldom came. Sometimes I worried that the nuts were the only food the two of them ate.

Well. No matter how many contract changes I was forced to make for Billie Attenborough, I kept telling myself to be patient. At age thirty-six, Billie was getting married for the first time, after two broken engagements. Unfortunately, Billie held an intense dislike for my godfather's pal, Doc Finn, and never tired of telling me how awful he was. According to Billie, Doc Finn had told both of her ex-fiancés—one with gastritis, the other with migraines—that they needed to break off their engagements to her. Since this didn't sound like any medical advice I'd ever heard, I asked Doc Finn about it. The kindly, white-haired general practitioner had rubbed his goatee thoughtfully, then looked at me over his half-glasses. He'd said that while he couldn't comment on any particular patient, he was in favor of everyone lowering levels of stress.

Now I knew what Doc Finn was talking about. Stress? *Stress?* I'd gotten to dreaming that I was throwing Billie off the nearest mountaintop. Too bad Doc Finn had hung up his stethoscope: I needed him to treat me for Billie-induced insanity. As I kneaded bread for the small baguettes Billie had insisted be served at her reception—instead of the croissants she'd demanded initially, or the corn bread muffins she'd wanted the second time around—I wondered how difficult it would be to dial 911 with a tray in my hand once I began to have the symptoms of a heart attack.

At least Billie was happy in love, I reflected. In fact, by her account, she was ecstatic, head over heels, and had found her true soul mate with her intended, a man eight years her junior, a newly minted general practitioner named Craig Miller.

Miller, quiet, good looking, with round horn-rimmed specs and an easy smile, had recently joined Spruce Medical Group to replace Doc Finn. Once, during a particularly excruciating lunch, Billie was again critical of Doc Finn, saying everyone knew he was senile and incompetent, and it was long past time for him to be replaced. Craig had joined us for this meal, and he calmly told Billie that Doc Finn had been a great asset to the community. Back when Spruce Medical Group was a small practice located in an old office building on Upper Cottonwood Creek Road, Finn had spent hours listening to, and talking to, patients who adored him. She should be kinder toward him. Billie had immediately shut up, and I wanted to ask Craig if he could come to all our lunches.

I kept telling myself, *Stay calm, stay calm, stay calm.* Eons ago, I'd majored in psychology, which had its uses in the catering biz. Billie just hadn't learned how to get along with people, I told myself. Even though she graduated from college, she'd never held a regular job. She'd been jilted by two fiancés; maybe she'd imagined them critiquing everything about her, and that was why her chief occupation in life was criticizing people. But I couldn't find a reason for what to me was Billie's main problem: the flakiness. Yes, she got lost; yes, she couldn't keep track of her calendar. But she'd also completely changed her menu six times.

Each time she changed the menu, she gave oddball reasons such as, "Oh, I tasted shrimp cocktail at the Pardee wedding, and knew we couldn't have it, too, because some of the guests would be the same. So I want calamari." When I told Billie's mother what that would cost, the menu was quietly changed to include deviled eggs topped with a spoonful of caviar. But then there was, "Last night Craig and I had a chicken satay at a Thai restaurant in Denver; could you make us a satay, but with duck?" Duck satay? Charlotte vetoed that one, too. But finally, Billie whined, "C'mon, it wouldn't be that much trouble for you to roast three or four suckling pigs, would it? You could dig the roasting pit outside your house." Right. Charlotte also vetoed the roasting pit, thank God.

"I'm giving up weddings," I told Tom, when I came home from that particular lunch.

Tom sagely commented, "Then you'd go nuts."

"I'm there, Tom. I'm totally bonkers. First I waited for her for two hours while she was lost trying to find the restaurant, and then she hit me with the roast suckling porkers."

Tom said, "Uh-oh."

"Billie Attenborough's wedding is killing me."

"Aw, you always say that."

"This time I mean it."

Chapter 2

The morning of August the twentieth dawned with rain, again, the same as we'd had since the month began. It was two days before Billie's twice-postponed nuptials. From our bedroom window, I looked out ruefully at the downpour. I had another wedding to cater today, Cecelia, aka Ceci, O'Neal's. Rain meant that the guests wouldn't be able to mingle outside, and we'd have the added problem of sixty raincoats to store.

I shook my head. It was a perplexing summer, weather wise. Even if the Colorado forecasters call July and sometimes August "monsoon season," the rain usually arrives in the late afternoon. And anyway, the term "monsoon season" is a laugh in itself, since we generally get an annual average of thirteen inches of rain. (Ten inches of snow equals one inch of rain, and we'd already had a winter featuring twelve total feet of snow. "You do the math," my sixteen-year-old son Arch had commented. To which I'd replied, "No, thanks.")

Still, three weeks of unremitting, incessant downpour was uncharacteristic. The New Age people over in Boulder would have said that all of Billie Attenborough's nutty behavior had brought on the bad weather. When I told Tom that interpretation, he pulled me in for a hug and whispered, "At least we know who to blame."

The Friday morning of Ceci's wedding, I decided that the first order of business was to take a freshly made sweet bread, richly studded with dried apricots, dried cranberries, and toasted pecans, across the street to my godfather. At fifty-eight, Jack was, by his own admission, a "recovering lawyer." Retiring from his practice, he said, and suffering through two heart attacks, had made him want to be closer to his son, Lucas, who had lived for over a decade on the other side of Aspen Meadow. But really, Jack had confided to me, he missed being a part of my life.

"And anyway," Jack admitted, "it's best for Lucas and me if we take each other in small doses. I know he's my son, but I'm telling the truth. I mean, after he got divorced, I paid for him to go to physician's assistant school. And when he graduated, what did he do? Told me to stop smoking and drinking. That's gratitude for you."

"You *should* stop drinking and smoking," I immediately countered.

Jack snorted. "You, too?"

To Lucas Carmichael's further dismay, Jack had not moved close to him when he'd moved to our town. Instead, Jack had bought a dilapidated mansion across the street from us. The house was a sixty-year-old Victorian-style monstrosity that had served as an inn, a restaurant, and a bar, all pretty much unsuccessfully. Now the old Painted Lady was in something of a state of disrepair, and Jack, a multimillionaire who confessed to knowing next to nothing about remodeling, was cheerfully bending his staccato energies to hiring people to fix up the place.

"Hey, Gertie Girl." Jack opened his newly sculpted oak door—one of the things he'd actually managed to get subcontracted and completed since he'd been here. "It's good to see you so early."

"I brought you something, Jack."

"You're wonderful."

"I just worry about you eating right."

"Don't you start." He peered out at the mailbox at the end of his driveway. "You bring me my mail from yesterday? I was a bit too trashed last night to get it."

"No, but I can—"

"Oh, Goldy, are you here again?" whined Lucas, who was standing behind his father. Lucas, who was about thirty, had a face like an inverted triangle—a broad, pale forehead, wide-set blue eyes, and a pointed chin—and that face reminded me, as it usually did, of a mouse having just recovered from a near drowning. He frowned at me. "Jack said you were catering a wedding today."

Jack said gently, "Goldy can bring me bread if she wants to, Lucas."

Lucas brushed back his blond bangs, then shoved his hands into the pockets of his rumpled jeans. "Well, I hope that it's not filled with ingredients that are bad for you." Lucas and I had always had an uneasy relationship. To me, he'd always seemed somewhat wretched, and no matter how many times I'd tried to be nice to him, he'd always held me at arm's length. I worried that Lucas was jealous of my relationship with Jack, and Jack moving in across the street from us hadn't eased that apprehension.

"Thanks for the bread." Jack took the proffered loaf from my hand. "I'll see you at Ceci's wedding. When does it start?"

"You're coming?" I asked, surprised.

"She adores Doc Finn, and he's an honored guest. I'm riding Finn's coattails to the party."

"Great."

I waved to Lucas and hightailed it out of there, unwilling to deal with Lucas's complaining or desperate-rodent appearance. The old anxiety about Lucas's competitive feelings toward me bloomed as I scampered back across the street. For it wasn't just the puzzles, games, toys, books, and fantastic birthday presents Jack had always given me that made me worry. In a moment of too-much-booze weakness, Jack had confessed to Lucas that I was in a terrible marriage—the one to my first husband, aka the Jerk—and that he, Jack, wanted to help me. Without warning, Jack had given me a large sum of money to get away from the Jerk. When Jack told his son about this, hoping to be congratulated for his generosity, Three Mile Island hadn't had a meltdown to match Lucas's.

Since then, Jack had told me not to tell Lucas about any gifts that came my way. I promised not to, but I still felt uncomfortable.

I ducked through the rain and into our house. In the kitchen, I was surprised to see Tom consulting my printed schedule for Cecelia O'Neal's wedding. Cecelia was due to get married at my conference center at noon.

"What are you doing?" I asked.

Tom raised an eyebrow in my direction, then shuffled to the walk-in, pulled out a box, and brought it to the counter.

"Helping you," he supplied. Tom was ever the master of laconic communication.

"Don't you have to go to work?"

"Got somebody filling in for me."

"Tom, what is going on?"

"Ceci's mother just called." Tom cocked an eyebrow at me. "Her name's Dodie O'Neal?" When I nodded, Tom went on, "It seems her ex-husband is threatening to show up at the wedding. Dodie's hired some security guards. And so I'm going to help you and Julian in the kitchen. When we get over there, I'll explain the situation."

Great, I thought, as Tom and I loaded my van. Two days before the twice-delayed wedding of Bridezilla

Billie, and I had been doing all in my power to put everything dealing with *those* worrisome nuptials out of my mind. What was it about nature, something about it abhorring a vacuum? Now we had a threatened disruption to what had promised to be a fairly straightforward wedding.

"Stay calm." I found myself whispering my new mantra to myself as I piloted my van through the downpour to my event center. Tom, behind me, was driving his own vehicle, in case he was called away by the department. "Stay calm, stay calm," I said again. "See?" I said to no one but myself, since I was alone in the van. "Talking aloud with no one there? I *am* going nuts."

Okay, well, security guards or no, I needed to concentrate on Ceci O'Neal's wedding. Cecelia, unlike Billie, had been easy to deal with. A tall, twenty-five-year-old woman who had a cap of short, black curls, Cecelia was unfailingly kind and gracious. She was also a selfless single mother. When she'd heard about an orphanage in Romania that needed adoptive parents, off she went on a discount flight to Eastern Europe, which was more than I would have done, and brought home little bawling Lissa, then an infant. Ceci doted on Lissa.

More than once, I'd thought of sending Ceci over to where Billie Attenborough lived with her mother in Flicker Ridge, an upscale development not far from Aspen Meadow Country Club. My idea was that Ceci would give Billie a class in Basic Civility.

But I frowned at the thought of security guards. I

already knew that Cecelia's biological father, Norman O'Neal, had decamped soon after Cecelia was born. This was right after Dodie had finished putting Norman through law school, which established good old Norm in the Jerk category. After a brief internship at a large firm, Norman had established a flourishing practice right here in Aspen Meadow. When we were doing the contracts, Dodie had related how Norman had wangled his way out of paying much in the way of child support. Still, for twenty years Dodie had proudly worked as a secretary—no euphemistic "administrative assistant" for her—down at the University of Denver.

My cell rang, interrupting my reverie. It was Dodie O'Neal.

"Sorry about the security guards," Dodie apologized.

"Tom told me. Don't worry about it."

Dodie said, "Last week, Norman announced to his firm that he would be giving his daughter away. And not only that, but he boasted that he'd been asked to give the first toast at the reception."

"Oh, Lord."

When I'd gently asked Dodie and Cecelia if there was a father in the picture, they had firmly replied that Norman O'Neal was having exactly no part in the wedding. Dodie would be giving her daughter away. And Doc Finn was doing the first toast. Period.

"Problem is," Dodie said now, "Norman has a terrible temper. I've always wondered how lawyers could get away with being bullies. Now I know."

I sighed, thinking of various scenarios, all of which ended in catastrophe. Before signing off, Dodie said she was confident everything would work out. She'd given an old photo of Norm to the security agency, and she believed the agency's claim that all would be well.

After ten minutes of carefully driving through the rain, I pulled into my gravel parking' lot. Tom was right behind me. I could hear his argument now: if armed guards were needed, so was he.

It was just before nine, three hours before the wedding was set to begin. The two guards, who were helping the valets, were already on duty. I told them we were the caterer and the caterer's husband, and they let us right through, no identification requested. Some security.

My cell phone buzzed and I glanced at the caller ID. Oh, I should have expected it: Billie Attenborough. Sometimes I wished I were a lawyer, and could charge for calls. With the way Billie was always phoning, phoning, phoning—why, I could have retired.

I could just imagine Billie tossing her blond mane and complaining, bitterly and loudly, that I was refusing to talk to her. I knew that losing weight could make people grouchy, but in Billie's case, it was making her certifiable.

I ignored the cell and parked as near the event center's side entrance as I could get. Tom was still behind me. Then I flipped up the hood on my rain jacket and hopped out of the van.

"Forget it," Tom called through the downpour.

"You're not unloading the van in this weather. I'll do it."

"Oh no you won't!" I replied.

I'd been single for a long time before marrying Tom, and he'd been unattached even longer. This had made us, as the saying goes, set in our ways, which is French for *stubborn*.

As Tom was sliding open the van's side door, my cell phone beeped again. Could it be Arch? My son was enjoying the last of his summer vacation by spending night after night either at the home of his half brother, Gus—the product of one of the Jerk's flings, whom I had embraced after his mother died— or at Arch's best friend Todd Druckman's house. Sometimes the three of them stayed at Todd's before decamping back to Gus's, or vice versa. There was no way Arch and his pals would be up this early, but I always worried. As I checked the caller ID again, I thought if it was Billie, I would disconnect the phone. Arch could call Tom if he was in a real jam.

It was not Arch. It was Julian. Even if most twenty-two-year-olds had trouble rousing themselves from bed to get to work, Julian's ambition of becoming a vegetarian chef meant he was always up early, scouring Boulder's farmers' markets, and then taking off to help me, or showing up to toil long hours in a vegetarian bistro near the University of Colorado.

"You're not going to believe this," he began, and I thought if his inherited Range Rover had broken down on the way over from Boulder, I would throw myself into the lake.

"Is whatever you're about to tell me going to upset me?" I asked as Tom heaved up a stack of plastic-wrapped trays.

"Hi, Billie!" Tom yelled into the cell phone before schlepping his load toward the kitchen door.

"What is Billie Attenborough doing at Ceci's wedding?" Julian asked in disbelief. "Was that Tom talking to her?"

"No, Julian, that was Tom trying to be funny. He thought I was on the phone with Bridezilla. Now, what am I not going to believe?"

"Billie just called me."

"What?"

"She's very pissed off that you're not answering your phone. She says she needs to talk to you, and if you don't start answering, she's going to come find you. She sounded as if she meant it."

"I hope you didn't tell her where I was going to be."

"Nope. But you know how she is."

I did indeed. Once when I'd refused to answer our home phone or my cell, Billie had driven over to our house and started knocking on the front door. I was busy cooking for a party, so instead of answering, I'd nipped into the bathroom. Billie traipsed around back and started tapping on the windows that Tom had installed to face our backyard. Still getting no response, Billie returned to her Mercedes convertible and leaned on the horn. I came out of the bathroom and watched through our partially closed blinds as Billie continued to honk. Finally, Jack came out of his house and yelled that he was calling the cops. His pal Doc Finn, who had preceded Jack out the front door to watch the action, had shaken his head.

Jack hollered, "They'll throw you in jail for disturbing the peace, Billie!"

Of course, Jack would never have reported Billie. But his years as a practicing lawyer always made him sound convincing. Billie had roared away in her convertible, but not before proffering an obscene gesture in my godfather's direction.

Yes, I said to Julian, as my call-waiting began to beep, I did indeed know how Billie was. I ignored the beeping.

Julian said he didn't want to worry me, just give me a heads-up. Then he asked how things were going. I told him about the security guards, and he wanted to know if there was anything he should say to them so he could be let into the parking lot.

"Just tell them you're with the caterer. They seem pretty bored."

Before signing off, Julian said that the rain was making everyone on the highway slow down, but he should be at our event center in less than an hour. I stepped into the chilly deluge, heaved up the last box of food, and splashed through the mud to the kitchen door.

There, Tom was already unpacking.

"Father Pete just called," Tom informed me. Father Pete was our parish priest at St. Luke's Episcopal Church, and was doing the O'Neal ceremony. "He couldn't get through to you. Anyway, he'll be here early."

"Great. I was on the phone with Julian. Billie called him, looking for me."

Tom shook his head. I thanked him for bringing in the lion's share of the boxes and said I would be right back, just after I checked on the dining room.

There, all was lovely. Rows of chairs had been custom fit by Dodie in a luscious pink sateen; she'd sewn the slipcovers, and made Cecelia's wedding dress, herself. For the twelve-top tables, now pushed to one side and hidden behind a curtain, Aspen Meadow Florist had done a phenomenal job. Centerpieces of pale pink carnations, baby's breath, and ivy had been Dodie O'Neal's low-cost choice. Pink faux-linen napkins, also sewn by Dodie, looked exquisite next to the snowy white tablecloths.

As if to reassure myself, I said aloud, "Everything's going to be great."

If only.

Chapter 3

Swathed in an apron, my handsome husband was refrigerating the trays of hors d'oeuvres that we would start to heat once the bridal procession began. Together, Tom and I finished unpacking and setting things in order. From time to time we consulted the printed schedule I had taped on the kitchen island. Julian arrived with the cake, a frothy pink and white three-layer confection that he had triple wrapped in plastic. Tom and I ooh'd and aah'd appropriately. Blushing with pride, Julian thanked us. With his wavy brown hair, clean-cut face, and compact swimmer's body, Julian would be sure to attract a few ooh's and aah's himself, especially from the unattached twenty-something females who would be in attendance.

The three of us worked for the next hour and a half finishing our setup. Julian set the cake on its own special table behind the curtain with the twelve tops. Tom laid out row upon row of martini glasses. When the guests began to filter into the main dining room,

Tom methodically filled each glass with shredded lettuce, then moved on to arranging poached shrimp on top. Just the sight of Tom bent so intently over his work warmed my heart. My good mood lasted until my cell phone tooted and I checked the caller ID again: Billie Attenborough. Aw, gee, why should I have been surprised?

Tom saw me make a face. "Now what?"

"Bridezilla Billie has some new demand."

"Remind me when her wedding is."

"Day after tomorrow." I set the phone to Vibrate and put it in my apron pocket. "I'm still not taking her call."

"Good idea," Julian interjected.

"She's nervous." Tom's tone was sympathetic. "Maybe she'll find somebody else to bother. Don't be too hard on her, Miss G."

I shook my head. Whatever reservoir of compassion I'd had for Billie Attenborough had dried up long ago.

When I was checking the temperature of the champagne Doc Finn would use for his toast, my cell phone buzzed against my skin. If it was Billie Attenborough again, I was going to turn it off. But it wasn't Billie. It was Jack Carmichael. I checked my watch: 11:30. He and Doc Finn couldn't have already started drinking, could they?

"Uncle Jack," I said, glad for the break. "I thought you were coming to Cecelia's wedding."

"Gertie Girl." He sounded a bit worried. "Is Finn there?"

"Doc Finn?"

"Yeah, yeah, Doc Finn, the old coot. He was supposed to pick me up, and he never came. Maybe he forgot. He does do that sometimes."

"Let me check."

I ducked into the dining room. About fifty guests had already taken their seats. They looked at me expectantly: Food already?

"I don't see him, Jack. Did you try his cell?"

"He's not answering. I'll just drive over to your center. Maybe he's in the parking lot visiting with somebody."

"Okeydoke. When you get here, come and say hi to us. We'll be in the kitchen."

He hung up, but before I could return to the kitchen, I saw a weaving figure duck into the dressing room, which was right next to the dining area. He was not a member of the wedding party. I was guessing it was Norman O'Neal, the difficult father of the bride. So much for the security guards.

Tom was ferrying the shrimp cocktails to the small refrigerator in the curtained-off dining area.

"It looks as if Norman O'Neal is here," I warned. "There could be trouble. He just walked in a very unsteady fashion right into the dressing area, where Ceci is supposed to be."

Tom bobbed swiftly behind the curtain to the dining area, and I followed, unsure of what to do. But Tom showed no signs of uncertainty. He slid his tray into the small refrigerator that we'd set up next to the cake stand, and headed to his left, right into the make-shift dressing room.

Behind him, I murmured, "Maybe you should be careful. This guy's an attorney."

"All the better," Tom replied without breaking stride.

There was no way I was going to stand by while my husband, who lifted weights and was in spectacular shape, flattened the father of the bride.

"You're my ex-dad," the bride was whispering angrily at the tottering male figure in a rumpled suit. The loveliness of Cecelia O'Neal, whose white dress fit her stunningly, was ruined by the flaming spots on her cheeks and her furious expression. "Please leave," Cecelia hissed when Norman O'Neal didn't move. "I don't want to see you."

"Where's your mother?" Norman demanded, pulling himself up straight. He was under six feet tall, and had a gray bottlebrush mustache and a puff of gray hair just above his forehead. He positively reeked of alcohol.

"Sir," Tom said calmly, "I'm going to have to ask you to leave. I'm asking you nicely. And I want you to leave nicely."

"Who the hell are you?" asked Norman O'Neal.

"I'm police," announced Tom, one eyebrow raised.

Norman O'Neal's rheumy blue eyes took in Tom, who was still wearing his apron. "I don't think so."

Lissa O'Neal, who was now an adorable eighteen-month-old with wisps of blond hair framing her face, clung to her mother's dress and began to whimper. In the main dining room, the hum of voices from more waves of arriving guests rose. I couldn't imagine that this little conflict—between Tom and an inebriated attorney, no less—was going to end well.

"Where's Harold Finn?" Norman O'Neal demanded querulously. With his index finger, he scratched his mustache. "If Doc Finn's in this wedding, then I'm going to be, too."

"Sir—," Tom began again, still patient.

The curtain swished open, and everyone except Tom jumped. It was not the first time I'd thought he had better hearing than I did, not to mention a sixth sense as to who was approaching.

"Dear me," said Father Pete, our short, corpulent priest. He cleared his throat and took in the anxious faces of our little tableau. All anxious, that is, except for Tom, whose eyes had never left Norman O'Neal.

"Who're you?" demanded Norman O'Neal, reeling unsteadily toward Father Pete.

Father Pete was as kind and pastoral as the midsummer days were long, but he didn't suffer fools gladly. "Where is your mother?" Father Pete asked Ceci, who had picked up the now-crying Lissa. Father Pete looked around the small makeshift room. "Cecelia? Where is Doc Finn? I thought he and your mother were walking you down the aisle."

"I don't know where any of them are," Cecelia wailed suddenly. She began to cry, too, which brought a fresh onslaught of tears from Lissa. As mother and daughter clung to each other, I thought, *There go the hair and makeup.* Two bridesmaids, both clothed in their floaty pink dresses, appeared at the curtain, widened their eyes at the scene, and whisked themselves away. "This is my ex-dad," Cecelia said, sobbing, to Father Pete. "He's insisting he's going to be part of the ceremony! Plus, he's wasted! He's going to ruin everything!"

There was a sudden hush in the large dining room on the other side of the curtains. All ears were apparently now attuned to the dressing room drama. Luckily, the DJ must have sensed something was amiss, as he started playing some Led Zeppelin a bit too loudly.

"He's not going to ruin anything," Father Pete was saying soothingly. "That's because he is going to get out of here right now. Off you go, ex-dad." At that point, Father Pete, who was wearing his robes and surplice, took hold of Norman O'Neal's elbow and began pulling him back toward the curtain.

Norman O'Neal hollered, "I'm not going to allow a cop in an apron and a priest in a dress to tell me what I am or am not going to do!" At that point, he took a wild swing at Father Pete. Tom moved swiftly to plant himself between the two men, but Father Pete was too fast even for Tom. Our priest caught Norman O'Neal's arm with one hand and delivered an uppercut to his chin with the other. Norman O'Neal flailed awkwardly, grasped bunches of the curtain to the area with the dining tables, and crashed backward, landing in Julian's perfect wedding cake.

"Oh, Christ," said Father Pete. "I didn't think I hit him that hard."

Norman O'Neal, his backside covered with frosting, didn't move. Tom bent down to feel his pulse.

"I'm going to call an ambulance," Tom announced quietly.

"You're not going to charge me with assault, are you?" Father Pete asked, his eyes filled with worry.

"Absolutely not," said Tom as he punched numbers into his cell phone. "That was textbook self-defense, Father." Tom asked me to send someone to find Julian, which I did. Father Pete, meanwhile, had moved to soothe Ceci and Lissa.

Two seconds later, Tom was giving quick directions to emergency services. He then hung up his cell and hoisted a still-unconscious, frosting-and-cake-covered Norman O'Neal.

"Any way I can get to the kitchen from here without going through the main dining room?" Tom asked me.

"Yes, I'll show you," I said quickly. I was trying to suppress a wave of nausea.

"Say, Father Pete," Tom said as he heaved Norman O'Neal toward the kitchen. "Where'd you learn to box like that?"

Father Pete stopped comforting Ceci and smiled shyly. "In my former life, I mean, before I was called to the ministry, I won the Golden Gloves." He beamed. "Twice."

Once Tom, a lolling, closed-eyed Norman O'Neal, and I were in the kitchen, there was a knock at the back door. Two uniformed security guards had heard they were needed.

"You are," Tom announced as he handed off a still-unconscious Norman O'Neal. "Lay this guy out on the gravel, and when the ambulance arrives, get him in there. I told the ambo guys no sirens or lights."

"But it's raining," one of the guards protested. "You put this guy on the ground, he's going to get wet."

"The rain will help clean him up," Tom said before turning back to the kitchen.

The guards obligingly took hold of Norman O'Neal and dragged him across the gravel outside the kitchen's back door. Once he was laid on the ground, Norman woke up enough to begin puking. Julian, meanwhile, had reappeared in the kitchen.

"What the hell happened to my cake?" he demanded.

"Norman O'Neal happened to it," I said. "Sorry. Can you do anything to make it look like . . . I don't know, a ski slope?"

Julian rolled his eyes and said he would try.

Tom, meanwhile, was concentrating on preheating the ovens. Out in the main dining room, the strains of the wedding march began.

"Okay, folks, here we go," I said.

We crowded together to watch the ceremony through the one-way mirrored panels I'd had put at eye level in the kitchen doors. The bridesmaids swarmed around Ceci, powdering her nose and cheeks with new makeup and patting her hair back into place. Then we only got to see Ceci coming down the aisle with Dodie, and Lissa in a lacy white flower girl outfit, before the back door to the kitchen was flung open, not by the security guards, or even Norman O'Neal, but by someone I dreaded even more: Billie Attenborough.

She swept in wearing a voluminous, silky-sounding black trench coat. Her blond-brown hair was soaked. Tall and bulky, she put her hands on her hips and tapped her foot. "Why can't any of you people answer your phones?"

"I'm doing another wedding today, Billie," I said evenly. "I'll be home tonight, when you are welcome to call me. Now, would you please leave?"

Billie lifted her small, dimpled chin. "I can't leave until I tell you the changes we're making to the wedding arrangements."

Tom groaned and lined another tray with rows of martini glasses filled with shrimp cocktail. Julian disappeared through the swinging doors.

"What's that?" Billie demanded as she peered over Tom's shoulder.

"Shrimp cocktail—what does it look like?" Tom replied.

Tom could move fast, but not as fast as Billie, who scooped one of the martini glasses off the chilled tray and began eating the shrimp with her fingers.

"Hey!" Tom yelled. He grabbed Billie by the wrist. She promptly dropped the martini glass on the floor, where it shattered. Noisily. I prayed the music in the dining room was somehow, *somehow* louder than Billie Attenborough.

"What is going on back here?" asked Jack Carmichael as he preceded Julian into the kitchen. Looking as dapper as ever in a custom-made dark gray suit, Jack's presence made me smile. "Sounds like either a food fight or a party." Jack glanced all around the kitchen. Julian started sweeping up the glass, while Tom quickly left the kitchen with his tray of shrimp cocktail. "Ah," Jack said in recognition. "If it isn't Bilious Billie. No wonder there was crashing and banging out here." Jack watched Billie push the shrimp she'd been eating into her mouth and shook his head.

"Don't say a word, you drunken old coot," Billie replied, once she'd swallowed. She wiped her hands on a kitchen towel.

"Nice talk," commented Julian as he dumped the broken glass into the trash.

I ignored all of them and put the first tray of hot appetizers into the oven.

"Gertie Girl," Jack said affectionately, "I'm here on an errand from Dodie. She says she hasn't seen Doc Finn. She wanted to know if I had, because they're going to want to start with the toasts once everybody's seated. I told her I'd already called you and asked if you'd seen him, but she wanted me to ask you again anyway."

Before I could answer that I still hadn't, Billie cried, "Doc Finn! That miserable old man. We could have a miserable-old-men convention right here."

"I have not seen him," I said quickly. I checked my watch: 12:15. "How far along are they?"

"About halfway," Jack replied. "I came in through the side dining room, so as not to disturb things any more than, say, Billie here breaking a glass."

"Shut up," said Billie.

There was a knock at the back door into the kitchen. Mentally, I cursed.

"Who is it?" I called through the heavy wood. If it was Norman O'Neal, he could just stay out in the rain.

"Craig Miller, Goldy. Is Billie in there?"

I shook my head and opened the door to Billie Attenborough's fiancé, Craig Miller. Wait, I forgot to think of him as Dr. Craig Miller. Important title, that. Before Billie and Craig were engaged, my best friend, Marla, had told me that Billie had told *her* that her next fiancé was going to be a doc. Marla had told Billie she might want to find someone with whom she shared mutual love. But Billie had dreamily countered that she'd always wanted to be introduced at Aspen Meadow Country Club as "Dr. and Mrs." So much for love, Marla had remarked, but Billie had ignored her. I'd said that I sincerely hoped the doc would be a psychiatrist.

"Billie, dear," Craig Miller pleaded now, running his short fingers through his brown hair as if he might tear it out, "please come back to your mother's house. Please don't bother Goldy now."

"I can't leave," Billie snapped. "She won't let me talk to her about what I came here to talk to her about."

"She hasn't been herself lately," Craig said to the group, his pale blue eyes wide with apology. "She's been trying to lose this weight—"

"Would everyone who is not a caterer please leave this kitchen?" I asked.

"Goldy," Billie said, "if you would just listen to me, I could tell you we've added fifty people to my guest list."

She finally had my full and undivided attention. "You've done *what*?"

Billie blithely closed her eyes. "My mother was supposed to tell you, and in all the rush of things, she forgot."

"I can't handle fifty more people here. Fire department regulations."

"Why do you think I've been trying to reach you and your assistant all day?" Billie asked. "We're having to move the wedding and reception to the Gold Gulch Spa."

"You're doing *what*?"

"Billie," Craig Miller tried again. "This can wait."

"It cannot wait," Billie announced. "Mother's calling everyone now, to make sure she hasn't forgotten anyone else."

Norman O'Neal may have lost his lunch already, but I was quite sure I would be next. Fifty extra people. A different venue. More food than I had ordered or had time to prepare.

When Tom returned to the kitchen, there was yet another knock at the back door. This was turning into one of the worst catering days of my entire career. Julian moved quickly across the kitchen floor to answer it.

"It's probably the ambo for Norman O'Neal," Tom said.

"Ambulance?" Craig Miller said softly. "Oh, I wish I had known. I just thought the fellow outside had had too much to drink—"

I shook my head while Julian conversed in quiet tones with whoever was at the back door.

"They want you, Tom," Julian said quietly.

Oh, God, I thought. Arch. Something's wrong. I glanced at my cell. My son had not tried to call. Nor had anyone else since the last time Billie had phoned.

Tom left, then stuck his head back into the kitchen. He looked very grave. He signaled me and I went out into the rain with him.

"I have to go, Miss G. They just found Doc Finn's Cayenne at the bottom of a canyon."

"And Doc Finn?"

"Inside the Cayenne. Dead."

Chapter 4

Somehow, I don't know how, Julian managed to get rid of Billie Attenborough and Craig Miller. Meanwhile, I pulled Jack aside and told him the terrible news. He turned ashen.

"Doc Finn?" His voice cracked, and he swallowed hard. "My friend? That's not possible. They must be wrong."

I shook my head. "I'm sorry. Can I get someone here to be with you?"

"How did it happen?" Jack asked.

I told him what I knew.

Jack rubbed his forehead. "I . . . we'd been talking a lot lately, Finn and I . . ." He broke off, and I signaled Julian for a chair. He rushed out, and returned with two.

"Oh, Jack, I'm so sorry," I said.

"My friend," Jack was mumbling. "Doc Finn. I can't believe it. I just—I don't believe it. How could this have happened?" His pale blue eyes beseeched me, all his energy drained.

"I don't know, Jack."

"And, oh my God, this endless rain." Jack's non sequitur took me by surprise. When I didn't respond, he said, "It's just that Finn was a great driver, and that SUV of his was excellent. A ravine? I don't understand."

I did not know what to do. Finn had been Jack's only friend in Aspen Meadow. But now I was worried about Jack. Maybe his son, Lucas, would be able to come be with him, and take him home.

"Can we go outside?" Jack asked me.

He was my godfather. He had brought me games and puzzles and endless days of joy when I was a child. I loved him unconditionally, totally, and forever. Now his best friend had died, and he was a mess. He had helped me when I desperately needed it. I simply could not abandon him.

I looked around helplessly for Julian. He understood the situation in an instant and brought me an umbrella.

"Tom told me what's going on." Julian's voice was low. "He didn't know what to do about Dodie and Ceci. But he thought the wedding shouldn't be more ruined than it already has been. They've got a couple of deputies stationed outside your French doors to tell Dodie when the ceremony's over—"

"Wait. As soon as the bride and groom say I do, pull Father Pete aside and clue him in. He'll know how to handle things."

"Good idea. How's Jack?"

I shook my head. Julian turned on his heel and moved quickly through the kitchen, intent on making this already-messed-up wedding seem as normal as possible.

When Jack and I stepped outside under the umbrella, the ambulance was just pulling away, presumably with Norman O'Neal inside. Jack wrinkled his face in puzzlement, and I murmured that a wedding guest had gotten sick.

One of the sheriff's department deputies had given Tom a windbreaker. Tom and two more investigators were deep in discussion. Tom's discarded apron lay, sodden and forgotten, on the ground.

Investigators? Julian had said two uniformed cops were outside the French doors, for when the time came to notify Dodie. So what was going on? It was as if I'd been in a mental fog, and now I grasped a situation that I hoped Jack did not. Beside me, he'd tilted his head forward and was rubbing his hand through his sparse gray hair.

I stared at Tom with his underlings. The Furman County Sheriff's Department did not handle car accidents. No Colorado county did, and that was because the state patrol was in charge of automobile accidents. The sheriff's department was only called in if there were other issues.

Criminal issues.

"Where's Lucas now?" I asked Jack. "Let me call him for you."

Jack gave me his son's number, and I punched it

into my cell. When I got voice mail, I identified myself and told Lucas his father needed him, as in, right now. I told Lucas where I was, and hoped his resentful attitude of that morning didn't mean he'd ignore my message.

Without thinking twice, I punched in Marla's number. Like me, she'd been unhappily married to the Jerk. Unlike me, she had inherited wealth and had no physical fear whatsover. Those two attributes had allowed her to clean his clock, financially and physically, when he'd come after her. We'd been fast friends ever since she divorced him. She had a wonderful heart, and although she might not particularly want to come take care of Jack, she'd do it anyway.

"Just a sec, Jack, take the umbrella, okay?" While he protested, I moved out into the rain. Marla's home phone rang and rang. "Pick up," I said to Marla's voice mail. "I know you're there and I need your help. This is an emergency, and I do mean a genuine bona fide emergency."

On the other end, the phone crashed and clicked.

"For God's sake, Goldy," Marla said dramatically. "Now what?"

"Marla—"

"I mean honestly, Goldy, tell me one time your life hasn't been a crisis. I have to get lots of sleep, just so I can deal with all the energy I have to expend—"

"Doc Finn's dead," I said quietly. Oh, why hadn't I brought two umbrellas outside? Jack had moved off to talk to Tom, which was not something I wanted. And I was getting soaked.

"Dead?" Marla echoed. "Doc Finn? What happened?"

"A car accident. Marla, please listen, I'm under a time crunch here. I'm at my event center, trying to do Cecelia O'Neal's wedding. But—" Oh, really, how could I summarize the events of the last two hours? I couldn't. "—I need you to come over and be with Jack, my godfather. Take him to your place, take him to his place, do whatever. Just be with him. He's a wreck, and I can't get hold of Lucas. Please?"

"All right, all right, why didn't you say so? I'll be there in ten minutes. Wait—did you try to reach Charlotte Attenborough? She and Jack have been going out for the last two months."

Oh, Lord, in the confusion I'd forgotten about Charlotte. She and Jack were indeed an item, maybe more in her mind than his, I'd gathered. Charlotte could be imperious and was used to getting what she wanted, but compared to her daughter, she was Mother Teresa. Still, I simply couldn't face any more Attenboroughs today, and I doubted Jack could either.

"No, I didn't call Charlotte, and I don't want to. It's a long story. Look, Marla, I'm outside and I'm totally sopping wet. Could you just please come over and get Jack? We'll be in the kitchen. I'll give him a drink or something."

"Do you even keep scotch in that event center of yours, or are you strictly a wine type of gal?"

"Marla, please?"

She groaned and signed off. I quick-stepped over to Jack, who was trying to elicit information from Tom.

"My friend Marla's coming to get you," I announced. "Please, Jack, could you come into the kitchen?"

Tom looked me up and down. "You have a dry outfit inside?"

I told him I did. Then I shepherded Jack back into the kitchen, where Julian was giving two of the servers instructions on how to serve the egg rolls.

"I shouldn't be bothering you," Jack announced suddenly. He looked around the kitchen, his eyes wild. "You've got other things to do here. And where's Dodie? I should be helping her. I should, I don't know, be doing the first toast or something." His face became even more agitated. "Do you know anything I could say about Ceci?" He rubbed his forehead. "I think Dodie just invited me because she wanted Finn to have company during the reception."

"Jack," I remonstrated, "you're in no condition to do any such thing." I reached into the cupboard behind the dry vermouth and drew out a bottle of Johnnie Walker Black Label. I poured Jack a hefty drink, plopped in some ice cubes, and drizzled in a bit—a very little bit—of water. Then I asked him please to sit down in one of the chairs Julian had brought.

Julian then wondered aloud if he should send Dodie outside to talk to the two uniforms, as she kept asking him if he'd seen Doc Finn.

"No," Jack said suddenly, draining his drink and setting the empty glass on the counter. "Don't ruin her special day with her daughter. Let me go talk to Dodie, tell her Finn was unaccountably delayed because of some . . . medical thing, I don't know what, and does she want me to make the toast. Now, Goldy, don't go getting stubborn on me, because I'm much more stubborn than you are, and I've been at it a lot longer. Dodie can learn what actually happened once the reception is over. And, godchild," he said tenderly, "you need to get into some dry clothes, take care of yourself for a change instead of everyone else."

Julian and Jack disappeared through the swinging doors. Two of the servers came back and said the guests had moved to the far end of the dining room for picture-taking, and all the tables had been moved back into the main dining room. Could they take out the shrimp cocktails, to start putting them on the plates? I gratefully said that would be super, then headed off to retrieve the clean uniform I kept in the restroom closet.

Somehow, we got through the next two hours. Jack did a wonderful toast, holding little Lissa with one arm and his glass with the other. Marla showed up as lunch was being served, and told Jack he was going home with her, no argument permitted. Besides, she added, she had a bottle of Johnnie Walker Blue Label, which he needed to open with her. Jack even managed a smile. He hugged me and said we'd talk later.

The lunch, a chilled curried chicken salad recipe I had been working on for a while, was served on a bed of baby lettuce alongside cold raisin-rice salad, and was a big success. The cake—which Julian had miraculously frosted with our back-up supplies into a replica of Keystone Mountain—was enjoyed by all. By the time the DJ started playing the music, I was ready to collapse with relief.

Guests at wedding receptions don't like to hear the sound of dishes being clanked around as they're washed. But I had asked the servers I had hired for the event to bring all the dinnerware and flatware to the kitchen as soon as the guests were done. I gave them their pay, told them I needed them to come to Gold Gulch Spa, and not my event center, for Billie Attenborough's wedding the day after next, and hustled them on their way. Julian and I then used our patented ability to clean silently, and washed, rinsed, dried, and packed up all the dishes, serving platters, trays, and flatware. By the time Dodie O'Neal appeared in the kitchen and handed me an envelope stuffed with bills, the cooking space was sparkling.

"Dodie, please, you've already given us the gratuity. It was part of your contract." I looked inside the envelope and realized the number of twenties she'd given us amounted to nearly a thousand dollars. "This is way, way too much extra money."

"Goldy, don't protest." Like some other women her age, Dodie managed to look older than her forty-five years. Her thin face was perpetually lined with wrinkles of worry, and she dyed her short blond hair at home. I didn't know if the cops had talked to her yet, but I doubted it. "I feel as if I ignored you throughout the proceedings," she went on, frowning.

"Have you, I mean, did you—," I faltered.

"Yes. After Ceci threw the bouquet, I finally asked the two policemen why they were guarding the French doors, since I'd hired security guards. They told me. What a disaster, and so sad."

"Yes," I said, remembering the times Doc Finn had treated me for bruises and cuts, all caused by my horrible ex-husband. Doc Finn had tried, in vain, to get me to report John Richard to the police, but I'd been too afraid. This had all taken place before doctors were required to inform law enforcement of suspected abuse, and I knew in my heart that Doc Finn never would have had any fear of the Jerk. A rock seemed to be forming in my chest. Poor, poor Doc Finn.

"Well," Dodie said now, "I want you to take the tip. Both of you. Give a good extra chunk to your servers, too. God knows you all deserve a big gratuity, since I understand Norman did show up, and caused a ruckus. And where were the security guards, I'd like to know? I didn't give them an extra tip."

"Please, Dodie, don't worry. Norman was just a nuisance. He created a temporary disturbance." I kept my tone nonchalant. Behind Dodie, Julian opened his eyes wide and cocked his head at me, as in, *You're kidding, right?*

"Where is Norman now?" Dodie asked nervously. She licked her lips and glanced around the kitchen as if Norman were going to jump out of the walk-in refrigerator. "Did he leave?"

"Yeah, he's gone," I said with a dismissive wave.

"But . . . where did he go?" Dodie pressed. "I suppose I should have checked on him before, but what with Cecelia being so upset, and Lissa starting to cry, I just didn't have the heart to come out and look for him."

"Your ex-husband, ah, became ill," I told Dodie.

"He's on his way down to, oh, one of the area hospitals, I think."

"He'll probably try to sue somebody." Dodie's voice was resigned. She pinched the bridge of her nose, sighed, then brushed the pleats of her beige dress. "That's what he always does when things don't go his way."

I thought of Tom's imposing presence, not at all diminished by the fact that he was wearing an apron as he towered over Norman O'Neal. I thought of Father Pete, the priest with the deadly swing. Norman was going to sue somebody? Who would that be, exactly?

"Well, he can try to sue people," I said. "But considering the forces arrayed against him, I don't think he'd have much chance of winning."

"Lissa started crying? Remind me who Lissa is?" Julian queried once we'd packed up the dishes—I'd given the leftovers to Dodie—and were walking through the rain back to my van. The precipitation had diminished to a whispering drizzle, which blended with the tumble of water over rocks in Upper Cottonwood Creek. The gray light made everything seem like dusk, even though it was not quite four in the afternoon, and the sun would not set until after eight.

I gave Julian an abbreviated version of Ceci's trip to Romania. He was impressed, and said he hoped to be that good-hearted one of these days.

"You already are," I said.

Julian pushed his boxes into the back of my van, and the two of us walked through the light rain to the kitchen door. When we arrived, Julian unlocked our storage door and brought out a shovel and a bag of sawdust. He dug into the bag and sprinkled it over the area where Norman O'Neal had hurled. We'd learned from unfortunate past experiences that the sawdust and shovel were necessary accoutrements for any catering venue where guests might be tempted to overindulge.

Julian stopped to lean on the shovel. "And, boss, what are you going to do about Billie Attenborough changing the venue for her wedding? She'll have to pay a cancellation fee for renting your space, too, right?"

"Absolutely. Charlotte knows that."

"Looks like you don't want to discuss it at the moment," Julian said with a kind grin.

"You're right." I really did not want to think about Billie Attenborough and her latest crisis. I could envision my entire evening—when I had wanted just to go home and cook for Tom—going down the proverbial tubes as I called the florist and all the other vendors. Of course, if Tom was involved in an investigation of Doc Finn's death, the evening was already shot. My heart squeezed again. Poor Doc Finn.

After a moment, I said to Julian, "Gold Gulch Spa is located at the old Creek Ranch Hotel."

"Yeah, the one with the hot spring. Way out Upper Cottonwood Creek. Near the Spruce Medical Group's building, isn't it?"

"Yes," I replied, "but Spruce Medical has relocated to town, and their old building is up for lease."

Julian shook his head. "This town is changing too fast."

"You know, with Gold Gulch Spa as the venue for Billie's wedding, we're going to have to deal with Victor Lane."

"That guy's an asshole," Julian remarked. "I wish somebody would dump him into a ravine."

"Now, now, Julian. Stiff upper lip."

"He thinks he knows about food and he doesn't know jack."

"He's going to know Jack, because Jack's coming to the wedding."

"Oh, super. Your godfather, the smoker who's had two heart attacks, coming face-to-face with the guy who thinks he knows all there is to know about healthful eating. I did a party where he was a guest. He tried to tell me what I should have served. I'm like, Welcome to the Vegetarian Revolution, Victor! You wanna cook, go ahead. But someone else is paying me to do it, so back off."

"I know the guy's a creep, but give him a break."

"No."

Great. I had to say, though, Julian was right. And in fact, I had as much, if not more, reason to dislike Victor Lane and his vaunted Gold Gulch Spa than Julian did. But I kept mum. After all, a job was just a job, right?

As Julian had said, No.

Chapter 5

As I headed home, tatters of dark cloud hung in front of a lighter sky. Gray drizzle continued to fall. Once I'd unpacked the boxes, I fixed myself what I called my Summertime Special: two to four shots of espresso—depending on how badly I needed the caffeine—with whipping cream and ice cubes, and sat at our oak kitchen table to collect myself. With some trepidation, I checked our blinking answering machine.

There was no message from Billie Attenborough—she probably figured she'd done enough damage for one day—nor was there one from Southwest Hospital, the place to which the ambulance had hauled away Norman O'Neal. Tom's deep, reassuring voice sounded strained when he said he hoped to be home by seven; the medical examiner was making a special trip in tonight.

That didn't sound good.

Arch was up next, announcing gleefully that he'd

been invited to spend another night at Gus's place, and was that okay? Todd was there with them, too, and Todd's mother had already said he could stay.

Charlotte Attenborough's voice greeted me next. She said she wanted to talk to me about the new arrangements for the reception, which Billie was supposed to tell me about, but had forgotten. I rolled my eyes. The daughter blamed the mother, and vice versa. Personally, I accepted Charlotte's version. I shook my head. If Arch had ever been as flaky as Billie Attenborough, he never would have made it through elementary school.

Did I, Charlotte went on, know where my godfather, Jack, was? There was no answer at his house. Could she come to my place this evening to talk?

"I sure don't want to see you," I said aloud to the empty kitchen. "But I suppose we're going to have to go over some things."

Adding fifty people and changing the venue of the reception? Letting me know a mere forty-eight hours in advance? I poured myself a small glass of sherry.

Finally, there was Marla. She and my godfather were getting comprehensively inebriated, and could they please come over? Not to worry, Marla had already called a Denver car service to do the chauffering.

"Call me as soon as you get this message, will you?" Marla demanded. "I'll have to tell the car service what time." She stopped to give Jack directions to her garage, where he'd find more scotch. "I know you live less than a mile from me, Goldy. But you can't be too careful with cops waiting around every corner, just dying to hand everyone DUI citations. I don't mean Tom, of course. Yeah, sure, bring the bourbon, too!" she shrieked at Jack. "Now listen"— here she lowered her voice—"I've got the church-women coming tonight for a fund-raising discussion. Remember that dessert you promised to make for me? I still need it. And I won't be able to stay at your place long, okay? So you need to take care of your godfa-ther once I get there. What, Jack?" she called. "You can find more ice in the refrigerator in the garage—"

She hung up.

So. At this point, I was left to worry about how much booze two former heart attack patients—Marla and Jack—were downing, whether I could come up with realistic contract changes for Charlotte Atten-borough, and making a dessert that I'd completely forgotten about. I wondered how the Episcopal churchwomen would feel about vanilla ice cream in a graham cracker crust. Probably not very good.

But I always had backup plans, so our walk-in or freezer should yield something.

I called Marla and told her to contact the car ser-vice. She replied that they'd be along as soon as hu-manly possible. How was Jack doing? I asked.

"About what you'd expect," was her cryptic reply. He must have been sitting right there.

Next I phoned Arch and said it was fine for him to stay with Gus. He thanked me profusely and prom-ised they'd be over the next night. I told him not to worry about it.

I called Charlotte Attenborough, got her voice mail,

and said sure, she could come over this evening, as long as it was before ten.

I opened the walk-in and looked around for dessert ingredients for Marla. My eyes lit on a coeur à la crème that I'd drained overnight, with the intention of serving it to Tom to celebrate our love, it being wedding season and all. I could fix Tom another one, and the churchwomen would be more likely to open up their checkbooks if they were actually served something that Marla said was "incomparably rich."

It was just past five. Marla was due to come over with Jack, but what with a car service having to make it up the mountain, that was probably at least an hour away. I drank my sherry, and thought about Doc Finn.

He had been a wonderful man, absolutely dedicated to healing. When Arch had been running a high fever during one of our periodic blizzards, his pediatrician's office had not been answering their phone. Nor had Arch's father, the Jerk, chosen to come home. He'd said he was staying in Denver—although I knew he was with his girlfriend. In desperation, I'd called Spruce Medical, and Doc Finn had jumped into his Jeep and driven out to us that night. I'd told him I didn't know doctors still made house calls. Doc Finn had tried to touch my swollen cheek—another gift from the Jerk—and I'd shied away from him. I'd said Arch was in bed, and didn't he want to see him?

Doc Finn had been kind and gentle with Arch. He'd taken my son's temperature, listened to his chest, and checked his ears. Doc Finn's verdict: Arch had pneumonia. But Doc Finn had brought a bag of meds, including antibiotics, and we had weathered the storm, literally and figuratively.

As Doc Finn was leaving that night, he turned to me thoughtfully and said, "Doctors are supposed to heal, not hurt." I'd burst out crying, and taken the card Doc Finn had proffered. It hadn't been his card; it had belonged to a divorce lawyer.

I finished the sherry and traipsed upstairs, where I peeled off my catering clothes and decided on a shower. Doc Finn had been such a wonderful man, so thorough in his diagnoses, so good with patients young and old—the town would miss him terribly. As would Jack Carmichael. My heart was wrenched, thinking of my godfather and his dear friend. What would Jack do without Doc Finn?

While the hot water soothed my body, I tried to put the image of Doc Finn at the bottom of a ravine out of my mind. But when I did, the vision of today's wedding crashers—Norman O'Neal, plus Billie Attenborough with her fiancé, Craig Miller, in tow—came up. Better to dispense with them, too.

Instead, I pondered Marla's pie. I had pecans in the walk-in, and could make a nut-and-butter crust. This I would pack with the chilled coeur filling. On top I'd put concentric circles of blueberries and raspberries, and I'd give Marla a bowl of whipped cream to place on the side. All this would go over well with the churchwomen, I had no doubt.

With the least of my problems solved, I dried off and donned jeans and a sweatshirt. It was still cool and drizzly outside, so a hot dinner for Tom and me, and Jack if I could convince him to stay, would work well. I always wanted Jack to feel welcome to eat with us, but he seldom did. Said he'd been a bachelor for so long, he resisted mothering.

I opened the freezer side of the walk-in and surveyed the contents. In February, I'd made and frozen a pork ragout. With penne pasta and a Romaine salad with vinaigrette, it would be perfect.

Once I'd mixed up Marla's butter crust with toasted pecans, I patted the crumbly mixture into a pie pan, then put it into the oven to bake. I set the table for three and thawed the ragout. It looked luscious. Finally, I located the penne, washed and dried the Romaine leaves, and whisked together a Dijon vinaigrette.

I pulled the hot pie plate out of the oven, set it aside to cool, and booted up my kitchen computer. Reluctantly, I pulled up Billie Attenborough's menu. I had my basic moneymaking formulas for different recipes. They all allowed for some overage, because you had to, but not for an extra fifty people. I was a true believer in love and all that, but if you were a caterer, weddings were the last place you should be feeling charitable.

I stared at the menu. On such short notice, how in the hell was I supposed to come up with fifty extra guests' worth of crab cakes with sauce gribiche, labor-intensive deviled eggs with caviar, artichoke skewers, and the two salads? Plus, would the wedding cake Julian was making even be big enough? And what about having enough servers? Well, Billie had said

Victor Lane's staff would be willing to help, and dog-gone it, help they were going to have to.

I printed out a list of extra foodstuffs we would need, plus the recipes that would go with those ingredients. I knew the chef at Gold Gulch Spa. Yolanda was actually an old friend who had trained with my mentor, André. She had a prickly exterior, but once you got to know her, Yolanda was a generous soul. Still, I knew she would not be happy to add more duties to all she had to do in the spa kitchen. I shook my head. What ailed Billie Attenborough anyway?

The phone rang and I checked the caller ID. It was Julian.

"Are you all right?" I immediately demanded.

"Of course I'm all right, why wouldn't I be? A drunk crashed into the cake I'd spent zillions of hours making for his daughter's wedding, and why? Because apparently the priest flattened him. And then while I was trying to fix the cake, the bitch whose wedding we're doing the day after tomorrow showed up in the kitchen with a whole new set of demands, which include adding fifty people to her guest list. What about that strikes you as not all right?"

"Oh, Julian, I'm sorry. I just was worried about you."

"And I'm worried about you, boss. I was just sitting here thinking of all that extra work Billie's dumped on you, and wondering how you're going to manage casing a new venue while buying more supplies while doing a kick-ass new amount of new cooking. So . . . are you staring at your computer now, or what?"

I sighed. "You've got it."

"All right, e-mail me your shopping list and recipes, and I'll get it done tomorrow. Plus, I know, I'll have to make an extra layer or two for the wedding cake. I always leave the assembly to the last thing, so that'll work. And I've already asked for the day off from the bistro."

"But Saturday is your busy day there! And you can't possibly do all this in one day!"

"Don't worry, okay? You've got enough on your plate. Speaking of which, boss, have you eaten anything?"

"I'm heating up dinner now. Jack's with Marla, and she's going to bring him over. Tom will be home late, and Arch is with Gus and Todd."

"Okay." He sounded relieved. "Now tell me you're not sweating seeing that prick of a spa owner Victor Lane too much."

"I'm not sweating it," I lied.

"You don't sound convinced." When I said nothing, he said, "All right, just e-mail that stuff over, and I'll get cracking. I know a fancy-food store here that carries caviar by the case, and they have organic free-range eggs, too. I can get some fresh new potatoes, dill, artichokes, and haricots verts at the farmers' market first thing in the morning."

"Okay, listen, I've got plenty of pasteurized crab to do an extra hundred crab cakes, plus sauce. That should be way more than enough. You're welcome to do all the rest. Please know I'm grateful. I'm so glad we don't have to dump all the extra work on Yolanda out at the spa."

"Wouldn't she just love that?"

"No, she wouldn't. And by the way, you're the best."

"Oh, and don't I know it," he said. But he didn't. Julian was the most humble twenty-something I'd ever met. "Now be sure to get plenty of rest tonight. Any word from the Attenborough coven?"

"Charlotte called. She's going to have to come over tonight so we can do the extra contract. But my big worry is Jack. I have to try to comfort him. I mean, he's just lost his best friend. I'm going to try to convince him to eat here."

"Yeah, good plan. Did they ever find out exactly what happened to Doc Finn?"

"Car accident is all I know. Tom should be able to tell me more later."

He signed off after again urging me not to worry about the Attenborough wedding. "Just think," he said, trying to sound jovial, "in just forty-eight hours, it'll be over!" When I didn't say anything, Julian concluded, "And don't worry about Victor Lane either."

Right, I thought as I checked the pecan-butter crust. It was cool enough to fill, so I set about picking over and carefully washing the raspberries and blueberries Julian had brought from the same Boulder farmers' market where he'd be going tomorrow.

Don't worry about Victor Lane, Julian had said. But how could I not worry about the obstreperous owner of Gold Gulch Spa? Victor Lane had stabbed me in the back once. Figuratively speaking, of course. Still, what was to prevent him from doing it again?

I spooned the luscious coeur filling into the cooled crust, and carefully dried enough berries to make the top of Marla's pie both gorgeous and appetizing. Then I told myself, *Don't think about Billie Attenborough, don't think about Doc Finn, don't think about Victor Lane.* Yeah, especially that.

But as I dropped the berries into precise place, I reflected, trying not to, on Victor Lane. When I'd finished my Denver apprenticeship to André Hibbard, I applied to work at the only catering business serving the mountain area, an enterprise with the ridiculously unappetizing name Victor's Vittles, owned and operated by Victor Lane. As far as I knew, Victor had gotten into the food business because he'd seen the need the wealthy of Aspen Meadow had for giving parties. He'd seen an easy way to make money, and he'd taken it.

I thought back to those difficult years right after I'd divorced the Jerk. I'd gotten the house, in the parlance of divorced people, and I wanted to be able to do food service when Arch was in school or with babysitters, without subjecting him to the grueling routine of restaurant work. I thought I'd have a perfect fit with Victor's Vittles.

Boy, was I wrong.

Victor did not like to work with food—far from it. His idea of catering a summer party was to go down to one of the warehouse clubs in Denver, buy corn chips and cheese dip, several tubs of prepared potato salad, a variety of packages of hot dogs, hamburgers, steaks, and/or chicken legs, all of which he slathered with bottled barbecue sauce and threw onto the grill while he tossed packaged salads with ranch dressing made from a mix. For dessert, he ordered either the warehouse chocolate cake, carrot cake, or cheesecake.

I'd learned from one of the young men who worked for Victor that he tripled the cost of his "ingredients," as he called the processed foods he bought . . . and he made out like the kind of bandito who'd once populated Aspen Meadow.

So I'd made an appointment to see Victor, and promised him—modestly? immodestly? I still didn't know—some new taste sensations. I showed up at his door with platters of homemade new-potato salad with handpicked dill and crème fraîche—the same recipe we were going to have at Billie's reception—marinated grilled chicken breasts, a flawless baby spinach salad, a loaf of homemade Cuban Bread, and a flourless chocolate cake. He'd tasted everything and curled his lip. Then he'd leaned back in his chair, crossed his arms, and turned me away with a curt, "Women don't know how to cook."

Pushing the memories away, I put the pie in the walk-in, pulled out a case of crab, and printed out my recipe for crab cakes. Then I checked that I had plenty of fresh celery, my only concern, and began mixing up the ingredients for all the extra crab cakes I would need for Billie Attenborough's reception.

Women don't know how to cook. How Victor Lane's cruel assessment had rung in my ears all the way home that day. As my van had chugged away from his house, I berated myself for allowing tears to sting my eyes, and slapped them away when they rolled down my cheeks. Still, self-pity ruled only until I swung my van into our gravel driveway. Don't know how to cook, huh? We would just see about that.

Oddly, my own beloved godfather featured in this story early on. Jack happened to call me after I had stomped back into my kitchen with the remains of my offerings for Victor Lane. Jack had been saying for months how worried he was about me since I'd kicked out the Jerk. He repeatedly asked if there was anything he could do for me. Would I consider moving back to New Jersey? Did I need money? Could he at least pay for housekeeping help for me? No, no, no thank you, I'd always said.

When Jack had called this particular time, I was still so upset I ended up giving him a blow by blow of my interview—a euphemism for rejection, if ever there was one—with Victor Lane, although I didn't use his name. I think I was too afraid Jack might fly out and shoot him—Jack was a crack shot. But Jack had made no threats. He had only said quietly, "I think you should open your own catering business. And I'm going to send you the money to do it."

I protested, of course, the way I always did. I wanted to make it on my own. Jack had said, "Gertie Girl? You got merit scholarships to go to prep school and college. You had a child while that creep treated you like dirt. You dumped the creep, you worked your way through an apprenticeship at a restaurant to learn the food business, and you think you haven't already made it on your own?"

"Jack, don't." And then I burst out crying again.

"Gertie Girl! Don't say another word. And stop crying. I'm sending you a check. No loan, mind you. A gift, and I'm paying the gift tax. I've made more money in the lawyering business than I know what to do with. Now get used to receiving a gift, dammit, and make this catering business work so you can show this new creep just who knows how to cook and who doesn't."

The next day, FedEx delivered a check for fifty thousand dollars. Aghast, I called Jack. I simply couldn't accept a gift that large. Or maybe I could, I didn't know . . . but I needed to thank my godfather, or do something. But Jack's secretary said he was in court. He'd told his secretary to say he didn't want to hear from me until I'd driven "some stupid creep," as she gleefully put it, "into the poorhouse."

It had taken only six months. I'd bought equipment and had my kitchen retrofitted to pass the vulture's eye of the county health inspector. I'd found Alicia, my supplier; I'd had cards and brochures made up; I'd given clients who referred me to new clients a 10 percent discount. And I'd cooked. Madly, insanely, with all the energy of a woman scorned. Victor's Vittles had quietly closed its doors.

But Victor Lane had not allowed me to take the processed cheese out of his mouth so quickly. He'd wormed his way into the affections of two food critics—one at a Denver newspaper, the other at a glossy magazine, *Front Range Quarterly*. He'd made sure that both critics skewered my business, *Goldilocks' Catering, Where Everything Is Just Right!* The critics said my food was unoriginal, boring, and left them hungry. Since André had taught me to have photos posted in my kitchen of every food critic working in the greater Denver metropolitan area, I'd been quite sure that neither of the poseurs had ever tasted my food or even attended one of my parties.

"Don't ever let anyone tell you this behind-your-back stuff isn't personal," Jack had told me. "It's as personal as it can be. But if you keep doing the work you were hired to do by clients who love you, then this new creep can blow his despair over you driving him out of business out his ass."

Like most lawyers, Jack did have a way with words. I'd refused to give up my catering business, which had continued to thrive, thank you very much. And Victor Lane had bought the Creek Ranch Hotel . . . and turned it into Gold Gulch Spa. The most delicious irony of all was that he'd hired a woman to run his kitchen. Yolanda, my friend, had confided that Victor was an absolute pain in the behind, but the spa clients, 99 percent of whom were women, were as addicted to Gold Gulch Spa as crack smokers were to their pipes. Even though Victor never, but ever, gave her any credit, she knew she deserved it . . . and, she said, the women who slipped hundred-dollar bills into her apron pocket at the end of their stays seemed to agree.

Whatever, as Arch would say. I didn't wish Victor Lane harm. I just wanted him to stay out of my way. Over the last four years, we'd been successful at dodging each other. But with Billie Attenborough scheduling her wedding and reception at Gold Gulch Spa, my carefully crafted avoidance of Victor Lane was about to come to an abrupt halt.

I finished molding the last crab cake, and counted them. I figured Billie could invite an extra seventy-five people to her guest list and we'd still be in good shape. I covered the platter and placed it in the walk-in, just in the nick of time, as it turned out. The door-bell rang: Jack and Marla.

Through the peephole, Marla waved at me with crazed, teen-type enthusiasm. I wondered how much of that scotch and bourbon they'd had time to ingest.

"Finally, finally!" Marla shrieked when I let her inside. The two of them stomped inside in a cloud of whiskey scent. "We're starving, do you have anything cooking?"

"Crab cakes or pork ragout? I've got plenty of extra crab cakes for the Attenborough reception, and the pork ragout is yummy—"

"Both, then!" Marla replied.

I took their coats while they ushered themselves into the kitchen. Marla's joviality was forced, while Jack, who had tightness around his eyes and wore a strained expression, looked as if he'd just lost his best friend. Which, of course, he had.

What, oh what, could I do to help my dear, sweet godfather recover? He had been uncompromisingly generous and kind to me my entire life, and I had no idea—none—how to help him.

Chapter 6

I thought you were having the churchwomen over for dinner," I said to Marla as she dug into a crab cake I'd sautéed for her.

"Dessert. You made my pie, didn't you?" When I nodded, Marla lifted her chin in Jack's direction. He was rubbing his forehead. He'd refused any food. Marla caught my eye and shook her head.

"Jack," I said gently, "let me call Craig Miller for you. He's a doctor, maybe you should have a tranquilizer or something." When Jack grunted, I went on, "Look, maybe Craig knows a psychologist or a psychiatrist or someone professional, anyway, someone who could come out to the house to talk to you. Will you let me, please?"

"Absolutely not," said Jack. He took a deep breath. "No doctors, please. I'm a big boy. I can handle this."

"Jack!" I exclaimed as Marla shrugged. "How about Father Pete?" I persisted. "Or Lucas? I know either one of them would want to be with you, if that would somehow make you feel better—"

Jack managed a wan smile. "Gertie Girl. I'm fine. Just tired." He frowned and looked around the kitchen, as if noticing for the first time that it was only the three of us there. "Where's Tom? Arch?"

"Arch is at his half brother's house. Tom's coming home late." I checked the clock: almost 6. "When are the churchwomen arriving, Marla?"

"Seven, but I have to be back home by half past six. The car-service guy is coming back for me. Do you have any more crab cakes? And how about a bowl of that ragout?"

I fixed her both. Since Marla had had her heart attack, I automatically prepared most of my main dishes with low-fat this, low-carbohydrate that, or reduced-calorie the other thing. If she ate dessert, I figured that was her problem. Jack, who'd had two heart attacks, had no desire to have me lecture him about anything, as he said he already got plenty of "that kind of tripe," as he called it, from his son, Lucas.

I didn't want to bring up Doc Finn's death, and it was clear that neither Marla nor Jack did either. But since Jack's conversations with me usually centered on the issues he was having adjusting to life in the West, or where he and Finn had just gone fishing, we suddenly had a cavernous space in our conversation. When Marla hopped up to heat another crab cake, I finally grabbed at a conversational straw.

"You're going to get sick of those before Billie

Attenborough's wedding," I commented. "It's day after tomorrow, remember?"

Marla and Jack groaned in unison.

Marla said, "I got a call today from a secretarial service that Charlotte is using. All the guests are being notified of the new venue for the wedding. Gold Gulch Spa? Please. What are we supposed to do, stuff ourselves silly at the reception, then go work out, then relax in the hot springs pool?"

"How 'bout," Jack interjected, "we just pig out, then go rest in the hot pool?" After asking that question, though, he went back into the daze that had enveloped him since he'd arrived at the house.

"Sounds good to me," replied Marla. "But get this—directions are being e-mailed, faxed, or delivered by messenger to each and every wedding guest, depending on how technologically current you are. Changing where the festivities are being held must mess up your plans somewhat, eh, Goldy?"

"I don't even want to go there," I replied. "I mean, I'll go to the spa, but I sure don't want to talk about how Billie's addition of fifty more guests is screwing up my life. Charlotte's coming over tonight so we can hammer out the details. I have to drive to Gold Gulch tomorrow morning, to see what our flow is going to be, where the tables will be set up, all that jazz."

"And then there's the dreaded Victor Lane to deal with," Marla added. She knew all about my dealings with the man who thought women couldn't cook.

"Victor Lane?" Jack suddenly seemed to come out of his stupor, and his gray eyebrows knit in puzzlement. "Victor Lane? Why does that name sound depressingly familiar?"

Oh, dear. I found it hard to believe that Jack, the man who'd been going out with Charlotte Attenborough virtually since he arrived in town, would not have heard of Victor Lane and his vaunted Gold Gulch Spa. Charlotte was well known as a Gold Gulch fixture. To forestall discussion of a subject that could upset Jack even more, I offered Jack and Marla something else to drink. When they declined, I poured myself another glass of sherry.

But Marla didn't take to forestallment. "Don't tell me Goldy hasn't told you about Victor Lane of Victor's Vittles. Victor Lane told Goldy that women don't know how to cook!"

Jack nodded at me appraisingly. "That son of a bitch? That same guy from all those years ago?"

I nodded and took a large slug of sherry.

"All those years ago?" Marla asked in puzzlement. "This is the guy from all what years ago?" Marla shook a bejeweled finger at me accusingly. "Goldy, did you have a fling with Victor Lane and not tell me?"

I laughed so hard sherry shot out of my nose and I started to cough. Marla took that as confirmation that I had *not* rolled in the hay with Victor.

"I wonder why he would ever say that women don't know how to cook," Jack said. "Tell that to all the women across America who find themselves standing over a stove for much of their lives."

"Look, Jack," I said soothingly, "if you hadn't

helped me see that Victor was as full of crap as he was of himself, there might well be no Goldilocks' Catering here in Aspen Meadow."

The doorbell rang, and Marla groaned.

"Just as I'm about to get some truly juicy gossip about Aspen Meadow's renowned asshole spa owner," she said, "my car-service guy arrives. Dammit! Now you two need to hold that thought, because I want to hear all about Victor Lane when we get together next." She eyed the platter. "May I take a couple of crab cakes, Goldy? I'm so hungry."

"Yeah, sure. I made lots extra for Billie Attenborough's shindig. And don't forget your pie."

I loaded her down with goodies, and she took off for the front door, where whoever was there was persistently knocking.

"Oops, it's not my guy," said Marla, as she checked the peephole. "It's an Attenborough," she singsonged, "incoming!" She put her platters of food down on the hall table.

"Already?" I asked.

"Yes yes," Marla singsonged again.

"I haven't called her all day. She's going to be angry," Jack said dejectedly.

"Charlotte, darling!" Marla swept the front door open. "Don't tell me you're not coming to the dessert fund-raiser tonight at my place? Don't break my heart."

"I'm coming, I'm coming," Charlotte trilled. "What are you doing here, Marla? Don't you have guests to get ready for? You smell like liquor. Where's Goldy?"

Jack uttered a swear word under his breath.

"In the kitchen!" Marla sang. "Oops, there's my car service!" She picked up her food platters and sashayed out. "See you later, everybody!"

I knew I should have been more ready for Charlotte, but I wasn't. The thought occurred to me that maybe she should tend to Jack. Charlotte Attenborough had been a nurse in her previous life, before her well-insured husband died of his bleeding ulcer. According to Marla, Charlotte had used the insurance money to buy a struggling local magazine with the uninspiring name *Aspen Meadow Monthly*. She'd transformed the publication into a glossy, widely read and admired lifestyle rag, *Mountain Homes*. Charlotte herself was owner, editor, and chief pooh-bah, and as such was greatly admired around town. She'd offered me free monthly full-page advertising for a year as an added incentive for doing her daughter's wedding. I'd joyously accepted . . . but that had all been nine months ago, and since then, I'd had second, third, fourth, ad infinitum thoughts telling me that no advertising was worth getting a bleeding ulcer myself.

"Goldy, do you have my new contract?"

"No. Sorry, Charlotte," I said. I didn't offer any excuses, such as having my godfather's best friend found dead in a ravine, dealing with a combative biological father at a wedding, or even actually having had another wedding reception to cater today. "I'll get right on it." I turned to my computer, booted it up, and began typing changes to our contract that would reflect additional guests and a change of venue. "Would you like a drink, or some food?" I asked as I pressed Print. "We have lots of everything."

"Jack," Charlotte said, surprised, "what are you doing here?"

I stopped what I was doing to turn back to them. I'd told Tom that Charlotte was perfectly preserved. Like jam? he'd asked. I'd merely shaken my head.

I knew Billie was thirty-six, and Charlotte had made a point of telling me she'd given birth to her only child when she was twenty. But there was no way Charlotte Attenborough was in her midfifties; she was sixty-five if she was a day. She wore her short gray-blond hair swept up in what boys from the fifties would have called a ducktail. She was at least five feet eight inches tall, but the ramrod-straight way she held her slender self, shoulders back, abs tight, made her look more like six feet. This night, she wore a mid-calf, dark gray sheath-style dress. Despite its fashionable draping, her attire gave her the look of a drill sergeant.

"Well?" she said to Jack.

As if on cue, both of our family's animals—a big, floppy, exceptionally affectionate bloodhound named Jake, and a long-haired feline named Scout—made their presence known at our back door. I'd called them to come in when I'd first arrived home, but neither had been interested then.

"I'll let in the pets." Jack leaped up from his chair and went to the back door before I could say, *Careful, they're going to be muddy!*

Which, in retrospect, would have been a very good idea, but not nearly as much fun. Charlotte, who clearly did not like dogs, flinched when Jake came bounding in. She screamed when he jumped up on her and muddied her impeccable sheath. The thick mud on his paws might not have done so much damage to Charlotte's dress if she hadn't then shrieked, "Stop, you!" and tried to whack Jake away. Even though I called him and tried to snag his collar, Charlotte's recoiling move made Jake want to be friends even more, so that he sprang up again on Charlotte, who tried to bat him away. "You stupid dog!" she cried. "Go away!"

Jake, who didn't like to be called stupid, began whimpering, and again vaulted up on Charlotte, who had turned her backside on him, which meant Jake's paws landed on the reverse side of the sheath, which I figured was now pretty much ruined.

"I'm so sorry, Charlotte, I'm so sorry, I'm so sorry," I kept repeating. My godfather, who had tried less successfully than I had to contain Jake, slumped in defeat on a kitchen chair.

When I finally managed to snag Jake's leash, I led him out of the kitchen. Scout the cat, who was much better at figuring out when he wasn't wanted, had already slunk away. I managed to corral the two of them in the pet-containment area, where I gave them a perfunctory drying off with fresh towels that I kept in their little home for just this purpose.

Oh, Lord, but I wished Tom would come home.

"Well, Charlotte," I said in my conciliatory voice

when I returned to the kitchen, "again, I'm sorry. Would you like to see the contract?"

She was at our sink, where she was rubbing her muddied dress with a wet paper towel. When she faced me, her eyes were slits. "This is a disaster," she said, and a cold finger of guilt ran down my spine.

"Dogs do get muddy when it rains," Jack said, attempting mournfulness. "It's, what do you call it? A force of nature."

"Stop it," Charlotte retorted. "I've been trying to phone *you* all day, too, but you won't return my calls."

Now Jack's voice was genuinely mournful. "My best friend was found dead in a ravine, Charlotte."

She turned to him, startled. "Who, Finn? What was he doing in a ravine?" Her tone implied that death could be avoided if one could but stay out of ravines. Jack just shook his head.

"It was a car accident, Charlotte," I said in a low voice.

"Was anyone else hurt?"

"I don't think so."

"This is a tragedy," she said to Jack. "I'm so sorry."

"Thanks," said Jack disconsolately.

Nobody said anything for a few minutes, and so I took a deep breath. "Now, Charlotte, here are the contract changes." I handed her the sheet.

She perused the paper. "This looks fine."

Charlotte kept glancing at Jack, who would not meet her gaze. I reflected once more on how much beyond me it was to know how or why these two had managed to keep a relationship going for a day, much less four months. Charlotte was elegant, perfectionistic, and expected to get her way, even if she had to pay for it. Her house in Flicker Ridge looked like a furniture showcase. Jack was generous, openhearted, and a slob, and the house he was renovating looked like a tornado had blown off the roof and thoroughly jumbled the interior . . . and no one had bothered to clean up since.

From the beginning of their odd relationship, I'd suspected that there was more desire to keep things going on Charlotte's side than there was on Jack's. He told me he'd been gentle, but firm, when she said she wanted him to stop spending so much time with Doc Finn. Doc Finn was his friend, and Jack wanted to go fishing and do . . . well, whatever his friend wanted. Charlotte had said he should want to spend more time with her.

Jack had demurred. But Charlotte had persevered. In fact, the previous month, she had confided to me that she expected to become engaged to Jack very soon. After a couple of weeks had gone by, I'd gently hinted around to Jack about this, as in, "Do you think you'd ever be wanting me to do your wedding reception?" He'd shaken his head at the suggestion, and told me he had no plans to get married again. His first wife had died of cancer before I'd known her. All this made me think that there were no nuptial festivities for Jack and Charlotte in the foreseeable future.

"I suppose that's the cleanest I'm going to get it."

Charlotte had put the contract down and was working on her dress again. Now she turned away from the sink and gave me a forlorn look, as if the dog, and Jack's unhelpfulness, had hurt her deeply, and I was supposed to do something about it.

But I didn't know what to do. "So, Charlotte, what do you think of the figures?" I tried again.

"They're fine." But she'd spent only a moment looking at them. She pulled out her checkbook and wrote me a check. "Goldy?" she asked. "Can you be out at Gold Gulch Spa at eight o'clock tomorrow morning, so we can do the walk-through, and you can figure out how to use their kitchen?"

"Sure," I replied, although I didn't feel too sure of it, frankly.

"Yes," said Jack, "I'll bring her."

"That's not necessary, Jack," I said.

"Jack," said Charlotte, attempting to be mollifying, "you don't need to be there. I want to spend time with you, but not there, not tomorrow. If you need to grieve for your friend, then you should do that. Out at the spa, you'll just get in the way, sweetheart."

Sweetheart?

When nobody said anything, Charlotte said, "Will you call me tonight, Jack, if you need me?" He looked up at her hopefully and nodded. "Well then," she went on, "I guess I need to go home and change before the fund-raiser."

When the door had closed, I turned to my godfather. "Jack, you don't have to take me out to Gold Gulch tomorrow. I can manage."

Jack made his face blank, a practice I'd seen him do before. "No, but I want to go. To protect you from this Victor Lane character."

"I don't need protecting, thanks."

"Uh-huh. Last time I looked, your first husband disproved that particular theorem."

"Oh, Jack, don't—"

"Now," he interrupted, "tell me why Tom is investigating the death of my best friend."

"I have no idea that that's what he's doing."

"Bull. When I had too much to drink and hit a tree with the seventy-one Mercedes I had before I got the seventy-three, the whole thing was handled by state patrol. That's how they do accidents in this state. I know, 'cuz I asked."

"Jack, I don't know—"

"Yeah, yeah, you said that already." He stood up. "All right, I'm walking across the street to my own house."

"Jack? You're not angry, are you?" I asked anxiously as I walked him to the door. "I really don't know what Tom is doing now. But I want to help with . . . with you feeling better about Doc Finn."

"Uh-huh." He heaved on his jacket and opened the front door. "Let me tell you something I learned in the years before I became a recovering lawyer."

"Jack—," I began, but he held up his hand.

"I always know when a witness is lying."

Doggone it, I thought, as I cleaned up Marla's dishes. I wasn't lying. Okay, I did suspect that Tom's disappearance from the O'Neal wedding was related to the discovery of Doc Finn's body. But I knew no more about the situation than Jack did.

When Tom finally came home, it was almost nine o'clock. I'd kept the ragout going on a low simmer, just in case.

"Miss G. You should have gone to bed. I'm sorry I'm so late."

"Did you eat?"

"No. I'll fix myself a plate."

"Sit," I commanded. Tom washed his hands and slumped at the table. He shut his eyes tight, either from exhaustion or to block out what he'd seen that evening. When I put a dish of cooked penne, steamed broccoli, and ragout in front of him, you'd have thought it was steak on the *QE2*.

"Oh my," he said. "This looks wonderful."

While he ate, I gave him an animated account of the rest of the day after he'd left, the reception, packing up with Julian, the visits from Marla, Jack, and Charlotte Attenborough. He shook his head and smiled briefly. But then the smile vanished.

"Can you tell me what kept you down at the department?" I asked.

"I can, but you can't mention a word of it to anyone, especially that nosy lawyer godfather of yours."

"Don't worry."

"Last night, a driver going west up the canyon spotted a reflection in the rain. Called in that she thought a vehicle might have gone off the road and landed down in that deep ravine where folks dump trash sometimes."

"Yeah, I know the spot." Despite the NO DUMPING sign, people didn't chuck their unwanted furniture and garbage down that hillside sometimes; they did it as a matter of routine.

"Last night, state patrol had their hands full with accidents in the rain, but they finally got around to checking that ravine. And there was Doc Finn's Porsche Cayenne, on its side."

"Did he slide off the road?"

"The mud has made it impossible to tell exactly what happened. But state patrol called us after they'd spent about an hour down in the ravine."

The taste of acid filled my mouth.

"Somebody," Tom continued as he pushed his plate away, "came down into the ravine and used a rock to break the driver's-side window. It looks as if whoever the person was then used another rock, or something, to smash in Doc Finn's skull."

"The rocks couldn't have come loose somehow, when the Porsche slid into the ravine?"

"No, Miss G. That's why state patrol is good at what they do." He shook his head. "Doc Finn was murdered."

Chapter 7

I slumped into the kitchen chair closest to Tom. My feet and hands were suddenly freezing. "So, what are they up to now, down at the department?"

"The ME's been called. They'll try to do the autopsy as soon as they can. And our department is analyzing the contents of Finn's car, to see if that will give us any leads. There are only a couple of houses nearby, and our guys have canvassed the whole area. But nobody saw anything."

"Do they have any idea where Doc Finn was going?"

"Yeah. He had his cell in the car. According to the Received Calls on there, he got a call from your godfather last night, but that went straight to voice mail. Before that, there was a longer call. It came around half past seven Wednesday night, from Southwest Hospital, from inside a patient's room. He saw a neighbor as he was backing his car out of his driveway, and he said he was off to see an old patient. Only

problem is, that room is on the maternity ward, and
the patient in that room was out with her husband
looking at their baby at the time. And she's never
been a patient of Doc Finn's. She's never even heard
of him."

"No security cameras recording the goings in and
out of the patient's room, I take it."

"Nope. My gut tells me we're talking about a clever
killer here. Of course, during visiting hours there are
all kinds of people in the hospital, so basically it
could have been anyone."

"Did Doc Finn even have any patients in Southwest
Hospital at the time?"

"That's something we're checking on."

I hugged my shoulders, but that couldn't dispel the
chill I was feeling. "You know Jack's going to be dev-
astated that his pal was murdered."

Tom nodded. "I figured."

"He really wanted to talk to you tonight. He waited
here a long time, wondering where you were, asking
questions. Said when he hit a tree, remember, not long
after he got here? State patrol handled the whole
thing. He kept asking me why you were down at the
department. It was almost as if he knew something
was wrong with Doc Finn's accident."

Tom pulled out his small notebook. "Almost as if
he knew something was wrong, huh?"

"Oh, Tom, for heaven's sake. Doc Finn was Jack's
best friend." My tone grew hot and defensive. "And
anyway, Jack wanted to talk to you."

Tom pushed his chair back from the table. "Well

then, maybe we should oblige him. Care to take a walk across the street?"

"You're going to interrogate my godfather?"

"I'm just going to ask him a few questions."

"Tom!"

"Trust me, Goldy, your godfather is a wily old coot. He can read people the way preachers recite Bible verses. If he even sniffs this is an interrogation, he'll lawyer up faster than you can say, Glory Be."

I gritted my teeth and reached for my trench coat in the hall closet. While Tom waited for me on the porch, I felt a pang of guilt that we were going over to Jack's with the intention of . . . well, whatever it was we were intending to do. I dashed back into the kitchen and grabbed a bottle of Sauternes, a little seventy-five-dollar-a-bottle number that a grateful client had given me. So far, I hadn't had the heart to open it.

"What do you think you're doing?" Tom asked me when I appeared on the porch with the wine.

"I'm taking Jack this bottle—"

"Put it back."

"Can't I just—?"

"Absolutely not. Y'ever hear of the old saying, 'Beware the gift giver'?"

"I can give Jack something if I want to!" I retorted. "I just brought him bread this morning!"

"He sees us coming? With you holding that? He'll think, *Here comes Tom the cop with his wife, my god-child, and she's holding a bottle of wine that she*

*thinks she's going to pimp me with, so I'll tell them all
the dirt on Doc Finn."*

"Tom!"

"You trust me on this, or not?"

Well, of couse I did. I put the bottle back. But I felt
my nerves becoming even more frayed . . . and they'd
been unraveling ever since Tom had arrived home.

"Tom, Gertie Girl, come in." Jack's tone was grateful as he opened his massive door, a large sculpted
oak number that he had picked up at a salvage yard.

And so we entered Jack's Jumble, as Arch called it.
My godfather kept saying he was renovating, but as
yet, there were few visible signs of improvement, either on the exterior or the interior. I could see why the
persistently rainy weather would have prevented him
from putting up new cedar-shake shingle siding,
which was what he claimed he intended to do. But on
the inside, he had no excuse that I could see. Fishing
and carousing tended to derail motivation, in my
view.

As we stepped into the gray-walled foyer that still
showed the rectangular outlines of the previous owner's pictures, it was clear Jack hadn't made much
progress. He'd gutted the first floor, so that instead of
having a parlor, dining room, and who-knew-what-
all Victorian-type rooms, he now had a big, open
space. In the far-left corner, he'd put state-of-the-art
appliances into what was going to be an open-plan
kitchen . . . but he still had no cabinets or counter-
tops. My feet gritted across the hardwood floors that

Jack had uncovered when he'd torn up the old green-and-brown shag carpeting. As far as I knew, Jack had not made a move to refinish the floors, or even to call someone to get an estimate to have them done.

"Thanks for coming over." He was trying to sound cheerful, but his voice was as forlorn as the long, high-ceilinged room that, he'd told me, would eventually double as both living and dining room. The whole area contained only a few pieces of furniture that Jack had bought from the local secondhand store, while his "good furniture," as he called it, stayed in storage.

"Sit," Jack invited us, sweeping his hand toward a threadbare, Victorian-style maroon velvet couch that had seen better days, I guessed, in a brothel. On each side of the couch, and in front of it, stood out-of-context teak Danish-modern tables that, more than the couch, had seen much better days. And then there were the two director's chairs that looked as if they'd been fished out of a well, back when Orson Welles had been a director.

Tom sat in one of the director's chairs, while I took my place at the far end of what I affectionately thought of as the johns' couch.

Tom grinned. "I can see you've been keeping your nose to the remodeling grindstone." He liked Jack, and the feeling was mutual.

"Can't rush these things," Jack commented. He gestured to an open bottle of scotch on the table, where there were also, I noted, three glasses, a carafe of water, and an ice bucket. Next to these cocktail fixings was a yellow legal pad and a pen, two lawyerly accoutrements that Jack had never been able to give up. "Drink?"

To my astonishment, Tom replied, "Sure." I blinked, and tried to catch Tom's eye. I had never once witnessed him take a drink from someone he wanted to question. He was always circumspect, if not downright wary.

"Gertie Girl?" Jack asked. "Same as usual?"

"With a lot of water, please, Jack. I've already had some sherry."

"Tom?"

"Straight with a bit of ice, thanks, Jack."

"Well, Tom-boy." Jack shook his head. "You must really suspect me of doing something." So, Tom was drinking and Jack was acting suspicious, and I was left to wonder what was going on. Muttering unintelligibly to himself, Jack poured us each a couple of fingers of scotch, added some water and ice to both, and handed them across. "Trying to throw me off guard, eh, Tom? Drink my scotch, see if you can get me to drink more than you do, loosen up my tongue, find out what I know about Doc Finn. Is that it?"

"Hey, neighbor, back off a bit," Tom replied. He took a long swig of the proffered drink. "I know you were friends with Finn, and I'm sorry he's gone." Tom paused. "Goldy said you wanted to talk to me, that's all."

"I do."

When no one said anything, Tom sipped his drink again and said finally, "So, you know anyone who wanted to hurt Doc Finn? Did he have any enemies?"

Jack surprised me again, this time by putting his head in his hands and starting to sob.

"Jack, Jack," I said. I moved over next to him and put my arms around his heaving shoulders.

"This is my fault," he howled. "It's all my fault."

I looked at Tom helplessly. Tom, in turn, gave me a warning glance that I knew meant—*Say nothing, do nothing.* But Jack was my godfather, I'd always loved him. For crying out loud, I'd known him before I'd even met Tom. So there was no way I was going to follow Tom's directive.

"It's not your fault, Jack," I protested. "It's the fault of the person who—"

"Goldy!" Tom shouted.

"Person who what?" Jack asked. He didn't seem to be crying anymore, and he'd picked up the pen he'd put by the legal pad.

I took a deep breath and settled back into the lumpy couch. In front of the couch was a large picture window that had been put in by a previous owner, so Jack had a perfect view of our house. I resolved to look at our house and say not a word. If Tom and Jack were playing some kind of cat-and-mouse game, I didn't have a rule book.

"Why is Doc Finn dying all your fault?" Tom asked gently.

"He was murdered, wasn't he?"

"Yes," Tom replied. "Is that your fault?"

Jack shook his head. "It's too complicated," he said,

his somber mood reasserting itself. He threw down the pen.

"I work all day at complicated," Tom commented.

"Can you tell me how he was killed?" Jack asked.

"No can do, you know that, Counselor."

"Gertie Girl?" Jack's large eyes implored me.

"Don't start with her, Jack," Tom said sharply. "Or else we're going to have to leave. Now tell me why it's all your fault, okay? Or else tell me who Doc Finn's enemies were."

Jack considered. Time stretched out for so long that I finally looked around for a clock. Big problem: this was Jack's mostly empty house, and there was no clock. He wore a Rolex, so he probably figured he didn't need another timepiece.

"All right," Jack said finally. "But if I talk to you, will you tell me what you know?"

Tom said, "Nope."

"Did someone run him off the road? Shoot him while he was driving?"

Tom shrugged.

Jack exhaled and stared at the legal pad. "I don't know too much about Finn's enemies. There were a few women who wanted to get married, and he didn't." Jack stopped talking and considered. "You know Finn had retired. But recently, he had a few patients. There . . . were problems, I don't know what."

"What kind of problems?" Tom asked sharply. "Medical problems? Financial problems?"

"I don't know," Jack replied, still disconsolate, still staring at the legal pad. "Finn just told me there were problems, and that he was doing some research. But then before I could find out what kind of research, exactly, he stopped answering his home phone and his cell. I went over to his house and banged on the door. No answer there either."

Tom grunted and refilled his drink. I wondered if he meant to rattle Jack by doing this. Ordinarily he'd have taken out his notebook to write down what Jack was saying; I knew that much about my husband.

"How recently was all this, Jack?" Tom asked. "Today's Friday. When, exactly, did Finn stop answering his home phone and his cell?"

"Why?"

"I'm just trying to figure out what you're telling me, how it fits with our timeline."

"What's your timeline?"

"I'm very tired, Jack," Tom replied. "Goldy's even more tired, and she and I both have to get up early tomorrow morning, even though it's a Saturday."

"Okay," Jack said. He set his glass down on the table. "Today's Friday." He cast his eyes up to his ceiling. "I was supposed to meet with Finn, let's see, last night. I didn't see him or hear from him after yesterday afternoon. I went to his place real late last night, but he wasn't there. Then this morning, he was supposed to pick me up for the O'Neal wedding, but he didn't show."

Tom pondered this. "So you were supposed to meet with Finn last night to find out what kind of research he was doing, and he didn't show. You called him on both his home phone and his cell, and then you went over to his place. Did you call anybody else, another friend, say, to see where he might be?"

"Nope."

"After Finn said he was doing some research, he suddenly disappeared and didn't call. Did you suspect foul play?"

Jack shook his head in frustration. "I didn't know what to think. Now could you please tell me what is going on?"

"I can't," said Tom.

And so Tom and I went home. I hugged Jack before we left, and he hugged me back and muttered something about seeing me in the morning.

"Where're you going with him in the morning?" Tom asked me, once we'd come into our house and put the animals back outside.

"Gold Gulch Spa. Jack's insisting on coming. Why? You don't think I'm in danger when I'm with him, do you?"

"No," Tom said thoughtfully. "I'm just trying to figure out what he's not telling us. There's something, I just can't put my finger on it."

"He's secretive, you know that. He . . . loves puzzles. He used to give me all kinds of different ones when I was growing up. Plus, he's a risk junkie. Maybe he's sure he can figure out what happened to Doc Finn . . . on his own."

"Oh, man, that's all we need. Another amateur sleuth mucking things up. What do you mean, he's secretive?"

We moved into the kitchen and sat down.

I said, "I didn't even know until a week before he got here that he was moving to Aspen Meadow from New Jersey. And that he'd bought that decrepit old place across the street."

"You didn't know anything?"

"Nope. And that was only six months ago, as you know. Plus, I think the only reason he told me about the move was that he had told his son, Lucas, what he was doing, and Lucas had had a fit that Jack wasn't moving across the street from *him*. So to avert Lucas showing up on our porch and accusing me of trying to steal Jack's affections, which he'd done before, mind you, Jack calmly called and told me his plans."

"Huh." Tom looked around our kitchen and insisted on tidying up. "It'll give me a chance to think."

While he was washing dishes, I said, "Listen, Tom, you've probably already heard this from six different people—"

Tom turned off the water, wiped his hands, and gave me his full attention. "Go ahead."

"Well, just some of those questions you were asking Jack . . ." Tom waited. Finally, I said, "Enemies Doc Finn had? Billie Attenborough didn't like Doc Finn."

"Stop while I get my notebook."

"You know," I went on, "she always blamed him for losing her first two fiancés. She blamed him loudly."

"Billie does everything loudly. And," he added thoughtfully, "you know how nothing is ever her fault? She doesn't take responsibility for a thing. Everything is always *your* fault." When I looked stricken, he said, "No, not you, Miss G. At least, not all the time." When I frowned, he went on, laughing, "Don't go getting paranoid on me. Guys down at the department are always saying women are just too sensitive." This time I narrowed my eyes. "Okay," Tom concluded, his tone apologetic, "for Billie, everything is always somebody else's fault." He closed his notebook. "We'll check this out, thanks. Now, let me finish these dishes."

I thanked him and put my feet up on a chair. When the phone rang, it startled me. Quarter after ten? Jack calling to try to get information out of Tom? Billie Attenborough phoning with a new demand?

It was neither. The caller ID said merely, SOUTHWEST HOSPITAL.

"Looks like somebody might be trying to set up one of us," I commented, and told Tom about the call's provenance.

"I'll deal with it." With wet hands, Tom took the phone. After a moment, he said, "Actually, you want my wife."

I shot him a murderous glance, but only sang into the phone, *"Goldilocks' Catering, Where Everything Is Just Right!* Whoever this is, I usually don't do business this late in the evening!"

"Is this Goldy?" a tentative male voice asked.

"It is." I wracked my brain to figure out who I knew in Southwest Hospital at the moment. Someone from church? Someone I was supposed to do a party for?

"This is, uh, Norman O'Neal."

I shook my head. Cecelia O'Neal's didn't-want-to-be-irresponsible-anymore ex-dad. "Norman. Last time I saw you, you didn't look too good."

"Okay, yeah, sorry. It's just that I can't remember today very well. I'm down here in the hospital, and I can't figure out what I did to get here. I'm not sick, or at least, I don't think I am. One of the nurses told me I busted up my daughter's wedding, and I'm really hoping that isn't true."

"Well—"

"Oh, God, I did bust up Cecelia's wedding, didn't I?"

"Not really. You just busted up the cake. I am curious, though. Why are you calling me? Why not call Cecelia if you want to apologize?"

"She's on her honeymoon, I guess, and her mother isn't answering. I, I'm desperate. I looked in the yellow pages for caterers and churches in Aspen Meadow, and your name sort of sounded familiar, so I called you."

"But why—"

"Oh, right, right. Well, to make a long story short, I want to get back into my daughter Cecelia's life."

I'd majored in psychology, and I knew Carl Rogers would have wanted me to spit that right back at him. And anyway, I didn't know what else to do. "You want to get back into your daughter's life," I said slowly.

Tom raised his eyebrow and gave me a quizzical look. I shook my head: *You don't want to know.*

Norman O'Neal's voice rose hopefully. "Do you think I have a chance? Of getting back into Ceci's life?"

I licked my lips and tried to think of what to say. "Let's put it this way, Norman," I said, finally. "I'd say you're going about it in the wrong way. You could start by apologizing to Cecelia and Dodie, and sending them a big check."

"Please, Goldy, help me." Norman O'Neal took an unsteady breath. "Have you ever had a close brush with death, Mrs. Schulz? You're married, aren't you? Should I call you Mrs. Schulz?"

"Mrs. Schulz is fine. And yes, I've had a close brush with death."

"Doesn't it make you reorder your priorities?"

"Mr. O'Neal. Norman. Tell me what's going on."

"Look, I have a granddaughter I've never seen. I know she's just adopted, I mean, not Cecelia's by blood, oh, that didn't come out right. But still, I want to be part of Cecelia's life, sort of start over, you know? I want to get to know this granddaughter, even if she is just adopted, you know."

"Just adopted?" I thought of Julian, who was "just adopted," and had turned out just fine, thank you very so much. "You might want to rethink your diction when it comes to referring to your granddaughter, Norm. And where does the brush with death part come in?"

"I heard my granddaughter almost died! So I wanted to reorder my priorities. Please, won't you help me? Wait, wait a second—"

"Almost died? What do you mean?"

There was no reply, just some gargling from the other end.

"Norm," I said, "really, I'd love to help you—," but was interrupted by the sound of Norman O'Neal once again puking his guts out, this time on the hospital floor.

Chapter 8

I hung up rather than listen to those horrible noises. I then told Tom about the remorseful, confused, and oh-so-sick Norman O'Neal.

"Sounds like your typical alcoholic after a blackout," Tom said. "He wants like hell to make amends, at least he likes the idea of making amends. Only thing is, he wants somebody else to make them for him."

"Maybe I should go see him in the hospital," I replied. "He did sound pretty awful. Plus, he said Cecelia's daughter almost died! Have you heard anything about that?"

"No, I haven't. And you're kidding about visiting Norman O'Neal in the hospital, right? As if you don't have enough on your plate already."

"Never tell a caterer she has too much on her plate."

"Miss G., please. You want to go see Norman O'Neal, I'll go with you. But at least wait until you've done Billie Attenborough's wedding," Tom advised. "By then the dust and/or mush may have settled in Norman O'Neal's brain, and the three of us might be able to have a civilized conversation. Although I doubt it."

"By then he'll have gone home from the hospital."

"I'm sure Dodie O'Neal will tell you where he lives."

"Or maybe he'll be in rehab," I said. "Then I'd never be able to reach him, or at least, not for thirty days, or whatever it is. Now I'm all worried about Cecelia's daughter. I'm going to call her."

"It's almost eleven."

But I dialed Dodie O'Neal anyway.

"Hey, Goldy," she said. "Saw your name on the caller ID. I gave you the right amount of money, didn't I?"

"Of course, Dodie. But Norman just called me from the hospital."

"Oh, is that what the calls have been about from Southwest? Please tell me he's dying."

I cleared my throat. "He said Cecelia's daughter had a brush with death. I just wanted to make sure she was okay."

"She's in bed, fast asleep. Was Norman still drunk?"

"He was pretty sick. But he sounded as if he wants to make amends, or to have a relationship, or something."

Dodie snorted. "He calls you again, tell him to contact my lawyer."

"I felt sorry for him," I said lamely.

"Goldy, don't fall for his act. He's a son of a bitch. He manipulates women into bed with him, he gets women to do his work for him, he gets women who are going through divorces to pay him more money than is sane. He would manipulate the boulders in my front yard, if he could."

"I just wanted to let you know about his call." I told her again what a lovely wedding Cecelia had had—even though I'd missed most of it, of course—and signed off.

Tom was emptying his pockets, carefully placing his keys, badge, notebook, and wallet on the counter. He stopped for a moment to give his words their full effect. "I don't get you, Goldy. A drunk—a lawyer, no less—comes and almost screws up the wedding of one of your favorite clients. He makes said client—the bride, no less—cry. He makes his granddaughter cry. The lawyer takes a swing at our priest. Our priest pops him one, and the offending father-of-the-bride, who, let us not forget, was entirely in absentia as his daughter was growing up, passes out. The drunk lawyer gets hauled off to the hospital, where, when he wakes up, he probably begins preparing his papers to sue Father Pete. But he takes a break from preparing those papers, and calls you to blubber. And you feel sorry for this asshole?"

"Oh, Tom, he just wants to have a relationship with Cecelia and her daughter. And you make it sound so—"

"You want to do something for a few drunks? Make

cookies for the AA meetings we have down at the jail. Trust me, drunks who are drying out love sweets. But do nothing for that SOB Norman O'Neal. You do anything? Visit him, send him flowers? He'll say in court, 'See, even the caterer felt remorse over what happened, she brought me roses.'"

I shook my head. "I married a cynic."

"No, you married a realist." He leaned over and gave me a kiss. "Not meaning to bring up the past. I mean, with the Jerk and all. But you've already felt sorry enough for one asshole to last an entire lifetime."

"That's hitting below the belt, Tom."

"My dear sweet wife," Tom said as he gathered me into his arms, "first of all, I would never hit you. Second, there are any number of fun things I would love to do with you that involve activities below the belt."

And so we went to bed, although we didn't actually go to sleep for a while. Tom had a number of those activities in mind, and I was more than willing to try them out.

As I was drifting off to dreamland, I realized that unlike many of the people I worked for, I hadn't thought getting married was any big deal. It was being married—to Tom, that is—that, along with having Arch, had been the very biggest deal of my life.

Saturday morning dawned with weak sunshine and birdsong. I lay in bed thinking how much better the night before, with Tom, had been than the day I was about to have was probably going to be. The prospect of spending my Saturday with Charlotte Attenborough and the dreaded Victor Lane at Gold Gulch Spa did not fill me with joy. Even the leavening presence of my godfather wouldn't help. I wished fervently for rain, lots of it, and a cancellation of all plans.

"Come on, Miss G." Tom leaned over and kissed my cheek. I luxuriated in his scent of aftershave and soap. He placed an iced espresso with cream on the night table. "I have to go meet with the medical examiner."

"The medical examiner? Do you really think he'll get to Doc Finn so soon?"

"Yup. Our guy was an old friend of Finn's."

"And he wants to perform that procedure on his old friend?" I shivered as I stood up and eased into black pants and a white shirt. "That's awful."

"He called me early on my cell. Said he doesn't want anybody else to do it, and that he was coming in early and wanted me there. Finn was going to the top of his list."

We were interrupted by the sound of Jack's horn, a custom contraption he'd had installed in the old sedan. *Tweep-tweep-twoop-tweep* declared his presence out front. I glanced at the clock: not quite 6:30? If the neighbors didn't love me because of my godfather habitually rolling in noisily after a night of carousing with Doc Finn, they sure as heck didn't love me now, with him beeping to indicate he was ready to go.

"Guy lives across the street," Tom commented, "and he can't phone or come over when he's ready to go? He has to honk the horn on that dad-blasted car of his?"

"He's from New Jersey. They honk there. And you know how he loves that horn."

"It may be after eight o'clock on the East Coast, but it isn't here. Six months ought to be long enough for someone to get used to changing over from Eastern Standard to Mountain Daylight Time, don't you think?"

"Tom."

"That secretive slob of a godfather of yours isn't always as loving as you think he is, that's all I'm saying. All right. Let me go and talk to him."

"Please be nice."

"I'm always nice."

While Tom went out front, I slipped down to the kitchen and looked around frantically. What did I need for the trip out to Gold Gulch Spa? Whatever it was, I needed to gather it up quickly, because Jack was not a patient man. I booted up my kitchen computer, brought up Billie Attenborough's revised menu, numbers, and table settings, inserted a new flash drive, and backed up the files for Yolanda. Bless Yolanda's heart, I knew she would be out there this early, as the overnight guests had to have breakfast.

I also quickly opened a morning e-mail from Charlotte. She said she was bringing extra place cards, linens, candles, centerpieces, china, and flatware to the spa. Maybe she should be leaving all this up to Billie, since Her Flakiness, Bridezilla, was the one screwing up this whole thing.

Except for the crab cakes, at least dear Julian was making all the extra food. Bless his heart.

I pressed the button on my espresso maker to make myself another Summertime Special. When I'd poured the espresso and cream into a thermal mug with a lid and showered it with ice, I grabbed my purse, the flash drive, and a raincoat, and raced out the door.

Tom and Jack were engaged in amicable conversation as they leaned against Jack's shiny red Mercedes. How someone could keep his house such a mess and be so careful to keep his classic car so meticulously clean was one of the mysteries of the universe, at least to my way of thinking.

Jack, looking dapper in a white Brooks Brothers shirt, navy blazer, and navy trousers, held the passenger door open for me. "Gertie Girl! Tom says you weren't quite ready to go. Sorry if I bothered you."

I shook my head at Tom, who was grinning widely. "I'm ready, Jack. I just don't understand why we have to leave so early. The spa's only twenty, twenty-five minutes away, and I don't think they serve breakfast to the overnight guests until seven or so."

"We have to get Charlotte. She called me at six and asked if we would pick her up. I felt bad for . . . not doing better with her last night."

"But your best friend had died!"

He gave me a sidelong glance. "My little Gertie Girl. Always making excuses for me. Well, let me warn you. Trying to pry Charlotte out of that house of hers is like trying to chip cement off a brick. Plus, you probably want to talk to Billie, don't you?"

"Not particularly," I replied.

Jack folded himself into the driver's seat and gave me a devilish grin. "If you don't want to talk to Billie, then that's why we have to get there early. That lazy, unemployed thirty-six-year-old wouldn't get out of bed before nine o'clock if her life depended on it."

Jack fishtailed away from the curb.

"Jack!"

"Oops, sorry. Buckle up, would ya? Tom's watching."

I wrenched on my seat belt and checked the rearview mirror. Tom was indeed eyeing our departure . . . but he was grinning and shaking his head.

I glanced around the interior of the Mercedes. It was black leather accented with wood grain, not the easiest color combination to keep clean in the mountains, where the summer weather was often dry, dusty, and windy . . . unless you'd had a ton of rain, which we had. But then you'd expect mud on the outside and inside of a vehicle. I was always struggling with either dust or mud in the van. But Jack's car was impeccable, as usual.

"Jack, I don't understand why your house is . . . the way it is, and your car is, uh, the way it is."

"I'm a study in contrasts." He checked his Rolex. "What do you bet Charlotte will be completely dressed this early?"

"She's already sent me an e-mail. I thought you said it would be harder to pry her out of her place than chipping cement off . . . what did you say?"

Jack chuckled. "Drink your coffee so you can wake

up." Jack pulled the Mercedes onto Main Street. "I didn't say Charlotte wouldn't be dressed, I said she wouldn't be ready to leave."

"Maybe she's used to you showing up early."

Jack shrugged. "That woman doesn't like to be surprised. She is utterly predictable."

"Not a study in contrasts, then."

Jack laughed all the way to the Attenboroughs' big place in Flicker Ridge.

"Ah, Jack," said Charlotte. "Thank you for coming." She'd opened the door before we'd even mounted the steps. She wore a loosely draped pantsuit of an undoubtedly expensive silvery material, and matching silver-gray heels. She looked Jack over approvingly, and smiled at me.

Jack, though, pulled his face into a pained expression. I couldn't read whether it was genuine or not. "Charlotte, dear. It's my pleasure."

Charlotte arched an eyebrow, as if she didn't believe him. "Well, thank you. Would either of you like a cup of coffee? I still have a few things to pull together here."

"No thanks," said Jack.

"Thank you," I said. "I'd love some."

Charlotte turned her attention back to Jack. "I have some pictures to show you of how you could decorate your living room. I think they're wonderful, and would really tie the whole Victorian scheme together for you."

"Thanks," said Jack, "I like things untied."

Charlotte drew her perfectly colored brown-pink lips together in a frown. "It will just take a minute."

Jack ground his teeth, then said that of course he'd look at some pictures. He stepped across the threshold into the cavernous house and gestured for me to follow him, which I did.

Charlotte had done a spectacular job on her own place, I would give her that. It was one of those mountain homes that have been filled with lots of expensive furniture made out of elaborate handmade configurations of . . . twigs. I knew the sofas, tables, and chairs-from-twigs were extremely pricey, because I'd catered the opening of the twig-furniture shop. Oversize crimson and green cushions, table lamps made from iron-in-the-shape-of-twigs, and patterned green-and-red rugs and quilts completed the effect.

"Here you go," said Charlotte, handing my godfather a folder marked JACK. It was neatly stuffed with photographs cut from magazines. Jack gave me a knowing wink while Charlotte disappeared around a corner.

"She's gone to check her makeup," Jack said. "Now watch this."

I followed him into the kitchen, a vision in periwinkle-blue-glazed tiles and pale hickory cabinets, complete with matching blue-glazed drawer and cabinet pulls. Jack pulled out a drawer beneath the counter, and pointed inside. It was not a drawer but a new-fangled, miniature trash compactor. In went the file marked JACK. My godfather flipped a switch, and a terrifying grinding noise filled the kitchen.

"Jack!" I whispered. "She'll hear you."

"No, she won't. It's a big house, completely sound-proofed, so neither Charlotte nor Billie can hear the elk bugling in mating season. It drives them nuts."

Soundproofing or no soundproofing, I tiptoed back to the living room anyway. I hadn't felt this guilty since I'd substituted homemade fudge sauce for some horrid low-calorie stuff a hostess had insisted I use at her daughter's engagement party.

"God, I need a cigarette," Jack said. "I think I'm going to step outside and have one. If she comes back, tell her I went to put the decorating file in my trunk, God forbid."

"Better hurry up," I warned.

"Will you calm down?" Jack winked again, and was gone.

I eyed a neat display of home-decorating magazines, afraid of mussing them up. Suddenly, I felt overwhelmingly tired. Where was the caffeine-delivery machine in that kitchen? I wondered. Charlotte had offered me some coffee, after all. Did I dare sneak back and look for it?

I did. A moment later I was frowning at an expensive wall-mounted unit with a computer and digital readout. After staring at it for a few moments, in which I was becoming increasingly nervous that Charlotte might reappear, I figured out that the thing ground the beans, then dripped the goods into a thermos. *Damn*, I thought. I didn't dare mess with it without having a look at the manual.

The phone rang, and I looked around for it. Another wall-mounted unit held both the apparatus and a blackboard. The phone rang and rang. It wasn't even seven o'clock in the morning. Should I answer the thing, I wondered, and take a message for Charlotte? I moved over to the blackboard just as someone picked up the phone—either a person or voice mail. I stared at the board, with its chalk hanging on a string. Then for some reason—probably lack of caffeine—I got the giggles. Did I dare write "Goldy was here" on the board? I did not.

There was a name that had been written in chalk, then erased. *O'Neal*. I wasn't aware that the Attenboroughs knew the O'Neals. In fact, I couldn't imagine them moving in the same, as the phrase went, social circles.

I looked over longingly at the coffee machine, but when I heard Charlotte's heels clicking along the hardwood floor, I raced back into the living room and flopped onto the uncomfortable sofa.

When Charlotte reappeared, she looked as lovely as she had when she left.

"Where's Jack?" she demanded.

"Outside."

"Doing what, may I ask?" When I shrugged, she said, "Oh, for God's sake, let's hurry up. I don't want to keep Victor waiting."

Whatever, I thought, *we're still an hour early.* But I didn't want to point this out to the client.

Out on the porch, Charlotte sniffed the air suspiciously, then squinted at Jack.

"You've been smoking."

"Last time I checked, that wasn't a crime."

Charlotte turned to me. "Could you work on your godfather, try to get him to stop his unhealthy habit?"

I swallowed. Wasn't there some law in this country called "I'm not in charge of what he does"? Jack shot me an apologetic glance. Just for good measure, he hit the doorbell. It donged mercilessly in the interior.

"Jack, what in the world are you doing?" Charlotte demanded.

"Trying to wake up that daughter of yours." He hit the bell again.

"She's getting married tomorrow! She needs her beauty sleep!" Charlotte protested.

"She needs something," Jack admitted before opening the sedan's back door so I could climb in.

Maybe I shouldn't have agreed to let Jack drive the two of us out to Gold Gulch Spa. Jack was teasing Charlotte, and it wasn't going well. As Tom had pointed out, men teased each other and they thought it was fine. When men teased women, though, we took it as pure cruel aggression.

Well, anyway, while dealing with Charlotte and Jack, I was beginning to feel like one of those spots on the globe that's set between warring factions. Alsace-Lorraine. Kuwait. Somebody always wants it, and the place ends up getting smashed in every conflict. I took a deep breath and closed my eyes, trying to visualize myself as Switzerland.

In the front seat, I could hear Charlotte Attenborough asking again about Finn. Was she trying to find out what had happened, or was she pumping Jack for information? I didn't know, but it made me uncomfortable. Tom said my paranoia antennae were the best functioning he'd ever encountered.

"I am not controlling," Charlotte was insisting now. "If anything, I'm too accommodating. I put up with that pigpen you call a house—"

"It's being renovated," Jack said calmly. "And no one is forcing you to come over. In fact, if you would call before you showed up one of these times, I'd have a chance to clean it up."

Charlotte tsked. "I dial your number, but you don't answer. And anyway, the only person I should be phoning is the county health inspector."

"That's going a bit far," Jack murmured as he turned out of Flicker Ridge and headed back toward the lake. An icy silence descended in Jack's Mercedes. When he turned, to head west on Upper Cottonwood Creek Road toward Gold Gulch Spa, Charlotte reopened . . . well, what were they? Negotiations? Hostilities?

"You know, Jack," she said, "I'm acquainted with any number of contractors who could have had that place of yours completely done, cleaned up, and ready to be lived in a month ago."

"I like to do things my own way," Jack replied, his tone stubborn.

"And now who's being controlling?" Charlotte retorted sharply. "If you just didn't spend so much time with—" But here she stopped short, and what felt like the refrain of a practiced argument was left dangling.

Jack's face in the rearview mirror turned an ashen gray, and I realized Charlotte had finally gotten to him. Charlotte had meant to say, I was willing to bet, that Jack was spending too much time with Doc Finn. That's why the house wasn't getting renovated fast enough; why Jack didn't answer when Charlotte called—he was fishing with Doc Finn; that's why Charlotte felt she had to show up at Jack's house unannounced, and I was willing to bet it was why there was this undercurrent of rancor in their relationship. Charlotte, I was also willing to bet, had only at the last moment remembered that Doc Finn was dead.

At the right-hand turnoff to the spa, I noticed on the left side of the street the forlorn-looking building that had formerly housed Spruce Medical Group. Most of the tenants had long since abandoned these digs for the posh new medical building on the north side of Aspen Meadow. But still. In a raging snowstorm, Doc Finn had set out from here, from this spot, when I'd called about Arch's fever. He'd overlooked his own peril to bring kindness and healing into our house. I'd be forever grateful to him for it.

But Doc Finn was gone, the victim of foul play. My heart twisted in my chest.

Chapter 9

Ah, the prodigal mother of the bride!" Victor Lane cried when we pulled up and disembarked. "I'm so happy to see you, Charlotte dearest!"

While Victor Lane ostentatiously kissed Charlotte Attenborough on both cheeks, Jack inverted his eyebrows, pointed to Victor with his thumb, and gave me his patented *Who-the-hell-is-this-guy* look. I shrugged and shook my head. Let Charlotte introduce them to each other; I knew I was invisible to Victor Lane, too. He just wanted to show me how unimportant I was.

Victor continued to fuss over Charlotte, who cooed back. Victor was a slender, unattractive man with pit-marked cheeks, a shaved head, and virtually no chin. His facial skin seemed to be pulled too tightly over the bones, giving him a skeletal appearance. In truth, I decided, he looked like a reject from the bowling ball factory.

This day, he was wearing a ridiculous-looking pale green sweat suit and black high-top sneakers, which gave him the appearance of being as innocuous as a lime lollipop. Still, I knew not to underestimate him.

In the distance, a bell gonged, and women emerged from the various dormitory doors and began to move along the dirt trails that led, according to signs, to the weeklong-spa check-in, the day-spa check-in, the living room, the dining room, the gym, the hiking trails, the regular pool, and the hot pool. I looked at my watch: seven forty-five. When had all these guests had breakfast, I wondered, and when was lunch? From the longing looks the gals were casting at the dining room, I had the feeling breakfast was in the distant past, and lunch was in the even more distant future.

"This is Jack Carmichael," I said loudly to Victor Lane, once he'd disengaged from Charlotte. "My godfather."

"Of course!" said Victor, extending a skinny hand. "The happily retired attorney. Charlotte has told me so much about you."

"And you remember Goldy?" Jack rejoined, with a smile and exaggerated politeness. He bowed in my direction, then straightened up. "She's the vastly successful caterer whom you believed couldn't cook."

So much for a peaceful visit. I smiled brightly, trying to envision Geneva, or Lake Lucerne, or some other sunny spot in neutral Switzerland.

"Yes, of course." Victor's smiling mouth full of yellow teeth and exaggerated enthusiasm made me cringe. "I knew your ex-husband, of course. Great doctor. And, ah, our chef, Yolanda? She's looking forward to visiting with you." He turned back to Charlotte. "We want everything to be perfect for our Billie!"

"Our Billie?" Jack asked, but I nudged him.

I interrupted the conversation to ask for directions to the ladies' room. Victor said it was off the TV room, next to the dining room. He then invited the three of us to come inside. I hustled ahead of them to the TV room, a pine-paneled space with overstuffed faux–Early American sofas. I stared at the far wall: there were four unmarked doors hidden in the paneling. I knocked on one, heard no response, and opened the door, praying all the while that it wasn't reserved for men, and that one was not lurking inside. Did men even come to this spa? I had no idea.

The restroom was unisex: a one-seater. I opened the window, an old-fashioned crank type, and inhaled fresh, moist, pine-scented air. I closed my eyes, did some yoga breathing, and listened to the sounds of women calling to one another about where they were going: massage? hot pool? aerobics?

Why, this might as well be camp, right?

I had loved camp. I'd gone to the same one on Cape Cod for five years, from age seven to twelve. I'd done swimming and boating, and when it rained, arts and crafts, where I'd made lanyards in every shade of the rainbow. There'd been lots of rib-sticking food, too, and with all the activity, you were always ravenous for it. This was like that, I said to myself, breathing deeply. And the wedding tomorrow evening? Why, I was just fixing a really big dinner for all the campers, who'd be dressed up in costumes.

With my new positive attitude firmly in place, I reached to close the window, and saw Jack hustling off toward the hiking trails, a lit cigarette dangling from his mouth. Apparently he'd had enough of both Charlotte and Victor.

Okay, but I was being positive. I straightened my back and stepped out of the restroom, where I immediately came face-to-face with a thin, black-haired woman who'd had such a bad face-lift—tight skin, eyes pulled back—she looked like a cat who'd learned how to stand up.

"Didn't you flush?" she demanded.

"Uh, I was just using the, uh, window."

She tsked, pulled open the door of one of the other restrooms, and slammed it behind her. Guess she and I wouldn't be sharing s'mores tonight!

I hustled into the dining room, where one of the staff members was giving a talk to a group of women. Charlotte and Victor were waiting for her to finish, and this appeared to make the speaker nervous.

"Gold Gulch Spa," the tour-group leader said, flicking her eyes over to Victor, who made a circling motion with his hand to hurry her along, "was at various times a mining camp, a hot springs retreat for the wealthy from Denver, who would make the horse-and-buggy trek before there were roads—"

"All right, Isabelle," Victor Lane interrupted. "Could you please take the ladies out to the hiking trail that leads up to Mount Red-tail Hawk? I'm sure they'd enjoy that. I mixed up a batch of smoothies about twenty minutes ago. Why don't you pour them now so the ladies can have smoothies for their walk?" The ladies murmured their appreciation. "When you get halfway up the mountain, you can give them the background on the spa. Here's the key to the Smoothie Cabin."

"Yes, Mr. Lane," Isabelle replied with alacrity. Thin, fine boned, and what my mother would have called "interesting looking" (which meant, not really pretty), Isabelle was about twenty, had thick bunches of curly red hair, and freckles everywhere. "This way, ladies, to the Smoothie Cabin. How do fruit smoothies sound?"

It sounded pretty darn good, apparently, because I wouldn't have thought that many overweight women could move so quickly.

"We use less than half this space at any one time," Victor began, sweeping his hands to indicate the huge dining room. "We give our clients lots of individual attention, so the spa accommodates no more than sixty-five weeklong clients at a time, plus staff. We average between ten and twelve day-spa clients, every day except Sunday. On Sunday, we clean the rooms and get ready for a new group of guests, who arrive on Monday morning. So a Sunday wedding is perfect."

The room contained a collection of extremely large round tables, each of which was surrounded by eight chairs. "We'll have ten of these moved out, with just enough set up for Billie's guests. Then we'll save this side of the dining room for the head table. . . ."

And on and on he droned. He seemed to have thought this out fairly well for someone who had just been asked to have the wedding and reception at the spa. Maybe he'd done it before. I certainly hadn't heard of Victor giving parties out here, but after all, he used to be a caterer, so maybe this kind of thing came easily.

"But, Victor," Charlotte protested, "are you sure all these women will be completely gone by Sunday morning?"

I couldn't help smiling. Maybe she'd noticed how quickly they'd all repaired to the kitchen in search of "smoothies," which was the term health foodies used for "milk shakes."

"I absolutely promise," Victor reassured her. "And I've already lit a fire under our staff, saying they have to be done cleaning the whole place by lunchtime, otherwise they don't eat!"

Great. Starving the staff didn't usually work as a motivator. Maybe I should see if I could hire a couple of extra cleaning people—

"Oh, Victor," Charlotte said flirtatiously. "You're such a card."

"Well," Victor continued, all smiles now, "I suppose you have your servers lined up, Goldy?"

Oh my God, the extra servers! I'd forgotten. I said, "I have six servers lined up, Victor. But that was for a hundred people, and Billie has invited an extra fifty—"

"Oh, dear, what a mess," Charlotte murmured.

"Not to worry, Charlotte dearest." Victor had that oily way of speaking that reminded one of Uriah Heep. "I will arrange for extra—"

"Mother!" came an all-too-familiar shriek. Billie Attenborough, pulling Dr. Craig Miller, stomped into the dining room. Did Craig Miller have any hobbies besides Billie? This being Saturday, shouldn't he be playing golf or tennis or being a good Coloradan and hiking up a mountain? Somehow, I doubted Billie allowed Craig to do much of anything in his spare time except take care of her.

Billie was wearing a flaming-red pantsuit, which I thought fit her mood, if not her figure, to a T. "How could you come out here without me?"

"Sweetheart, I thought you'd want to sleep—"

"And how was I supposed to sleep with someone dinging on the doorbell?"

"Well, that was Jack—"

"Jack, huh?" Billie said. "Where is he? I'll ring his bell for him!"

"Billie dear—"

"So, you're here," Billie said to me, lifting her dimpled chin.

"Your mother requested my presence," I said, trying to keep the defensiveness out of my voice.

"And I suppose you're charging us for your time?" Billie's eyes blazed at me.

Come to think of it, that wasn't a half-bad idea.

"Billie, my sweet," Craig Miller began, pushing his mop of dark curly hair out of his face with his free hand, "Goldy has been more than generous with you, for numerous extra hours of planning." He held up his hand when she began to interrupt him. "And your mother has been the soul of kindness—"

"What about me?" Victor Lane's high-pitched voice caught me off guard. "Got any kind words for me, Doc?"

Craig Miller actually laughed, a wonderful snuffling noise that made me smile. He wore a navy polo shirt and khaki slacks, looking casual, relaxed, and not at all worried about the upcoming nuptials. Well, if he was relaxed about it all, he was the only one present who was. "How about," Craig addressed Victor, "if the two of us guys let the women work things out in here?"

"Great idea," agreed Victor Lane, smoothly following Craig Miller out of the dining room.

I wanted to scream, *No, no, don't leave me here with the Harpies!* But I didn't. Plus, we hadn't exactly worked out the flow issues.

"I think I need to get to the kitchen to meet with the chef," I said quietly.

"You're not going into that spa kitchen without me!" Billie cried. "I want to hear what you two talk about!"

Yolanda Garcia looked up in surprise when an unexpected trio of women—yours truly, plus Billie and Charlotte Attenborough—invaded her culinary space. Yolanda, who was Cuban, wasn't just pretty, she was beautiful, with creamy brown skin, lots of dark hair that she had pulled up under a hairnet, liquid brown eyes, and a smile that would break your heart. If the smile didn't do it, her cooking would. Her homemade Cuban Bread, which she served with a Tomato-Camembert Salad, made even Julian swoon.

"Yolanda," I said apologetically, "is this a good time for us to talk to you about the wedding plans for Sunday?"

"Goldy, sweetie," Yolanda said, "so good to see you! It's a fine time for you to come. Come whenever you want." She wore a brilliant white, starched uniform and apron, and moved quickly to embrace me in a hug. "I've got some flan that you're just going to love, and none of the women here—"

"Who the hell is Yolanda?" Billie Attenborough demanded. I was pretty sure Billie knew full well exactly to whom I was talking.

Yolanda drew herself up straight. She couldn't have been more than five feet tall, but she was imposing nonetheless. "I am Yolanda. Who are you?"

Aw jeez, I thought. Was there anyone Billie Attenborough came in contact with whom she *did* get along with? I wished Craig Miller would come back.

"Wait, wait," I said. I felt in my purse for the flash drive with the menus and recipes. On the counter on the far side of the sink, there was a computer, thank goodness.

"Are you the cook?" Billie demanded, pointing a finger in Yolanda's face. "Because we have a very big wedding coming in here tomorrow!" Billie cast a derogatory look all around. The other kitchen workers, sensing fireworks, had made themselves as scarce as Craig Miller. "This is your kitchen? How in the hell can you work in such a small—"

"Hey, chica!" Yolanda retorted, one hand on a hip, the other picking up a frying pan that she held in a somewhat, ah, aggressive manner. "This is my space! My kitchen!"

"Do you know who I am?" Billie demanded, pointing a finger in Yolanda's face.

Yolanda frowned in mock horror. "Do I look like I care who you are? Do you know who I am? Now, if you don't mind, I need to talk to Goldy—"

Billie turned to her mother and fell against her chest. "I can't work with this woman!" she wailed. "And I can't call everyone again and have the wedding changed one more time, to some new place!"

"Now, Billie dear," said Charlotte, patting her daughter on the back, "you know perfectly well who Yolanda is, and you've told me how well you do with the diet here, so this is no time—"

Oh, dear, I thought, when's the next flight to Anchorage? Maybe Julian could handle the whole Billie wedding. No, I wouldn't do that to him.

Craig Miller burst into the kitchen. "What in the world is going on in here? What's all the yelling about? What is wrong, for heaven's sake?"

I waved in Billie's direction, and managed not to say, "Craig, if you want to keep your mental health, you should cancel your wedding."

Craig Miller eased Billie's heaving body away from her mother and onto his own chest. "There, there, dear," he soothed, patting Billie's back. "Everything's going to be all right. We probably shouldn't have come here and worried your pretty head about details. Let's go out in the hall."

Great idea, I thought as Billie allowed herself to be led into the hall. In fact, forget the hall and just get Billie out of here, period.

"I think we should probably go," Charlotte said to me.

"Will this flash drive work on your computer?" I said quickly to Yolanda.

She scowled at it. "Yeah. Sure."

"All the menus and recipes are on it. I've made extra crab cakes and sauce already, and my assistant is doing more of the other dishes. But we'll need to be set up for a hundred and fifty, and we'll probably need an extra, oh, eight to ten servers, if that's okay."

"No problem," said Yolanda.

"Goldy?" said Charlotte.

Yolanda rolled her eyes at me. I wanted to tell her she should get out while the getting was good, as in, before this wedding started the next day. But I didn't have a chance.

Once Charlotte, Craig, Billie, and I were out in the pine-paneled space, I wondered what we were supposed to do next. We hadn't yet done the walk-through, and with Victor off somewhere, I doubted we were going to get to it. Billie was still sobbing. Were we having fun yet?

Craig finally said, "Billie dear? Why don't you let me ask Victor to fix you a nice smoothie? Peach?"

Billie kept sobbing, but nodded against what had been Craig's clean polo shirt. When Billie lifted her head to take a tissue from her mother, a great wet blob indicated where Billie had lain her head. Lovely. "There now." Craig kept his tone comforting. "A peach smoothie that's sweet like you? Does that sound good? How about you, Charlotte?"

"Oh, I'd love a strawberry one, please!"

"Goldy?" Craig asked.

"If they have coffee flavor, I'd love it."

Craig ruefully shook his head. "Victor's rules. No coffee in the whole place. Sorry."

"Not to worry," I replied. "Thanks for asking."

"Now," Craig said to Billie and Charlotte, "we just need to go find Victor, to get the key to the Smoothie Cabin—"

I turned away. Actually, what I really wanted was another iced latte, preferably with two or three big scoops of coffee ice cream jammed on top, and a spiral of whipped cream on top of that. I doubted Gold Gulch Spa offered such a treat, so I decided to go in search of my godfather instead.

I didn't want to bother Yolanda again, not when she was probably still upset about our last intrusion, and anyway, Jack hadn't gone by us. Billie, Charlotte, and Craig were moving down the hall away from me and speculating among themselves as to whether there would be any other place where the wedding could be held at this late date. Aspen Meadow Country Club? A country club in Denver? Would all the dates in August have been booked long ago?

Charlotte, hearing me, turned back. "Don't worry," she whispered, "we're having the wedding and reception here. I'm just letting Billie ventilate." She frowned. "Could you go see if you can find Jack?"

"Sure." I walked away and pushed through the swinging doors. After a moment of indecision, I chose the path that led to the hiking trails. Boulders had been placed along the way, and late-blooming bushes of pink muskmallow and perennial daisies hugged the crevices between the rocks. All the recent rain we'd been getting had left swaths of puddles along the trail, and as I hopped, skipped, and jumped along, I almost missed the sign that said SMOOTHIES! with an arrow pointing toward the very last section of the building, which also housed the kitchen, dining room, and TV and living rooms.

The woman who had been shepherding the ladies along on their walk—the twenty-something Isabelle—was nowhere in sight, but the ladies themselves were lolling about on freestanding porch-style swings. And they were all sipping pastel-colored drinks from large clear plastic cups.

"Best thing about this place," one was saying to another.

"I'm so glad Isabelle said we could skip the hike. This smoothie is yum. I can't believe it's low fat."

"Me either. I wanted to have two yesterday, even offered to pay, and Victor said I couldn't, that it was too many calories. Mean!"

I asked first one, then another gaggle of women if they'd seen a dapper fellow in his fifties walking past,

maybe smoking a cigarette. I worked my way through
the groups of women, and they all replied in the nega-
tive.

I looked up the boulder-lined path, then drew back
as the odor of sulfur invaded my nose. Clouds of
steam were drifting down from a place up the path,
and with my marvelous powers of deduction, I figured that was where the hot springs pool was. I
scanned the woods and what I could see of the paths
again. Jack really couldn't have gone hiking by himself, could he? Not after two heart attacks—both the
results of his lawyering days, he said—plus, he
smoked, and he hated exercising. But then where
could he have gotten to in such a short time?

Nearby, two women were swinging contentedly.

"Maybe their smoothies really do have sugar and
cream in them," one of the women commented. "It
sure tastes like it. I could just kill for another one before lunch!"

Talk about a fixation. I'd have to get the recipe for
this concoction before I left the next day.

"Maybe that's why they won't let you have two in
one day—they really are fattening."

"We're being weighed tomorrow morning, Sara
Ann. That's why they won't let us have more than one
at a time."

"Well, yesterday my roommate didn't want the
mango one she ordered, so she gave it to me. I drank
it right after I had my blueberry one, and I felt so mel-
low, I decided to sunbathe instead of exercising!"

"Uh-oh, Sara Ann! You risked the wrath of Victor

by not showing up for water aerobics? Did he get in your face later?"

"Yeah. But it was worth it. And anyway, I told him I wasn't paying for him to yell at me, so he backed off."

At that moment, both women looked up at me expectantly. *Was I eavesdropping, or did I have another problem?* their look said.

"You still haven't seen my godfather?" I asked lamely.

"No," said Sara Ann. "Why don't you check in the bushes beside the dining hall? That's where people go to smoke sometimes. When they're hiding out, that is."

"Thanks."

I got the bright idea to try Jack on my cell. But the screen said no service. I tried again, heard the characteristic chirp of Jack's phone, then lost the service again. I glanced around once more. No Jack.

The door to the Smoothie Cabin was firmly closed, and as if that weren't enough, a SHUT sign hung by a rope over the door. I moved closer to the sign, retried Jack's cell, and heard it chirp again, but only once. Before it could go to voice mail, I lost the service again.

Well, doggone it. I tiptoed right up next to the Smoothie Cabin, where whispering voices were just audible within. If the smoothies made you want to sunbathe instead of go to water aerobics, had somebody figured they wanted to get a really good tan this afternoon? I knocked on the door, and there was sudden silence.

"Jack!" I called in a stage whisper. "It's me, Goldy! Charlotte's looking for you! Are you in there?"

There was still no response. By this time, I was very curious as to what was going on behind the Smoothie Cabin door. Could Jack be inside? Could he be in trouble? He didn't seem like the getting-into-trouble type, somehow. He seemed like the causing-trouble type.

But still. I did worry about him. At least, that was what I told myself as I traipsed through mud and puddles and around two Dumpsters to get to the other side of the building. I jiggled the locked door handle, then realized the door was ever so slightly ajar. This must be the entrance that the staff used for taking out the trash, and for receiving deliveries of supplies.

I was careful not to bang the door as I entered. Yet for the second time that day I found myself tiptoeing . . . this time to where I judged the Smoothie Cabin wall began. There was some kind of window there.

The window looked into the Smoothie Cabin. And there I gave a start and gasped.

To my astonishment, Jack was inside the Smoothie Cabin—really just a glorified closet—and he was with Isabelle. I waved and waved to them, but they could not see me. For crying out loud, I was not looking through a window: I was gazing into a one-way mirror, the reflective side of which was facing Jack and Isabelle.

They were not doing anything untoward, but were looking through cabinets. Jack was holding what looked like a small key. I could barely hear Jack's whispered words.

"Do you have any more keys? Does anyone?"

I could not understand Isabelle's response. What were they looking for, protein powder? Whey whip?

My fist was poised, next to the glass, to knock and alert them to my presence. But I was frozen. I wasn't really spying on them, I told myself, more in bewilderment than anything else; I was just trying to figure out exactly what was going on. But before I could do anything, I heard the raised voices of Craig Miller—and Billie and Charlotte Attenborough.

"Quick!" Jack whispered. "Put it all back together!" And he and Isabelle began to zip around the Smoothie Cabin interior, putting away containers and closing cabinet doors.

Suddenly the main door of the Smoothie Cabin was wrenched open, revealing Victor Lane, Craig, Billie, and Charlotte. Then—in order to cover up his real purpose for being there, I guessed, meaning, to snoop—Jack grabbed Isabelle and kissed her. Victor, surprised, jumped back.

Unfortunately, it was the Jack-Isabelle clench that Craig, Billie, and Charlotte witnessed. Charlotte, screaming an obscenity, slammed the Smoothie Cabin door on Billie's hand. Billie shrieked and began sobbing again.

As confused as ever, I stood, openmouthed, and waited for Jack to finish kissing Isabelle. He did not. As soon as Victor firmly closed the Smoothie Cabin door, though, Jack and Isabelle unclenched and began checking that every open cabinet door was firmly closed.

At that point, I noticed the security cameras at the upper corners of the one-way mirror. One was pointing inside the Smoothie Cabin, and had recorded everything that had transpired within.

The other was pointed at me.

Chapter 10

Luckily, I was able to get out of there quickly, before Victor Lane or one of his surrogates could chase me down. Maybe Victor really, really didn't want any of his charges breaking into the Smoothie Cabin to get extra calories.

Then again, as Tom always said, I was of a somewhat paranoid nature. Jack didn't need or want extra calories, I thought as I hurried along to his car. So what had he been looking for? And why did he have to cover up what he was doing by pulling Isabelle in for a smooch?

In any event, I was expecting a very long, very chilly ride home. But then Charlotte announced she was going with Billie. Jack began to speak to Charlotte's turned back in low tones. Bottom line: Charlotte relented. This time, I let myself into the rear seat, only to have Jack surprise me by asking me to drive. He and Charlotte wanted to be chauffered, he said with a smile.

"Whatever," I replied happily, and took his key ring from him. "Are we going to the Attenborough place or to your house?"

"Let me see how my peacemaking mission goes," he whispered. "Her place first, if that's okay."

What the heck, sure, it was fine. My stomach was growling from the lack of both breakfast and lunch; I was massively irritated at having to endure yet another temper tantrum from Billie Attenborough; and I had about a hundred details of the next day's wedding to go over. But, drive? Be a chauffeur? No problem!

At first, Charlotte and Jack were so quiet in the backseat, I couldn't tell how the peacemaking was going. After a while, I could tell that Charlotte was weeping softly. Even though I knew, or suspected, that Jack smooching Isabelle was fake, designed to cover up whatever he was doing in the Smoothie Cabin, if it had been Tom kissing a girl who was younger and thinner than yours truly, well, there would have been more than gentle crying.

Jack said, "Oh, my sweet girl, please don't. C'mon, dear sweet Charlotte. Come be close to me."

Eventually Charlotte sniffed and whispered that with Jack always off with Doc Finn, and ignoring her ideas for fixing up his place, and not wanting to spend tons of time with her, well, she didn't know why she even kept seeing him. Clearly, she wasn't his girlfriend, and he seemed to be making it clear he didn't want to get married. So what was she to him? She wanted to know.

Jack said that Isabelle was supposed to be making

him a smoothie, and all of a sudden, she'd grabbed him and started kissing. This was a lie, of course. I wondered if Charlotte would buy it. Why not just say, "Isabelle and I were hunting around for something in the Smoothie Cabin. So when you, Victor, Billie, and Craig suddenly opened the door, I had to conceal what we were doing. I couldn't think, so I grabbed her and made it look as if we were hiding out to smooch. I know it looked bad, but . . . ?"

How would that work?

"Do you mean to tell me," Charlotte whispered fiercely, "that a fifty-something man would prove to be so attractive to a twenty-something woman, an employee of the spa, no less, that she would grab him on spa property and start kissing him? You must think I'm awfully naive, Jack."

"Let me ask you this, Charlotte," Jack replied, his voice low. "Do you think Isabelle is nice looking?"

Charlotte sniffed again. "No, I don't. She's . . . too thin."

"Not all the women in the world are as lovely as you, my dear."

"Jack, don't—"

"I'm not done. Do you think it's even possible that she would want to try her making-out skills on an old guy like me? Maybe because she thought I wouldn't say no?"

I rolled my eyes.

Charlotte said, "Oh, Jack, come on."

Jack said, "Look, Charlotte, I'm sorry. Isabelle was

helping me look for something. I heard people coming, so I grabbed her. End of story."

"What were you looking for?"

"Just . . . something that didn't belong there. That's all. Look, will you come over and spend the night with me? Please?"

Again I had to remind myself to keep my eyes on the road, as it twisted and wound all the way back to Aspen Meadow. As far as I knew, aside from Finn, Jack had never had overnight guests. I didn't want to ponder why he was suddenly offering Charlotte an invite.

Unless . . . unless he thought she had some information about Doc Finn? Maybe Billie had confessed something untoward to her mother? I wondered.

Jack liked Charlotte. He didn't love her. I wondered if that was enough for Charlotte. And if it was too much for Jack.

Man, relationships! You think once you get out of high school, all the mucky mess and emotions and expectations and disappointments are behind you. News flash to the uninformed: they last your whole life.

Charlotte was saying, "Stay in your house? Tonight? Jack. Thank you. Please listen, though. My only daughter is getting married tomorrow afternoon, and I have a thousand things—"

"May I come over to your place, then? You're always inviting me. This afternoon, I'll take you out to lunch, and then we can have some fun, and then I'll take you out to dinner, and we can have some more fun."

"I thought you were taking me to the rehearsal dinner tonight."

"Oh, yeah, the rehearsal dinner. Forgot about that. Where is it?"

"Well," Charlotte said tentatively, "since we changed the venue, we're doing the walk-through, a rehearsal, yes, at Aspen Meadow Country Club. Then I'm throwing a dinner party for the bridal party, also at Aspen Meadow Country Club. You are invited. You've always been invited."

Jack said, "May I take you out to lunch? Wherever you want to go."

Charlotte paused. I couldn't resist: I looked in the rearview mirror. Jack was kissing Charlotte on the neck. It sure as heck wasn't Charlotte who was all charm.

Charlotte sighed. "All right, then," she whispered at last. "But you have to promise to be out of the house by eight tomorrow morning."

As I piloted my godfather's Mercedes down Upper Cottonwood Creek Road, I called Tom on my cell phone. There was no answer. He was probably still with the county medical examiner. Reluctantly, I punched the numbers for Arch's cell.

"Jeez, Mom," he said when he finally picked up. "It's summer, and I'm still in bed over at Gus's house."

"Sorry, buddy." One of the conditions of our buying Arch a cell phone was that he was not allowed to turn it off, ever. Unfortunately, Arch's teenage sleeping pattern didn't match my grown-up working one, and invariably we were at odds over who was bothering whom. I said sweetly, "Listen, bud, can you get up and come get me over in Flicker Ridge?"

"Now? You have got to be kidding me."

"Yes, now. Sorry." Just after his sixteenth birthday in April, Tom and I had bought Arch a used VW Passat. One of the conditions of that purchase had been that he would help out occasionally with running errands. Since Arch's driver's license had been freshly minted, he'd been very happy to "get a ride," as he put it, although it seemed to me that what he was getting was not a ride, but wheels. Another Mom job: learn how nomenclature differs from one generation to the next.

Arch said, "Do you remember that Gus and Todd are coming with me, and spending the night?"

"Oh my, I forgot."

"We're not going to bother you, Mom. And it's way past our turn to have everybody."

Actually, he was right. This summer, the Druckmans and the Vikarioses had done the heavy lifting in the Entertain-the-Kids department. They'd always insisted that they loved having the boys as much as possible. And I believed them, but my gut still gnawed with guilt. The Druckmans were leaving on Monday for a family fishing trip in Montana. When they came back, school would be starting. I needed to do my bit, as Arch had reminded me. Over the protestations of

Jack, I gave Arch the address of the Attenborough residence.

"Just take my car home," Jack said. "Charlotte can run me back to my place in the morning."

"I cannot run you anywhere," Charlotte said huffily. "I'll be too busy!"

At the Attenborough place, I told Charlotte and Jack I would just wait inside Jack's car until Arch arrived. Jack said that was fine, but please would I lock the car and bring him the keys? I agreed, and the two of them took off for the house.

Truth to tell, I also wanted to stay in the car because I figured the last place Billie would look for me was right out in front of her own house. To make sure, though, when Craig Miller drove up in his Lexus, I ducked. I felt childish, but I really, really didn't want Billie to catch sight of me.

After what I thought was a safe interval, I lifted my head, only to scream when I saw Craig Miller smirking at me through the driver's-side window. He had his hands in the pockets of his khaki pants, and he was rocking back and forth on his loafers, the preppy Cat Who Swallowed the Canary.

"You about scared me to death!" I said after I finally found the proper button to bring down the window.

"Are you hiding from Billie?"

"I, well, I . . . yes. Is she coming out here to tell me she wants some more changes to the menu?"

"I doubt it. I saw you, but she didn't. She was too busy complaining about the spa venue. All the way back I heard about how impossible it was all going to be. It was really a fun drive. But don't worry, she's going to stick with having everything there. Since the date has been changed so much, we had to go with some later reservations to the Greek isles, so we'll actually be staying at the spa for the first couple of days of the honeymoon." He laughed that snuffly laugh of his, but I wasn't disarmed by it. When Craig glanced up at the house, I felt a twinge of fear that he would signal Billie. I was ever mindful of Henry Kissinger's dictum: *Even a paranoid has real enemies.* Craig turned back to me and asked, "May I get into the car with you?"

"Billie's not going to be looking out the window, and see you out here, is she?"

For answer, Craig chuckled again. As he rounded the front of Jack's car, I wondered for at least the fiftieth time what this handsome, well-built doctor saw in Billie. He was a self-assured professional who, Marla had told me, was only twenty-eight. Billie was thirty-six, not terribly attractive, and a bitch. Her mother was nice, and she was rich, but Craig wasn't marrying Charlotte.

Then again, who was I to decipher the motivations of love? My first time around, I'd married a violent narcissist, which showed you how much I knew.

"I know I've said this to you before, Goldy," Craig began, once he was sitting in the passenger seat. He turned to face me, his expression all earnestness. "Billie and I are just very, very appreciative of all the work you've done for us."

"I'm just doing my job, Craig."

He smiled. "Seems to me you've gone above and beyond the requirements of your job."

"Thanks." I really did not want to talk about the wedding, or Billie, or anything related to Billie or the wedding, so I plunged in with, "Actually, I knew a doctor once with the last name Miller. Philip Miller? Ever heard of him? He went to the University of Colorado Medical School—"

"No, can't say that I have. What kind of doc is he?"

"Was. He's deceased."

"I'm sorry. It sounds as if he was a friend."

"Yes, that's true." Was I so transparent, or was Craig Miller just really good at reading people? Well, that was his job, I supposed. Philip Miller had been able to read people, too, and it had gotten him killed.

"Do you want to talk about it?" Craig asked, again all earnestness.

"No, thanks." I tried hard to think of how to change the subject. "Um," I said finally, "where did you get your medical training?"

"The Caribbean," Craig said. "And after living there year-round for four years, I swore up and down I was going to live in a place with a really cold winter and lots of snow."

I burst out laughing. "D'you think you ended up in the right place?"

His smile filled the car. "Oh, don't I know it!" I was afraid he might go back to talking about the wedding, but he didn't. Come to think of it, it's women who love talking about weddings, not guys. Craig eyed me with the sly expression Arch used to employ when he wanted something from the cookie jar. "That was quite a stunt your uncle pulled at the spa."

"He's my godfather, not my uncle. And trust me, he pulls stunts all the time. Which one were you talking about?"

Craig raised an eyebrow. "Making out with a twenty-year-old in the Smoothie Cabin? Has he no shame?"

I gave Jack's it-wasn't-my-fault version of the kiss in question. I even managed not to smile when I said that Isabelle was the aggressor.

"You expect me to believe that?" Craig asked. "That a spa employee tricked an older man into a glorified closet? So she could kiss him? Why not just ask him out on a date?"

I shrugged. At that moment, Arch's battered Passat drove into view. I explained that I needed to get going, as I still had so much to do before the you-know-what the next day. Craig said that he understood, and hopped out of the car. He offered to take the keys up to Jack, but I said I'd promised to deliver them myself. I locked the Mercedes and followed Craig up the steps to the house.

When Jack came to the door, I said, "Jack." Once Craig disappeared through the living room, I hesitated. Should I bawl out my godfather for a) honking his horn this morning, b) disappearing during the spa visit, and c) pulling the stunt with the Smoothie Cabin?

"I've upset you," Jack said. "I screwed things up out at Gold Gulch, didn't I?"

"Sort of." I felt uncomfortable.

"You know how much I love you, don't you, Gertie Girl?" When I nodded, he pulled me in for a hug. "I'm sorry. There was a reason for my stuff at the spa. I . . . I'm just not ready to tell you yet. Will you forgive me?"

With my head on his shoulder, I said, "Of course."

He thanked me, hugged me again, and took his keys. He said he'd see me the next day.

"You want to drive, Mom?" Arch asked. From the backseat, Todd and Gus gave me sleepy greetings.

"Not particularly," I began, "I just drove all the way—"

But then I had a good look at Arch. He appeared to have slept in his rumpled, none-too-clean shorts and T-shirt. He had dark bags under his eyes, which he could only manage to keep half open. So maybe he hadn't actually slept at all. While he was waiting for me to answer, he yawned.

I said, "Yeah, sure, give me the keys, hon."

Arch, Todd, and Gus all fell asleep on the way back to our house, which was less than twenty minutes away. I shook my head. When Arch was an infant, he'd had numerous sleepless nights. Sometimes I'd found that the only solution was to take him out for a ride in the car. As soon as we'd gone half a block, he'd always be in dreamland. Looks as if things hadn't changed that much.

Marla called on my cell when we were halfway

home. The buzzing of the phone did not seem to bother the boys, and I resolved to call Marla back later. But she would not be deterred. She called again, and again, and again, until I finally answered.

"I need to see you," she said breathlessly. "Where are you now?"

"Almost to our house. Want to come over? I have extra crab cakes."

"Ah, the promise of food. Yes, please. And I have such a juicy and delicious piece of gossip for you, you won't believe it."

The boys groaned when the car stopped and didn't move again. Finally, they piled out, extending their arms, cracking their joints, and complaining more than Rip Van Winkle with a backache. Arch yawned and asked if he could make his pals pancakes, if he promised not to get in my way. They were *so* hungry, he added. And he wouldn't make any mess.

Right, I thought. But I only said, "Yes, Arch, I think that's a great idea." I glanced at the clock: 1:00 in the afternoon already? "And could you make enough for me, too, please? I'm ravenous."

Arch was pleased. Although I'd often offered to teach Arch to cook, he'd always resisted. But making flapjacks was a skill he'd learned in Cub Scouts, and he still loved whipping up big batches. He'd even perfected the art of dropping dollops of batter into a hot pan when it was just the right temperature. Plus, he always insisted on melting real butter for the batter and then pouring more on top of the flapjacks themselves. He'd even learned to make clarified butter, which he made and froze in small batches, to use in the pan so the fat wouldn't burn before he ladled in the batter. I guess he was his mother's son, after all.

Even better than all that, Arch was always particularly pleased with his creations when my dear Tom would tuck into a stack of eight or more of the creations, and invariably pronounce them the absolute best pancakes he'd ever tasted in his entire life.

While Arch gave directions to Todd and Gus on setting the table, I checked the messages. Julian had called to say he had located plenty of new potatoes to make our salad for the additional fifty people. Was I doing okay? I left a voice mail message on Julian's cell saying I was fine, no problem.

Was I fine? Did I have enough food for the Attenborough wedding? Suddenly, I wasn't so sure.

So while Arch sizzled clarified butter in our flapjack pan, I began measuring out the ingredients for extra crab cakes.

"Gosh," Gus asked, "who is all the crab for?"

"A wedding tomorrow."

"Who's getting married?" Todd wanted to know as he frowned over the cutlery drawer.

"Billie Attenborough and Dr. Craig Miller. He's a doctor at Spruce Medical Group."

"Oh, man," Todd commented, "my mom hates Spruce Medical Group. She took me there when I had that torn rotator cuff, you know, the one I had the operation for at the beginning of the summer? My mom wanted an MRI, but whoever was in charge there said I only had a sprained arm. Anyway, the guy told me to start lifting weights. He even showed me how to lift the weights, especially with my left arm, which was the one that was hurting so much, especially at night."

"Which guy did you see?" I asked.

"Aw, I don't remember his name," Todd said.

"You're such a wuss," Gus interjected, which brought some spectacular left jabs from Todd. "Okay, okay, you're not a wuss!" Gus hollered in defeat.

"So did lifting the weights help?" I asked.

"Not even, Steven," Todd replied. "I did those stupid weights every day for a couple of weeks, and by then the upper part of my left arm felt as if it was falling off."

"Hello?" said Arch, as he measured out buttermilk. "Your upper arm can't fall off. Only your whole arm can fall off."

"And it's called resistance training, Todd," Gus said, laughing.

"Thanks for the updates, guys," Todd replied. "Okay, it felt as if my whole arm was coming off when I did resistance training, how's that? Anyway, my mom took me someplace else, and whoever was in charge there said I needed an MRI, which showed, duh, that I had a torn rotator cuff. And so I had surgery. I told her we should sue Spruce Medical, but she said people make mistakes all the time, and I should just cool it."

Gus sighed dramatically. "Don't we live in a litigious society? That's what my grandparents say. I had no idea what that meant, so I looked up *litigious*. It means we all sue each other too much."

Arch said, "Will you guys quit yakking and get out the butter and the maple syrup? They're both in the walk-in refrigerator."

When Marla arrived, Arch, Todd, and Gus had polished off seconds in the pancake department, and I was just starting on my own. They were delicious: Arch whizzed cottage cheese in the blender to add to the batter, and this gave them a nubbly texture, a modicum of protein, and a tangy taste that people invariably asked about. By the time I started on my second stack, my mood had improved considerably.

"Ooh, flapjacks!" Marla cooed as she admired the table. "Are these from Arch's extra-special recipe?"

Arch blushed but said they were, and he'd made lots of batter, and would Marla like some?

"You bet." Marla put her hands on her hips, which were swathed in an ample burnt orange and lime green Marimekko shift. When she wiggled, I noticed she was wearing large dangly lime green earrings. She looked like a big orange tulip. "I've already had lunch, so this will count as my dessert, I guess. Maybe I'll have to break down and visit Gold Gulch Spa one of these days, eh?"

While Arch was frying Marla's "dessert," Todd and Gus did their dishes, then told Arch they were going out to the Passat to get their stuff. Meanwhile, I gave Marla an abbreviated version of that morning's trip up to Gold Gulch.

"Smooching with Smoothie?" Marla asked. "Sounds like a horror novel."

"It wasn't Smooching with Smoothie—"

"Oh, don't get technical." She shoveled in the last bite of pancake. "That was great. You know that T-shirt, *Life Is Short, Eat Dessert First?* What else have you got around here?"

"Marla, I have to make sure I really do have enough crab cakes, even if Billie adds another fifty people to her hundred and fifty guests—"

"So, make your sauce gribiche, then keep going on the crab cakes, give me the first one to taste, and I'll tell you whether it has too much salt, that kind of thing."

"I try to put in somewhat less salt than a dish might need, then—"

"There you go getting technical again. You want to hear my news or not? You're going to like it. The first part has to do with Doc Finn and your godfather. The second is incredibly juicy, and has to do with this wedding you're doing tomorrow."

I hauled out industrial-size jars of mayonnaise, bulbs of fresh garlic, and other things I would chop to go into the sauce.

"Uh," I said to Marla, with her dubious cardiac history, "maybe you shouldn't be having this."

Marla tsked. "Okay, remember I was having that fund-raiser for the church at my place last night?"

"How could I forget? It was just dessert, right?"

"Oh, hell no. Well, actually, I thought it was just dessert, but then somebody called and said did I remember it was snacks and dessert? Think, light dinner, heavy dessert. I don't know. And I cursed and said I didn't have any snacks, and she said to just put out what I had. Well, I didn't have enough wine to serve thirty people, and I did have cheese for an appetizer, but I didn't have more than twenty crackers, that'll teach me. But! I did have a case of hundred and ten proof vodka, which I could serve either neat or as martinis. Plus, I had lots of olives. Nut-stuffed olives, pimento-stuffed olives, kalamata olives, you name it. And when people haven't had dinner but only have olives and vodka? You get great gossip."

"I hope nobody was driving."

"No, Goldy, they all walked to my house and then stumbled home. For crying out loud! One of the perks of this little event is that I had the car service again, in case people needed to be ferried to and fro. I'd forgotten the wine and appetizers, but I'd remembered the cars. You can't have everything."

"Marla—"

She heaved a voluminous sigh. "Are you going to let me tell my story or not?" When I said nothing, she went on, "You know Lucas Carmichael?"

"Unfortunately, yes."

Marla's ears perked up. "Why unfortunately?"

I tried to make myself sound nonchalant. "He just doesn't like me."

Marla cocked a knowing eyebrow. "He's jealous of how much love, attention, and money Jack's lavished on you."

I sighed. "'Fraid so."

"Well. You know Lucas's ex-wife Paula is an attorney?"

"Yeah. Down in Denver?"

"Yup."

"Then why was she at—?"

Marla held up her hand. "Paula has kept her membership at St. Luke's, which was the reason she was at the fund-raising shindig. She even told me it's her way of keeping tabs on wealthy potential clients. After three martinis and only a couple of olives, what Paula also told me is that she's still unbelievably pissed at having to pay spousal support to mousey little Lucas. But if she has to dish out dough, she can also dish dirt, eh? And check this out: now she does prenuptial agreements exclusively. She didn't do one for herself, but now, oh, man! The irony!"

I couldn't imagine where this was going, but I'd already been bawled out enough by Marla for interrupting that I just printed out my recipe for the crab cakes, and began spooning mayonnaise into glass measuring cups.

"Yesterday, Paula had a hard day in the trenches trying to keep money away from grasping potential spouses," Marla went on. "Or at least so she said. I'm telling you, she kept slinging back dirty vodka martinis so fast, she was like the Before poster for Alcoholics Anonymous. I even told her to take it easy, and you know I never do that. She laughed and said she wanted to get her money's worth, five hundred dollars a person for new cabinets for the church kitchen? And no dinner for the donors? Well, she was pissed, in every sense of the word."

"Marla—"

"I'm getting there, Goldy, hold on to your gearshift.

Okay, you know how we ex-wives occasionally are weak enough to sleep with our ex-husbands?"

"Not among my finest moments after kicking out the Jerk," I admitted.

"Nor mine," Marla agreed. "But anyway, Lucas and Paula got all intimate a couple of weeks ago, and Lucas confided that he'd been hoping Paula would not be having to pay alimony to him much longer."

"He'd been hoping?"

"Yup." Marla raised an eyebrow. "He'd asked Jack if he could have his inheritance, or part of it, early. But Jack said no. It seems Lucas was quite bitter, in spite of just having scored free sex."

"Nice talk. Good thing Arch is out of earshot."

Marla waved this away. "Anyway, according to Paula, your dear godfather Jack had not only told Lucas he couldn't have any money now, Jack was also thinking of changing his will completely. Changing it, that is, so that Lucas was cut out, I should add. And the proponent of the change, according to Lucas? Dr. Harold Finn."

"Doc Finn?"

"One and the same. Doc Finn went to Duke University Medical School, and apparently he'd convinced Jack to stop in Durham after one of their drinking-and-fishing trips back East."

"I knew this," I said. "Jack told me about the trip, that he almost got eaten alive by mosquitoes."

"Did he tell you the med school wined and dined him? Did he tell you the powers that be promised him that if he donated twenty million to the school, they'd name a building after him?"

"No. But I'm not sure I believe all this, or even any of it. There's no way Jack has twenty million dollars. Jack and Lucas don't always get along, and this sounds like some joke Jack is playing on his son."

"You think?" Marla looked around the kitchen. "Any chance of some espresso? If I'm going to think, I need some. I might have had one or two too many martinis myself. Plus, I've got such a damn headache, my cranium feels as if it's been splitting rocks all night."

Shaking my head, I dutifully fixed my friend a double espresso. I knew Jack had enough money to live comfortably. But I simply could not believe he had twenty million smackers squirreled away somewhere. Otherwise, why buy a house that needed to be gutted and redone? Why not just buy a new place in Flicker Ridge, plus a house in, I don't know, Belize or someplace, for the snowy months?

Finally I said, "Sounds to me as if my godfather just wanted to stop Lucas from asking for money. I think he was also pulling his son's leg."

"I voiced those very sentiments to Paula. She shrugged. She'd told Lucas the same thing, but he was disconsolate. First, he was pissed that Jack would even have twenty mil that he hadn't shared with his own young whippersnapper—"

"He sent him to physician's assistant school," I inserted.

"And second, that he would even think about leaving it to, as Lucas put it, some stupid med school."

"Oh, dear. Sounds as if Lucas is still bitter that he didn't go to med school."

"But wait," Marla said after slurping some coffee. "It seems young Lucas's main beef was not with his father, but with Doc Finn. According to Paula, after she and Lucas had their roll in the hay a couple of weeks ago, it was all Lucas talked about—how much he hated Doc Finn."

No. I just wouldn't admit to the sickening possibility that was turning my gut.

"So I was thinking I should tell you," Marla concluded.

I sighed and looked out the window over the sink.

There had been the nighttime call from Southwest Hospital that had summoned Doc Finn. But before he'd gotten there, his car had landed in a ravine. Perhaps he'd been hit from behind?

Then somebody had traipsed down into that ravine, and killed the old doctor.

I said, "I'd better call Tom."

Chapter 11

Tom still wasn't answering his cell phone, but a helpful person at the sheriff's department informed me he'd just left to run some errands. After that, he'd said, he was going to come home for a few hours.

I looked at the clock. It was just after two. If Tom was only coming home for a little bit, that meant he and his team were going to be working late, very late, and he wanted to give me the bad news in person. Or maybe it was something else; I didn't know. Still. Usually when there was a fresh homicide, Tom worked the case almost continually for at least forty-eight hours.

"You haven't heard the rest of my news," Marla said, pouting.

"Ah yes, this is something juicy about the wedding I'm doing tomorrow?"

"Juice is my middle name, girl. Given the food connotation, maybe it should be yours, I don't know.

But it's mine. Your middle name can be Coffee."

I gave her an exasperated look and began to chop the celery for the sauce gribiche. Then I drained the capers. A pungent, fresh scent filled the kitchen.

"All right, getting to this wedding you're catering tomorrow. Ever heard of an old-fashioned dowry?"

"Of course I have, silly." I paused. "Don't tell me Billie Attenborough has a big old dowry."

Marla waved a dismissive hand. "Not exactly, honey bunch. But you're close. Anyway, they don't call it a dowry these days. They call it making a marriage contract that involves a lot of money."

"What in the world are you talking about?" I had to be careful that I didn't slice my hand open with the knife. But Marla's revelations were messing with my head. The information she had gleaned sounded distinctly fishy, and made me think the sheriff's department should attend more church fund-raisers. I put the knife down and faced her. "Is there a prenuptial agreement between Billie Attenborough and Craig Miller that involves lots of dough?"

"Ah, my dear, not between Craig and Billie. Between Craig and *Charlotte*."

"What are you talking about?" I demanded. "And who was your source of information this time?"

"Same drunken one as before. I told you Paula Carmichael, Lucas's ex, did those kinds of contracts, right? After the whole story about the alimony that isn't going to end because Jack won't give Lucas money, Paula said I couldn't imagine how boring her work was. I murmured sympathies and poured her some more vodka. This time, she waved away the vermouth and olives and asked if I had a bigger glass. So I gave her a big tumbler, with a few ice cubes thrown in."

Thank God for the car service, I thought. I would hate to think what could have happened if Paula Carmichael had downed that much liquor and then gotten behind the wheel. Reflecting on Arch driving while drunk drivers were wreaking havoc on the roadways was almost more than I could bear.

"Are you telling me that Paula Carmichael got so smashed she just happened to spill the details of a prenuptial agreement?" I picked up my knife and moved on to the smooth, pale cloves of garlic, which I began to crush.

"It wasn't that easy," Marla huffed. "I had to dig for it, darling. Lucky for me, it was after Charlotte Attenborough had left."

"Lucky for you?"

"Wait for it. What happened was that I said to Paula, 'Always boring? What about prenuptial agreements between really, really rich people? Can't they be pretty exciting?' She said, 'No, they're depressing, because they always remind me of what I should have done before marrying Lucas.' Then she got all pensive, as if she was thinking hard about whether to tell me something, but she was so comprehensively inebriated, I could have gotten anything out of her, I think. She was slumping precariously on my sofa, and I had to prop her up with one hand. Finally she said, 'I did do a contract, not prenuptial. It wasn't like anything I'd done before. But it did involve a marriage, or it will when the wedding takes place.' "

"She made sense like that?"

"Not really, I'm interpreting. But after a while, Paula said, 'Okay, picture this: a woman has a loud-mouthed brat for a daughter, and that daughter has just turned thirty-six, with no marital prospects in sight. I mean, who would want to marry a monster?' "

"Try catering for her."

"Then Paula says, 'So this mother goes to her doctor for bunions. The doctor is a cute young thing, age twenty-eight. And he complains to Charlotte about his medical school loans, and how he's never going to get out from under the debt load, never be able to afford a house, never be able to raise a family, et cetera, et cetera.' "

"You know," I said, folding the ingredients into the sauce base, "it just breaks my heart how doctors can't make ends meet in this country."

"Cry me a river," Marla agreed. "Lawyers can't make any money either, according to Paula, but that's only when they're stupid enough to have to pay spousal support ad infinitum."

"So," I said, trying to hurry Marla along, "Charlotte's left your party, so Paula can spill this dirt, although she doesn't say the person she's talking about is Charlotte. But anyway, there's Charlotte with her doctor—did Paula ever tell you it was Charlotte when she told you this story?"

Marla raised her eyebrow. "Give me a little credit,

Goldy. I figured that part out. See, hanging out with you and Tom has really sharpened my deductive skills—"

I gave her an absolutely sour look, and pulled out my long knife, plus the cutting board.

"You don't need to threaten me with sharp instruments," Marla said in mock horror. "Anyway, back to this doctor. Charlotte, hereinafter known as the client—"

"Marla!"

"Okay, okay. Charlotte described the doctor to Paula as very attractive, just without money. And there Charlotte is, with lots of money and an unattractive, unwed daughter. This daughter has no job, a fluffy education at a second-rate school, where she got Cs, and no skills apart from spending money. Up until that moment, Charlotte must have been thinking she was never going to be able to catapult Billie out of the family homestead. So after Craig moaned and groaned about his financial situation, Charlotte said, 'I have a lovely daughter I'd like you to meet. I mean, you've been such a great doctor to me, taking you out to dinner would make this old lady so happy.'"

I stopped slicing. "Charlotte called herself an old lady?"

Marla nodded, grinning broadly. "I guess she wanted Craig to feel sorry for her. You know, with her bunions and all."

"So they had dinner, and Craig and Billie fell in love—"

"Ha! You're such a romantic, Goldy. Billie might

have fallen in love, but Craig would have to be living in the next solar system to think Billie is someone he'd want to spend the rest of his life with."

"Try the next galaxy."

"So after this dinner," Marla continued, "which went okay, apparently, Charlotte found out from her boyfriend Jack about his ex-daughter-in-law, Paula, who does prenuptial agreements. Charlotte called Paula for clarification on how to set things up. Then Charlotte called Craig with a proposition. 'I want to do a contract with you,' Charlotte said. 'It's not a pre-nuptial contract, because that's just between a bride and a groom. This is a regular old contract. Marry my daughter, stay married to her for at least five years, and I'll give you four million dollars on signing and another million a year after the five are up.'" Marla crossed her arms in triumph.

"Jeez!" I exclaimed. "I've heard of the cost of free agency in baseball, but this is ridiculous!"

Marla raised an eyebrow. "Do you think? Paula still hadn't told me who the doctor and the lady with the problematic daughter were, but at the end of the story, she said, 'I did the contract. And the doctor and the lady's daughter are getting married this Sunday, right here in Aspen Meadow.' So that's when I fired up Ye Olde Deductive Reasoning again and concluded, ladies and gentlemen of the jury, that the couple she was talking about consisted of Billie Attenborough and Craig Miller."

I carefully blended the crab cake ingredients in an enormous bowl, then began forming and rolling. As

Marla ran water over her dishes, I remembered earlier in the day, when Craig had circled Jack's Mercedes. At the time, I'd wondered why I couldn't decipher the motivations of love. A cute late-twenties doctor bonding with a difficult midthirties woman? I think I finally had the answer to the motivation, and love had nothing to do with it.

Marla left not long after relating all her gossip. I called Yolanda through the main switchboard at the spa, and asked her if she'd had a chance to look at the menus and arrangements. She said yes, and that all would be well. She apologized for yelling at Billie, but I told her to forget it.

After I'd finished forming the final batch of crab cakes, I hopped up the stairs to check on Arch and his pals. There were murmurings going on behind the door, so I knocked. When Arch opened up, I noticed that the boys were stuffing their backpacks with M&M's, granola, salmon eggs, hooks, and other hiking and fishing essentials.

"Going on an expedition?" I asked. "It's a mite late in the day to be starting out."

"Time is relative, Mom." Arch frowned, his brown eyes serious. "These days? The sun doesn't set until after eight. Todd is going to Montana on Monday, and we're trying to take advantage of the last days of summer."

I took a deep breath. "So, where are you going?"

"Up into the Aspen Meadow Wildlife Preserve. Don't worry," he said, smiling, "we'll be back in time for a late supper. We're hoping to snag a few trout that we can grill."

"Take rain gear," I advised. "You never know. And cell phones, you know how I worry."

Once Arch and his pals had roared off in the Passat, I finished the gribiche and took a shower. By the time I was out and getting dressed, Tom had arrived home. Incredibly enough, I didn't have any more cooking to do for Billie Attenborough's wedding, as Julian was doing the extra food, including the rest of the rolls, which he could get from a marvelous Boulder bakery, the green beans vinaigrette, and the cake. The first batch of rolls was made and frozen. Perhaps before the boys got home with our fish to grill, Tom and I would have a chance to kick back, have some fun together—

One look at Tom's face, exhausted and slack with worry, made me cancel the have-some-fun idea. Even though it was only four o'clock, he sat at the kitchen table with a glass of scotch in front of him.

"Tom?"

I knew better than to ask whether he was all right. Clearly, he wasn't. He was a veteran; he'd headed hundreds of death investigations. I didn't know how he could do what he did, but he kept on, claiming he loved the work. He spoke for the dead, he said. He championed them. But the work took its toll, and I was looking at it.

"Tom, what can I do for you? Is there something I can get for you?"

He looked up and gave me a rueful smile. "Nothing except yourself, Miss G. Come sit down with me."

First I poured myself a glass of water, then I sat next to him and sipped my water. Mindful of the story Marla had just told me about overimbibing, I didn't want to be tempted to overindulge. Anyway, I knew that after Tom told me what was going on—which was his way to unburden himself—I was going to want to cook. Not have to cook. Want to cook.

I put my glass on the table, sat down, and scooted my chair over by Tom's. Then I gave my husband a long, wordless hug. He embraced me back, holding tight.

When he let go, he looked around the kitchen as if registering his surroundings for the first time. "Don't you have prep to do for the wedding tomorrow?"

"It's done. I did extra crab cakes and gribiche, just in case. Julian offered to do the rest of the extra cooking for the added guests. Arch and his pals are here, though, or at least, they're in the Aspen Meadow Wildlife Preserve, ostensibly fishing for dinner. We'll see. Maybe I should get out some steaks."

"Good idea. If the boys bring home trout, great, I'll throw it on the grill." His expression turned pensive. "I can eat here, but then I have to go back. Tonight." He smiled thinly. "Got any salad to go with grilled trout?"

"Tom, I've got enough fancy balsamic vinegar to make a salad to serve the entire armed services— army, navy, air force, coast guard. The Attenborough wedding reception will only consume enough for an army, I think. Plus, with it being held at Gold Gulch Spa, maybe the guests will feel guilty and not touch the potato salad. They'll see all that exercise equipment and figure they should be losing weight instead of stuffing themselves."

"Gold Gulch Spa, eh?" Tom was perusing the contents of the walk-in. "That's where the reception is?"

"Tom, I told you, remember? Bridezilla decided she was having an extra fifty people, and moved the whole show out to where she was trying to lose weight to fit into her wedding gown. She just neglected to tell me until yesterday."

Tom shook his head, lost in thought. "Yeah, I remember, and that's why Jack picked you up this morning. Listen, I want Boyd to go with you."

I thought, but did not say, Oh, brother, here we go. But Tom was right in being suspicious, I supposed, as some of the people who'd apparently disliked Doc Finn were going to be at the wedding, making it a volatile situation.

Tom smiled at me. "Why don't you fix that salad now? I don't remember having any lunch. I'll cook after I've had some of your good food, how's that?"

I returned his smile, wrapped a baguette in foil, and put it in the oven. Then I melted a knob of butter in my sauté pan, cracked in three organic eggs, salted and peppered them, and made a quick salad of frisée and arugula, which I drizzled with a freshly made balsamic vinaigrette. I brought out the baguette, which was steaming, put it on one side of the plate, then arranged the frisée on the other side. Finally I slid the luscious-looking eggs on top of the frisée.

"Wow, Miss G. I wasn't expecting all this."

"Do you want to talk about the case?"

He nodded, and talked as he ate. "It ticks me off when people kill other people, but I especially get ticked off when someone kills a child or an older person. Especially a nice older person like Doc Finn, whom almost everybody seemed to love."

"Yeah, almost everybody."

"Did you hear that?" Tom glanced out the window. Sure enough, periwinkle gray clouds were darkening the horizon, but I hadn't heard thunder. I frowned and hoped Arch would have the sense to stop fishing if it began to storm.

"So, Tom, have your guys figured out any more particulars about who didn't like Doc Finn?" Of course, I had a couple of answers to that myself, but I would wait until Tom finished telling me what he'd learned.

"Since you mention Gold Gulch, Miss G., I'll tell you first off that Doc Finn was out there the day he died. Thursday."

"Doing what?" I imagined the easygoing, flinty-faced doctor out at the spa, frowning at all the baby boomers tearing up their tendons and muscles, and putting way too much stress on their joints.

"Having a fight with Billie Attenborough, apparently."

"I know Billie didn't like him. Do you know why they were fighting?"

"Nobody seems to remember that, exactly. Doc Finn was talking in low tones. But everybody could hear Billie. He would say something, and she would yell at him to mind his own business. Then he would start to talk, or try to, and she would scream at him not to be so nosy."

I sighed and got up to wash the pan I'd used to fry Tom's eggs. Charlotte Attenborough's magazine, *Mountain Homes,* had recently run an article entitled "How to Spot Good Breeding." She should have had a caption: "Don't Look at My Daughter."

I said, "Won't Billie tell you what Doc Finn was talking to her about?"

"She says he told her she was losing weight too fast, and that it wasn't good for her." Tom took a last bite of his lunch. "Thanks, that was great. Here's the deal with Billie: She's lying. I've been in this business long enough to be able to spot that. So I took a different tack and told her we'd heard she was angry when Doc Finn ran off her two fiancés. She shrugged. Plus, we've got access to Finn's files, and Billie wasn't even a patient of his. When we asked her when the last time she'd seen a doctor was, and when exactly he had weighed her, she clammed up and told us that if we wanted to talk to her further, she needed to have her attorney present."

"Did you tell her you were in the middle of a homicide investigation, for God's sake?"

"She already knew. The higher-ups in the sheriff's department thought we should announce that Doc Finn's death was a homicide. No particulars, of course, just the usual, that we were looking for help with the investigation. But none of that made any difference to Billie."

"Oh, God. That publicity is probably killing Jack."

"Nothing we can do about that."

"Do you think I should go over there?"

"No. If he wants to contact us, he will." He looked expectantly around the kitchen. "I know you've got some cookies stashed around here somewhere."

I shook my head. "You're not going to want any trout."

"Speaking of which, you better get out those steaks. I think I just heard hail on the roof."

I don't know where Tom got his supersonic sense of hearing, but just at that moment, a flash of lightning and an almost simultaneous loud clap of thunder announced that, indeed, a hailstorm was upon us. The lights went off, then came back on again.

In the walk-in, I found half a dozen individually wrapped filets mignon, which was a good thing. If I knew Arch and his pals, they'd come racing home from their fishing trip, soaked, starving . . . and, if the hail kept up, empty-handed.

"Do you want some cookies?" I asked Tom. "We don't have anything on hand. I could bake some, though."

"Please don't go to the trouble. I was just wondering."

"I'll do some baking while you're barbecuing, how 'bout that?"

"Super."

"Now, Tom," I said, as I began to melt butter with brown sugar, "tell me why you want Boyd to go out to the spa with me. Is it just that Finn and Billie fought out there?"

Tom opened his palms. "No. It's more of a feeling. Too many things going on that don't add up. Doc Finn goes out there and has a big fight with a spa client. Then that night, somebody makes a bogus call to him from Southwest Hospital. The rear of his Porsche Cayenne was badly dented, so we figured someone ran him off the road. And get this: we found a towel from Gold Gulch in the back of Finn's car."

"Maybe he had a shower out there."

"He didn't, we checked. Plus, the towel was behind the seats. Who takes a shower and then puts the towel in the very back of his SUV?"

"Nobody I know."

"Exactly. And guess what else we found in his car? Not with the towel, mind you, but on the floor of the front seat. A pair of women's shoes."

The hail was hammering on the roof now. "No name inside, I suppose."

"No, but when we went to talk to Billie Attenborough, we took the shoes, and asked her about them. She recognized them, no question, but she wouldn't say whose they were. Then her mother walked into the living room, and said, 'Oh, there are my silver pumps. Did you borrow them, Billie?'"

"They were Charlotte's shoes? So, did Billie borrow them?"

"Who knows? 'Cuz just at that moment, Billie said, 'Don't say or do anything, Mom.'"

"Jeez, Tom."

"I know."

I said, "I certainly hope their house gets broken

into, so the sheriff's department can answer their call with, 'We can't say or do anything.' Is there anything else you found out?"

Tom said, "Out at Doc Finn's house? There was a vial in the trash can out back. We also found a note to himself that said, 'Have analyzed.'"

"What was in the vial?"

"Don't know yet. We're trying to see if there are traces of anything in there that we can send off for analysis. We also don't know if the note goes with the vial."

"Hmm. That's it?"

"So far."

"All right, well, listen." I told him about Jack charging around in the Smoothie Cabin, apparently looking for something.

"I don't suppose he told you what he was looking for."

"Nope, but I'll bet you it's related to whatever was in that vial in Doc Finn's trash. Do you think Victor's hiding drugs out there? That he's some kind of dealer?"

Tom said, "Hmm. So we've got a faked call from a hospital, a dented car, an argument at Gold Gulch Spa, a pair of shoes, a towel, a vial, a cryptic note, and Jack rummaging around in the Smoothie Cabin. All very strange."

I removed the cocoa-butter mixture from the stove to cool, then measured out oats, baking powder, and salt. "And none of it adds up," I said as I began beating an egg in our mixer, "at least not yet. But listen, I have some things to tell you."

I wasn't five words into what Marla had learned at her fund-raiser when Tom pulled out his notebook and began to write down what I was saying. When I got to the monetary details of the contract between Billie's mother and Craig Miller, Tom whistled.

"Have you ever heard of such a thing?" I asked.

"Nope. Jack's son's ex-wife, Paula, the drunk lawyer with the big mouth? Did Paula mention if she'd shared this information about the four million with anyone else, specifically, Billie Attenborough?"

"She didn't say. Why?"

Tom tilted his chin. "I was just wondering how Billie would have reacted. I mean, how would you have felt if your mother had paid John Richard to marry you?"

"I'd have gone ballistic."

"What do you think it would have told you?"

"That my mother didn't have any confidence that I could attract anyone on my own."

"Uh-huh. Now I'm wondering if Doc Finn could have gotten wind of the contract somehow, and told Billie about it. That could have made her go ballistic." Tom rubbed his forehead. "But if Billie wouldn't even let her mother talk about a pair of shoes, she sure as hell isn't going to tell us what she and Doc Finn really talked about."

I looked at all the ingredients I'd assembled, unsure of exactly what kind of cookie I was going to make for Tom, Arch, and the boys.

"You had something else to tell me?" Tom asked.

"'Cuz I'd like to go have a shower before I get called upon for grilling duties."

"Do you know anything about Doc Finn's will?"

Tom seemed surprised. "We've had a preliminary talk with his lawyer. Doc Finn left everything to Duke University Medical School."

"Right. Well, according to Lucas, or rather, according to his inebriated ex-wife, Paula, Lucas was upset that Doc Finn was trying to get Jack to change his will to leave everything he has to Duke, too."

"What?"

I spooned some flour into the cookie batter. "Yup. And Lucas was very put out about it, because if Jack did that, it meant Lucas would never get out from under depending on Paula for spousal support. Which isn't that great for the old ego."

"Yeah, why rely on spousal support when you can inherit money? Sounds as if Lucas might have had a reason to hate Doc Finn." Tom stood up and reached for the phone.

"I thought you were going to take a shower! Who are you calling?"

"Southwest Hospital. I'm going to find out if Lucas was on duty Thursday night."

Chapter 12

No, Lucas Carmichael had not been on duty. Interestingly, though, the nurse to whom Tom identified himself mentioned that she had seen Lucas in the cafeteria around ten Thursday night. She was sure of the time, because her nephew had called her during her dinner break, which began at a quarter to ten. She'd been in the cafeteria drinking coffee, asking herself if it was ever going to stop raining, when her cell phone had buzzed.

Lucas had been there, too, the nurse remembered. He'd been alone, looking out the dark window. Before her cell phone beeped, she'd been thinking that Lucas, too, might have been wondering if the rain was going to go on forever.

How long had Lucas stayed there? Tom asked. The nurse didn't know. She'd gone outside, under a porch roof, to get better reception on her cell; also, the hospital didn't like people to use cell phones in the building. When she came back, Lucas was gone.

Tom promised to follow up, then called his office to get someone to go over to Southwest Hospital, to talk to the nurse, to other medical personnel, to anyone who could have seen Lucas Carmichael using the phone in a specific maternity-ward room on the fourth floor. It was from that room that the call had come to Doc Finn's home phone just after ten Thursday night. The maternity ward, incidentally, was not far from the cafeteria entrance. Then he directed one of his investigators to go talk to Lucas Carmichael, to feel him out, get his alibi, and see if he acted guilty, defensive, or both.

"Thursday night it was pouring like nobody's business," I observed. "I don't suppose you found any usable footprint in the ravine."

"No, that's part of the problem." He rapped his fingers on the counter. Then he put in another call to the department, and asked the fellow on duty about Finn's impounded car. Had the computer on board the Cayenne yielded any more information? If so, he needed to know ASAP, he said.

"That might help," Tom concluded after hanging up the phone. "We work out times and who was where when, we might have something."

I'd decided to make chocolate lace cookies for the boys, then sandwich ice cream between them for a very special dessert. To Tom, I said, "Charlotte? Billie? Lucas? You looking at anyone else who might not have liked Doc Finn?"

Tom shook his head. "According to the elderly receptionist who still works for Spruce Medical Group, everyone loved him. Former patients, church friends, you name it. And before you ask, no, nobody from Duke University Medical School has shown up on our radar."

"Hey, Tom, take it easy. You're always telling me you have to look for the person due to benefit from someone's death." I hesitated. "I just can't believe that Lucas is a murderer. That he would have killed Doc Finn. I just can't." And, I wondered, if he would kill Doc Finn to keep him from convincing Jack to bequeath these questionable millions to Duke, was *Jack* safe? I shook my head. No, I didn't believe it.

Tom tilted his head. "How's Jack doing?"

I thought back to Jack's antics that morning. "Would you say rummaging around in the spa's Smoothie Cabin, then smooching a much younger woman was normal behavior for someone grieving?"

Tom cocked an eyebrow at me. "Normal for Jack, I'd say."

"Yeah, well, by the time I'd driven Jack and Charlotte home, they'd made up. And get this: the Smoothie Cabin has a one-way mirror, with security cameras pointed inside and out, just to make sure nobody steals the vitamin C."

"Hmm. Not enough for a search warrant, I'd say, but enough to go ask Victor Lane some more questions."

"Did you ask Victor Lane about the vial you found at Finn's place?"

"Miss G., we don't even know if the vial came from Victor, and so far, we don't know what was inside it."

I reflected for a moment, remembering Jack and Isabelle's frantic search through the drawers and cupboards of the Smoothie Cabin. "What do you suppose Jack and Isabelle were really looking for?" I asked.

Tom shook his head. "Maybe something to do with Doc Finn, maybe not. Maybe something that makes you lose weight. Maybe drugs. Unfortunately, knowing Jack, I'd say, first guess?" He raised his eyebrows at me. "Booze."

By the time Tom returned to the kitchen, showered and wearing clean khakis and an open-necked white shirt, I had made and refrigerated a tomato salad with fresh basil and chopped garlic, Camembert, and red wine pear vinaigrette. I'd baked the first batch of cookies. Once they'd cooled, I reasoned, they would taste deliciously crunchy and flaky with either the ice cream I'd planned, or frosting as the cookie sandwich "filling." Or at least, I hoped so. As I was putting the second sheet of goodies into the oven, Arch, Gus, and Todd traipsed onto the deck. Gus triumphantly held up a line of brown trout.

Predictably, Jake and Scout made a sudden appearance. They then began their own chorus of howling and meowing. We weren't the only ones who were going to get fish, they insisted.

"Yeah, yeah, down, boy," Arch called to Jake, who would have devoured every fish on the line if allowed to do so.

"Okay, boys," said Tom, "who wants to learn how to clean fish?"

"Oh, man, I need a shower," said Arch.

"Me, too," Todd and Gus chimed in. Soon the three of them were clomping madly up the stairs. Anything to avoid fish guts, apparently.

"Do not clean those fish with your lovely clean clothes on," I told Tom. "You start the fire, and I'll do the fish."

"Forget it," said Tom. "Make some more cookies, will you, please? I'll start the fire and then find my rubber apron that I keep expressly for this purpose."

I sighed but started filling the next batch of cookies with ice cream, then freezing them. As I rummaged around for the tomato salad, I figured one of us had put the covered glass salad bowl as deep in the dad-blasted walk-in as his rubber apron must be in the garage. When I finally located the bowl, I tasted a few tomato slices, deemed the concoction exceedingly wonderful, and spooned the whole thing onto a bed of lightly dressed field greens circling a crystal platter. By the time I'd set the table for five, Tom had made the fire and cleaned the fish. The man was a marvel.

The boys appeared looking freshly scrubbed, if a bit sheepish for skipping out on fish-gutting duty. They promised to do the dishes, to which I added a mental uh-huh, but said nothing. I didn't want them to have to clean up, as it was almost the end of summer. Todd was leaving on Monday for the Montana trip. Gus's grandparents had fussily informed me that they were planning to spend the last couple of weeks before classes buying Gus back-to-school supplies, a task to which I never devoted more than a single evening. And anyway, now that Arch could drive, I figured I would give him some cash and he could buy his own supplies. There were some benefits to having a teenage driver in the family, after all.

The dinner was fabulous. I shoved the steaks back in the refrigerator so the boys would never know we'd doubted their fishing abilities. Tom's grilled trout was succulent, with crisp skin and lusciously moist flesh. The boys scarfed it down faster than you could say, "Freshly caught and grilled fish taste remarkable!" Gus, ever the diplomat, said the tomato salad was so delicious, he just knew his grandmother would love the recipe, which Tom promised to print out. Todd said he was going to save room for dessert.

As soon as we finished, I shooed the boys upstairs and told them I would do the dishes, no sweat. They hustled off before I had a chance to change my mind.

"You sure you're all right cleaning up all this?" Tom asked as we cleared the table. "I promised the guys at the department I'd be back by eight."

"I am absolutely fine," I assured him. "The prep for Billie's wedding is done. Go down to the department and find out what happened to Doc Finn."

"Remember, Boyd is working with you tomorrow," Tom warned.

"That really isn't necessary," I protested.

"I'll decide what's necessary," Tom said quietly. "And you'll have a free pair of hands to help you with the serving and whatnot."

Well, I wasn't going to argue with him. Still, having Boyd underfoot in the small Gold Gulch Spa kitchen wouldn't be quite as wonderful as Tom envisioned. Like allowing Arch and his pals to do the dishes, sometimes having an extra person to help with the work was more trouble than it was worth.

After Tom left, I took the boys a plate of ice-cream-filled cookies to share while they watched television. Then I put in a call to Julian to make sure all was set for the next day.

"You bet, boss. Just think, tomorrow night at this time, we'll have Billie Attenborough out of our hair, forever."

"Maybe I'll shave my head, to commemorate the occasion."

Julian waited for me to tell him I was kidding, which I finally did. We promised to meet at the spa at noon, even though the wedding wasn't until six.

"Tomorrow at this time," Julian repeated.

"Bring a razor."

Immediately after I hung up, the phone rang. With dread, I checked the caller ID. But it was not Billie; it was Marla.

"Well?" she demanded. "Have you learned anything about this prenuptial agreement?"

"You mean the four mil? I thought you said it wasn't technically a prenuptial—"

"All right, all right, this *contract,*" she conceded.

"How can I find out anything when you're the source of my information?" I pointed out.

"Oh, for God's sake, can't Tom get a subpoena or something?"

"Marla," I explained patiently as I boxed up the leftover cookies, "in order to get a subpoena, you have to have a reason—"

"Stop right there," she interjected. "Legal terminology gives me a headache. So . . . what are you serving at the wedding tomorrow?"

Although the last thing I wanted to do was discuss yet again the menu for Billie Attenborough's dinner, I did it anyway. Marla loved to anticipate food.

"Omigod, it sounds yummy," she said when I finished. "I'd better wear a dress that's a size too big."

"You know you can have any of this you want, anytime. You don't have to wait for a wedding!"

"Yeah, yeah. I don't even have a date for this thing. Date? Listen to me. My invitation said 'Marla Korman and Escort,' like I was going to hire a male prostitute."

"Oh, Marla, come on. By the way, Sergeant Boyd will be there. He's supposed to be helping me in the kitchen, but I'd just love it if you asked him to dance with you."

"Really?" she said cautiously. "He is cute."

"Oh, Lord, if you could take care of him, that would take an enormous load off my mind."

"But won't he be wearing a caterer's uniform?" she said dubiously. "Black pants, white shirt? And oh man, I can just imagine what Charlotte would say if I started waltzing around the spa dining room with a cop wearing an apron."

"Don't worry, I'll have him remove his apron. He'll

look smashing, and if anyone threatens to disrupt the proceedings, say, like Billie herself, well, we'll have a built-in cop, which is what Tom wanted anyway."

"If you're sure it's no trouble," Marla said plaintively, and I realized then, painfully, how much Marla wanted to have male company for the wedding, and how unwilling she was to ask for it.

"No trouble at all," I assured her.

"It's just that Victor Lane made me feel so damn insecure the last time I was out there," she blurted out.

"What are you talking about?"

"Like all the rest of society, he's nice to the slender women, and mean and judgmental to the overweight ones. And to think he owns a damn spa! He told me if I exercised and lost some weight, I'd have a much better social life. I asked him how did he know I didn't have a smashing social life, thank you very much?"

I shook my head. "He's a son of a bitch. Always has been, always will be."

"I resolved never to go out there again. I mean, if I want abuse, I don't have to look any farther than talk radio."

"I'm so sorry, Marla." Then, mischievously, I added, "Maybe in the not-too-distant future, I'll be catering a wedding for you."

She made exaggerated choking noises. "No way, I'm done with being married. Once is enough. Oh, but wait! I thought of something I meant to tell you!" She inhaled for dramatic effect. "There I was out at Aspen Meadow Country Club today, resolved to do some laps at the pool but indulging in a lobster roll instead, and you'll never guess what I heard through the grapevine."

I couldn't imagine. Marla's grapevine stretched and twined through every layer of Aspen Meadow society.

"Charlotte Attenborough told her bridge club that she expects to get married soon, maybe next year!"

"What? Get married to whom?"

"Why, your dear godfather, Jack, that's to whom."

I glanced around the kitchen and shook my head. "I don't *think* so. Furthermore, Charlotte's aware of Jack's stance on this. Jack is as confirmed in his determination to remain single as you are."

Marla raised her voice to a singsong. "That's what Charlotte said."

"Well, I don't believe it," I asserted. "Not for one second."

"Yeah, me either. But I thought you'd be interested to hear."

"Thanks. Maybe I should warn Jack about what Charlotte is saying behind his back."

"I think your godfather can stand on his own two feet."

We signed off, and I put the finishing touches on the clean kitchen. Then I printed out my schedules for the next day, along with the list of all the foodstuffs we would need. Feeling slightly self-indulgent, I crept upstairs and drew myself a hot bath. I was determined to be as relaxed as possible for Billie's ceremony, knowing full well that she would turn anything that did not go well around to being my fault.

But Charlotte marrying Jack? How could Charlotte ever get such a crazy-ass notion? Jack didn't love Charlotte, of that I was sure. More than anything, he seemed to upset her, which he made up for by pandering to her. This wasn't love, it was masochism.

But if it suited them, I thought as I sank into the steaming, bubbly water, why should I worry? Jack, as Marla had pointed out, was fully capable of taking care of himself.

All right, I promised myself as I toweled off, no more obsessing about Jack's future.

Sufficient unto the day are the evils thereof, I thought as I buttoned myself into my pajamas.

If only I'd had any idea just how bad those evils were actually going to be, I'd have canceled Billie's wedding myself.

Chapter 13

The alarm burbled at six, and it seemed to me to be very far off. A distant rendition of Handel's Water Music made me imagine I was floating on a raft down Cottonwood Creek. Tom had come in very late, and I'd only vaguely registered his warm presence beside me. Now I wanted him on the raft with me, so I rolled over and curled myself around him. He responded by pulling me in close.

"Could you turn off the music?" he murmured. "I'd enjoy this more."

So I did. We made slow, affectionate, and very quiet love. I doubted we would wake up the boys, but still, I didn't want to risk it.

Afterward, I thought, *That was the best thing that will happen today.*

"Boyd's meeting you out at the spa at noon," Tom whispered warmly in my ear.

"That is so unnecessary. We'll be fine."

"It'll make me feel better to have him there."

"Tom. Julian will be there. Jack will be there."

"Miss G., I doubt even a twenty-two would fit underneath whatever natty outfit your gun-loving godfather is wearing. Then again, he could whack someone over the head with a liquor bottle."

"Go back to sleep."

I tiptoed into the bathroom, where I took a long, hot shower that felt great. Back in our bedroom, I slid onto the floor and began doing yoga. I'd already told myself my routine should be twice as long as normal so I could build up a reservoir of calm before the day's stresses began.

Feeling serene, cool, and unable to be ruffled, I crept down to the kitchen, fired up the espresso maker, and pulled four shots, which I used for a high-test Summertime Special. I might feel composed, but I needed to get the old energy going, that was certain.

I'd turned the ringer on our phone off when I'd gone to bed, and it was a good thing, as two messages had come in while we were sleeping. After turning the volume to Low, I pressed the button. The first message was from Charlotte Attenborough. Of course I wasn't surprised.

"Goldy," she whispered. "Jack's fixing me a drink in the next room, but I just wanted to let you know how sorry we are that we had to change the venue at the last minute. It was because of all the rain. Since Billie had wanted guests to be inside and outside at your center, she was afraid everyone wouldn't fit inside if the rain kept up."

And the fifty extra people? I wondered. Where did they come from? But that was coming.

"The extra people are all my best advertisers. I decided at the last minute that they should be included, and they all said they wanted to honor Billie and Craig."

I giggled so suddenly that I choked on my latte. Right! You mean you were hitting them up for big donations to your daughter's wedding-gift haul! Well, she would need presents from other people, as that four mil you used to pay off Craig must be putting a dent in your finances, eh, Charlotte?

That message had come in at eleven o'clock the previous evening. If my godfather was fixing Charlotte a drink then, the likelihood of her getting enough beauty sleep was slim.

But then the second message was from Charlotte, too.

"Goldy," she said urgently. "Billie's having a meltdown. Craig's been trying to calm her, to no avail. So she's going out to the spa this morning."

My heart sank. Billie underfoot in the spa kitchen? That was all I needed.

"I told her she'd feel better if she had something to do, so she's going to oversee the putting up of the decorations in the spa dining room."

Better and better, I thought. *Not.*

"I'm going to take her dress and veil out there. I don't want to leave that up to her. I figured, better safe than sorry."

Man, I was already sorry. I slid a new, chilled glass

under the espresso spout and watched four more shots spurt inside. I dumped in more cream and ice cubes, and wondered if Marla had any Valium in the massive pharmacopeia she kept in her house. But would it be better if I took it, if I gave it to Billie, or both?

After printing out the last of my checklists, I started packing the boxes I would be taking out to the spa. A sudden sharp rap at the back door startled me so that I spilled the latte all over the floor. First I choked on it, then I spilled it on the floor.

"Jeez, boss," said Julian when he came through the back door, "you look like you saw a ghost or something. What's wrong?"

"This wedding, that's what's wrong," I replied bitterly. I glanced at the clock: 7:30? Julian was supposed to meet me out at Gold Gulch.

"I was worried about you getting everything packed up. My Rover's full, but I can help you get your gear out to your van."

"Thanks," I said, and meant it. Catering was always a hundred times easier with Julian there.

"I took an early call from Charlotte Attenborough this morning," Julian said, heaving up a box and giving me a mischievous grin. "I mean a very early morning call. Try half past five."

"Oh, Lord, Julian, I'm sorry. I wish a thousand times over that I'd never agreed to do this wedding."

"Oh, no, man, it's great! The stories we'll have for the next twenty years, are you kidding me? We'll be saying, 'Remember when Billie bit the other lady who wanted her dress at the sample sale?'"

I sighed. I hadn't heard about that, which was probably a good thing. "She bit somebody?"

"Yup." Julian placed his box in my van. "Marla told me, I can't believe she didn't tell you. Apparently, the two of them, Billie and this other girl, wanted the same dress, and Billie placed her chompers on the other gal's arm and bit down hard. The shop owner called the cops, the bitten lady filed a complaint, and Charlotte had to hire a lawyer to bargain the charge down to misdemeanor assault, with probation. And the other lady got to buy the dress. Plus, Billie had to pay the lady with the bite marks a pretty hefty fee."

"I can only imagine."

We traipsed back to the house, where Julian fixed himself a quadruple espresso, which he then doused with four teaspoons of sugar. I tried unsuccessfully not to shudder. Warming up to his tale, he went on about Billie.

"At the O'Neal wedding?" He slugged his coffee, then put the cup in the dishwasher. "When Billie appeared and threatened to mess that up? I think that's why Craig came with her. He didn't want her biting again. He even said so, you know, in that low voice of his. 'I don't want a repeat of the bridal shop situation,' he muttered, and Billie loudly exclaimed, 'I'd bite that bitch again in a heartbeat!'"

"Wonderful." We picked up the last two boxes and started out to my van. "So what did Charlotte want this morning?"

"I'll show you."

We placed the boxes in the van and Julian led me

over to his old Range Rover, inherited from former clients. He leaned into the front seat and pulled out a florist's box. Inside was a large bridal bouquet.

"You didn't have to make that," I protested.

"At five this morning? No way. But I did take some of the ingredients over to this florist I know, and she put it together."

"A florist you know? A new girlfriend?" I speculated.

"I'm not telling you anything about my social life. But take a sniff of the bouquet."

I did as ordered. The fragrance was pungent, and . . . culinary. "It smells like something you'd put in a stew."

"Garlic, bay leaves, and chives," Julian reported. "Charlotte was insistent and is paying me big bucks to bring it today, to replace the one she already ordered."

"Why the garlic, et cetera?"

"In medieval times," Julian said, "at least according to Charlotte, that mixture warded off evil spirits."

"Oh, for God's sake."

"Yeah, well, I thought I'd tell Father Pete, see what he thinks." He closed the door to the Rover. "All right, let's bounce."

I'd gotten used to Julian-speak, and sometimes it even helped me with clients in their early twenties. We were bouncing up to Gold Gulch Spa, i.e., we were driving, and once again, weak sunshine lit the way.

The weather was cool, though, in the low fifties. I hoped the guests would bring jackets. I didn't know if rain was predicted again, and cared even less. All I wanted was for this thing to be over.

My cell phone buzzed when we made the turn that led to the spa.

"Where are you?" Charlotte Attenborough demanded.

"Charlotte, I'm almost at the spa. I'm getting ready to set up. Where are you?"

"At home, at home. Jack's here with me, and I'm just so worried." Her voice was mildly hysterical. "Billie's not answering her cell!"

"Cell reception out here is pretty bad. You want me to go look for her?"

"Yes! Then call me!"

"Okay, but Charlotte—"

I'd either lost the signal or she had disconnected. Somehow, I suspected the latter. There had been no please, no thank you, just do it. As if that was what she was paying me for. One thing I was beginning to learn: where Billie got her bitchiness from.

I told Julian what was going on. He rolled his eyes and said I should go look for Billie; he would unload our boxes.

The spa had been transformed. I had to give it to Aspen Meadow Florist: They'd done wonders with the designs Charlotte had given them. Had Billie helped? I wondered.

Garlands of lights hung on every aspen and pine that surrounded the main building of the spa. Ropes of fresh white flowers and ivy had been draped at six-foot intervals under the eaves of the building, and the main door itself was also bedecked with flowers.

The dining room had undergone an even more spectacular metamorphosis. The theme of Billie and Craig's wedding was medicine, I guess so Billie would be sure everyone knew she was marrying a doctor. Even though I thought that was as tacky as a bride, even a biting one, could possibly get, Aspen Meadow Florist had once again outdone themselves. The table-cloths had a black underskirt and a white tablecloth on top, onto which rows of buttons had been sewn, à la lab coat, with *Billie and Craig* machine-embroidered in fanciful black script in between. In the center of each table, stethoscopes had somehow been placed upright, and they were surrounded by lilies and ivy.

In the front of the dining room, where the ceremony would take place, bright white-and-black slip-covers festooned the chairs, which had been placed in neat rows. A new dance floor had been placed over the dining room's old cement one, and there were more swags of white flowers and ivy between the rows of chairs. Aspen Meadow Florist must have worked all night.

But there was no one in the dining room. Specifically, there was no Billie in the dining room.

The clang of pans issuing from the kitchen told me someone was here, though, so I headed in that direction.

Yolanda, her face creased with exhaustion, was working with three other cooks. Julian, who was pil-

ing up the boxes, gave me a warning look: *Don't ask.*
But I was puzzled, and upset that she was even here.

"Yolanda!" I exclaimed. "You really didn't have to
be here. Julian and I already have all the food for the
wedding reception made, and we have all kinds of
helpers coming—"

Yolanda tossed her head. "Yeah? Well, I need to
keep my job, okay? And Victor said that Charlotte,
the mother of that bitch, the bride, what's her
name—?"

"Billie," Julian and I supplied in unison.

"Yeah, well, Charlotte told Victor, who's my
pendejo boss, that I upset Billie the Bitch, so my pun-
ishment is that my cooks and I have to make three
more appetizers for this stupid reception—"

"But, Yolanda," I protested, "we're already making
two appetizers—"

"Now you got five, then," Yolanda said. "We all got
five appetizers, right, girls?" she asked her crew.

"Yeah, we got five," they replied.

"Yolanda, I'm so sorry—," I began.

Yolanda put her hand on her hip. "What they gonna
do with five appetizers if you're giving them dinner,
too?"

I shook my head, then took a deep breath. "You
happen to know where Billie the Bitch is? She was
supposed to be decorating the dining room."

"The dining room's all decorated," Yolanda said.
"So Billie couldn't find anything to do, or anyone to
bother, and I wouldn't talk to her, I'm telling you,
when she came out here. She seemed all smug and

whatnot, being happy that I had to do all this extra work, so she started asking me questions, 'Where is this and where is that?' But I said, *'No hablo ingles, chingada.'* And then I just spoke Spanish to my girls here, didn't I?"

"Sí," they replied.

I swallowed and said, "Please tell me you didn't really call Billie a *chingada*." Beside me, Julian was laughing. I sure as hell hoped Billie didn't speak Spanish.

"Yeah, I did." Yolanda was defiant. "And she finally left."

"Her car's still here," Julian pointed out.

"I hope she's up in the gym exercising," Yolanda said. "And that she's sweating so hard it hurts."

"Better stick to Spanish," Julian advised before he and I took off for the gym.

But the gym was locked and dark, as was the entrance to the indoor pool. The guest rooms were arrayed on three floors of large houses, or dorms, and each floor boasted a large front porch. Cleaning crews were working their way through the guest rooms, as their carts were lined up on different porches, and people in uniforms ducked in and out of the rooms. Since I very much doubted Billie did cleaning of any kind, I figured the dorms were a no-go.

My cell phone beeped: Charlotte Attenborough again. So in some spots out here, I did get a signal. I ignored it anyway.

"We should split up," Julian said. "There are hiking trails all over this place."

"Wait," I said. "Did you see the sign for the Smoothie Cabin?"

"Yup."

"Try there. It's easy to find. I'll go up to the hot pool. Maybe she's relaxing, or trying to."

Julian took off down the sidewalk that led back to the spa's main building, while I began to negotiate the rocky path that led to the geothermal pool. Trees lined the path, and I thought that if you became really relaxed in the ultrahot water, a single misstep on the way back to your dorm could be, if not fatal, at least injurious.

Not far down the path, a thick cloud of steam billowing through the trees indicated I was getting close.

"Billie?" I called tentatively.

"Yes?" came her response. Her voice sounded, for once, positively languorous. "Who is it? I'm taking a break."

"It's Goldy."

"What do you want?" she asked, back to her normal sharp-glass vocal intonation. "I've already checked in with the kitchen. Everything's moving forward."

"Your mother can't reach you," I replied as I finally reached the side of the pool. The steam had made the pavement slippery, so I backed off a bit.

Billie heaved a voluminous sigh. I finally saw her, naked, in the pool. Great.

"Hand me a towel, honey," Billie said.

I looked around for a towel, then realized suddenly

that she wasn't talking to me. Craig Miller was with Billie. I could barely make him out, but it looked as if he, at least, was wearing a bathing suit.

"Here you go," said Craig. Through the steam, he appeared to be handing her a towel.

"Take these dishes and glasses, Goldy," Billie ordered. "Victor made us some Bellinis and sandwiches and cookies. He said he'd be back up for everything, but I don't want him to be bothered."

Of course, it was okay for me to be bothered. But I was used to Billie by now. I'd get her damn dishes, and soon, as Julian had pointed out, this day would be over.

"Call your mother," I barked. "She's worried about you."

"She's always worried about me. To hell with her."

Oh-kay. No wonder Charlotte was willing to pay four mil to be rid of her thirty-six-year-old brat. This time, I noticed, Craig hadn't been able to say he was sorry for the way Billie was acting. Too bad. Better get in the habit of always apologizing for your wife, buddy!

As Craig and Billie strolled back down the path, giggling and murmuring to each other, I edged over to the table from which Craig had picked up the towels. There were at least half a dozen glasses and dishes, sets of silverware, and crumpled paper napkins. Apparently, Craig and Billie hadn't been the first couple to think of having a minipicnic up here. Of course, I had not brought a tray with me, which would have proved helpful.

The dishes were littered with crumbs and were already attracting rows of ants. Wonderful. One of the glasses was almost full of a pink liquid; a drowned bee was floating in it. Other glasses were empty or almost so, and hadn't yet attracted any insect life. I started stacking up the dishware, then thought better of it.

I pulled out my cell and punched in Charlotte's home number. To my surprise, not only was the cell connected, but Jack answered on the first ring.

"Where's Charlotte?" I demanded.

"Happy to speak to you, too, godchild." I could hear the smile in his voice.

"Sorry. It's just that Charlotte sent me on a wild goose chase to find Billie, and I found her, up in the spa's hot pool. She was with Craig. She's fine, or as fine as any monster about to be married can be."

"I'll tell her, sweetheart. Calm down, will you? You sound stressed out."

"I am very stressed out. When will you be here?"

"Around four, Charlotte says. I'll come looking for you."

"Thank God for that," I said. "You're the best," I added impulsively.

"As are you," he replied. "Just hang in there. Weddings are like olives. They can be the pits."

I didn't mention that Charlotte thought she and Jack themselves were soon to be wed. I was pretty sure that would be news to him. If so, would their wedding be a kalamata or a California olive?

"See you soon," I said.

"Will Tom be there?" he asked suddenly. It sounded like a casual question posed as an afterthought, but I knew Jack too well for that. He'd probably seen my caller ID on Charlotte's phone, and immediately picked up just so he could inquire about where my husband would be and when.

"Why?" I asked.

"I'd like to see how he's making out on the Finn case, that's all."

"He's working the Finn case today, actually. I know he'll keep you posted, Jack."

"Will anybody else from the sheriff's department be at Billie's wedding?"

I paused for a moment. What was going on here? I had the feeling Jack was fishing for information, but for what kind of information?

"One of Tom's associates will be here," I said cautiously. "His name is Sergeant Boyd."

"Is he a guest?"

"No, he's helping me in the kitchen. Jack, what is going on? Why are you asking me these questions? You know, you can always leave a message for Tom if you want to."

"Hey, Gertie Girl, back off!" He laughed. "I just want to know what they've found out."

"I doubt Boyd will know anything."

"All right, then."

We signed off, and I continued piling up the dishes and silverware. The conversation with Jack troubled me. Did he know something about Finn's death that he had withheld from the sheriff's department? If Finn was his friend, why not tell all to Tom?

I tried to put these questions aside as I worked on figuring out how to balance all the plates and glasses. I started with the dishes, then put the napkins on top, then the glasses, then the silverware inside the glasses. I was immensely proud of myself when I'd constructed a mountain of china that looked like something out of Arch's old magic books.

With great care, I picked up the whole thing. Unfortunately, I hadn't figured on the hot pool's steam covering the surrounding flagstones and my carefully constructed stack with condensed moisture. I slipped, fell on my knees, and watched in despair as my castle of dishware plunged into the depths of the pool.

I cursed, rubbed my knees, and tried to think of what to do. I peered into the murky water, but could not see the glass. The famous Creekside Ranch hot pond, about fourteen feet across, was fed by genuine geothermal springs. There were two ladders, but the bottom was invisible because the soaking pool was constructed of dark, and undoubtedly slippery, rocks.

"Dammit to hell," I muttered.

What would happen if someone drank to excess at the wedding reception, came up here, and decided to have a soak? And what if he or she cut a major artery on broken glass? Unlikely, perhaps, but I didn't carry enough insurance to cover stupidity, my own for losing my grip on all those dishes, or others', for drinking too much.

I prayed that no one, absolutely no one, was anywhere nearby. I pulled up my sleeve, knelt, and reached into the steaming water.

It was so hot that I gasped. But I got used to it after a few moments. Scooting forward and feeling a couple of feet down along the edge of the pool with my fingers, I realized that a bench of some kind had been constructed around the inside perimeter. Marvelous. Only one plate had landed—and broken—on the bench.

I decided to make another grabbing circuit of the hot-spring pool. Unfortunately, when I extended my right arm as far as I could, my knees gave way yet again on the slippery stones and I fell in.

Cursing as wildly as one can while one's mouth is full of foul-tasting water, I tried to get some purchase on the bottom. Underneath the bench was another shelf, probably meant as a footrest. I used it to propel myself upward, where I emerged, choking and coughing.

I heaved myself onto the pool's bench, shivering and thinking. Thank God I kept a clean change of catering clothes in my van.

Since I had dropped the load in the first place, Victor would no doubt blame me—endlessly—for the broken dishes and glasses.

What the hell, I was already wet.

I took a deep breath and plunged down, down, down. How deep was this thing, anyway? Finally, at a depth that I judged to be about eight feet, I touched an uneven bottom. I pushed off and up for more oxygen, as I didn't want to risk hurting my eyes by opening them. Then down I went again, and began to feel, ever so carefully, for more dishes and glasses.

The water was hot, really hot, and I wondered if anyone ever scalded him- or herself. There was only one warning sign indicating that the very old or very young should not expose themselves to extreme temperatures for more than ten minutes. Peachy.

After what had to have been twenty minutes of probing, I had found four glasses and five plates. Had there been more? I could not remember. My hair stank of sulfur, and I was so light-headed I thought I might pass out. Had I just heard Julian yelling for me?

I had. He seemed to be hollering from a distance that might not be too far off. Was he on the path, maybe?

"Yeah, I'm here!" I croaked, sputtering.

"Goldy?" he called.

"Yeah, I'm in the pool! Just don't come all the way up, 'cuz I fell into the water and my clothes are stuck to me!"

Julian laughed, sounding relieved. "All right, I've got my back turned. Jeez, it's misty up here."

I clambered out of the pool and immediately felt even more light-headed. "No kidding," I said.

"I couldn't imagine what had happened to you! Look, why don't you have a shower in the spa gym? They're cleaning in there and it's open. I'll bring you your clean clothes from the van. We've got lots of work in front of us, boss." He paused. "What're you doing up here, anyway?"

I told him about finding Billie, then being ordered to pick up all the dishes and glasses, then dropping all of same into the pool, then feeling guilty and worried and reaching for the stuff, and finally, falling in, which was when I started looking everywhere for the still missing glasses, *et cetera*.

"This is easy," Julian called from the path. "We tell Victor about what happened. He puts a sign up saying the pool is being cleaned or something, and then he finds somebody to fix the problem. I'll meet you in the gym in ten minutes?"

"Okay," I said reluctantly. I clomped down the path toward the gym.

I simply could not wait for this day to be over.

Chapter 14

Sergeant Boyd, whom we'd always only ever called "Boyd," had arrived and immediately gone off looking for me up one of the hiking trails. Billie, apparently, had not bothered to tell anyone where I was.

"Man, I thought I was going to lose my job over you being abducted or something," he said, running his carrot-shaped fingers through his unfashionable black crew cut when I reappeared in the kitchen, showered, shampooed, and dressed in clean clothes. "In fact, lose my job? Forget my job. Schulz would'a killed me."

Julian just shook his head. Yolanda, who wore her hair up in an intricate cascade of curls, giggled. Apparently, she thought Boyd was kidding. Yolanda looked happy, anyway. After their set-to the other day, maybe Billie was giving Yolanda a wide berth.

"C'mon, Sergeant," she said playfully, "taste one of these. You won't want to go looking for anyone else the rest of your time here."

She plucked a paper napkin from a pile and put what looked like an empanada on top. I peered more closely at the napkins. They said *Billie and Craig* in embossed silver letters. I supposed with all the scheduling changes, Charlotte had given up on having a date printed on them.

"Here's one for you, Goldy," Yolanda said demurely. "Julian won't want one, because it has meat in it."

I tasted her offering: it was crunchy on the outside, with a smooth pork filling and a chile finish with a definite kick. "Yum," I said. After all my time in the hot pool, I was strangely famished. I was also strangely *dizzy*. When black spots appeared in front of my eyes, I reached for the kitchen counter and swayed.

Julian grabbed me. "You need to drink some water or a sports drink or something. You're dehydrated from being in that hot pool for so long."

"You were in the pool *all* that time?" Yolanda demanded. "Why?"

I gave them an abbreviated version of Charlotte's request to find Billie, my hunting expedition, the mishap with the plates, and finally, my sulphur-water diving escapade.

Yolanda held her hand up in an almost-closed position, as if she were handling an invisible potato. "Ay, that woman Billie! I curse her and her wedding—"

"You don't need to go that far," I protested, ever wary of evil people bent on providing real curses. "We'll all be fine."

Yolanda lifted her chin. "I curse her anyway."

Boyd and Julian, who were apparently impervious

to Yolanda's cursing, ducked out of her way as they ferried plates from the spa cupboards to the counter where Julian had taped my signs showing where everything should go.

"Victor told Isabelle she had to help with the serving!" Yolanda said, her face ablaze. "We're going to have too many servers as it is, and now Isabelle? And it's all because Charlotte complained about her, too." Yolanda lowered her voice. "Isabelle? She was kissing the boyfriend of Charlotte?"

"Well," I began, "he was kissing her . . . I'm just so sorry you and Isabelle are having to give up your Sunday."

"Don't be," she said, playful again. "I kind of like your friend Boyd. I just broke up with my boyfriend, so I'm available. And Boyd is cute! Get it? Boyd-friend?"

I didn't mention that I'd half-promised Boyd to Marla for a dance at the reception. Man, these things could get complicated.

But before we could chitchat further, Julian bolted into the kitchen.

"Boss man's coming," he hissed.

Yolanda immediately turned back to her deep fryer, and I opened the first box I could find, which contained the chilled crab cakes.

"I see you've begun working," Victor boomed. "Yolanda volunteered to help you," he went on, and only I could hear Yolanda's tiny groan at this blatant lie. "Isabelle will be along around five. She's also offered to help."

"I really don't need them—," I began, but Victor held up his hand.

"They absolutely insisted," he lied again. He squinted at me. "You want to tell me what you were staring at inside the Smoothie Cabin?"

I shrugged. "I was looking for my godfather, Jack."

"And what was he looking for in there?" Victor pressed.

"I don't know," I said truthfully. "Have you asked him?"

Victor pursed his lips and gave me an angry look. "You just happened to be going by there just when your godfather just happened to be scrounging around for something, after breaking into private property—"

"Oh, that reminds me," Julian said. "Speaking of breaking? There was an accident up at the hot pool."

Victor blanched. "An accident? Was someone hurt? Did you call an ambulance? What happened?"

"If you'll be quiet, I'll tell you," Julian said evenly. Everybody else was cowed by Victor Lane, but not my assistant. Hooray.

"Young man, what is your name? Maybe we need to clarify your relationship to this spa," Victor said. "You are here because I allowed you to be here. I can easily ban you from the premises, starting right now." Victor snapped his fingers to make his point.

"You want to hear about this accident, or not?" Julian said, unfazed.

I really, really needed Julian to help me with this

wedding reception, so I plunged in with, "Billie and Craig were up at the pool with some dishes and whatnot. They asked me to pick up after them, which I did, but the dishes slipped out of my hand and into the pool, and I couldn't find them all, so they're probably at the bottom of the—"

Victor Lane turned on his heel. As he stomped out of the kitchen, he shouted over his shoulder, "This is why I refused to hire you!"

"And you're showing why she wouldn't work for you!" Julian called after him.

I closed my eyes. When I opened them, Julian and Yolanda were laughing so hard, Julian was doubled over and Yolanda had tears coming out of her eyes.

"Since this is undoubtedly the last time I'll be working here," I said calmly, "could we please, please get going on this reception?"

"Sure, boss," said Julian. His face had turned bright pink from all the delirium, but he made an effort to read over my checklist.

Boyd shuffled back into the kitchen. "What's so funny?" he demanded. "Victor Lane told me he wanted some mulch spread in the new flower beds. So I spread the mulch, rewashed my hands, and now I've missed out on the big joke."

I told Julian to take Boyd out to the dining room, along with their checklist, if the latest tale in the Victor Lane saga absolutely, positively had to be repeated. Spreading mulch in the new flower beds? What was the matter with Victor Lane, anyway?

Thank goodness, I couldn't contemplate that

question because we had too much to do. We worked
diligently over the next two hours, making sure every detail was being attended to. Yolanda kept us
supplied with scrumptious Mexican appetizers, and
Julian had even brought some nonalcoholic beer
that we could have with them.

The ceremony itself was due to start at six, which
meant guests would start to show up around half past
five. Charlotte and Jack arrived, but I didn't get a
chance to visit with Jack, as the photographers showed
up at the same time. Charlotte, who was wearing a
flounced scarlet blouse and black pencil skirt, told the
photographers to take lots of pictures of the spa exterior until it was half an hour before the wedding, at
which point they were to come and find her. She then
announced that she needed Jack to help with getting
the groomsmen ready. Jack, who looked dapper in a
white shirt and navy suit, winked at me.

Charlotte caught the wink and cleared her throat.
She said she was just checking in the kitchen to make
sure we were on schedule. Then, once Jack was helping the groomsmen, she was off to make sure the
hairdresser and makeup artist were hard at work on
Billie and the bridesmaids.

"Billie and the Bridesmaids!" Yolanda singsonged.
"Sounds like a rock group!"

Charlotte narrowed her eyes at Yolanda, unsure
whether she was being made fun of, which of course
she was. But clearly, Charlotte had more important
things to do at that moment than force Victor to pun-
ish Yolanda again. Everyone departed for various

dressing rooms, Julian announced he was going to start the grill for the artichoke skewers, and I was glad once again to be working with Boyd and Yolanda.

Various servicepeople arrived. Boyd showed the bartender to his lair in the dining room. The bartender, a tall, slender fellow with a bald pate, began arranging the glasses, ice, sliced fruit, and bottles of wine and hard liquor to his liking. To my question when Boyd returned to the kitchen, he announced that the bartender was sober. This in itself was cause for rejoicing.

Father Pete poked his chubby face into the kitchen. "I'm looking for a handout."

"Ooh, the priest!" Yolanda trilled. "You like quesadillas, Father?"

"Do I!"

While Father Pete was feasting on Yolanda's offerings, Boyd once again checked every table; every place card; every setting of china, silverware, and crystal in the dining room. He reported that everything looked A-OK.

Billie had insisted on a miniature organ being set up in the room's far corner. When the opening strains of Jeremiah Clarke's "Trumpet Voluntary in D Major" startled me, I asked Boyd to make another quick check. He disappeared and returned, saying the organist was just warming up.

"Still, though," he cautioned, "one of the ushers warned me that the guests will probably start arriving in about ten minutes. You ready?"

I surveyed the kitchen. Yolanda's offerings of empanadas, quesadillas, and fish minitacos were ready to be slid into one of the spa's large ovens. The enticing scent of wood smoke drifted through the windows; this meant Julian's fire would be ready in time for the artichoke skewers. Like the caviar-topped deviled eggs, the rémoulade sauce was still in the spa's enormous walk-in refrigerator, as were the crab cakes—also on baking sheets, ready to be heated— the new-potato salad, and the haricots verts, with their vinaigrette only needing a final shake. The butter and baguettes were covered with plastic wrap on the center island. And the cake, another of Julian's phenomenal creations, was on a separate wheeled cart, along with a stack of plates, napkins, and dessert forks.

"We're ready," I said under my breath, just as the organist started in on Jeremiah Clarke in earnest, and the murmurings of guests being led to their seats beside the makeshift aisle began. Before long, the strains of the processional indicated the bridesmaids were making their way toward Father Pete. And, at long last, Wagner's "Wedding March" commenced.

Julian popped into the kitchen through the back door. "Fire's ready. Oh, man, you should see Billie. That dress does not fit her. She looks like a whale inside a white girdle that's, like, two sizes too small."

I groaned. "Don't say that. If she thinks the guests are judging her, she'll be in an even more vile mood than usual." I gave him a worried look. "Will they notice?"

He shook his head confidently. "Not if they're blind."

Boyd snickered. "Man, I'd like to work with you people every day. You're certainly a lot more fun than the sheriff's department."

Yolanda tilted her chin provocatively. "We would like to have you work here. In fact, I would like it very much."

"Is that so?" Boyd asked. "How are your cheese enchiladas?"

This banter went on for about twenty minutes as we worked. When we took a short break, I handed out the tip money from Dodie O'Neal, including Yolanda and her servers in the disbursement. Then, suddenly, from out in the dining room, Father Pete's sonorous voice announced something, and the guests clapped.

"Boy, that was quick," Julian said in surprise. "Guess the bride and groom didn't write their own long, elaborate vows. I'll go start the skewers."

As prearranged, Boyd and the rest of the servers worked to move the chairs away from the aisle. That side of the big room would be the dance floor, while the dining tables and their chairs would be reserved for people who just wanted to sit and relax. The wedding party, meanwhile, was outside having their photos taken.

Yolanda worked with alacrity on her appetizers, while out in the dining room, the sound of popping corks came in quick succession. Luckily, the weather was cool, so guests wouldn't be tempted to down multiple glasses of champagne just to slake their thirst. I'd seen that happen more times than I wanted to count, and the vision of guests passed out in the spa's flower beds—newly mulched by Boyd—was not something I wanted to contemplate.

Jack made an unexpected appearance in the kitchen. "How you doing, Gertie Girl? Anything I can help with?"

"Oh, thank you, but no," I said quickly, intent on the tray of Deviled Eggs with Caviar in front of me. "We've got everything under control. Why don't you just go enjoy the party?"

"I'd rather not. Where's your bodyguard?"

I gave him a quizzical look. "You mean, Sergeant Boyd? What makes you think he's my bodyguard?"

"Gertie Girl, I may have been born at night, but I wasn't born last night. Where is he?"

"Moving chairs," I said impatiently.

"I want to talk to him," Jack said.

I took the rémoulade out of the refrigerator and stirred it, then began to spoon it into small crystal bowls. "Jack, please. If you want to talk to Sergeant Boyd, he's out there somewhere. But please, please don't give him a lecture on taking care of me. He will."

Jack held up his hands in protest. "Okay, okay!" He grinned widely, then disappeared.

I forgot about Jack, Billie, Charlotte, Victor, and everyone else as our crew worked quickly to serve the appetizers, then start the crab cakes heating and get everyone seated. I didn't know who was making the first toast and didn't care. Julian gave me the high sign when it was time to start serving the dinner, and the servers whisked away with their trays.

The satisfying clink of silverware against china

mixed with the incidental music being provided by Aspen Meadow's one disc jockey, who had arrived without my noticing. The organist had apparently been dispatched, and this had not made a ripple in my consciousness, either.

"How're we doing?" I asked Julian when all the dinners had been served.

"Great. The guests are loving the food. When we were serving the appetizers, several people asked if you'd share the recipe for the deviled eggs. I've never had that happen before."

"Julian!"

"I mean, they're great, boss." He colored, then smiled. "It's just that people don't go to the trouble to make deviled eggs so much anymore, that's all."

When the conversational noise rose again, it was a sign that the meal was coming to a close. The servers zipped out of the kitchen with trays and began what I hoped was a subtle clearing of the tables. Yolanda filled the kitchen's tublike sinks with scalding water and soap, and, with one of her coworkers, began a quick, quiet, professional dishwashing enterprise. After ten minutes of clearing, one of the servers announced that the tables were ready.

"I'm taking out the cake," Julian announced as he rolled the cake stand toward the dining room.

"The ice cream!" Yolanda shrieked as she peeled off her rubber gloves. "We never have it here in the spa, and I forgot to let it soften!"

"If that's the worst that happens during this meal," I said, "then we'll be in good shape."

But it was not the worst that would happen. The toasts did not take long, nor did the serving of the cake, which was a miracle, considering Julian had to use his swimmer's arm muscles to dig ice cream out of the big containers. I helped Yolanda with the dishes, and soon the dance music began. I didn't see Billie and Craig perform their first waltz, which was probably just as well.

But I was genuinely surprised when Lucas Carmichael slammed into the kitchen and marched right up to me. I pulled away from him, which only made him lean in close to my face.

"Did you sic the cops on me?" he demanded. He wore a pale blue suit that must have had heavily padded shoulders. Instead of making him appear more fit, which was probably the effect he was after, the suit made him look like a kid who'd been dressed up for a Sunday School presentation. "I'm really tired of you and your manipulations, Goldy. I mean, we both know my father's an easy touch. So you worm your way into his affections," Lucas said, "with all your crying and moaning about your ex-husband. Then, when he decides to move out here, you convince him to buy a decrepit house across the street from you, not near me."

"I didn't!" I protested. "I didn't even know Jack was leaving New Jersey until he was practically here."

But Lucas had closed his eyes and was shaking his head. "You feed him food full of stuff he shouldn't have."

"I don't," I tried again. "I try to give him heart-healthy meals."

Lucas pointed his right index finger at my nose. "And if all that weren't enough, you tell the cops that I was involved in the death of Doc Finn—"

After my years with the Jerk, I'd learned to stand my ground. "You are exaggerating, Lucas," I said evenly. "You've got problems with your father? Or with law enforcement? Those are your issues, Lucas. Not mine."

But Lucas was going to have his say. "This past Thursday night, I happened to be at Southwest Hospital checking on a patient on my own time, not calling Doc Finn to set up . . . eek!"

Sergeant Boyd had come up quietly behind Lucas, circled the young man's chest with his powerful policeman's arms, and lifted him off the floor. Lucas's feet flailed wildly, and he was suddenly finding it difficult to breathe, much less bawl me out.

"Listen up, pal," Boyd said huskily into Lucas's ear. "You don't belong in this kitchen, understand? It's for food workers only. Got it?"

When Lucas did not reply, Boyd loosened his grip a tiny bit.

"Put me down!" Lucas managed to squeak.

Boyd retightened his hold on Lucas. "Got it?" the sergeant repeated. Yolanda and two of the servers were frozen, their mouths open, staring first at Boyd, then at Lucas, then back at Boyd again. I wasn't doing much better. I wanted Lucas out of the kitchen, but I certainly didn't want to alienate the young whippersnapper any more than I already had.

Into this unfortunate scene Marla happened to

appear. She breezed into the kitchen wearing a rosy pink satin designer dress with a matching shawl; in her hair and ears and around her neck were barrettes, earrings, and a necklace constructed of masses of pink sapphires. She smiled at our little tableau.

"Well, well, Lucas Carmichael!" she exclaimed, as if she ran into cops holding physician's assistants in death grips every day. "When I saw you slip in here, I knew you weren't coming for another crab cake. Now, Sergeant Boyd," Marla scolded mildly, "whatever it is you want from Lucas Carmichael, I can guarantee he'll give it to you. Right, Lucas?"

Boyd released Lucas, who despite his light weight dropped heavily onto the kitchen floor.

"C'mon, Lucas," Marla spoke down smoothly to where Lucas was kneeling on the floor, coughing, panting, and rubbing his eyes. "It looks as if they want you out of the kitchen. Am I right or am I right? Okay, I'm right. And anyway, I want you to dance with me."

"I, I—" Lucas struggled to his feet, narrowed his eyes to give me a dark look, then glanced over at Boyd. Boyd crossed his arms and raised his thick black eyebrows in a threatening manner. "Okay," Lucas said grudgingly, straightening his pale blue tie. "But I was just trying to—"

"Don't start with the excuses, buddy," Boyd said. "Or I'll lift you up by your ankles."

Marla tapped her foot. "Lucas? I'm waiting." She leaned over and whispered in Boyd's ear, I suspect to say she was going to take Lucas off Boyd's hands instead of asking Boyd to dance. "Lucas?" she asked again. "Are you going to dance with me?"

"God, Marla," Lucas said, recovering himself, "dance with you? You're old enough to be my mother."

"Take it easy, dear boy," Marla said, taking Lucas's arm. "Does your mother have a ten-million-dollar slush fund?"

Lucas gazed at Marla with sudden interest. "Do you?"

Marla's expression twinkled as brightly as her sapphires. "Well, I suppose you'll have to dance with me to find out!"

Yolanda, her coworkers, and I hadn't worked more than ten more minutes when Julian stuck his head in the kitchen.

"Boss," he said to me, "you'd better come have a look at this."

"Oh, hell, Julian, if it's Lucas Carmichael again, then I'll bring Boyd with me, and we can—"

"It's not Lucas," Julian replied. "It's Jack."

"Oh, crap," I muttered under my breath. Jack and Lucas fighting? Jack and Billie fighting?

When I sidled into the dining room, which had been skillfully turned into an enormous dance floor, I tried to focus on the crowd, to look for Jack. It was a slow dance, which was unusual for a wedding, and made distinguishing people via their backsides somewhat challenging. Finally, though, I saw him. He was dancing, very close, with Isabelle. Again. Oh, hell. She was supposed to be there in a server capacity, not a guest capacity. Yes, the serving was over, but I could imagine the kerfuffle if Victor saw Isabelle with Jack again.

Aw, jeez, now it looked as if Jack was whispering something in Isabelle's ear. When she turned away to laugh and shake her head, I noticed she wore a red lace dress with lots of décolletage.

So Isabelle was breaking all kinds of rules here. First of all, nobody at a wedding was supposed to wear lace except the bride. And no one, no woman anyway, is supposed to look sexier at a wedding than the bride. Take it from me, I'd heard from plenty of mothers of the brides who were outraged at the provocative dresses some of the female guests had turned up in, that this was a huge no-no. Worst of all, Isabelle was dancing and flirting with a man—okay, my godfather—who was old enough to be her father, and he had come with Charlotte Attenborough. Plus, Isabelle was a server, not a guest . . .

Which all might have been okay in this day of relaxed standards. But leaning against a nearby wall, Charlotte Attenborough was ostensibly talking to a friend—someone I recognized from a *Mountain Homes* photo display—while casting murderous glances at Jack.

Would he never learn?

Chapter 15

I repaired back to the kitchen, where any crisis was worth dealing with as long as it didn't actually involve the wedding. Boyd and Julian were engaged in a conversation that was important enough that they'd stopped washing the cake dishes. Julian finally faced me with the bad news.

"Four guests have come in saying they smelled pot smoke coming from the area of the Smoothie Cabin," he announced.

I glanced at Boyd. "Do we have to do something about it?" I said, ever one to duck responsibility when it came to law enforcement at catered functions.

"You don't," he said simply. "How do I get to the Smoothie Cabin?" I told him. "Keep an eye on her," he ordered Julian, "don't let her out of your sight." Then he checked that his cell phone was working and marched out the back door of the kitchen.

I eyed the remains of Julian's cake. There wasn't much left. "What should we do with this?"

"Charlotte came in and said we were to wrap it well and put it in our van. She didn't want any hungry spa guests delving into it, and she wants to save some for a magazine staff meeting tomorrow morning."

I sighed. "Of course."

Five minutes later, Boyd had not returned, but Julian and I had wrapped the lowest cake layer in plastic.

"I can take this to the van," I told Julian.

"The hell you say. I'm sticking to you like, well, what? Epoxy? Cement?"

"Dried royal icing."

"Fine," he conceded. "Let's boogie."

We, too, marched out the back door, with Julian holding the cake and me being, well, his escort. There was indeed a strong scent of marijuana drifting from somewhere, but it was hard to tell from where. Where was Boyd? Had he decided to get stoned with the party? Unlikely.

After we'd stowed the cake, Julian and I were walking back to the main house when we heard a soft, low moaning.

"Somebody having sex?" Julian whispered to me. "They needed the grass to get them going?"

"Wait. Listen."

The low groaning was there again, along with faint coughing. It did not sound as if whoever-it-was was enjoying himself.

"Could it be Boyd?" I asked Julian fearfully. "Maybe he caught somebody smoking, and whoever it was hit him, or something."

"I think Boyd can take care of himself."

The moaning was there again, less distinct this time. But I was sure it was a man in pain.

"I want to find out who's hurting," I said firmly.

"We've got a lot of dishes still to do," Julian warned as I set off in the direction of the newly landscaped area.

"They'll keep!"

Julian cursed under his breath, but true to his promise, stuck close to me.

"Where are you?" I called into the night. "Boyd? Are you hurt?"

There was a kind of whimpering coming from the bushes. Oh, how I wished cheap old Victor Lane had installed some real perimeter lighting instead of relying on Christmas-in-summer strands of lights.

"Boyd!" I called again when the sounds stopped. "Where are you?"

"I'm right behind you," Sergeant Boyd announced, and Julian and I almost jumped out of our epidermi.

"Did you find the pot smokers?" Julian asked.

"Nope."

"Well, we heard somebody moaning and groaning and crying," I said. "Somebody's hurt."

"More like somebody's drunk or having sex," Boyd said.

But it was neither. Beside the bushes, a body was sprawled at an unnatural angle. It looked like a man clad in dark colors. In the strings of lights, he was visible by his bright white shirt. Julian and I rushed over.

"Oh, Christ," Julian said. Breathless, I fell to my knees beside the man.

"Gertie Girl," Jack Carmichael managed to say before he lost consciousness.

Boyd was right behind us, and quickly took command of the scene. Thank God, he got a cell signal. He summoned an ambulance and law enforcement, while Julian judged Jack's condition.

"His heart's beating fine," Julian said to me. I was still speechless, but I was vaguely aware of tears streaming down my cheeks. "It just looks as if he was knocked out or something. Oh, Christ," he said again, as he reached around to the back of Jack's head. When he pulled his hand back, he held it up to show me. His fingers were covered with blood.

I'd seen plenty of trauma in my day, but it was different when it was someone you loved. "Jack!" I called down to the inert form. "Please, Jack!"

"Move away, Goldy," Boyd ordered. "You, too, Julian."

"He's been hit in the back of the head, and he's bleeding," Julian said. "I should hold on to the wound until the medics get here."

Curious wedding guests were gathering outside to watch the drama before them.

"Dammit," Boyd muttered when he saw the crowd. "All right, then, Julian, stay where you are. But do not move a muscle from that spot. Goldy, I've called Tom. We had a bad connection, but he's coming. Now, I want you to move these people back inside. Get Yolanda to help you. Victor, too. Tell everyone . . . tell them Jack's had an apparent heart attack and we need the guests to stay away until the ambo gets here. You got it?" he asked. "You going to be all right to do that? You're not going to pass out on me, are you? Or throw up?"

I pressed my lips together and nodded. "I am fine," I said evenly, "and I'll do exactly what you want. But what the hell happened? Is he going to be all right?"

"He's going to be fine as long as you can keep people out of here. Oh, and isn't the groom a doctor? Get him out here. ASAP."

"All right," I acquiesced. "But," I continued stubbornly, "why would someone do this?"

"Goddamn it, Goldy," Boyd said angrily, "I don't know. Isn't your godfather wealthy? Maybe someone wanted his wallet."

"His Rolex is gone," Julian said. "Uh-oh, he's conscious now. And he's going to puke."

"Roll him on his side," Boyd commanded. Julian did as commanded, and I really did think I was going to pass out when my godfather began to throw up weakly into the grass. Boyd shouted, "Get the damn doctor, Goldy!"

I blinked, overcame my immobilization, and walked quickly over to where the crowd was gathered. "Please go back inside," I begged them. "Someone is just sick, that's all."

"Serves him right," a guest commented.

"I'm sure as hell not having any more of that punch."

"Cake either!" Someone else cackled.

"Does anybody know where Dr. Miller is?" I asked, my voice suddenly high and imperious.

"Inside, I expect," an anonymous voice from the

crowd announced. "Which is where all of you should be." The voice was Victor Lane's. "Let's go, everybody. The show's over."

Victor was better at directing people around than I was, perhaps because he'd had more practice.

I pushed through the crowd, future clients be damned. "I need Dr. Craig Miller," I said urgently to Victor.

"He's still inside, Goldy. At least, he was the last time I saw him."

I sped through the dining hall doors and searched the hundred or so faces. Near me, Isabelle was listening uncomfortably to a lecture from Charlotte Attenborough. Out on the dance floor, Marla was swaying jovially from side to side, while Lucas Carmichael tried desperately to find the music's rhythm. He seemed as ill at ease as Isabelle. I threaded my way through the tables and immediately was aware of people's glares. *Now what does she want? Isn't the dinner over?*

Finally, Billie's loud laugh exploded from the far side of the dining room, and I made a beeline toward that noise. I realized I hadn't yet seen her in the fancy cream wedding dress that, when you included all the fees for change orders, Marla reported had cost over two thousand bucks.

"Craig, you are so funny!" Billie announced loudly, and the doctor, obviously pleased with amusing his bride, broke into a wide smile. Father Pete, who sat with them, wore a perplexed expression, as if the joke had entirely eluded him.

"Excuse me, Dr. Miller," I said, trying to sound as

formal as possible. "One of the guests is sick, and we need you. Please. Sergeant Boyd thinks this guest may be having a heart attack—"

"Goldy!" Billie shrieked at me, her face ugly with rage. "Go find another doctor!"

And then, all the months of dealing with Billie Attenborough's narcissism caught up with me, rising in my throat like so much bile.

"There isn't another one! I need Dr. Miller," I cried. "Please, Craig, Jack has been hurt. If you could just come out to the side entrance—"

Billie Attenborough sprang to her feet, and with her wide body encased in the cream dress, she blocked my view of her new husband. Unheeding, I peered around her to Craig Miller, who looked as if he'd swallowed half a dozen goldfish, live. "Dr. Miller," I began again, "please—"

Before I knew what was happening, Billie Attenborough reared back and slapped me across the face.

Tears exploded in my eyes. Still, even though my cheek flamed with pain, I was so frantic about Jack's condition, and so desperate to get Craig Miller's help, that I ignored my own distress.

When Billie saw I wasn't going to react to her, she began to sob.

"Dr. Miller!" I screamed over Billie's blubbering. "We need you outside! Jack's hurt!"

"Don't go, Craig!" Billie wailed. "I need you!" With great drama, she fell to the ground.

"Goldy," said Father Pete into my ear. "Tell me where this sick person is, and I'll take Dr. Miller to him. Then I want you to go out to the kitchen, and stay there."

"I am not going into the kitchen," I said, my jaw firmly clenched. "I'll take Craig out to Jack. You can tend to Billie Attenborough. Please," I added, as tears stung the slap on my cheek.

"All right," said Father Pete, resigned. He knelt next to Billie, who lifted herself slightly, then crumpled onto him.

"Let's go," Craig Miller said from beside me. He'd regained his composure, thank God. "Show me where this patient is."

I grabbed his upper arm and pulled him toward the closest exit, which happened to be about ten steps away. Billie was still doing her fraught moaning, and Father Pete was speaking to her in low, comforting tones. *Better him than me,* I thought, and I wondered if Craig Miller was thinking the same thing.

By the time we got outside, the ambulance had arrived. Thank God. Craig Miller hurried his pace toward Jack. To my surprise, Lucas Carmichael had magically appeared at Jack's side, too. He must have heard me yelling at Billie that it was his father who was hurt.

Despite the presence of two paramedics, Craig Miller was able skillfully to take control of the scene. He assessed Jack's injuries and ordered the medics to get a stretcher and a brace to stabilize Jack's neck. The medics sprinted back to their vehicle and returned with the stretcher. Boyd, standing over Jack, shook his head. This brought a fresh onslaught of tears down my stinging cheek, although no sound issued from my mouth.

"What happened?" Lucas demanded first of Boyd, who shook his head again, and then of me.

"I don't know," I said. "He was moaning. Julian and I heard him, and came over. His scalp is bleeding."

"His Rolex is missing," Lucas said to me, his tone angry. "Do you know where it is?"

This time I knew better than to say or do anything. I'd already lost my cool with Billie Attenborough, and the fact that the only thing Lucas could think about was Jack's expensive watch made me realize once again, for at least the hundredth time since I'd known him, that what Lucas really cared about was his father's possessions. The brat. Poor Jack, I thought, to have such a grasping materialist for a son—

"They're taking him now," Craig announced to Boyd, Lucas, and me.

"I'm going in the ambo," Lucas announced. "Does he have his wallet? He'll need his insurance card at the hospital."

I prayed to God to give me patience with Lucas. But this was just the way he was. Still, Craig Miller called to the medics, who stopped in their tracks with the stretcher.

A moment later, Craig called back to us, "No wallet!"

"Motive was probably robbery," Boyd said, his tone low. "It might not be here."

"Oh, look," Lucas said, reaching down. The wallet was right at his feet. "I've got it. Let's go."

"Let me come with you," I begged Lucas.

"I'm family," Lucas said. He seemed to be savoring

the moment, and his superiority over me. "You're not family. And there's not enough room in the ambo for all of us."

"Will you call me?" I pleaded.

Lucas didn't answer me, but merely hurried along behind the stretcher. Openmouthed, I watched them go.

"Who was that smarmy guy who said he was family?" Boyd wanted to know.

"Jack's son, Lucas. He's a creep."

"No kidding. Was that wallet right there at his feet?" Boyd asked. " 'Cuz I didn't see it when I was here with Jack."

"I didn't notice," I said truthfully, although it did seem a bit coincidental that Lucas had arrived and suddenly found Jack's wallet right in front of him.

A police car pulled up, lights flashing. Two cops jumped out and called to Boyd, who started walking toward them.

Meanwhile, I turned and trudged slowly back toward the dining hall, Billie Attenborough, and all her guests. I so didn't want to go back there. And I wished, desperately, that Tom was here.

A glimmer in the muddy grass distracted me. I bent down and saw, barely, the gleam of gold. I didn't look around to see if the cops were watching me. I just fluffed out my apron and scooped up Jack's Rolex from the dark spa lawn. Working to appear casual, I stood up, straightened my apron, and dropped the watch into one of its pockets.

Robbery was the motive? I wondered.

Chapter 16

Somehow, Julian, Yolanda, the servers, and I finished the reception. Billie had left with her mother, one of the servers informed me. Craig Miller and Father Pete had accompanied them.

"They said they were going to Southwest Hospital," the server said. She gave me a quizzical look. "Why would a bride and groom go to the hospital?"

"Was it the bride's mother's idea?" I asked.

"Actually, I think it was. But why wouldn't you just leave on your honeymoon?"

Because the bride's mother pulls the strings, I supplied mentally. In this case, Charlotte Attenborough pulled purse strings, as strongly wired as a ship's ropes. If Charlotte said, "Drive me to the hospital, Billie," then that was where everyone was going to go.

"Take my keys and go home," Julian said, once we were down to washing pots and pans. "Wait there for someone to call you about Jack. The cell phone reception out here sucks, so how would you know if someone was trying to call you? We can handle the rest of the cleanup."

"That's not what she's being paid for," said Victor Lane, who'd swished through the kitchen doors.

"Victor," said Yolanda, pointing a crimson-painted fingernail at him. "You want me to keep working for you? I did all this wedding, no charge. Now, let Goldy go. This man who was hurt on your property? He's family for her. I know you don't want to upset the family of someone who was hurt on your property."

Victor heard the threat in Yolanda's words, the threat that a family member might sue him for allowing someone to be hurt on spa property. Victor seemed to waver for a minute, then looked at me defiantly. "I'm going to have to tell Billie Attenborough that you left before everything was cleaned up."

"Victor!" exclaimed Yolanda.

"No, that's fine, Victor," I said, my voice flat. "Tell her. Tell Billie all about it, I don't mind." I would be so happy if I never had to work for Billie Attenborough again, in any capacity.

"What did you do to your cheek?" Victor demanded, staring at me. "Did you hurt yourself on spa property? And while we're at it, could you please tell me what you were doing yesterday, when you were looking through the glass into the Smoothie Cabin?"

"I told you. I was searching for Jack," I said. "He was inside the Smoothie Cabin with Isabelle, as you no doubt noticed when you checked the film."

"Jack is her family," Yolanda said. "He's the one who's been seriously injured on your property, and

now he's on his way to the hospital. And you're asking her a bunch of questions? Why don't you let her
go, and let us finish here?"

Victor was unmoved. "I want to know what you did
to your cheek." His tone was still stubborn.

"I didn't do anything to my cheek," I replied. "Billie the bride did that."

"Christ," said Victor Lane.

I ignored him and stalked out. Meanwhile, Yolanda
was peppering Victor with reasons why he should just
leave, so she could prepare the kitchen for the new
guests coming in that morning, actually, since it was
past midnight. I didn't wait to hear a reply. Victor
Lane was a pill, but my money was on Yolanda in any
conflict.

"Wait. Maybe I should come with you," Julian said
from behind me.

"You gave me your keys. You don't need to baby
me, big J."

"Yeah, and what if the same person who attacked
Jack attacks you? Then Tom really would kill me.
Which wouldn't work for his career, him being a
homicide cop and all."

Outside, a gentle rain had begun to fall. The cops
had cordoned off the area where we'd found Jack.
They'd set up a spotlight that shone in the mist. An
investigator was talking to one of the valets. Should I
tell them about the Rolex? Probably. But I didn't. I
wanted to tell Tom.

"You have your cell?" Julian asked.

I felt in my other apron pocket, the one that didn't

have a fifty-thousand-dollar watch in it. "Yup." I rummaged in my purse, and handed Julian the keys to the van. "Thanks for loaning me your Rover."

"No sweat. Soon as you get out on the road, you should get good reception. I'd feel better if you called Tom and told him you were on your way."

"All right. Jeez, Julian, you're as bad as he is."

"I'll take that as a compliment. Now get going, will you?"

And so I took off in Julian's Rover, which splashed through the muddy ruts in the dirt road leading to the spa. When the rain intensified, I was blinded by it, and when I failed to find the windshield wipers, I pulled over. Once I located the interior lights, I managed to turn on the wipers. But still, I sat.

I didn't want to go home, even though every muscle in my back and legs, and my swollen cheek, said that was exactly what I should do. I felt helpless and hopeless. I hated not having any information on how Jack was doing. I told myself I would call the hospital when I arrived home. If I had to get Tom on the phone with them, I would pry out some information on Jack's condition.

I figured out how to turn on the wipers and got going again, slowly. Eventually I reached the main road back to Aspen Meadow. When my cell phone rang, it startled me. I pulled over again, and prayed that this was not bad news about Jack.

"Miss G." Tom's voice was as comforting as dark chocolate.

"Where are you?" I hadn't checked the caller ID.

"Home. You out on the main road yet?"

"Yes, Julian gave me his—"

"I know," Tom interrupted me. "I called the spa's land line."

Terror rose in my throat. "What's going on?"

"First of all," said Tom, "I heard about Jack going out for a smoke and being attacked and robbed. And a little while ago, Lucas Carmichael called here," Tom went on, with amusement in his voice. "It seems your Uncle Jack woke up in Southwest Hospital and had a request."

"Request?"

"Actually, Lucas said Jack stopped breathing in the ambo, and the paramedic had to give him a trach. At the hospital, the first thing Mr. Impatient Attorney wanted was a pad of paper." I laughed with relief. This was so typical. "Wait," said Tom, "there's more. It sounded as if what really upset Lucas was the fact that Jack wrote your name down as soon as he got the pad. Apparently, the person he wants to see is you, his goddaughter. Not Lucas, his son."

"I'm going down to Southwest Hospital."

"Yeah, I thought you'd say that. I tried to tell Lucas that would be what you wanted to do, and would he allow you to see Jack. He said he would." Tom paused. "Will you call me when you leave there?"

"Sure. And, Tom? I have to tell you something."

"Uh-oh, sounds like confession time."

"Well, first of all, I sort of got into a physical fight with Billie the Bride at the reception."

"Super. Did you get your final check before this altercation?"

"'Fraid not. I was trying to get to Craig Miller, so he could come help Jack. Billie wouldn't let me through. She ended up slapping me."

"Oh, for God's sake. You were trying to get to a doctor. Are you all right?"

"I'm fine. But the second thing is, this wasn't a robbery."

Tom's voice was immediately sharp. "What makes you say that?"

"I, uh, picked up Jack's Rolex from the grass."

"Goldy, I swear, you never learn."

"I didn't touch it with my hands!"

"Better and better. You had an evidence bag with you, and you gave the cops on the scene the watch, inside the bag."

"Well, no."

"Where is it now?" Tom asked.

"Inside my apron pocket. Sorry, Tom."

"Yeah, yeah. Okay, I want that watch. Do not touch it."

"I never did!"

"Uh-huh."

We signed off, and I headed through the dark, rainy night to Southwest Hospital. Why would you rob someone, and then not take his expensive watch and his wallet? Was the robber interrupted? Or was he up to something else?

Once I'd parked in the hospital lot, I pulled off my apron, folded it, and stowed it on the floor of Julian's Rover. The rain was still falling, so I hunted around for a slicker of some kind, and found a folded plastic poncho in Julian's glove compartment. I opened it, pulled it over my head, and trotted into Southwest Hospital.

After assuring the receptionist that I was not here about my swollen cheek, I was directed to the fourth floor, and Jack's room.

I knocked on the door, which was pulled open by Lucas. He looked incongruous in his fancy suit that had become muddy and creased. Since I was ensconced in the brown poncho, a look of incomprehension wrinkled his thin face.

"It's me, Goldy," I said.

Lucas's face dissolved into irritation, which I tried to ignore. "He's conscious, but I just don't have the feeling that he knows what's going on. He choked on his own vomit in the ambulance; that's why they had to give him the tracheotomy. Then he was moaning and groaning, as if he was in pain, so they've given him morphine in his IV, for the head injury."

"Stitches?"

"Not yet. Not until he's stabilized. They butterflied it."

"I'm so sorry, Lucas."

"Yeah," he said bitterly. "I'll bet you are."

As usual, I couldn't read Lucas's vinegary tone, and didn't want to waste time trying to.

"You might as well come in, then," Lucas said.

I'd had more enthusiastic invitations in my day, but again, I didn't care. I was so eager to make sure Jack was his old hale and hearty self that I plunged into the room, then recoiled when I saw how gray and helpless he looked. His eyes appeared rheumy, but when he saw me, he motioned me forward.

"Don't upset him," Lucas warned me, as if I would.

"Jack," I said gently. "I'm so glad to see you."

Jack reached out the hand with the IV in it and clasped one of mine.

"I don't suppose you've washed your hands any-time recently," Lucas's voice intoned from behind me.

I turned. In a low voice, I said, "Lucas? Shut. Up."

"All right, listen," Lucas said, as if I hadn't spoken. "Here's what happened. We got him here, and he woke up, and because of the trach, he couldn't talk. But he was acting all impatient in that way he does. So I gave him the pad of paper and a pen. He wrote, 'Gold.' And I said, 'Goldy?' And he shook his head no, but then he nodded yes. I'm telling you, it's the morphine."

Behind me, Jack's ring banging on the bar of the hospital bed brought me back to his side. He had a yellow legal pad—where had the hospital found one?—and on the same piece of paper that he'd written "Gold," he now penned, "Feel bad, Lucas. Need time with G."

Lucas, who after months had finally shown me a teensy bit of politeness and restraint, raced out of the room in a huff.

"You know, Jack," I said, attempting humor, "you might want to try to be nice to Lucas so that he and I could get along and share you—"

Jack grunted and tapped the legal pad. I said, "Do you want something?"

He groaned and made a scribbling motion with his hand. Where had the pen gone? Eventually I found a pencil in a table drawer. He took it and tried to get purchase on the pad of paper, then looked at it in puzzlement. He growled in frustration.

"Do you want me to write something down for you?" I asked. "Do you want to tell me who hurt you?"

Jack frowned and shook his head. His gray face and the wrinkled skin of his chest visible above the hospital gown made me feel sick to my stomach. Hadn't Jack just told Lucas he felt bad and needed to be with me? What did he need me for? What was he trying to say? Unable to decipher his grunts and movements, I felt as frustrated as he clearly was.

The door swished open. I thought it must be Lucas, back already. He'd been gone only a few minutes, which might upset Jack. Still, for once I was grateful that Lucas was showing up. Maybe his presence would clarify whatever it was Jack wanted to write to me—

But it was not Lucas. To my astonishment, Charlotte Attenborough, Craig Miller, and Bridezilla Billie all swept into Jack's room. Charlotte was still wearing her mother-of-the bride outfit, but Billie had changed into a navy blue skirt and paisley blouse. Craig looked as dapper as ever in khaki pants and a maroon shirt. But why were they here? What the hell was going on?

"What do you want?" I asked, suddenly angry that they would see Jack looking so vulnerable.

"Shut up, Goldy," Billie scolded.

"Shut up yourself," I replied. "Jack doesn't want to see you, trust me." As if in complete assent to what I was saying, Jack let loose with a mighty groan.

"You see, Goldy?" Charlotte's voice was triumphant. "He does indeed want to see us, or at least me, because I am the one he really, really loves—"

"We just wanted to check up on you, old boy," Craig said with exaggerated cheer. "I told Billie there was no way we could go back to the reception right after you'd been hurt so badly—"

In response, Jack picked up the pencil and finally, finally scribbled something. His hand shaking, he passed the pad to Craig. Billie grabbed the pad first. She read aloud, " 'Go on your honeymoon.' You see, Craig, I told you the old coot would be just fine." She tossed the pad back on Jack's chest, and he moaned in pain.

Omigod, I hated this woman. But I wasn't going to upset Jack any more than necessary. My godfather's two previous heart attacks loomed large in my mind.

"Do you miss me, Jack?" Charlotte asked. To my astonishment, tears pooled in her eyes and spilled onto the hospital sheets. "Do you want me to stay? I will, you know. I'll stay forever."

She must be drunk, I concluded. I hadn't seen how much booze people had imbibed at the reception, although I usually kept a close check on the alcohol consumption. I'd had too many buffets and cakes ruined by inebriated guests not to know when to tell the bartender to slow things down. But too much had been going on at Billie's wedding. There had been half again as many guests as I usually had to deal with, and too much had happened in too short a time.

"Don't you want me to stay?" Charlotte demanded of Jack. "I will, you know." Jack closed his eyes and shook his head. "Jack," Charlotte implored, "won't you even look at me?"

In reply, Jack moaned and kept his eyes closed.

"He might be in pain," Craig Miller said. "Perhaps it would be best if we left."

"Why does *she* get to stay, then?" Billie demanded, pointing at me. The fact that she'd changed her mind about wanting to go on her honeymoon hadn't seemed to occur to her. Billie should be a politician, I thought, she flip-flopped so often.

"Come on, everybody," Craig said, finally showing a bit of leadership ability. "Charlotte? Billie?" He gave his new wife a penetrating look. Billie, demure in the face of—spare me—actual authority she respected, flounced out. Charlotte, sobbing, followed her.

"Craig?" I asked, once the two women were in the hall. "Why did all of you come down here?"

"Charlotte insisted," he said, shaking his head. "She's had too much to drink, as you can no doubt tell, and I didn't want her to drive. So we all came." Behind us, Jack groaned again. Craig gave him a worried glance. "Should I get the nurse?"

"I don't think so. He has the call button right next to him, and he knows what to do if he's in pain. He's trying to communicate something, but I don't know what. He seems confused."

Craig's face scrunched in alarm. "I don't like the sound of this."

"I'll go ask him," I said. "But if you could just take Charlotte and Billie away, I think that would be the best thing."

Craig nodded and swept out.

"Jack?" I asked him. "Do you need the nurse? Do you want pain medication?"

This time his head shaking was unequivocal. He did not want the nurse or meds. But what did he want?

As if in answer, Jack's hand went to the legal pad. Swift and sure, he wrote a word, then tapped on the paper for me to come see.

He'd written "Keys."

"You want your keys?" I prompted.

Jack, looking confused again, wrote "Fin."

But the door was opening. No wonder people said they couldn't get any rest in the hospital. Jack quickly tore off the piece of paper, handed it to me, and gestured to the hospital closet.

"Oh, Dad," said Lucas. "Did she finally leave you in peace?"

Next to the closet, with Jack's piece of paper in my hand, I froze. As if in answer to Lucas, Jack let out his most fearsome groan yet. I pushed the paper into my pants pocket and turned around. Instead of meeting a chilly stare from Lucas, I saw him leaning over the bed, trying to read what Jack was writing now.

"Pain?" Lucas asked. "They just put morphine into your drip, Dad, I don't think—"

But Jack groaned again, and Lucas, cursing, took

off through the door. As soon as he was gone, I opened the closet and began showing Jack pieces of his clothing.

Jacket? He shook his head impatiently, and sure enough, there were no keys in either pocket. Shirt? No keys. When I held up the pants, Jack grunted, and I felt in each of the pockets. Finally, I pulled out his bundle of keys. They were covered with a gritty substance. Jack nodded, so I put the keys into my pocket, next to the piece of paper.

"Okay, here we are," Lucas said as he reentered with a uniformed male companion. Doctor? Nurse? I had no idea. Nor did Jack seem to care, as he just closed his eyes again.

"I'll be going," I announced. Jack's eyes didn't flicker. "Get well soon," I called to him. He didn't open his eyes.

The next morning, our doorbell clanged very early. It was so early, in fact, that as I stared at our bedroom clock, I was convinced that the alarm had gone off by accident. It was not quite half past five.

Tom was not beside me. So he'd gone in extra early to work on the Finn case? Where was he?

The doorbell continued to ring. I squeezed my eyes shut tight, trying to remember the events of the night before. When I'd come home from the hospital, I'd found a note Arch had left me. Since Todd and his family were on their way to a fishing trip, he and Gus were going to the Rockies game with Gus's grandparents, then staying at Gus's place. He would call.

Not continue to press and press and press the doorbell. Cursing mightily, I pulled on a robe and half-raced, half-tripped down the stairs.

My peephole revealed Father Pete. His gray face was unusually somber; his clerical collar was as tight as a noose.

Oh, God, I thought. It's bad news about Jack.

My mind immediately developed into denial. Didn't Father Pete have to go get ready for church? No, wait, it was Monday, not Sunday . . .

I opened the door and avoided our priest's eyes. "Father Pete, I don't understand—"

"Let's go into the living room, Goldy."

I wished desperately for coffee, for Father Pete not to be here. But I moved into the living room anyway, and turned on two lamps. When Father Pete sat heavily in a wing chair, I lowered myself onto the edge of the couch.

My denial threatened to slither away. "I don't want to hear bad news," I said weakly.

Father Pete's eyes were filled with sadness. I cursed inside. I cursed and cursed, waiting for his announcement. "I'm sorry, Goldy, I do have bad news. Very bad, I'm afraid. Your godfather, Jack Carmichael, died last night. He had a heart attack."

Chapter 17

"I'm very sorry, Goldy," Father Pete said. I blinked and blinked at him. "Would you like me to come sit next to you?"

"No." My voice sounded disembodied.

"I'm so sorry, Goldy."

"I don't believe you. I don't believe something has happened to Jack," I said. In the distant reaches of my brain, a tiny voice said, *Yeah, but he'd had two heart attacks already, he was a smoker, and he looked like hell when you saw him. Why are you surprised?* I told the inner voice to shut up. "There's been some mistake," my actual voice said weakly. "An error. I just saw him a few hours ago. He was getting better."

"I know, I know." Father Pete's voice seemed to be coming from far away. "But he had a history of heart attacks, and—"

"Who called you?" I whispered.

"Lucas," Father Pete said gently, keeping his large eyes on me. He leaned forward in the chair. "Lucas was with Jack when he died. The hospital staff tried and tried to revive him, but it was just too sudden and too strong an attack—"

I groaned.

"I couldn't reach Tom," Father Pete persisted. "But one of his associates said he'd find him and tell him to come home. Meanwhile, I called Marla, and she'll be over here shortly. She's going to stay with you until Tom gets here."

"Are you wanting me to help with funeral arrangements?" I asked.

"Goldy. Eventually, we can talk about that, if you want." Father Pete's big, brown, Greek eyes regarded me. "I know how much he meant to you, and how much you meant to him. He often told me—"

"Please, don't. Not now." Tears were sliding down my face, but I was as unaware of where they had come from as I was aware of my irrational desire to get Father Pete out of our house. I made a fist and pushed it against my closed mouth.

"I will call you later." Father Pete stood up. "Again, Goldy, please know how very sorry I am. Marla is supposed to phone me and tell me whether or not you want meals sent in."

I took a deep breath and removed my fist from my lips. "I don't want or need food." Then I forced myself to say, "Thank you."

"Goldy." Father Pete was hovering next to the couch. I didn't want to look at him, so I closed my eyes. "You need to take time to grieve. I will be at the church if you need me. Call anytime. If I'm not at the church, you can call my cell . . ."

I said, "Thank you." I forced myself up, and wordlessly saw Father Pete out.

The front door closed behind him with a soft *chook*.

I waited for something to happen, but nothing did. A car rumbled by outside, then another. I went back out to the living room and sat down. When Father Pete had been here, the light in the living room had been wan, the illumination of early morning darkened by the incessant cloud cover that had marked the unending rain.

When I stood up again, I still felt as if it wasn't quite my body that was moving, not really my own hands that were punching the espresso machine. I pulled myself four shots, added an ounce of Irish whiskey, then drank that down straight, no cream.

Then I moved without thinking over to one of the kitchen cabinets Tom had installed. I opened it and pulled out a large crystal bowl, an item I'd splurged on after Jack had sent me his generous check. I looked at it in my hands, then let it fall to the floor, where it crashed and broke into smithereens.

By the time Marla pounded on our front door, I almost had the mess cleaned up. I would have been ashamed to tell her what I was doing, or what I had done, so I took an extra few seconds to wet a paper towel, then wiped up the last of the shards. "Just a second, just a second," I said under my breath. But Marla would not quit banging.

"Sheesh!" I said. "I'm alive, if that's what you were worried about."

Marla, who wore a sparkly purple sweat suit, lifted an eyebrow as she appraised my bathrobe, tear-streaked face, and, I saw too late, a cut on my foot that had left bloody streaks in the hallway.

"Barely alive, apparently." She used her plump self to push the door all the way open, then pointed at my foot and the scarlet trail back to the kitchen. "I've heard of stigmata, but this is ridiculous."

I couldn't help myself: I laughed.

Marla, meanwhile, had made her way to the kitchen, where she was assessing the damage. "Okay!" she called. "This is interesting. What did you break?"

I started to walk toward her. Suddenly my right foot hurt like the dickens.

"A bowl. A crystal—"

Marla turned back toward me and held up her hand. "Stop where you are. I'm going to get a wet wash-cloth, some alcohol or peroxide or something, and have a look at that foot."

Truly, she is a great friend, I thought as I sat on the hall floor and waited for her to come back. The tears were still slipping down my face, and I was snuffling, trying to catch my breath.

"Denial, anger, bargaining, grief, acceptance," said Marla as she inspected my foot and used the wash-cloth to gently remove a sliver of glass. She'd filled a large porcelain serving bowl with warm water and dipped my foot into it, then blotted the foot with— typically Marla—a cotton ball soaked with Irish whiskey. "Sorry, this was all I could find in a hurry. All right, where was I? You, o psychology major, should know about those stages of grief, brought to you courtesy of Dr. Elizabeth Kübler-Ross." She patted my foot dry and placed a bandage on the worst cut. "I'd say the broken bowl was anger. Father Pete called my cell, as he was convinced you were still stuck in denial. You're moving along quickly, you precocious girl."

I couldn't help the high-pitched giggle that escaped my lips. "Marla, don't make me laugh."

"No way. But what I am going to make you do is go take a shower. Go on, I'll clean the kitchen floor, as you missed a few spots. Then you're going to make me something to eat, because I am ravenous." She leaned in to my face and I recoiled. "You've been drinking," she accused.

"Not much. Just—"

"I'm not saying it's a bad thing. I may have to get half lit just to do some mopping. Say, how do you use a mop, anyway?"

"Marla, stop—"

"I will if you'll just get your butt upstairs and hop into the shower. When you come back down, I'll inspect your foot and make sure I don't need to take you in for stitches."

Southwest Hospital, I thought, as my throat closed again. I wasn't sure I was up to going back there anytime soon.

I ran the hot water, took my shower, which actually did help me feel better, and got dressed in a clean polo shirt and much-laundered sweatpants. A breeze ruffled the curtain and I walked over to the window. I couldn't help it: I looked out, across the street to Jack's house.

He'd wanted to start his renovation on the outside, although Tom and I tried to dissuade him from doing so. It had snowed off and on all through April in Aspen Meadow, as it always did. Jack, ever cheerful, had said okay, he was willing to wait until summer to work on his house, after I'd told him for the umpteenth time that we didn't really have "spring" in the mountains. So off Jack had gone with Doc Finn, who'd promised to teach Jack ice fishing. Occasionally, they brought their catch to us, and along with Arch, the five of us had some merry pan-fried-trout suppers, with Jack holding forth on how much fun it was to spend cold days with Doc Finn.

"We're just two old farts who like to drink and fish, not necessarily in that order," Jack said, with a wide smile. "We get too plastered, Gertie Girl? We can just walk across the street and sleep at my place."

"You have beds with sheets on them for you and Finn?" I asked. "Because you can always stay here."

"Oh, dear godchild," Jack had said with mock ruefulness. "The things you don't know about me." When I'd given him a puzzled expression, he'd gone on: "Of course I have beds with clean linens."

I sighed, not wanting to think about what would happen to Jack's house, or anything else of his, because basically I didn't want to think. Still, as a neighbor walked her dog up our street, I thought, *How can she do that? How can she just go on with her life, as if nothing has happened?*

I felt dizzy and sat down on our bed. After a few minutes, Marla came looking for me. She plopped down on our bedroom chair.

"I put something together that's vaguely eggy, and now it's in the oven."

I smiled in spite of myself. "Vaguely eggy, huh?"

"Only very tangentially eggy, but very cheesy. Why don't you come down to the kitchen? 'Cuz I have no idea how long this thing should cook."

I shook my head, but heaved myself up off the bed anyway. A moment later, I was gazing at Marla's concoction in the oven, asking her how many eggs, exactly, she'd put into her creation, and how much cheese, and so on. She said she couldn't remember. Well, at least a dozen eggs, she said as an afterthought.

"Marvelous," I said, and set the timer for forty-five minutes. Since I didn't want to be as rude to Marla as I was afraid I'd already been to Father Pete, I immediately apologized. I added, "I'm sure it'll be great."

"I'm not even sure it'll be edible." Marla paused, then sniffed. "Tom called while you were in the shower. He's on his way." She regarded me closely. "Tell me how you're feeling."

"I'm feeling like crap is how I'm feeling. I just think I should have been able to prevent this."

"Whoa, whoa, whoa, Goldy. Your godfather had already had two heart attacks, and he was a heavy smoker and drinker. At the wedding, he was violently mugged and lost consciousness, or at least that's what Julian told me." When I didn't contradict her, she said, "Then one of our church pals from Med Wives 101 called me late last night. She was down at Southwest because her son tore his ACL playing soccer, and they were there until all hours. Anyway, while they were waiting to be seen, she'd been wandering the halls, and stopped in when she saw Jack's name on a door. She said how awful Jack looked, because he'd stopped breathing and had to have a trach in the ambulance." Marla took a sip of her own Irish coffee. "That's a whole lot of stress for an older man to deal with, and you're wondering how all that could have precipitated another heart attack? Come on." Marla's eyebrows rose, inverted commas surprised by my naiveté. "Jeez, Goldy, better to ask why wouldn't he have had a heart attack?" She rose to make us each another coffee—this time with no whiskey, but with added whipping cream.

"I should have stayed with him," I said stubbornly. "If his heart attack was inevitable, then I should have called his cardiologist and told him he had to come down to Southwest Hospital."

"You're going to tell a doctor what to do? Last time I looked, that didn't work out for either one of us, even when we were married to the doctor in question."

"I should have done something for Jack. There must have been something I could have done."

"There was nothing you could have done. Sunday was yesterday, so would you please quit with the messiah routine? It's aggravating."

Marla was the only one in the world who could talk to me like this and get away with it, and actually, I treasured her for it. Father Pete had done the right thing to call her, and for that, too, I was thankful.

"Hey!" I noticed for the first time that the whole kitchen floor was immaculate. "Thanks for cleaning the floor. I'm surprised you could find the mop—"

"Every now and then," Marla rejoined as she got up to set the table, "even a blind chipmunk runs into an acorn. Or a mop, as the case may be."

"You should let me set the table," I began, but shut up when Marla gave me a withering glance. I sighed, and suddenly felt tears sting my eyes again. When a sob left my lips, Marla turned suddenly.

"Okay, okay! You can set the table!"

I half-laughed, half-sobbed as Marla pulled me to my feet and hugged me. I allowed myself to cry. Into this scenario walked Tom. I hadn't even heard him drive up.

"Miss G.," he said as Marla passed me off to my husband. "I'm so sorry about Jack. I really, really am."

"I know. Thanks for coming up."

"I'm going to have to go back down in a bit." He gave me a hooded look that said, *Not in front of Marla,* which she immediately interpreted.

"Why don't you just use your cell to call Goldy from the living room?" Marla queried. She turned to the oven and brought out her puffy, golden pan of whatever-it-was. "Then you could tell her what it is that's such a big secret."

"I've gotten used to you, Marla," Tom said jovially.

"Oh, hell," said Marla, as she plunged a spoon into the pan and pulled up a serving of her concoction, only to have a puddle of uncooked egg pool out like batter from the center of the dish. "What did I do wrong?"

"Not let it cook long enough?" asked Tom. "Want me to fix us some ham and eggs?"

And so, twenty minutes later, we had Marla's egg dish in front of us, as well as an enormous ham-and-egg omelet, courtesy of Tom. Unfortunately, I took one bite of Marla's concoction, and simply could not swallow it. Not that it wasn't good; it was. I not only wasn't hungry, I suddenly thought I was going to puke. When I put my fork down, Marla gave me a worried look.

"That bad, huh?"

"No, Marla, I'm just not that hungry. Thanks anyway."

A worried glance passed between Tom and Marla. I never lost my appetite.

Marla's cell buzzed. It was Father Pete, wanting to know how I was doing. Marla said I was okay, considering. Then Marla said, "Well, I'm sure she didn't mean to hide them. I mean, I'm sure they're not hidden, they're just . . . not where you can find them. There's a difference." I could hear Father Pete's despairing voice on the other end of the line. Then Marla said, "All right, all right, let me come help you."

When she disconnected, she said, "Are you going to be all right, Goldy, now that Tom's here? Because Father Pete says there are letters from the diocesan office he can't find in the church files, and was wondering if I could go help him try to figure out how the new secretary's mind works. Since I recommended that he hire this woman, it's all my fault, apparently, that the diocesan letters were placed in some random file drawer instead of on Father Pete's desk. I even warned him she had ADD, but he just said he didn't think that would mean needing CIA assistance to find some random letters from the diocesan office."

"It's fine, go," I said. "Thanks for coming."

"Oh," she continued, "and Father Pete told me to tell you you should take a few days off from catering, maybe get Julian to fill in, so you can grieve."

"Wonderful," I said, unable to conceal my sarcasm. "That just sounds super, grieving all day. And anyway, I don't need to take off from work, because I don't have any catered events until next weekend. And I've got plenty of money from all the work I've been doing lately, so I don't have to go out and drum up business."

"Do you want some work?" asked Marla as she gathered up her purse. "If we don't find those diocesan letters, I'll bet the position of St. Luke's church secretary will be opening up mighty quick."

I said, "Gee thanks!" We hugged again and she rushed away.

Tom said, "I know how much Jack meant to you,

Miss G." He regarded me with his wonderful sea green eyes, then pulled me in for a hug. "Tell me what I can do to help," he murmured in my ear.

I exhaled. "I don't know. Truly, Tom, I don't. One thing I do know, though, I don't want to sit around and *grieve*." I pulled away from him. "You tell me— when you have a case that's really bothering you, that you can't get over, what do you do? I know you don't grieve."

"People grieve in different ways, Miss G. Some people need to sit around and cry. Other people need to be doing something, something they find meaningful, that will help them deal with a death. I fall in that second category. As do most homicide investigators, I might add."

I canted my head at him. "What did you just call me?"

Tom, genuinely surprised, tucked in his chin. "Miss G. The way I always do. Why?"

"Because Jack always called me Gertie Girl. He never called me anything but."

"And this is significant because . . . ?"

Where was that piece of paper Jack had scribbled on in the hospital? "Hold on a sec."

I raced upstairs and found Jack's note, and his keys, as well as—oops—his Rolex, which I'd meant to give Tom first thing, except the news of Jack's death had intervened. I wanted to give Tom the watch and show him the note, but I certainly didn't want to hand over Jack's keys until I knew exactly why he had wanted me to have them in the first place.

With only a small pang of guilt, I stuffed Jack's keys into my pajama drawer, then brought the note, plus the watch, still wrapped inside my apron, down to the kitchen.

"'Gold. Keys. Fin,'" Tom read, after he'd shaken his head, given me a dubious look, and put the Rolex into a brown paper evidence bag. "What's that supposed to mean?"

"Well, I don't know, but he sure was eager to be writing something for my eyes only," I said. "Lucas called and told me about the trach Jack had had in the ambo, and how he seemed to be wanting to talk to me, because he'd written 'Gold.' Lucas thought Jack wanted him to summon Goldy. But Jack never, ever called me Goldy. He called me Gertie Girl."

"And what do you think he meant?"

My shoulders slumped. "I haven't figured that out. Something gold in his house?"

"Did he give you keys to get into his house?" Tom raised one eyebrow at me. "So you could go in there and get whatever it was?"

"I don't know why he wanted me to have an extra set of keys. I already had a set of keys to his house."

"You'd better hand over those keys he gave you, Goldy." He held out his palm expectantly.

Tears streamed down my cheeks. "He didn't want anybody else to have these keys. He wanted me to have them. Don't make me give them up, Tom. Please."

"Don't use either set to go into his house, Goldy. If he died as a result of this attack on him, then it's felony murder, and we'll be going through every inch of that house." He paused. "Somebody broke into Finn's house after he was killed."

"Oh, no."

Tom said, "Oh, yes. We don't know what was taken, if anything. But at this point, please, please don't screw things up for us. I'm begging you."

"I won't," I promised.

Tom groaned, then looked back at the note. "What do you suppose he meant by Fin? Talking about his pal, Doc Finn?"

"I don't know. You know, sometimes you see that at the end of French movies. *Fin*. It means the end. Maybe he had a premonition he was going to die."

"You ever know Jack to go to a French film, read all those irritating subtitles? I sure didn't. And anyway, I think if he meant End, then that's what he would have written."

"Maybe. Except he was pretty out of it at the hospital."

"Out of it enough to misspell his best friend's name?"

Tom's cell phone buzzed, and he answered it. Meanwhile, I stared at the cryptic note my secrecy-oriented godfather had left for me. "Gold. Keys. Fin." I had no idea what Jack had been trying to say.

"I've got to go back down to the department," Tom said. He gave me a worried look. "Let me get Trudy over here to be with you."

"Gosh, what am I, an invalid? First Father Pete, now you. I'll be fine." I glanced at the clock: 7:40.

"How about this? I'll go to church and help Marla with some stuff she's doing for Father Pete. Finding letters either to or from the diocese, I'm not sure which."

Tom appeared unconvinced.

"I'll be fine, Tom," I assured him.

"Church." He waggled a warning index finger in my direction.

"Church!" I replied. "For crying out loud, give me a little credit!"

He eyed me skeptically. "Yeah, yeah. I don't give you too little credit, Miss G. I give you too much credit."

Once I'd heard Tom's Chrysler rumble away, I went upstairs, pulled out the set of keys I'd taken from Jack's jacket in the hospital, and stuffed them into my sweatpants pocket. I slammed my pajama drawer with such violence that it startled me.

Cool it, I said to myself.

All right. I needed to think, and to cook. These would help me grieve, not sitting around crying. In any event, going to St. Luke's was the very last thing I wanted to do, of that I was sure.

Chapter 18

In the kitchen, I located my recipe for coeur à la crème. I'd had to give the one I'd made earlier for Tom to Marla for her shindig, so I needed to make another one. No, I thought after a moment. I'd make another coeur, and then . . . a plain old cream pie for someone else I'd suddenly decided to see. I sighed, then told myself to get going.

The walk-in offered up mascarpone and whipping cream, and the pantry held confectioners' sugar and imported Mexican vanilla. I beat the cheese, sugar, and vanilla to a smooth, delectable mass, then set it aside and whipped the cream. I lined a sieve with cheesecloth, set it over a bowl, folded the two mixtures together, and scraped half of this concoction into the cloth-lined sieve. After I'd placed one of these into the refrigerator to drain, I put the second mixture—the one for the cream pie—into a separate bowl. Then I located fresh berries of all varieties. These would go on top.

I wanted to offer the cream pie as an attempt to elicit information.

I hoped offering the coeur to Tom would allow him to forgive me for doing stuff behind his back as I tried to figure out what in the hell had happened to my godfather.

And, I added mentally, I wanted to find out what had happened to my godfather's best friend, Doc Finn. Because now the two deaths, one definitely a murder and the other a death possibly as the result of an attack, seemed more and more inextricably linked.

I made myself a quadruple espresso for a heavy-duty Summertime Special. Then I went out to the living room to think. I unfolded Jack's note. "Gold. Keys. Fin." Jack's clutch of keys jangled as I dropped them onto the table.

As I'd told Tom, it was extremely doubtful that Jack had meant to summon me to the hospital when he had written "Gold." So what did the "Gold" stand for? Did he have a stash of gold somewhere that neither Lucas nor I knew about? Was he trying to alert somebody to that stash?

What other possibilities were there?

I hiccuped violently and succumbed to a fresh onslaught of tears and sobbing. I wished suddenly for Arch to be here, just so I could hug him and tell him how much I loved and needed him. Maybe I should have let Tom summon Trudy to be with me.

You've got to move forward, Gertie Girl, Jack had said to me before he'd sent the fifty thousand that had gotten me into my own business and out of the marriage to the Jerk.

I nabbed some tissues, splashed cold water on my face, rubbed it virtually raw, and looked at my tired eyes and red-slapped cheek. Beauty contest? No. Able to move forward? Yes.

I went back to the living room, took a healthy slug of the iced latte, and looked again at the note. "Gold." *Think. Move forward.*

Gold could stand for Gold Gulch Spa. Jack had been digging around in the Smoothie Cabin just a couple of days ago. Had he found what he was looking for? And what exactly had he been looking for?

I made a note to talk to Isabelle. Unfortunately, I didn't even know her last name. What had she and Jack been up to? When Jack had heard someone coming in, he'd grabbed Isabelle and started smooching her. Then at the reception, he'd been snuggling up to her again. Why?

Jack was secretive, that was certain. Maybe he hadn't told Isabelle anything. Maybe this note didn't mean anything; maybe it was just, oh, I didn't know what.

Doubt squeezed my heart again as I looked at the word "Fin." Doc Finn had been lured out onto the highway at night, hit from behind, and then killed. Jack Carmichael, his closest friend, had been attacked three days later in a robbery-that-wasn't-a-robbery. I had to believe the sheriff's department would demand an autopsy on Jack's body to determine the exact cause of his death. If the injuries sustained in the attack had led to Jack's death, then it was felony murder, as Tom had said. Maybe the sheriff's department was already investigating, and I didn't even know about it.

I exhaled in frustration, then stared at the extra set of Jack's keys. Why had he wanted me to have them? I saw the Mercedes keys on this set, plus some others I didn't recognize. Had he wanted me to go back out to Gold Gulch Spa and get his Mercedes? If so, then why not write that down? Had his mind been wandering so much in the hospital that his notes, and his desires, didn't really make any sense?

A shiver went down my spine. What if his beloved car was not the issue? If he had wanted Lucas, who already had a set of keys to Jack's house, to go to Jack's house for some reason, then why insist on my having this set?

I needed to think some more. First I checked for my keys. Thank God for Julian, who had returned my van during the night, and taken back his Rover.

Then I quick-stepped into the kitchen and made a graham cracker crust. Then I spooned the luscious filling into the crust, scattered blueberries on top, and melted some apricot preserves on top of the stove. Once I'd strained the liquid from the preserves onto the pie, I carefully placed the pie in the bottom of a cardboard box, stabilized my offering with crumpled newspapers, and placed the box in my van.

Then I took off for the Attenborough haunt in Flicker Ridge.

* * *

Charlotte answered the door. I'd called on the way over, saying we'd never finished our business the previous evening. Charlotte, confused, had said she didn't know what I was talking about. As delicately as possible, I had reminded her that I had not received the last payment for the wedding reception.

"Oh yes, yes, of course," Charlotte had replied. "I thought you meant, that is, I thought you were talking about Jack."

"Yes, it's very sad. I can't stand to stay in my house. Is this, is it a bad time?"

Her breath caught when she sighed. "No. Come on over, you might as well. I'm just getting packed to go to the spa. I . . . have to get away. I guess I can't stand to stay in my house either."

"I'm bringing you something," I said, which sounded lame, even to me.

"I hope it's not flowers." She exhaled so forcefully, I didn't have the heart to ask her to explain herself.

When Charlotte ushered me into her living room, I knew immediately what the flower comment meant: at least twenty bouquets from the banquet tables were ranged around the immense living space. The place looked like a funeral parlor and smelled like a perfume factory.

"Well," I said, unsure of what words to use.

"Horrible, isn't it?" asked Charlotte, as she swept an arm to indicate the room. She wore a bright pink pleated blouse and designer jeans. But her face was a wreck: deep, dark bags creased the area under her eyes, her eyes were bloodshot, and her skin was mottled.

I handed her the wrapped blueberry-cream pie. "Don't know how long you're going to be at the spa, but this should keep a few days in the refrigerator."

"I don't know how long I'm going to be there either. Until I feel better, I suppose. Victor's been trying to convince me to invest in the place. I told him before I did that, he'd have to improve the food. He said I had no idea how much it cost to provide lovely meals to the clients. But he'd let me stay for as many days as I wanted until he closed in October—" She stopped suddenly and regarded me. "Sorry, I'm running on at the mouth, which is what I do when I'm upset." She pressed her hands into her closed eyes.

Charlotte most definitely was not someone you hugged, even in church, even if she was crying.

"I'm sorry," I said, my voice low. "It's just terribly sad. We all . . . we all loved him."

"I'm not being very polite," Charlotte said as she walked quickly into the kitchen. "Would you like some coffee?"

I thought of all the caffeine I'd already had that day, and asked if she had decaf. She said she did. Once she'd put the pie in the refrigerator, set the coffee to brew, and placed cups, saucers, spoons, cream, sugar, and an insulated carafe on her breakfast bar, she seemed to have recovered somewhat. As she poured the decaf into the carafe, she even smiled at me.

"It's good to have company. Oops, I forgot your check." She reached into her purse, pulled out an envelope with my name on it, and handed it to me. "With all the chaos last night, I just . . ."

"Don't worry about it. Thank you."

She took a tentative sip of her coffee and asked, "Do the police have any idea what happened to Jack when he went outside?"

I shook my head. "I have no idea. Didn't someone from the sheriff's department come talk to you?"

She snorted. "A young fellow asked me questions very early this morning. Did I see anyone leave the dining room with Jack? No. Did I see anyone leave the dining room right after Jack left? No. So why did Jack leave the dining room? To have a cigarette, I told this young fellow, didn't you find a butt outside? And he said they found marijuana outside. He thought I was trying to make a joke, which of course I never would."

"Huh," I said noncommittally.

"Before Jack was attacked, there just seemed to be a lot of organized chaos," Charlotte went on bitterly. "Afterward, there was just chaos, period."

"Chaos," I agreed.

"Oh, God, I do wish I'd paid attention, but I'm afraid I was more focused on the music getting going, the tables, I don't know, it all seems like such trivia now. So . . . have they figured anything out?"

"Nobody's told me anything."

"It was probably one of the landscapers, staying to see if he could mug a wealthy guest."

Inwardly, I bristled, since whenever there's a theft or any other problem at a party, it had been my experience that the help—which includes yours truly—is always blamed. More often than not, though, it's one of the guests who starts rifling through pockets and purses in the guest room, not a staff person. We're much too busy. But I knew in order to get information out of Charlotte, which, I admitted, was my chief purpose in racing over here this morning, I would have to park my proletarian sensibilities at the door.

"Have they talked to the landscapers?" Charlotte demanded. "Were *they* smoking marijuana?"

"I don't know. Sorry." We were both silent for a moment. I glanced down at Charlotte's shoes—metallic flats—and said, as if it had just occurred to me, "Oh, nice shoes. Very pretty."

Charlotte looked at me as if I were crazy. "You're admiring my shoes? Why, do you want to order some to wear at your next catered event?"

"Sorry, Charlotte. I just think they're lovely. Wait a minute—didn't Màrla or someone tell me you lost a pair in Doc Finn's car?"

Charlotte rolled her eyes. "That was another thing this young fellow asked me about. Did I remember when I had left my shoes in Doc Finn's car? No, I told him, because I'd never been in Doc Finn's car. I have no idea how they got there. And when I heard they'd been in the car of a person who'd died in a car accident, I wanted to throw them away, but the police insisted on keeping them as evidence."

"Poor Doc Finn," I said. "We waited and waited for him at Ceci O'Neal's wedding, but he never showed. We didn't know he was dead."

At the mention of Ceci O'Neal, Charlotte's eyes became hooded. Well. So . . . judging by Charlotte's guilty reaction, the erased name "O'Neal" on the Attenborough blackboard meant something. I just didn't know what.

"Do you know the O'Neals?" I ventured. "I thought I saw their name on your blackboard when I came over with Jack. But I didn't see you at the O'Neal wedding—"

Charlotte stood up. "The O'Neals? How are you spelling that?" When I told her, she said, "No, that doesn't ring a bell. Well, I must be getting over to Gold Gulch. Thank you for the pie."

"You're certainly welcome," I said, feeling uncomfortable. I got to my feet and gathered up my purse. Doggone it, so much for active investigation as a substitute for grieving. I was zero for three in my questioning of Charlotte. She hadn't seen anyone leave the spa dining room when Jack did—or so she said. She had no idea how her shoes had ended up in Doc Finn's Cayenne—or so she said. And whatever her connection was to the O'Neals, she wasn't going to share it.

I had gleaned one possibly useful nugget, though: Victor Lane had asked Charlotte to invest in his spa. So . . . the spa was having money problems? Was that what Jack had been looking for in the Smoothie Cabin? Indications of money problems at the spa? Why would he do that? I had no idea.

Charlotte had turned to her large living room window, where birds were flocking to her feeder. She'd pulled a hankie from out of nowhere and was dabbing her eyes. My feeling of being ill at ease increased. Funny how we get used to hugging people as a way to comfort them, and then when that's not an option—

"Do you think he loved me?" Charlotte blurted out. She continued to stare out the window. "He never said he did."

My mouth turned dry. In fact, I'd been unsure of what Jack's true intentions, emotions, et cetera in the Charlotte Department had been. But what good—or bad—would it do to say that now? I settled for the verbal equivalent of a hug.

"I know he loved you," I said emphatically. "He told me he did."

Charlotte quickly wiped her eyes, tucked the hankie into a pocket of her jeans, and began bustling around the living room. "Take these flowers to the church, would you please, Goldy? They'll all be faded by the time I get back from the spa."

And so I said I would. I had to roll the windows down to dispel the pungent, cinnamon scent of the stock in the bouquets. When I got to the church, neither Marla, Father Pete, nor the secretary was in evidence. Luckily, I knew the hiding place for the key to the heavy doors. I placed all the flowers in the sacristy, wrote a quick note to Father Pete, and drove slowly back home.

But again, the thought of going back into our house was not something I could bear. Tom's car wasn't anywhere in evidence, but I wouldn't have expected him to be home yet.

I turned off the ignition in my van and looked disconsolately up at Jack's house, much as Charlotte had stared at the wild birds on her deck. Without thinking, I reached into my sweatpants pocket and felt for the keys Jack had insisted I take in the hospital. Luckily, I'd also put the note in there that he had written.

If Jack was directing me to go into that mess he called a residence, or more properly, a residence being renovated, then what did he want me to find?

I suddenly and with unexpected vividness remembered Jack coming into the spa kitchen the previous night. He'd asked if he could talk to Boyd. Jack had wanted to talk to Sergeant Boyd, who worked for the sheriff's department.

About what?

Well. I looked back at Jack's house. There was no doubt that Lucas, whom I perhaps unfairly thought of as a materialist, would eventually have his way with Jack's house. Lucas was the son, the heir. Marla had heard he needed money. So Lucas would probably get in, finish the renovation as quickly and cheaply as possible, then put the place on the market. This made me extraordinarily sad. I forced my mind to veer away from this line of thinking.

The problem was, I was having trouble breathing. I didn't want to have anything in my mind. I didn't want to feel anything.

I pulled out the keys Jack had told me to take, and without thinking about it, jumped out of the van.

Watery sunshine was breaking through the clouds. Finally. It felt as if we'd been underwater for a month. More sadness: now that it was finally nice, Jack wasn't here to enjoy it. *Stop,* I ordered myself.

A breeze shuffled through the pines and aspens as I

hopped up the steps to Jack's house, and I wished I'd worn a jacket or a sweater. But if I went back home, my nerve would fail and I would rethink the advisability of going into Jack's house. I didn't think it was illegal, but I certainly did not want to consult an attorney on the subject.

The key squeaked as I turned it in the lock, the mechanism itself infected with the humidity that had been our constant summer companion. I tiptoed into the house, and immediately felt as if things had changed. Things had changed? What things?

The interior was as disordered as usual. Jack had apparently left a few windows open, and the fresh scent of recent rain filled the air. Jack's old sofa was piled with clothes and towels—a dump of clean laundry awaiting folding, probably. The end tables and coffee tables held precariously piled stacks of books and magazines.

I allowed my gaze to travel around the room, thinking the whole time: What's different? What had Jack wanted me to see in here, if anything? If Jack had been so anxious for me to see something in his living room, then he should have been clearer about it—*wait*.

Beside the door was a set of golf clubs in a beautiful leather bag. Golf clubs? The clubs and the bag looked brand new. But Jack had bursitis in both of his elbows. It had pained him, and he was always rubbing in this or that new anti-inflammatory cream.

Why new golf clubs? Had Jack bought them as a gift for someone? If so, for whom? Were they for Doc

Finn, Lucas, or Craig Miller, as a wedding gift? They hadn't been here when Tom and I had come over to visit the other night.

Jack could not possibly have thought he would be able to play eighteen holes, or even nine, as his aches would have made the outing disastrous. The bursitis didn't bother him fishing, he always told me, just doing something strenuous, like . . . sports. And anyway, with whom would Jack have played golf? He and Doc Finn had engaged in fishing and drinking, not necessarily, as Jack had always said, in that order.

Then I saw something else that had not been there on any of my previous visits. A small gold travel clock was folded into the open position, on a tiny end table right in front of the picture window that gave someone looking out a view of our house. If somebody were sitting on the couch, that person would look right at the clock, and then to our house across the street.

Golf clubs, when he didn't play golf. A travel clock, when he kept no clock in his house. Hmm.

Okay, I was anxious and grief crazed, and who knew what all. But I couldn't help seizing on the idea that Jack had left the clubs and the clock here because he wanted me to find them. They were one of his puzzles, left for me.

Without thinking about it, I moved across to the table and picked up the clock. It was not telling the correct time, and when I tried to turn the tiny crank on the side, nothing happened. Without thinking, I folded the clock back into a square, and slipped it into my sweatpants pocket. I walked over to the golf clubs, and ran my hands over the golf bag, which was made of a lovely buttery yellow leather. Maybe it belonged to somebody else? But when I looked closely, I saw a price tag dangling from the bag's handle.

I simply would not accept what other people might have said, that the clubs and bag and nonworking clock were evidence of mental decline on Jack's part. I supposed it was possible he had bought the golf accoutrements, then remembered he didn't actually play golf . . . and then had wanted to return what he'd bought.

As improbable as it seemed, I found myself returning to the puzzle idea. I began to remove one club after another from the bag. I didn't know what I was looking for, or even if I would recognize it if I found it.

I had just put a five iron on the floor when I felt a slight movement of air behind me. I started to turn around, but I wasn't quite fast enough. For all my worry and care about why Jack had given me his keys, I was rewarded with a glancing blow off the side of my skull.

My knees crumpled. My mind's eye brought up my dear Arch and Tom. But then pain exploded on the side of my head, and I thought, *What the hell?*

The first oddity facing me as I sputtered, blinked, and coughed uncontrollably was to figure out who was waving spirits of ammonia under my nose. This person had to be stopped. I screamed that I hadn't blacked out, I was perfectly conscious, thank you very much. The ammonia disappeared.

The second problem had to do with my mother's pet bird, a canary named George who'd lived in a cage in our New Jersey home while I was growing up. George the canary had not died, as I had been told, but had grown as large as a human and now was fully alive, leaning over me. What kind of badly scented alternative universe had I entered?

Eventually the big canary resolved into the avian facial features and yellow hair of Lucas Carmichael. Next to him were two policemen. I was looking up at them from a prone position on the floor.

"Would you please get my husband? Tom Schulz?" I asked one of the policemen, a fellow with sparse red hair who looked familiar. Then again, I'd just thought the son of my godfather was a canary, so maybe I did not in fact know this guy. Still, in as authoritative a voice as I could muster, I said, "Please call Tom Schulz. Right now. He needs to be here. Please," I added again.

"Oh, Christ," said the other policeman, who had dark, slicked-back hair and a youthful face. "Schulz? This is Schulz's wife?" He looked down at me. "This isn't Schulz's house, is it?"

"No, it isn't," said Lucas Carmichael.

I narrowed my eyes at Lucas. "Please tell me you weren't the one who hit me on the side of the head."

"I didn't know it was you," he said, his tone humble. "I'm sorry. I just didn't recognize you from the back."

While the policeman I had spoken to summoned Tom on the radio, the other one glanced up questioningly at Lucas.

"She did break in," Lucas protested defensively.

From my ignoble position on the floor, I fastened my gaze on Lucas. "Don't you watch any TV, Lucas? You're supposed to say, 'Freeze, asshole!'"

"I am not an asshole," Lucas said. "And do you ever think not to break into people's houses?"

"I wasn't breaking in, and I wasn't calling you an asshole. Sorry, Lucas." Suddenly, I felt consumed with guilt. Lucas appeared bleary-eyed and defeated. He'd just lost his father. "Sorry," I said again. "I was—"

"Mrs. Schulz?" the sandy-haired policeman interrupted. His name tag said his name was Katz. "Your husband will be here directly. He was in the area and shouldn't be long." Officer Katz smiled at me. "So I'm finally getting to meet the infamous Mrs. Schulz."

"She's infamous?" Lucas asked.

"Hey, buddy?" Katz said to Lucas. "Don't talk unless I ask you a question, okay?" To me, he said, "You want to tell me why you're in this house?"

"Will you help me up first?"

Katz offered me a strong hand, and soon I was sitting on Jack's couch. The dark-haired policeman, not wanting, I figured, to be bawled out by Tom for being unhelpful to his wife, scrambled to get me a glass of water from the kitchen. I felt dizzy and in pain. On the floor not far from where I'd fallen was a small brass lamp with a broken bulb and smashed shade. It was the bulb and shade, I figured, that Lucas had swung at the side of my head, leaving me stunned, confused, and lying on the floor. I wondered if he could be arrested for assault.

"I'll tell you exactly what I was doing here." I felt in my sweatpants pocket that held the keys, not the one with the travel clock. Seeing Katz's immediate look of alarm, I pulled out my hand. "I'm not going for a weapon," I assured him. "You want to feel in my pocket? I was getting the keys Jack gave me, and the note in his handwriting saying he wanted me to have them." I gave Lucas another angry look. Lucas shrugged and stared at the ceiling.

"It's okay," said Katz, "I trust you. Get out the keys and the note. I'm not going to go feeling around in the pockets of the wife of my superior officer, thanks."

I withdrew the note and the keys, which Katz studied. If he wanted to make sure the keys worked, then he could go and test them on the door. But I had the feeling he believed me.

The dark-haired policeman came over and handed me the water. His badge indicated his name was Allen. He furrowed his eyebrows at Jack's handwriting.

I had, of course, left the travel clock securely in the bottom of my other pocket.

"This your father's writing?" Katz asked Lucas, who stared down at the note. "These his keys?"

"Yes," said Lucas. "I'm sorry I panicked and hit Goldy—"

"All right, then," Katz interrupted noncommittally as he handed the keys and the note back to me.

"Don't give those keys back to her," pleaded Lucas. "She doesn't belong here."

"Could you give it a rest, please, Lucas?" I asked gently. I trained my gaze on Katz. "Let me explain.

We live across the street." My breath hitched, and I fought to maintain calm. "Jack Carmichael was my godfather." Tears began their unwanted streaming down my face. "He . . . died last night, in Southwest Hospital," I managed to say. I cleared my throat and paused to compose myself. As they're taught to do, the two cops waited patiently. Lucas was shifting his weight from foot to foot. I went on, "Here's what happened. Last night, Jack Carmichael was attacked at a wedding I was catering out at Gold Gulch Spa. He actually died early this morning. Our priest came to tell me, and I thought, since Jack had insisted in the hospital that I take the keys, maybe he wanted me to . . . I don't know, water his plants, feed a pet—"

"But he has no plants and no pets," Lucas interjected. "As you very well know, Goldy."

"Lucas," I began again, "could you please just stop? Why are you here, anyway?"

He reddened. "Well, I do have keys to the house."

I asked, "So what were you doing here, then?"

"Hold on, kids," said Katz. He and Allen exchanged an unreadable look. Before Lucas and I could keep arguing, there was a sharp knock on the door. Lucas and I both jumped. Allen held up both hands, indicating everyone should stay where they were. Then he walked over quickly and opened the door. When Tom strode into the room, my shoulders relaxed in relief, while Lucas groaned even louder.

"Schulz," said Katz. "Thank God." He was clearly relieved not to have to sort out what was going on between Schulz's wife and the dead man's son.

But alas. Tom did not seem relieved. I recognized the attitude he assumed, but was usually successful at concealing, when he was mightily ticked off. He gave me a bitter look, and I could just imagine the questions he'd pepper me with as soon as we got back to our house: So, how'd you do with Marla at St. Luke's? Get those diocesan letters straightened out, did you? Oh, wait, you didn't do that.

The cops briefed Tom as to Lucas's phone call to 911: he'd heard an intruder in the living room, who had been me, and he needed law enforcement to come as quickly as possible. Then he proceeded to side-swipe me with a lampshade.

"I want this house sealed," Tom said to Katz and Allen. "Nobody else comes in except our guys, understand? We're looking into a suspicious death, and this residence is off limits to anyone not involved in the investigation."

"Oh no, you are not going to seal this house," Lucas protested. "My father had a history of heart attack and he had another, fatal one early this morning. It is simply not fair for you to—"

Tom's stance—not menacing, but not even close to conciliatory—his penetrating green eyes, his lifted chin, all these he trained on Lucas Carmichael, who closed his yappy mouth. Thank God.

"Okay, everybody out," Katz ordered, and I was only too glad to meekly follow Tom out of Jack's house.

* * *

"Goldy," said Tom, once we were in our kitchen and I had downed some aspirin for my sorely aching head. "What were you thinking?"

"I wasn't really thinking."

"That much is obvious. Down at the department, they're going to have a field day with this. 'Schulz's wife broke into the house of a guy whose death was suspicious. What d'you suppose she was looking for?'"

"Katz and Allen will say all that? Why?"

"Because they're cops, Goldy, and they've got to talk about something when they come off their shift. And the more trouble you get into, the more news you make, Miss G."

"I wasn't getting into trouble! I just wanted to find out why Jack left me his keys!"

"And did you?" Tom moved over to the espresso machine.

"No."

There was a pause while we looked at each other. Then Tom exhaled, smiled, and shook his head. "You want some coffee?"

"I've been thinking I should switch to decaf."

Tom laughed. "You?"

"All right, all right, the good stuff." While Tom rattled around retrieving cups, I said, "There was a new set of golf clubs in his living room." I didn't elaborate, as I didn't want to mention the clock. Stealing merchandise from a potential crime scene? Not something I wanted to share with Tom. My head hung, and I felt an acute sense of misery. I could barely form the words, but I had to know. "So did Jack die, you know, naturally? Of a heart attack, I mean. Or was the death suspicious?"

"Miss G." Tom pulled shots of espresso for each of us, brought them over to the table, and sat down. "Why are you doing this to yourself? You know that since Jack was attacked, and died shortly thereafter, his death is suspicious by definition. I've already called down to Southwest Hospital to have the body sent up to our pathologist. We have to determine cause and manner." He reached out for my free hand. "You know this."

Yeah, okay, I knew it, but the knowledge just increased my misery. The mental image of Jack being cut open, his parts being dissected and weighed, made me ill.

"Drink your coffee," said Tom, as he placed an espresso in front of me.

Just to placate him, I took a tiny sip. It was hot and scalded my tongue. "Have you found out anything else?"

Tom said, "We're still working on getting the analysis back on the vial from Finn's trash. These things take time. But we found out a bit more about the break-in at his house."

"What?"

"A neighbor came forward and said she saw someone over there on Friday afternoon. Don't know why she didn't call us sooner, but people get scared."

"Any description?"

"Nope, just a man, she thought. Maybe older."

"Was it Jack?"

"We don't know who it was. If the woman had come forward sooner, we'd know more. We still don't know what he took, if anything. The neighbor says the person wasn't carrying anything when he—or she—came out of Finn's house. So that's why the analysis on the vial is so important." Tom stood up. "I have to go back. Will you promise me, pretty please, with a cherry on top, that you'll stay home until I get back? I can call Marla to come over and be with you."

"I'll call her. Just hand me the phone."

"Goldy," said Tom seriously, "do not go back into Jack's house, understand? It has been sealed."

"I won't." Almost as an afterthought, I said, "Before Billie's wedding last night, Jack said he wanted to talk to you."

"About what?"

I shrugged. "You think he was going to tell me why he wanted to talk to you? You know how he was."

"I do indeed."

"Then he wanted to talk to Boyd. Do you know if he found him?"

Tom shook his head. "I asked Boyd if he'd seen Jack, or talked to him, and he said he had not. Sorry, Miss G."

Tom kissed me and left.

I drained my coffee, called Marla, got her voice mail, and invited her over. I had no idea when or even if she would show up. Then, very carefully, I pulled out the nonfunctioning travel clock.

I was still convinced, or I wanted to be convinced, that Jack had left this for me, as a puzzle. And if he had, then by God, I was determined to figure out what it contained.

There were initials, very faintly visible, I noticed belatedly, embossed in gold on the leather case: hwf. I blinked, and then it came to me. This old travel clock had belonged to Harold William Finn. Had Jack taken this out of Finn's house? But why? And had the brand-new golf clubs been Finn's, too? Why would Jack have those?

One thing at a time, I told myself. I turned the neatly folding travel clock over in my hand. I had to know why Jack had had it. Jack was not sentimental, and it seemed extremely unlikely to me that Finn would have given Jack a small travel clock to remember him by.

I opened the case once more and folded it into its triangular shape. Nothing.

Hans Bogen, the master jeweler at Aspen Meadow Jewelers, had fashioned the rings for Billie and Craig Miller. He had vociferously complained to me about Billie's constant changes of mind concerning the setting of her engagement ring, the size of the diamond(s), and the color of the metal: White gold or yellow? Or should we have platinum? Could Hans order the Versace china Billie had picked out, and give them a discount? Why not? And would he take back the "hideous" desk clock somebody had given them as a wedding present, even though the clock had not been bought from him? Like me, Hans had learned that when dealing with Billie, one had to become adept at caller ID.

But after the third change of mind about the setting for Billie's engagement ring, Hans had had enough. He'd told Marla that he'd informed Billie to take her business down to Tiffany's in Cherry Creek. "Enough is enough," said Marla, imitating Hans's Swiss accent.

Luckily for me, Hans Bogen and I had become partners-in-pain. He liked me, and had even ordered his wife's birthday cake from me, which I'd given to him gratis. He'd promised I could call on him if I had any jewelry problems, of any kind. Call him whenever I wanted to, he said.

He lived nearby, and after I'd dropped off his wife's cake, he'd repeated that Tom and I should drop in anytime.

Which was exactly what I intended to do, as Hans Bogen's specialty was clocks.

Chapter 19

This time, I had the sense to put on a cardigan before venturing out. While 'we'd been having all that rain earlier in the month, I'd actually relished going outside, as the wet pines and aspens had filled the air with a delicious scent. But I was still having trouble catching my breath, and my head continued to throb, so it was hard to smell anything. Jack's death had left me without the ability to use any of my senses, apparently. But I was determined to use my head, or at least that part of it that hadn't been smacked by Lucas Carmichael.

Anyway, using my head—that was what would get me through this mess. I couldn't even call it grief. If I did, that would mean Jack was really gone.

At the end of our street, I stared at the signs and tried to remember where the Bogens' house was. Finally I turned right, figuring I would recognize the Bogens' red-painted, white-trimmed Alpine-style A-frame, even if I couldn't remember the address.

And I did. When Hanna Bogen, brown haired, of medium height, and in her midforties, opened the door, she blinked. She wore a denim skirt and a T-shirt that read, WILL TEACH FOR FOOD.

"Goldy," Hanna said, without a trace of the Swiss accent that lay so heavily over Hans's speech, "you don't look so hot. Come in."

Within moments we were in Hanna's snug kitchen, which was so clean and scrubbed I wondered if I could hire her to help do cleanup for Goldilocks' Catering. But I knew she would never jump ship to catering, as she was dedicated to—of all things— teaching English literature at Elk Park Prep. She set down two steaming mugs of cinnamon tea, a plate of ginger cookies, sliced peaches, and a wedge of Swiss cheese.

"I'm not hungry," I protested. Mentally, I added, *And the day I drink herb tea is the day they have to put it in my IV, when I'm in a coma.* "But thank you."

"Pfft. When was the last time you had anything to eat? You look as if you're going to pass out."

"All right, thanks," I said, and downed a slice of peach. I'm sure it was wonderful, and under ordinary circumstances, I would have enjoyed the sweetness. "Is Hans around? I need to talk to him about a clock. It's really, really important, and after I, uh, made your birthday cake, he said I should come over anytime if I had—"

Hanna held up her index finger. "It is a truth universally acknowledged that Hans will never be here when clients drop in with their timepieces."

Omigod, please spare me the Jane Austen quotations at this moment. "Do you know where he is? Or, uh, when he'll be back? This is really, really important."

"Hans takes Monday off. Today, he went fishing. He usually doesn't get back in until the evening. And anyway, he would need all the tools he has at the shop." When she saw my downcast face, her brown eyes filled with sympathy. She said, "Look, I can loan you a clock, Goldy."

"It's not like that," I found myself protesting. "Could I leave Hans a note?"

Hanna produced pen and paper, and I wrote Hans a message that I hoped conveyed enough bafflement and desperation that he'd get cracking on Finn's travel clock, but not call the police. My godfather, I said, had left me the clock as sort of a puzzle. *I don't know why it doesn't work, I wrote, but I'd like you to open up all the machinery, if that's what you call it, and see if there's anything else in there, something that doesn't belong. Whatever that thing is, that's what I need. I know you're busy, but I really need this to be done as soon as possible. Not knowing why my godfather left me this clock is driving me batty. Thank you, Hans.* I signed it simply *Goldy,* with my business and home lines.

I bade Hanna farewell and took off for home. I hadn't gone ten paces when my cell phone buzzed.

"Where the hell are you?" Marla fumed. "I'm outside your house and you're not answering. Billie's wedding is over, Goldy. You can come out of hiding."

"I'm out taking a walk," I said. "I'll be there in less than ten minutes."

"Ten minutes?"

I actually smiled. "Just get in your Mercedes and wait for me."

"I'm going to need a drink when you finally let me in. Father Pete and I couldn't find the diocesan letters, and everyone was calling the church, wanting to know about arrangements for Jack. I've already had a heart attack myself, you know. So this is all just as depressing as hell."

"Tell me about it."

Soon I was outside our house, and I speedily let Marla in. I asked her if she wanted a sherry. She glanced at our kitchen clock—I was thankful we actually had one—and said to make it scotch with a splash of soda.

"I don't care that it's not technically cocktail time," Marla said. "I need the good stuff, calories be damned. Speaking of which, do you have any food left over from the wedding? I know we had eggs this morning, but I'm hungry again. And I didn't get very much of that fabulous-looking food during the reception, I'm sorry to say." She grinned widely. "But I'm hungry for it now."

"Julian packed up, sorry. I have some Brie and crackers. Will that do?"

Marla lifted an eyebrow. "Works for me. God, that spa was awful, with Victor hovering around, as if he was spying on you, on the wedding, on something. Victor gives me the creeps. He employs Lucas Carmichael there, did you know? The vaunted PA does in-take evaluations."

"Lucas?" My mind immediately leaped to the pos-sibility that Lucas and Victor, neither of whom was on my Favorite Persons list, were in cahoots. But in cahoots about what, exactly?

Marla was squinting at me. "Goldy, what in the world are you thinking? You look awful. Look, I know I said I'm sorry about Jack, but maybe I shouldn't—" Marla paused, then reached over and squeezed my hand. "Maybe I should go home. I'm sorry I brought up all this stuff."

"It's okay, you can talk about the spa or Victor." My throat closed momentarily. "You can talk about Jack." I felt Marla's friendship embrace me. Oddly, this meant that tears were able to run freely down my face.

Marla disappeared, then reappeared with a box of tissues. "C'mon, let it out."

So I did. But something Marla had said stuck in my head, and when I stopped crying I stared at her steadily.

"Dammit, what's wrong now?" She sipped her drink, set the glass on the table, and glared back at me. "You want some other brand of tissues?"

"No, I want you to go out to Gold Gulch Spa."

"Why?" She waited for me to say something, but my throat had closed again. "You want me to help you get Jack's car? I mean, it's still out there, isn't it?"

"No. I want you to go out there as a client. For a week."

She stuck a piece of Brie in her mouth. "Forget it," she mumbled around the cheese.

"It's not for me. It's for Jack."

Marla closed her mouth and chewed. Then she shut her eyes and rubbed them, as if she were trying to think of just the right words. Finally, she said, "Jack passed away last night, Goldy. He doesn't care whether I lose weight or not."

"Don't joke, okay? Just listen." I explained to her how Jack had written "Gold" on a piece of paper, and how Lucas had misunderstood Jack as wanting to summon me to his bedside. But, I said, it was my opinion that Jack had been referring to Gold Gulch Spa. I'd even seen him rummaging around in the Smoothie Cabin when I'd been out there. And, I added, I thought Victor Lane was having money problems. He'd asked Charlotte Attenborough to invest in Gold Gulch. So maybe Jack was looking for evidence of money problems, and Victor caught him . . . and attacked him.

"Goldy," Marla said after a few more minutes' thought, "I think you need a drink, too." When I sighed, she insisted, "Who knows what Jack meant? He'd just been attacked, he was probably on some megadose of painkiller, he could have meant anything. And anyway, Victor's been looking for a financial angel to help with that spa since he first took it over. He even asked me to invest in the place. I went out there once, as a day client? I told him he needed to serve better food if he wanted any of my bucks. Nothing against Yolanda, I think she's a great cook. But when I complained to her, she said Victor keeps a stranglehold on the regimen out there." Marla took a long pull on her drink. "Really, I think you should just—" She paused again. "Just—"

"Grieve?" I supplied. "I already tried that. I want to know what was going on with Jack, and why Doc Finn, his best friend, was killed." I reminded myself not to give away anything Tom had told me about Finn's peculiar murder. "Something is going on out at that spa," I insisted to Marla, "and I think Jack wanted me to find out what it was."

"But he didn't say anything to you about it, did he? He didn't leave you a note telling you something untoward was happening at Gold Gulch, did he? And he certainly didn't indicate what he wanted you, or better yet, Tom, to do about it. Did he?"

"No. Not really. But there's more." I told her about the crowd in the hospital: Lucas, Billie, Charlotte, and Craig. I told her about Jack's impatience to have them all gone, and how he'd written "Keys," and "Fin" on the paper, too. As if in proof, I drew the crumpled paper from my sweatpants pocket and laid it on the kitchen table.

Marla peered down at it. I suddenly saw Jack's shaky lettering through somebody else's eyes, and an arrow of doubt found its way to my heart.

"Goldy," said Marla, "he didn't even spell Finn's name right. And you think this word 'Gold' stands for Gold Gulch Spa?"

"I do," I said with more firmness than I felt. "I'm, uh, going to see if I can go out there and cook. Maybe help Yolanda in the kitchen or something. But I need you to be poking around, too. Like, for example, talk to the other, longtime guests about the Smoothie Cabin, about whether Victor is selling them something other than fruit drinks. Or try to find out more about whatever financial problems Victor might have."

"Why? Because Jack was scrounging around in the Smoothie Cabin? I'm sure that has all kinds of interesting things to do with Doc Finn's death."

"Something's going on out there in that Smoothie Cabin," I said stubbornly. "Victor Lane has cameras focused on the inside and the outside of a one-way mirror that looks into the space, and he keeps that cabin locked up tight—"

"Maybe he's worried the clients, desperate for extra food, will get in there and trash the place."

I sighed in exasperation. "Why won't you take me seriously?"

"But listen to yourself. You want *me* to go out to Gold Gulch Spa as a client, and exercise and eat a bunch of low-fat food for a week."

"Or high-protein meals," I corrected. "I don't know what kind of diet Victor has people on."

"Okay, so I go out there and eat and exercise for a week, and you'll be working in the kitchen, and in the meantime, I'm supposed to chat up the other guests and see if Victor Lane is a drug dealer. And that will help you find out why Doc Finn was killed?"

Okay, it sounded a teensy bit illogical. But I said, "Yes. Please."

Marla collapsed her head onto the table and banged it several times, for effect. She said, "You'd better fix me another drink."

Marla left soon after, to sleep, she said. "You know, Casanova's aunts used to have to nap for months before he showed up."

"Casanova?" I said. "What are you talking about? Are you planning on a tryst out at the spa?"

"I wish. No, I'm planning on withdrawing from booze and chocolate. Oh, and did I add the part about being exhausted from exercising?"

"Look at all the good being out there did for Billie."

"All the good that spa did for Billie was negligible," Marla immediately retorted. "Charlotte had to pay her dressmaker to let out that expensive wedding dress ad nauseam, well, maybe not ad nauseam, because that would have made Billie thinner. Billie lost a total of two pounds, and she still ended up postponing the wedding all those times."

"Who told you all this?" I asked absentmindedly as I walked Marla to her car. I'd thought getting outside would do me good, but when I saw Jack's empty house looming across the street, my stomach clenched.

Marla turned to me. "Goldy, are you listening? *Charlotte* told me. She figured Billie had some secret supply of fattening food out there. Plus, whenever Billie came home from Gold Gulch, within a few days she was a nervous wreck."

Hmm, I thought, and why would that be? But I said nothing because, to me, Billie always seemed to be a nervous wreck. But in the end, as I knew she would, Marla promised to call Victor Lane to see if she could book into Gold Gulch for the upcoming week.

Back in the house, I splashed cold water on my face and looked hard at myself in the mirror. If I wanted to find out what had happened to Finn and Jack, then Marla wasn't the only one who needed a spa visit. I really would have to go out to Gold Gulch. It wasn't that I didn't trust the police, and Tom especially. I did trust them. But what if Victor hid evidence, clammed up, or hired a lawyer? If Marla talked to the guests, and I talked to the staff—especially Isabelle—then I'd have a better chance of finding out the truth.

I paced around the kitchen. Victor Lane didn't like me, blast him. So how was I going to get out there?

I came back again to the idea of Yolanda. When we'd both worked at a restaurant down in Denver, we'd become good friends. She'd help me out with this, of that I was sure. I put in a call to her house and left a message on her voice mail.

Suddenly, before Yolanda had even agreed to let me help her, I had the same worry that Marla did about good food becoming scarce. Tom loved my Chilled Curried Chicken Salad. So I preheated the oven, washed my hands, and sprinkled olive oil, salt, and pepper on chicken breasts. If I was going to be going out to Gold Gulch, I reasoned, then Tom would need to have food ready for him, right?

Tom. What would he say to my plan, besides that it

was cockamamie? Figuring a good offense was the best defense, I called Tom and left a message: I was going out to Gold Gulch Spa to repay Yolanda for all the help she'd given me at the wedding. Could Tom spare Sergeant Boyd to come with me?

I speared the chicken breasts with a meat thermometer, put them in the oven, and began hunting for the other ingredients. When the phone rang, I was just finishing draining juice from the mandarin oranges and pineapple tidbits. I figured the ringing phone was Yolanda calling me back, and I picked it up quickly and delivered my singsongy business greeting.

"Goldy, are you out of your mind?" Tom spluttered.

"Oops. Guess I shouldn't have answered the phone."

"Oops? You don't need to help Yolanda. What? You want to go out and mess up another crime scene—"

"Wait a minute," I protested, as I measured out mayonnaise. "What was the first crime scene I messed up?"

"You know I'm talking about breaking into Jack's house," Tom said, with an attempt at patience. "And now we've had—"

"Hold on," I interrupted as I nabbed chutney from the walk-in. "I didn't break into Jack's house, and it isn't a crime scene—"

"Wait, now, Miss G. Within hours of Jack dying, you used a dubious legal basis to employ Jack's own keys to enter his house, without knocking or ringing, according to Lucas."

"Lucas needs to make fewer accusations, and hit fewer people on the side of the head," I replied, indignant. "Listen, Tom," I said, as I worked on my own patience, "I'm sorry if I upset you, as well as Lucas, but I was just trying to figure out why Jack—"

"Where's Marla?" Tom demanded.

"I sent her home to nap."

"Nap? Why does she need to nap?"

"She had too much to drink over here, what with the Irish coffee this morning, and scotch and soda this afternoon. Plus, she's going to try to come out to the spa this week, too. For that, she needed to rest up."

Tom said, "Jesus." Then he paused, thinking. "If Boyd can't go out there with you, you're not going."

"All right." The call-waiting beeped, and I glanced at the phone's readout, which is what I should have done before picking up to hear Tom being angry. "Yolanda's ready to talk to me. I've gotta go."

After Tom warned me again not to go into potentially dangerous situations, he signed off. Sighing, I clicked over to Yolanda.

"Are you out of your mind, Goldy?" Yolanda asked me.

"Don't start. Tom's already bawled me out."

"How long has it been since you worked in a restaurant?"

"Come on, Yolanda. Let me help. Oh, and Tom says I have to have Boyd with me if I'm going to be working out there."

"There's not enough room in that kitchen for you, me, my two assistants, and a cop," Yolanda said flatly, "even if the cop is kind of cute. There's hardly enough room as it is. Plus, Victor's such a jerk, he'd never let you work in there for no good reason."

"You can tell him I'm repaying you for helping with the wedding."

"He'll never buy it."

I pondered the salad dressing I was making, as well as the situation with Yolanda. She was right about the Victor piece of this.

"How about this," I proposed. "You call Victor and tell him you have appendicitis. Or something. And it's an ailment so sudden and dreadful that you have to go into the hospital. You tell him you've asked me to take over, since we used to work together in a restaurant, and I know what I'm doing. Then I take your place for two or three days, and Boyd helps me. We manage in the small space, you come back after those days off, and I pay you your entire salary for a week."

"Why do you want to get in there so badly?" Yolanda demanded. "I hate Victor, but I really need this job. If you make trouble for him, he might fire me."

"Oh, don't worry," I said, although in the far reaches of my brain, the ones that oversaw vengeance for not hiring me, I saw making trouble for Victor as a plus. Still, though, Victor was Yolanda's boss, and I really didn't want to create problems for my old friend.

"Uh, Goldy? You didn't answer my question. What

do you think you're going to find out at the spa?"

I set the blender on High and walked into the other room. Should I explain to Yolanda about the note from Jack? Well, if I was trusting her to lie for me, then perhaps I should. So I told her about Jack dying after being attacked at the spa. "Did you see anyone skulking around outside? Did anyone come through the kitchen to use your exit?"

"I've already talked to the cops about this. We were working hard, you know that. Did you notice anyone going in or out?"

"No. I wish I had."

"And if anyone came in or out, I certainly don't know when they were around. The one thing I remember? Jack crept through, made some kind of joke, and said he was going out for a smoke. Then he slipped through the door we use for putting out our dirty aprons and towels. He, uh, you know, didn't come back in."

I took a deep breath and told Yolanda about the note Jack had written for me in the hospital.

"Huh? He wrote 'Gold' on a piece of paper," said Yolanda, incredulous, "and you think he was referring to the spa, and not you?"

"He didn't call me Goldy. He called me Gertie Girl."

Yolanda paused. "Did he write anything else on the paper?"

"Yes. He wrote 'Keys' and 'Fin,' which was the name of his best friend. Although he didn't spell

Finn's name correctly. Look, Yolanda, does Victor ever have you make up smoothies in the Smoothie Cabin?"

"No, Victor does all that. He makes up batches of them, and then has some of the staff pour them for the guests, usually. It's not as if it's a secret recipe, he tells me, but he still won't let me do it. It's less work for me, anyway."

"Do you think he would let me do it?"

"I'm sure he would *not*. He says he has to monitor the calories the clients get."

Right, I thought. "Do you think Isabelle would let me into the Smoothie Cabin?"

"I doubt it, but she might, even though Victor told her he was going to fire her if she let anybody else in there."

"Okay, I'll talk to her when I get out there."

"She can't fake appendicitis, too."

"Don't worry, Yolanda. And thanks."

"Goldy," she replied, "you should have your head examined."

"Will you call Victor and pave the way for me?"

"Yes, and you don't have to pay me all that money."

"Yes, I do. Jack was my godfather." My voice cracked, and I silently cursed it. "I loved him, and I want to find out what he was looking for in the Smoothie Cabin. I want to find out what happened to him."

"The cops have been out at the spa all day!" She

sounded exasperated. "What do you think you'll find that they missed?"

"I don't know," I said truthfully. "But I know I'm not going to rest until I at least make an effort on behalf of Jack."

Yolanda exhaled again. "That's why you don't have to pay me." She paused. "I didn't need my appendix anyway."

Chapter 20

I woke in a sweat before the alarm went off. Our room wasn't hot, and I was not menopausal (yet). Hmm. I glanced at our clock: not quite five. I slid out of bed and tiptoed over to flip the switch, to keep the clock from awakening Tom. Perhaps worry about the upcoming day had jolted me out of sleep. Those worries included: Would Victor Lane, who long ago had insisted to me that women in general and I in particular couldn't cook, be nice to me? (Fat chance.) Would the spa clients like the food I prepared? (Not if they were anything like Billie.) Would I feel any better if I found out anything on the subject of why Jack had been attacked? (Too early to tell.)

Then again, maybe anxieties about the upcoming day had not awakened me. Our bedroom was filled with unusually bright light. I pulled back the curtain and couldn't believe that after all our weeks of rain, sunshine streaking through the pines and aspens now dappled our street.

I veered away from looking at Jack's house and instead spread out my yoga mat. I lay down and tried to summon an attitude of optimism to match the weather. But that would entail forgetting that my dear godfather was dead. It would also mean consigning to the River of Forgetfulness the colossal argument I'd had with Tom the night before.

As I stretched and breathed and tried unsuccessfully to clear my mind, I recalled how the first thing that had happened after dinner was that Yolanda had called me back. She'd phoned Victor with the bad news of her sudden attack of appendicitis and having to be down at Southwest Hospital. Instead of being compassionate, Victor had started yelling, no surprise. Yolanda had grunted and groaned her way through a fake pain attack and managed to say she'd hired a replacement, who was yours truly. Victor had been pissed, she said, laughing, but he'd agreed to let her off until Thursday dinner, when she'd "better be back, or be fired."

"Oh, for crying out loud," I said. "Who's he going to get if he lets you go?"

"Hey, Goldy, good question! But I groaned big, and he told me to stop. So I managed to thank him. I also told him I'd call my assistants so they could be there to help you with breakfast. You don't have to show up until quarter to six. Can you manage that?"

"Absolutely," I promised. "Do you think he suspects you were faking?"

"That's the only thing that worries me. I keep telling him he needs to see a shrink, get on some anti-paranoia medicine."

"Jeez." I remembered Victor blowing his top about Jack's search of the Smoothie Cabin, and how he'd questioned me as to what my godfather had been up to. Had I put on a good enough act? I wondered.

"Totally. But listen," she warned, "in addition to Boyd, you might need Julian to help you with dinner. It's not the extra cooking that makes the last meal of the day difficult. It's the serving. The clients just get really, really hungry by the end of the day."

"If Julian can't help, then I'll find someone else."

Yolanda had promised to e-mail me the menu for Tuesday so I would know what to expect. She also told me the recipes were stored in the spa's kitchen computer, and gave me the password: weight. She made me swear to call her if I needed her back. And she still didn't want me to pay her. I told her I'd had lots of catering assignments this summer, was up to my chef's hat in money, and had a free week, to boot. She laughed and said she was capable of making a rapid recovery. I thanked her again and signed off.

Then I called Julian, who said, "Oh no, I don't think I can do low-fat food." When I told him the emphasis was on health, not weight loss, he said, "Okay, I'm down for it." Which was Julian-speak for yes, he would help.

Tom, unfortunately, had been even angrier than Victor Lane when he heard I'd had Yolanda lie so I could do a fill-in job at Gold Gulch. I'd broken the news to him when we were chopping the last ingredients for the Chilled Curried Chicken Salad. Tom had stopped slicing, put down his knife, and shaken his head.

"I told you on the phone, Goldy, you're not going out there again unless Boyd goes with you."

"And I said that was fine! He just has to be there at a quarter to six."

Tom called Boyd with the specifics, and nodded curtly when he got off the phone. So Boyd must have been down for it, too.

I handed Tom a spoon with a dollop of the curry dressing. "It'll be better when it's chilled."

He tasted and nodded. "Know what, Miss G.? You'd be better if you chilled."

"Very funny."

"Not meaning to be. Look, investigating the Finn case is proving more difficult than we'd anticipated, because of all the mud and trash down in that ravine next to the highway. If I have to worry about you and what you're up to every minute, then my own work becomes more challenging than my cardiologist wants."

"What cardiologist?" I asked. I spooned the pineapple, mandarin oranges, raisins, shreds of roast chicken, and chopped red onion into a crystal bowl and tossed them together. Then I ladled on creamy dollops of the curry-and-chutney-laced dressing, and stirred again. "When did you start going to a cardiologist? And does this mean I should have used low-fat mayonnaise?"

Tom began washing the cutting boards. "Now

who's being the funny one? Anyway, all that is beside the point."

"Look, Tom, I'm insisting on going out to the spa because Jack wanted me to. I feel it in my bones."

"So much for empirical analysis," Tom said dryly. "Tell me: do you feel it in your bones that Jack wanted you to get hurt? Hurt the way he was, I mean?"

I gave him a look full of vinegar. "He wrote 'Gold' on a piece of paper—"

"Ah, the infamous meaningless note."

"And remember, Boyd will be with me—"

"Yeah, I had to take him off a security detail for the governor, so if the gov gets whacked in the next three days, it's on you."

I ignored this, because I knew Boyd wouldn't have been taken off an important security detail unless they'd found someone to replace him. "So," I went on, "Boyd will be helping me. The bistro where Julian works is closed for the month of August, and he's going to come over and lend a hand, too. And there will only be sixty-one guests at the spa. Piece of cake."

Tom rolled his eyes at the ceiling instead of making a joke about the cake.

"Tom! I will be fine."

He bristled. "Fine? Fine?"

"I'll take my cell phone."

"Service out there is spotty. That's what we discovered when we were looking into the attack on Jack." His shoulders slumped. "All right, if you're determined to do this, Boyd sticks to you like epoxy, and you go through the spa switchboard if you need me."

I agreed. I called Arch. Gus had already invited him to stay at his house for "their last free week before school starts." So much for Gus's grandparents' school-supply shopping plans.

"It's not like you're going to prison next week," I said to Arch.

Arch said, "Mom, you haven't been in an American high school lately."

I didn't want to argue, so I told him I'd be back Thursday. Still, I sensed Tom was worried about this little expedition, Yolanda was anxious that her fake illness would be found out, Marla was bitching about going to numerous exercise classes every day, and Julian was okay with healthful recipes, but was dead set against cooking low-fat food.

Other than all that, I thought as I stretched into my last asana, everything was, as we say in food service, peachy.

I took a quick shower and crept down to the kitchen, where I filled an insulated mug with ice, splashed in a goodly dose of whipping cream, and pulled four shots of espresso for a volcanic Summertime Special. I took a long swig, then shuddered when I thought of the menus Yolanda had e-mailed me for that day. For dessert, the clients were getting canned fruit with low-cal whipped topping. That didn't sound too healthful to me.

When I'd loaded the cooking equipment I couldn't live without into the van, my eye snagged on the facade of Jack's Victorian. The unfinished front porch, with its higgledy-piggledy assortment of flowerpots, made the place look even more forlorn. I looked away, down at the Grizzly Saloon, where an early-morning worker was sweeping the porch. By half past ten, the place would be filled with patrons—usually men, sad to say—who couldn't get through the day without booze, and plenty of it.

I gunned the engine: time to get out to Gold Gulch Spa. Even if Tom thought I was nuts, I knew what I wanted to do: find out why someone had killed Doc Finn. He'd been investigating something. Then Jack had searched the Smoothie Cabin. Maybe Doc Finn and/or Jack had found what they were looking for, and were threatening to go public with it.

If either one or both of them had gathered evidence proving some kind of wrongdoing, then that would be it—finito, fin, the end—for the spa.

If the whistleblower had been Doc Finn, then the note in his trash reading "Have analyzed" could be the key. Had Doc Finn taken a sample from the spa . . . from the Smoothie Cabin . . . and put it into a vial? And had he received the news back as to what was in the vial? Had he confronted Victor, and if so, had the old doctor been lethally punished for his efforts?

And how did Billie Attenborough, now Billie Miller, play into this, if at all? She and Doc Finn, whom she had already professed to hate, had been having a large, loud argument out at Gold Gulch Spa right before he was killed. Billie had said Doc Finn had told her she shouldn't try to lose weight so quickly. I still didn't believe this. I couldn't remember when Craig Miller had said he and Billie would be leaving

for the Greek Isles for their honeymoon . . . I just recalled how much I wanted them to be on it, instead of
hanging around Aspen Meadow.

I also wanted to know what the hell Charlotte was
up to. To my mind, she hadn't really explained what
her shoes were doing in Doc Finn's Porsche.

Was my theory about Victor possibly having it in
for Doc Finn and/or Jack likely or unlikely? What
was Lucas up to, if anything? Where did Charlotte,
Billie, and her new husband fit in, if at all?

I pressed my lips together and wound up Upper Cottonwood Creek Road on the way to Gold Gulch Spa.
No question, it would pay to be extremely vigilant.

My cell phone rang, startling me out of my reverie.

"Okay, boss," came Julian's crackling voice, "I'm
on the interstate and Sergeant Boyd is right behind
me. He said to call you and tell you not to drive into
the spa until we catch up. Tom's orders."

"Well," I said with a nervous laugh, "make it
snappy." I glanced at the car clock: half past five.

"I would," replied Julian, "but remember, Boyd's a
cop, and he's driving like a cop. Right behind me.
Slowly."

"Is he in a police car?"

"No, but I have a feeling that if I go twenty miles
per hour over the speed limit, he'll get out the hand-
cuffs."

Twenty minutes later, the five of us—Boyd, Julian,
Yolanda's two female assistants, and yours truly—
were madly scrambling eggs, toasting whole wheat

bread, and swirling soft tofu with spring water, to mix into oatmeal. The two breakfast servers were filling the skim milk and decaf coffee machines.

"I thought you said this was a high-class place," Boyd commented as he peered into the walk-in refrigerator. "I'm not seeing any expensive low-fat breakfast meat in here. In fact, I'm not seeing any kind of breakfast meat in here."

"Better for your arteries, Mr. Policeman," Julian commented.

"Yeah?" said Boyd. "Kiss my ass, Mr. Vegetarian."

"Boys, boys," I scolded gently, "this is no place for a food fight, even a verbal one."

But the two of them were already racing around the kitchen's big island like a couple of kids. Julian snapped a dish towel at Boyd. Boyd snatched a wet pot scrubber and hurled it at Julian. The two kitchen assistants began giggling as the fight escalated to Boyd and Julian swinging kitchen implements at each other. The assistants' laughter reached hyena levels. While the two guys banged around and yelled taunts, I prayed that Victor Lane was far away. I also began to wonder where the seven thousand dollars a week that each client paid to visit Gold Gulch went. The kitchen did not hold a single piece of fresh fruit, and only the most desultory collection of fresh vegetables. Frozen chickens, thawing for tonight's broiling and tomorrow's lunch, had been bought in bulk, as had the pork tenderloins that I was fixing for the next night's dinner. Why would Yolanda put up with preparing such foods, instead of insisting on high-quality, fresh ingredients? She must really need this paycheck. I frowned.

Of course, there was no way I was going to tell Victor Lane how to run his spa. Still, when I'd started out in catering, it had taken me awhile to figure out how to calculate what exactly I had to charge to make a profit in food service, and Victor, I was sure, had done the same thing. The basic rule of thumb was that you took your raw ingredients and tripled them. As far as I could figure, Victor Lane was paying less than two bucks a day per person for his raw materials. So if the clients were paying a thousand dollars a day for food, shelter, and exercise, I wondered how much the shelter, cleaning, and exercise classes cost.

Charlotte had told me Gold Gulch was almost always full, with a waiting list, even year-round. Victor must be making a killing. But if that was true, then why was he trying to convince Marla, Lucas, and Charlotte to invest in Gold Gulch?

While I was wondering about all this, Boyd and Julian picked up sauté pans and clanked them together like swords. I tried to filter out the racket while looking more closely at the menus Yolanda had posted in the kitchen: Scrambled Eggs and Canned Fruit Cocktail for this morning; Baked Tuna with Tomato Salad for lunch; Broiled Chicken, Cauliflower, and Broccoli for tonight, with packaged Angel Food Cake for dessert. If you were allergic to anything, you got yogurt. Whoopee!

Tomorrow the clients were getting more Scrambled

Eggs with Toast, or Oatmeal with Tofu and Sugarless
Applesauce for breakfast; Chicken Salad with fat-free
mayo for lunch—I gagged—and Roast Pork Tenderloin with more Sugarless Applesauce plus Steamed
Green Beans for dinner, with yet more Angel Food
Cake. Another day of Awful, or offal, depending on
how you looked at it.

Even when I'd gone to boarding school as a schol-
arship student, and we'd all complained about the
food, nothing had been as bad as this.

An enormous crash, squealing, and hollering on
the other side of the kitchen stopped me wondering
about anything. Julian, Boyd, and the sauté pans they
were wielding had collided with the plastic vat of
fruit cocktail, which in turn had spilled all over the
floor.

"Oh, hell, boss, I'm sorry," Julian apologized. "I'll
clean it up."

"No, no, I'll do that," Boyd said. But then he said,
"Wait. Don't move. Don't do anything." He looked a
tad ridiculous, I had to say, holding his pan aloft and
peering down at the floor, as if he'd seen a giant insect
and was about to whack it.

When Victor Lane bellowed, "Everybody out!" I
jumped. I hadn't heard or seen him come in. Nor had
the two combatants. Julian had murmured something
about looking for a mop, and Boyd was still staring in
confusion at the mess on the floor.

"Victor, I'm so sorry," I babbled. "These two, my,
my, er, staff people, that is, were just trying to help
me. I'll clean up the spilled fruit, I promise."

"Oh, no you won't," Victor Lane retorted. His skeletal face loomed too close to mine, and I reared back defensively. "I should have known Yolanda would screw up my place," he continued angrily. "Appendicitis, my ass. She's probably visiting relatives. And anyway, she should have let me choose a replacement. There are plenty of cooks out there who could use a job."

"Sir," said Boyd, "please—"

"Shut up!" screamed Victor, his back to us. "Get out of my kitchen!" He was at the sink, filling a bucket with water. He ignored Boyd and picked up the full bucket.

Then, to my astonishment, Victor doused the section of the floor covered with fruit cocktail with water. The water, syrup, and about half the fruit were whisked down a floor drain. Victor was cleaning up something? Why? I'd never seen him do anything other than give orders . . . or criticize.

"Sir!" said Boyd.

"Be quiet and get out!" cried Victor.

Chapter 21

T hat guy is a nut," said Boyd, his voice low.

"Naw," said Julian, "more of a legume. A peanut."

"Guys, you're driving me bonkers," I said.

We were sitting outside in my van, the only place we felt safe enough to talk, until we were sure Victor was out of the spa kitchen.

"Maybe he's a soybean," said Julian. "Full of protein but bitter."

"Don't the two of you start up again," I warned. They were sitting side by side in the backseat, wearing guilty-little-boy expressions. "I don't want us to get thrown out of here. Listen, Sergeant Boyd, what did you see in the fruit cocktail?"

He shook his head. "That wasn't just fruit cocktail. There was something in it. Something that didn't dissolve."

"What?" I asked, thinking of the Smoothie Cabin.

"I don't know," Boyd said carefully. "But you noticed the clients were only supposed to get small cups of it? One little cup each, no seconds?"

"Yes," I said thoughtfully. "Okay, look," I began. Then I told them about Jack searching the Smoothie Cabin, and my conviction that something suspicious was going on behind that particular locked door. "I need to get into that Smoothie Cabin," I concluded.

"We'll go together," said Boyd, his voice protective.

"Girls and boys?" said Julian. "How 'bout I take samples of all the food, to get tested?"

"You're on," I said. "I'm just wondering if I should warn—"

But I didn't get a chance to finish the thought, because the person I wanted to warn was Marla, now on a path leading from one of the dormitories. She wore a giant pink muumuu, pink sunglasses, and pink flip-flops. She raised one dramatic hand to her forehead, Tallulah Bankhead style, and waved with the other. When she came a bit closer and saw that Julian and Boyd were with me, her waving became genuinely enthusiastic.

"Three of my favorite people, all in one place!" she cried. "It's okay for me to be in the van, right? I mean, Victor warned us last night not to fraternize with the help."

"What?" I squealed.

"My sentiments exactly," said Marla. "We met all the exercise instructors last night, and not one of them is attractive, trust me."

"You mean, none of them is an attractive *guy*," Julian teased.

"Well," said Marla, fluffing out her hair and peering into the backseat, "none of them is as attractive as, say, Sergeant Boyd here."

I checked the rearview mirror, and tough-as-steel Sergeant Boyd was indeed blushing.

"I'm going to have to get back to the sheriff's department," Boyd said. "Working at this place is proving beyond my capacities."

"I doubt that," said Marla, keeping the flirtatious lilt in her voice. "And I certainly hope the three of you have been fixing a marvelous breakfast here. Last night we had an intake assessment and a demonstration of the athletic equipment, which we were all required to be involved in, Victor said, for insurance purposes. What the hell does that mean? If you die after the first night, it's not his fault? Well, anyway, I about dropped dead, but I didn't, 'cuz I only walked for ten minutes on that blasted treadmill. So now I'm famished, and if whatever you're giving us today is as pathetic as the fish and fruit they gave us last night, I'm going to quit now."

"Fish and fruit?" Boyd asked sharply. "What kind of fruit?"

Marla paused, then looked over the seat again. "Canned peaches! It's the middle of summer, and we're in a state that grows peaches, for God's sake! So why were we having canned peaches, will somebody please tell me?"

"What did Victor say?" I asked.

"Victor didn't say *nada*," Marla replied. "Yolanda was the one in charge last night, and she said Victor had done all the calorie calculating, and only canned peaches worked for his careful dietary whatever. Why?" She was suddenly curious, as if I might give her a gossipy tidbit that would get her through exercise class. "I'll tell you something else, though. The women say the smoothies are wonderful, and make them feel dreamy."

"Dreamy?" I asked. "How can a smoothie make you feel dreamy?"

"I don't know," Marla replied. "But we're all only allowed one a day, so maybe they limit dreaminess the way they limit calories."

A rustling emerged from the backseat. Then Boyd reached forward with two zipped plastic bags. "Could you save me some of your fruit cocktail this morning? And some of your smoothie this afternoon? Please?"

"Why?" asked the increasingly inquisitive Marla. "What do you think is in them?"

"I don't know," said Boyd flatly. "That's why I need you to gather some up for me. Preferably when no one is looking, if you can manage it."

"But you must suspect—," Marla had begun, when the bell rang for breakfast.

"Look, Marla," I said, "we do suspect Victor might be putting something in the food. We don't know what."

Another bell rang. "Oops, gotta run. Victor said we had one minute after the second bell rang to make it into the chow line, and then the line was closed. That's what he called it, too, a chow line, like we're a bunch of dogs who need to—oh, man, I have to run, I'm starving." She stuffed the plastic bags into a copious pocket of her muumuu, and opened the door. Then she pointed into the backseat with a pink-painted nail. "I'm doing you a favor, Sergeant Boyd, and I'm going to expect a favor in return!"

"Christ," said Boyd when Marla shut the door. "I wonder if Schulz will take me back now."

"Victor just left," said Julian. "We'd better hustle in there if we're going to help with breakfast." And off we went.

Inside, I dished out the scrambled eggs, using the little scoops marked EGG MEASUREMENT. Julian and Boyd spooned oatmeal into small bowls for the clients who wanted that instead of eggs. Yolanda's assistants sprayed butter substitute onto whole wheat toast and put little dabs of sugar-free jam on top. The very few male clients—four, to be exact—were stoic, but the women kept commenting that they were ravenous. It made me wish I'd brought some brownies for them.

"Well, well, what are you doing here?" asked Billie Attenborough Miller, the last woman in line.

I was so taken aback to hear her voice that I dropped the serving spoon. Julian came rushing over with another.

"Omigod," said Billie. "This kid's here, too? Where's Yolanda?"

"Sick!" I managed to squeak. Meanwhile, my brain was madly fluttering with questions. Dr. Craig Miller was nowhere in sight. Was he still in bed? Had they even consummated the marriage?

"Ah, the bride," said Boyd, more smoothly than I could have managed.

"You!" said Billie. "The cop! Why are you here?"

Boyd said solicitously, "I'm here helping Goldy, since Yolanda has appendicitis."

"Your tax dollars at work!" Billie sang. "Is someone going to use a new spoon to give me some eggs, or am I going to be standing here all day?"

Julian obligingly lifted a new, clean spoon and gave Billie a heaping spoonful of eggs. She eyed it warily. If she complained he'd given her too much, he could take some off her plate. If she complained he'd given her too little, he might say that was all she got, if she expected to lose weight.

"And why haven't you left for your honeymoon?" Boyd persisted.

"My husband wanted to stay here a few days before we leave for our honeymoon," Billie replied huffily. "Not that it's any of your business." With this, she picked up her plate and strode off.

In the kitchen, the presence of the other workers made conversation among Julian, Boyd, and me impossible. But when the two worker bees announced it was time for them to help the two servers clear the tables, Boyd and I lifted our eyebrows at each other.

I said, "Billie drove me crazy for months, then after changing the date twice, she finally got married, and they're staying here, eating this food? Is she trying to lose more weight to fit into her bathing suit? I remember now that Craig Miller told me he had to change their tickets for getting to Greece, but why not stay in a hotel?"

Boyd rubbed his forehead. "I don't know. It's a good thing I'm helping you, though. I don't like that woman. Whenever we get somebody who's real belligerent, we think he or she might have had something to do with the crime. And I'll tell you what, *she* was like a pit bull when we questioned her after Jack Carmichael was attacked."

"Tell me about it. And where is Craig Miller? Sleeping in?" I didn't really want to see either of the Millers, but I did have someone I wanted to talk to. I had the idea of checking the calendar of classes right outside the dining room. When I came back, I asked Boyd, "Any chance you and Julian could finish washing the dishes, and then set up for lunch? I need to go find someone named Isabelle. She works here, and is the only one who might have a key to the Smoothie Cabin, besides Victor," I added.

"I promised your husband I wouldn't let you out of my sight," said Boyd.

"Then look out the front kitchen windows," I said. "I'm going to pause out there, where Jack was attacked. Then I'll be walking along a highly visible path to the gym, which is a highly visible structure, where Isabelle is."

"Boss," said Julian, "we should really start fixing lunch as soon as we get breakfast cleanup done. Any chance you know what Yolanda wants us to make?"

I showed him the kitchen computer, then booted it

up, entered the password, and brought up the screen
with MONDAY LUNCH.

"Thanks, guys," I said. I removed my apron, and
walked quietly outside, while behind me, Julian
shrieked, "That's it? That's disgusting!"

The area where Jack had been hit was surrounded
by tattered yellow police ribbons. Since I'd already
picked up my godfather's Rolex and been bawled out
for it by Tom, I knew better than to go into the
cordoned-off section of lawn and garden, even though
the absence of police probably meant they'd finished
investigating this place. But . . . had they found anything out? I wondered if Tom would tell me. I took off
for the gym.

Isabelle was more energetic than I expected. She
was not attractive. Her freckled complexion was
blotchy, her red hair was pulled back in a low pony-
tail, and her too-thin ankles and wrists all canceled
out any femininity quotient. But she knew how to
move to a beat, and maybe her lack of prettiness gave
the guests confidence, in a perverse way. I was amazed
when she convinced even the most recalcitrant of the
bunch—always in the back row, just like elementary
school—to step up and wiggle their behinds. Billie
Miller was right in front of the room's big mirror, so I
ducked behind an exercise bike to avoid being seen by
her.

"What are you doing here?" Victor bellowed from
in back of me. I was so startled I crashed over into the
exercise bike, toppling it noisily to the floor. I tried to
right it, but was too weak. Victor did it one-handed,

all the while giving me a scalding look. I had to wonder: did this guy have an invisibility cloak that prevented me from seeing when he was sneaking up on me?

"I, I need to talk to Isabelle?" I proffered, scuttling around to put the newly upright exercise bike between the spa owner and myself. If Boyd was bothered by Billie's bellicosity, I was giving the Hostility Prize to Victor.

"If you have so much time on your hands, away from the kitchen, that you need to sneak around my spa—"

"I'm not sneaking around!" I protested. "I was waiting for Isabelle. She was practically the last person to see my godfather alive—"

Victor smirked. "Then get into her class, Goldy! Look, there's an empty spot right there in the front row—"

"The hell you say," I retorted.

Victor pointed. "You want to talk to Isabelle? Go exercise with her."

Omigod, why was this spa so popular? It just had to be one of those cases where the owner was nice to the clients, but hell on the help. Still, I was in no position to argue, because truth to tell, I *had* been sneaking around. Problem was, wherever it was I was intent on sneaking, Victor always seemed to be a step ahead of me.

Isabelle gave me a very sympathetic look. The class wasn't half bad, moving as it did from the cha-cha to a kind of rock-and-roll step that I managed to keep up

with. Of course, I looked ridiculous in my black catering pants and white shirt, which stood out painfully against all the brilliant hues spandex had to
offer. But for the most part, the clients really were
overweight, so it wasn't as if we were at the Aspen
Meadow Athletic Club, with its high-voltage classes
and even higher-voltage clientele.

"You wanted to see me?" Isabelle asked quietly,
once we'd gone through a stretch routine that was so
relaxing I almost fell asleep. "I don't have a class for
another hour."

"Yes, please." I paused to take a drink of water
from the conical cup Isabelle offered. "Thanks." I
tried to think of how to pose the questions I knew I
needed to ask. "My godfather, Jack Carmichael—"

"I heard he died. I'm sorry. He was a nice man.
And funny, you know? Not funny peculiar, but funny
ha-ha."

"Right. I saw you two in the Smoothie Cabin, and
then dancing together at the reception."

Isabelle blushed. "I don't know why he wanted me
in the Smoothie Cabin. I mean, he said it was for
'cover,' whatever that meant. He was searching for
something."

"What, do you know?"

She shook her head. "He said the less I knew, the
better. That's what I told the cops when they talked to
me."

"Please, Isabelle," I begged. "He must have given
you some idea of what he was up to."

Isabelle cast a furtive glance around. We were

alone. "He did ask me—" She stopped. "I don't want to lose my job. I mean, it's a crap minimum-wage job, but I need it."

"If he didn't ask you to do anything illegal, then you're fine. You saw how well Victor Lane and I get along, which is to say that we don't. So I'm not going to be talking to him about what you tell me." Meanwhile, I was thinking, *A crap minimum-wage job?* If Victor didn't buy high-quality foodstuffs, and he didn't pay his people anything, what was he doing with all the money he made from the spa? Maybe those insurance costs he'd mentioned at the meeting Marla went to were particularly onerous.

"Jack wanted to know about Doc Finn," Isabelle whispered. "Jack knew Doc Finn had been out here last week. Jack wanted to know every single thing Finn had done while he was at Gold Gulch. How much time Finn had spent, with whom, and what had happened. I did tell the cops all this," she concluded.

I thought of Jack's scribbled notes: "Fin." I said, "I heard that when Finn was here, he had a big fight with Billie Attenborough."

"He did." Isabelle's voice was barely audible.

"She told me Finn was mad at her for losing weight so fast."

Isabelle waited a moment and then shook her head. "Their argument," she whispered, "had nothing to do with weight."

"What did it have to do with?"

"Her wedding."

"Losing weight for her wedding?"

Isabelle shook her head. "I don't know, because at that point, they went into her room. That's what I told Jack, and that's what I told the cops. Jack asked me if Billie, in one of her many visits to the spa, had been seeing anyone else. Like a guy," she added, embarrassed. "I told him Billie had been here once when Lucas, Jack's son, was here. Jack shook his head, but I wasn't sure if he was disappointed in Lucas or in Billie."

"Did Lucas enjoy being here?"

"Hard to tell. He consults for Victor, but I don't think Victor pays him much. Lucas complained that the spa was too expensive. But he's back this week, so he must have found some money around somewhere."

No kidding. I said, "So go on about Jack."

"Well," Isabelle said, "there just isn't anything. Still, I figured Doc Finn must not have won the argument with Billie, because Billie and Craig Miller are here, enjoying one of the three suites. And talk about weird, Billie's mother is here, too. They sat together at the intake meeting last night. Around the staff room? Our theory is that Billie's mother wants to know if the wedding's been consummated."

I said, "I sort of wondered that same thing when Billie showed up in the dining room this morning, without her new husband."

"They brought food when they checked in," said Isabelle. "Two coolers' worth."

"Based on the menus I saw, I don't blame them." But I was puzzled. "What difference would it make if the wedding is consummated?"

Isabelle grinned for the first time since we'd begun talking. "The staff is taking bets on it. Our theory is that if Billie and Craig have consummated their union, then Craig can't give Billie back to Charlotte and say, 'No thanks.'"

"A wife is not something you can return to the store if you don't like her," I said.

Isabelle's lips quirked into a mischievous smile. "There's a first for everything."

"How about a second for everything?"

"What?" she asked, suddenly suspicious.

"I need you to get me into that Smoothie Cabin."

Isabelle said, "Victor will fire me."

"Do you know how to disable the security cameras?"

Isabelle looked at me as if I'd asked her to fix the transmission in a Korean sports car. "Uh, no way."

"Do you have any spray paint?" I asked. "We can do it the old-fashioned way."

Chapter 22

Julian and Boyd kept watch. I set up a ladder near the outside camera, the one that pointed into the Smoothie Cabin. Isabelle handed me a can of gold spray paint that they kept for when the clients made Christmas crafts. Then she buttoned a catering jacket onto my head, as a makeshift mask. When I said I could see through the front gap, I stepped up the ladder, pointed to the camera lens, and sprayed. Once Isabelle had let me into the Smoothie Cabin, I repeated the process. Then Isabelle joined Julian and Boyd in monitoring the door. Isabelle told me I probably had no more than five minutes, as Victor kept a close eye on the feed from the cameras in his office, near the reception area.

"You need to be methodical," Boyd had told me beforehand. "I wanted to go in with you, but I can't. I don't have a search warrant, so *you're* going to have to take samples of everything you find. If *I* take anything out of there, Schulz will have my badge."

The room was really like a large closet, about eight feet by eight feet. There was a small, humming refrigerator filled with yogurt, ice, strawberries, blueberries, and three tall bottles of what looked and smelled like jam, except they were labeled smoothie mix. I extracted the plastic bags Boyd had given me and quickly spooned in samples of mango, strawberry, and pineapple. Across the two counters, bunches of bananas were carefully arrayed between three blenders. A sink, a bottle of dishwashing liquid, and a drain looked innocuous enough. The first cupboard I checked held plastic glasses and spoons. The second contained about two dozen plastic canisters with healthful-sounding labels like protein powder, ginseng, echinacea, vitamin powder, chamomile, and the like. Each canister contained powders of various colors.

"Take samples of everything you find." Boyd's words echoed in my ears.

I was about halfway through when Julian knocked quickly on the door. "Boss!" he whispered urgently through the door. "He's coming!"

"Have Isabelle waylay him," I whispered back.

"Give me the samples," Boyd ordered me through the door. "I'll make my way to the van out the back door of the kitchen. Meet me there."

I did as directed. I stuffed the bags into a large grocery bag I'd brought expressly for this purpose and handed them to Boyd. Then I walked quickly through the cabin door, raced across the kitchen, and hauled myself out the kitchen's back door. There, I scooted around a half-full cart of dirty table linens and towels, and ran to where we had parked the van. Thank God Boyd had insisted we put the vehicle behind the spa's garage, where it could not be seen.

Boyd was already there. He'd placed the grocery bag in the back. He told me to walk calmly around the corner and start toward the dining room. He'd be right behind me.

In front of the Smoothie Cabin door, Isabelle was explaining to Victor that she had no idea who could have picked the lock to the Smoothie Cabin and vandalized the cameras.

When Victor saw me, he held up his hand for Isabelle to stop talking. He narrowed his eyes at me and said, "I don't suppose you know anything about this."

I said, "Anything about what?"

"If I find spray paint in that kitchen, you're done here."

I said, "Spray paint? For what?"

"Isabelle," Victor said loudly, "give me back that key I gave you to the Smoothie Cabin." When she sheepishly handed it over, Victor said she was done helping him with smoothies. Now, he concluded, he was on his way to the hardware store to get a padlock for the Smoothie Cabin door.

Somehow, we got through the rest of the day. I didn't discover anything else, and none of the food seemed to have anything odd about it. When Victor returned from the hardware store, he went straight to the Smoothie Cabin. I prayed that the clean-up job I'd done would convince Victor not to destroy any evidence, if indeed there was evidence to be had there. I hadn't found any vials, which wasn't encouraging. What *was* encouraging was that Victor hadn't fired Isabelle on the spot, or thrown me out of the spa altogether. *He must be desperate for cooks and aerobics instructors,* I thought.

I saw Lucas only briefly at lunch, and Charlotte, Billie, and Craig Miller for a moment at dinner. I didn't have a chance to speak to any of them, which was probably just as well. Boyd, meanwhile, hovered over me, which made me feel crowded. But I'd agreed to his being there, so I was compliant. Plus, I simply could not wait for him to get those samples analyzed.

The one time I saw Marla, Boyd instructed Julian to watch over me. Then Boyd sauntered off to go talk to Marla. Marla rummaged in her gym carrier and, as unobtrusively as possible—not easy if you were Marla—gave Boyd the plastic bags he'd given her that morning.

I was so tired by the time we finished cooking dinner that I wanted to go have a soak in the hot springs pool before heading home. I knew if I did, Victor would fire me for sure. I *was* still worried about those broken plates, though, and thought we should check on the status of the cleanup.

The spa servers were washing the dishes—their job, they insisted—while the clients were settling in for an evening of karaoke, which I'd always thought was a singularly foolish activity. But nobody was asking me.

"Let's go up and see if the hot pool has been re-opened," I suggested to Boyd. It was half past seven, and the twilight air smelled delicious. Shreds of sulfurous mist from the hot springs were unraveling overhead. There was a hint of fall in the breeze. Boyd, who was still tagging along beside me, lifted an expressive eyebrow.

"I'm not propositioning you," I insisted. "Don't give me that look."

"I'm not allowing you to go into any body of water. If I did, I'd lose my job."

I laughed so hard that my fatigue abated a bit. By the time we reached the top of the path that led to the steaming pool, I'd told him in no uncertain terms I only wanted to see if the mess I'd made had been cleaned up. He was visibly relieved that there was still a NO ENTRY sign by the pool. I was disappointed, as ribbons of hot mist floated invitingly our way. But still. Presumably, the remains of a couple dozen broken cups and plates lurked on the slimy bottom. Once again, I wondered where Victor Lane was putting all his money from running the spa. Not into handymen and cleaning crews, clearly.

"Tough luck," I said, trying hard to sound sincere.

"Yeah." A man of few words, was our Boyd. We turned back down the path.

"Can you help me?" asked a large, fleshy blond woman as she toiled up the path. She stopped to gasp for breath. "I . . . I followed you from the kitchen."

Boyd, ever watchful, stepped in front of me. "Help you with what?"

"I'm starving." She put her hands on her waist, bent over, and panted. She was about sixty, and her thin blond hair had dark gray roots. "I . . . I've been here before, and . . . Yolanda always gave me"—here she blushed—"gave us, some of us, that is, extra food. After dinner, at the back door to the kitchen." She straightened and wheezed. "We paid her," she added, then reached into the copious pocket of even-more-copious pants and pulled out a wad of cash. "I can pay you."

Boyd turned to face me, so that his back was to the woman. He gave me a *what-the-hell* bug-eyed look.

"It's all right," I said soothingly to the woman. "I don't have anything right now, but I can bring you something tomorrow."

"Oh, thank God," said the woman, who made her way back down the path while we waited behind.

"Didn't she come here to lose weight?" Boyd asked, once the woman was out of earshot. "Why sabotage yourself like that?"

"It's probably like being able to get drugs in rehab. Those clinics are one of the best places to score. So if she wants a dessert, I'll bring her one."

"Kee-rist," said Boyd. "And I thought cops were the most cynical guys in the world."

At home, Tom was upstairs taking a shower. I checked our voice mail: there was nothing from Bogen the jeweler about Jack's clock, and that irritated me. Finally I went upstairs, and on impulse, joined Tom in the shower. That proved more rejuvenating than any old hot springs pool.

"I'm hungry," Tom whispered in my ear, when we were embracing, afterward, in the steamy bathroom. "You?"

I nodded assent. We put on pajamas and trekked down to the kitchen.

"How was the spa?" Tom asked. He was ladling spoonfuls of Chilled Curried Chicken Salad onto glass plates.

"Exhausting." I opened bottles of imported beer—what I'd been told was the proper drink to go with curry—and placed cold glasses on our table. I told him about Isabelle's revelations, which were more puzzling than eye opening. I then said I had gone into the Smoothie Cabin to hunt around.

Tom closed his eyes and shook his head. "Yeah, Boyd confessed to me. Did you find anything?"

"Don't get mad at Boyd, okay?" I told him about Boyd suspecting that he saw "something" in the fruit cocktail, and how I had taken samples from jars of preserved fruit and powdered supplements.

"If Boyd comes back with anything," Tom said matter-of-factly, "we won't be able to use it in court. You know that, right?"

"I know, I know," I said, although I wasn't convinced. Plus, we still had Marla's smoothie and fruit cocktail to get analyzed. It had been served to her, so she had the right to have it analyzed, correct? I said, "Lucas was up there. It looks as if he's already starting to spend Jack's money."

"He's not going to be able to spend it until the coroner's office gives him a death certificate, and there won't be any death certificate until we know more—"

He stopped talking when he saw my eyes pooling. The day had been so bone-crushingly busy, I'd somehow put the fact that Jack was dead on the back burner of my mind. But now Tom's use of the term "death certificate" gave Jack's premature departure from this life a finality I wasn't ready to face.

"Miss G." His voice was warm. He took my hands in his. "We shouldn't be talking about this. Remember, Father Pete said you should take a couple of days to grieve."

"A couple of days. Right. If I were to spend a couple of days moping around the house, I'd go stark raving bonkers. Hold on a sec." I left the kitchen, blew my nose in the bathroom, washed my hands, and returned with a box of tissues. "Please tell me more about the case. I really want to know."

"You know we've tentatively linked Finn's death with Jack's? That's partly owing to the note Jack wrote you. It's not much of a link, but it's a link."

"So . . . did the pathologist confirm that the heart attack was directly caused by Jack being attacked?"

Tom shook his head. "The connection isn't certain. But given the head trauma that Jack did experience, it's clear that someone tried to kill him out at the spa, and almost succeeded. Well, did succeed, in the end, because he just died later." Tom narrowed his eyes at me. "You all right?"

"Fine. But the person who attacked Jack couldn't have counted on Jack having a heart attack in the hospital from his injuries."

"Exactly."

It took me a second to understand what Tom was implying, and when I did, it chilled me to the bone. "The call Doc Finn received the night he was murdered came from within Southwest Hospital. Are you saying that someone in the hospital might have . . . helped Jack to have a heart attack? Might have poisoned him or . . . ?"

"It's obviously a possibility. Jack had a history of heart disease and he'd been badly injured, but the heart attack was still very sudden. Even closely monitored the way he was, we can't rule out tampering. So the pathologist is checking everything in Jack's system against the meds he was taking for his heart condition. Those meds, by the way, were in his house."

"Right," I said. "And remember, Lucas was already inside the house when I used Jack's keys to get in. So maybe he planted something, or took something away."

"We've talked to him, again. He says he didn't touch anything, and we can check his house, if we want. You don't like Lucas, do you?"

My shoulders slumped. "I'm not sure he's a killer. But he's like the cousin you never really got along with, the cousin you suspected was trashing your toys and stealing from your mother's purse, but you could never prove anything."

Tom grinned. "Your professional psychiatric opinion, no doubt."

I shrugged. "What else have you found out?"

"Nothing. These tests take a bit of time, you know,

Goldy, even when you're doing things on an expedited schedule, which we are."

I rubbed my forehead. "I can't think of what to do."

Tom knew better than to tell me to do nothing. He said, "I'll tell you how you can help. We have all the technical expertise, the teams going out talking to witnesses, the labs doing their tests. But what you're particularly good at is dissecting . . . people's relationships. It's not the *how* that's really stumping us here, although we're working on that. It's the *why*. You want to help? Bring that intellect to bear on the reasons somebody or somebodies would want these two guys . . . to be gone."

I exhaled so disconsolately that I knew Tom sensed my frustration. Finn had stuck his nose into some kind of hornets' nest and had dragged Jack into it behind him. Had it been very odd, or even criminal, activities performed by Victor Lane at the spa, or an entirely different problem? I felt no closer to an answer than I'd been when I woke up Monday morning and learned of Jack's death.

Tom looked around the kitchen with a thoughtful gaze. "You want to cook?"

I was so startled by his suggestion that I actually laughed. It was already after ten, and I had to get up at five. But Tom knew what would make me feel better—apart from shenanigans in the shower, that is.

Thirty minutes later, Tom had finished the dishes,

and I'd made the same chocolate cookies I'd made the other day. They were so flaky, the first one I made broke off in my mouth. Hmm. While Tom was putting the dishes away, I decided not to spoon ice cream into the middle. Instead, I whipped together a buttery, extra-creamy vanilla frosting, and spread it between two of the cookies. Yum! Tom agreed.

I would give—not sell—the resulting cookie sandwiches to any person who presented herself at the spa kitchen's back door the next evening.

"I can't believe you're making those for these spa guests who are trying to lose weight," Tom commented.

"Boyd was right beside me," I said defensively, "when the lady wanting the treats approached us on the path."

"Sort of like getting drugs in rehab."

"That's what I told Boyd."

Two hours later, Tom was in a deep slumber beside me, and I should have been fast asleep, too. But this was one of those times when, despite my physical exhaustion, my mind was wide awake. Too wide.

You failed Jack, my hyped-up brain accused. *He wanted you to figure something out, and you're not doing it.*

I'm trying, some other part of my brain protested.

Not hard enough.

Finally, I gave up on sleep and crept down to the kitchen. What did the accusatory voice in my head expect me to do? Since that voice was now resolutely silent, I made myself another Summertime Special. What the hell, I had to get up in five hours anyway, why not just stay up all night?

I moved restlessly around the kitchen, picking up a cup here, checking my knives there. Something was indeed niggling at the back of my mind now, but what?

It was something I'd said to Tom. When I used the keys to get into Jack's house . . .

I rummaged around in the living room until I found the ring of keys Jack had wanted me to take, as well as the crumpled paper with Jack's scribbled notes: "Gold. Fin. Keys."

What was I missing? I sipped my coffee, and turned over Jack's keys, which jingled in my hand. The key to his house was there, plus the key to his car, which as far as I knew was still out at the spa. Maybe the cops had impounded the car and were searching it. Tom hadn't mentioned anything about that. There were keys to I-knew-not-what. Jack's liquor cabinet? A storage compartment I didn't know about? Maybe I should have given Tom these damn keys.

I turned over one, a smaller one, then turned it back. On one side were the initials AMCC. On the other was a letter and a number: M-71.

Omigosh, my golly, I thought. The brand-new golf clubs had been in Jack's living room, along with the old-new travel clock. But Jack eschewed clocks, and he had constantly complained that his bursitis had made it impossible for him to keep playing golf. I was having the clock examined and dissected, but I'd practically forgotten about the stupid golf clubs.

I glanced at the key again. It didn't belong to a liquor cabinet and it certainly wouldn't open a storage container. The key was from the Aspen Meadow Country Club, the AMCC.

Jack had given me the keys, I was willing to bet, and set up the clubs in his living room, in case something happened to him. He had safeguarded something, I had no idea what, and he'd wanted me to figure it out—a final puzzle for his godchild. That was why he'd given me the keys. He'd put whatever he wanted me to find in locker number 71, on the men's side of the changing rooms at the country club.

I didn't stop to think. Aspen Meadow Country Club served fancy dinners and offered dancing until two in the morning. The dining room did not close any particular night, Marla had told me, because members were required to eat there five times a month. I knew some of my clients found this requirement onerous, but then they'd reluctantly bought the diamonds and dresses to make it all possible.

If I went back upstairs, I'd awaken Tom, and I definitely didn't want to do that. I'd already put another change of clothes in the van, which was in the driveway. I wrote Tom a note: "Gone to Aspen Meadow Country Club, back by three." Then I disarmed the house's security system, grabbed my purse and Jack's and my keys, and was off.

* * *

In the parking lot of the AMCC, I changed into my catering uniform, which I hoped looked similar enough to the club's servers' uniforms for me to fit in. The parking lot was, dishearteningly, less than a quarter full. I certainly hoped the cars belonged to patrons, and not just worker bees.

I came in through the kitchen, where a couple of long-suffering workers were washing pots and pans and speaking in Spanish.

I said, *"Busco los clientes,"* which I hoped meant that I was looking for the clients, and not, I'm searching for my long-lost parents. I'd once asked the male manager of a Spanish grocery store, *"¿Tiene huevos?"* Which I thought meant "Do you have eggs?" but instead meant, "Do you have balls?" and not the the kind you bounce around on the playground. I never went back.

But one of the dishwashers nodded and said merely, *"Allá."* He pointed in the direction of the dining room, the location of which I knew very well. I nodded my thanks and took off through the kitchen doors. But instead of heading upstairs toward the dining room, from which some waltz music was playing too loudly, I headed downstairs, to the darkened locker rooms.

When I got to the side marked MEN, I opened the door, which creaked ominously. I called, "Hello? Maid service?" When no one answered, I turned on the overhead lights, which flickered gray, and then finally came on. I made my way cautiously inside.

I was gripping Jack's keys so hard that my palms were beginning to sweat. The locker numbers danced in front of my eyes, a function, no doubt, of my extreme fatigue. I told myself to relax, I'd be in bed soon enough, and I'd have the satisfaction of knowing what Jack and Doc Finn had been up to. That thought gave me a pop of energy, and I slowly began to peruse the lockers until I found number 71.

No sooner had I put the key in the lock than I heard the locker room door creak open. I cursed silently, and for once wished that I had Boyd back by my side to protect me.

"Maid service!" I called loudly. "We'll be done cleaning in here in fifteen minutes! Can you come back, please?"

To my very great relief, the door creaked back closed. Probably some inebriated fart had wandered away from his wife. He'd gotten confused and figured it was time to play golf.

I tried to downplay paranoid thoughts that I had been followed. No way, I told myself. What, was someone parked outside our house, ready to follow my van in the middle of the night?

I certainly hoped not.

I swallowed hard and turned the key in the lock. *Just get whatever it is and get out,* I told myself. Go back through the kitchen, where the dishwashing staff will still be at work. I'd ask one of them to accompany me back to my car. Would my crappy Spanish yield me the right phrases? Well, one problem at a time.

I opened locker M-71. I don't know what I was expecting, but a single piece of paper was not it. The writing was old-fashioned, not Jack's.

> *O'Neal—dehydration*
> *Parker—thyroid*
> *Druckman—rotator cuff*
> *Foster, White, Katchadourian—Symptoms of addiction withdrawal. All were told they were stressed out, should go back for a week or more. Once there, they said, they felt better. Home two days, more symptoms of withdrawal. Again told to go to back. Etc.*

I reread the paper. Symptoms of withdrawal? From what? They should go back for a week or more? Go back where? To Gold Gulch Spa? And what were Foster, White, and Katchadourian, none of whom I knew, withdrawing from? From the stuff in the fruit cocktail? From the smoothies? From something I had taken out of the Smoothie Cabin?

I wanted to scream at heaven: The next time you leave me a puzzle, Jack, make the solution clearer, won't you?

I heard nothing but silence.

Chapter 23

I tucked Jack's keys and the paper into my pocket and walked quickly, watchfully, back to the kitchen. I saw no one, and the band in the dining room was playing "Good Night, Ladies," the cue that the dancers' evening was winding down.

One of the workers kindly accompanied me to my van. My spotty memory of Spanish yielded up the phrase, *"Tengo miedo."* I'm afraid. Which I was. Alone, in the men's locker room, in a country club I didn't belong to, in the middle of the night, trying to figure out why someone had killed a kindly doctor and attacked my godfather so brutally he'd died of a heart attack? You bet your bippy I was full of *miedo*.

With the wiry Hispanic man there to protect me, I looked cautiously around the parking lot: were any of these cars new since my arrival? I couldn't tell. I thanked the worker, then offered him ten dollars as a tip, which he proudly declined. I thanked him again and hoped I hadn't offended him. Some cultural walls take time to hurdle, and my brain was too mushy to learn whatever lesson was being offered. I jumped into the van and raced home.

There were some cars out on the road, but it was hard to tell if anyone was following me. I didn't think so, and no one turned up our narrow road off Main Street. Still, I was massively relieved when I slouched into our kitchen. I guess I shouldn't have been too surprised to find Tom at our table, a glass of scotch in front of him.

"You needed to play nine holes of golf in the middle of the night?"

"I just didn't want to wake you—"

"You could have at least taken your cell phone," he said mildly, turning his green eyes in my direction. "Turned it on, too, in case your nervous husband woke up, didn't find you, but found this cryptic note about you waking up with a sudden desire to mix with the country-club set."

"I wasn't mixing with anyone, I was getting this." I handed him the paper and explained its provenance. I didn't tell him about my fear that someone might have followed me, then come into the locker room while I was there.

"I want you to give me Jack's keys right now." Tom held out his hand. "No excuses, and no more late-night ideas for investigating. You're not rational."

"Oh, don't pull that logical argument—," I began.

Tom held up his hand. "Enough, Miss G. I also need that paper. I'll make a copy for you." And off he went to the basement, where he kept his office equipment.

So, at just after three in the morning, Tom wordlessly handed me a duplicate of the scrawled note from the golf club locker. When we finally climbed into bed, I was grateful Tom hadn't bawled me out more than he had.

When the alarm went off at five, I thought I was going to die. Or maybe I was already dead. I slapped it, reset it for seven for Tom, and then went slowly through my yoga routine. Both my insides and outsides felt covered with grit, so I took a quick shower. Then I made my way down to the kitchen, fixed myself a quadruple espresso, and sat down to think.

I missed Jack. His absence was like an ache. If he had stayed in New Jersey, if he had never moved here this year, then I wouldn't have known what it was like to have my beloved godfather so close by, wouldn't have known how much fun it would be to renew a relationship that had meant everything to me when I was young.

Yes, I missed him.

I knew enough psychology to be aware that one ignored one's feelings at one's peril. But beyond acknowledging that yeah, okay, I was sad, what was I supposed to do? This was not the first time I'd reflected that academic psychology departments were long on analysis and short on advice. And in the long run, what did people need, analysis of their problems, or advice on how to fix them?

Well, I needed the latter, I thought as I pulled another four shots and dumped them over cream and ice. And then I felt another tug on my heart, because if there was one person who'd offered me support and advice in copious quantities, whenever I'd wanted or needed either, it was Jack Carmichael.

This line of thought wasn't getting me anywhere, so I looked at my copy of the paper I'd pulled from men's locker number 71 at the Aspen Meadow Country Club. Maybe it meant something, maybe it didn't. But as feeling depressed worked quite a bit less well for me than a quest for meaningfulness, I chose the latter.

This note *did* mean something; Jack had left it for me. Maybe he'd felt someone closing in, and left the piece of paper in the golf club locker as an insurance policy. But the problem with an insurance policy is that you have to understand it in order to get anything out of it.

The handwriting was unfamiliar. I had known that Todd Druckman had had a rotator cuff injury. But my calendar announced all too unfortunately that the Druckmans were off on their fishing trip in Montana. Todd had woefully told Arch that his mother had strictly forbidden the taking of any cell phones into the backcountry. You'd have thought she'd told him he couldn't have any food or water either.

I glanced at the clock: quarter past five. If I was going to fulfill my duties out at Gold Gulch Spa, I had to get cracking. I glanced back at the list, with its puzzle demanding a solution.

I called Julian, who was already on his way over from Boulder. Could he fix high-protein vegetable frittatas this morning, for sixty-one clients at Gold Gulch Spa? I'd pay him well, I assured him.

"Oh, boss," Julian said, relieved. "You bet. Victor says absolutely no fresh fruit, but I bought fresh vegetables at the farmers' market day before yesterday. I put them into bags to bring to the spa, just in case I could find a way to serve them. I can stop and pick up cheese and cream, too."

"I'll be there by lunchtime," I said. "Think you can handle it? Yolanda said there were plenty of foodstuffs, and the menus and recipes are there in her computer. You don't have to follow her recipes exactly."

"No problem," he said confidently. "I'll do my own Summertime Frittata. If you have any issues, call me through the spa switchboard, okay? I can't get cell reception out there to save my life."

"Absolutely. And thanks."

"Before you hang up," Julian said, at once awkward and shy, "tell me, what's going on?"

I gave him a brief summary of my evening's ramblings, and the list in front of me. He whistled. I asked him if any of the names sounded familiar to him, and he said, except for Druckman and O'Neal, no, sorry. We signed off and agreed I'd be out at Gold Gulch no later than eleven.

Next I punched in the numbers for Boyd's cell phone. He picked up on the first ring, and was oh-so-relieved not to have to do guard duty this morning. We arranged to meet at the spa at eleven, in time to prepare the lunch.

I went back to frowning at the list. If O'Neal was Dodie, then that looked like the best bet. If it referred to another O'Neal, or if it was Ceci, then I would be out of luck, as I didn't know any other O'Neals, and Ceci was on her honeymoon.

The clock still indicated it was too early to call the O'Neal residence. I took the time to go through the Aspen Meadow phone book, looking for any Parker I knew—there were twenty-seven of them—but none was familiar. There were three pages of Whites, so I gave up on those right away. There were only four Fosters, and I wrote down those names. There was no Katchadourian in the phone book, so I called directory information, which told me that the number was unlisted.

I cursed and slammed the phone book closed. Tom was still asleep, Marla was at Gold Gulch Spa, out of cell phone reach . . . but what about Arch? I'd told him he had to keep his own cell phone on at all times. So I called him.

"Oh, Mom," came his sleepy voice. "What is it? Is something wrong?"

"Not really." I hesitated, as I could just imagine him encased in his sleeping bag over at his half brother's house.

"Well, then why are you calling me? I'm so tired!"

"Sorry, hon." I tried to make my voice nonchalant. "I was just calling to see if you remembered Todd's rotator cuff problems."

"What?"

"Remember when Todd had his shoulder problems?"

"Mom, I'm so tired. Can't this wait? Why do you need to know about this now?" Sudden tears welled in my eyes, and I couldn't find my voice. When I didn't speak for a couple of minutes, Arch said, "Mom? Are you still there? Hello?"

"It has to do with your Uncle Jack," I whispered. And then I further embarrassed myself by starting to cry.

"Oh, Mom, I'm sorry." He groaned, and I heard the unmistakable slither of body against nylon sleeping bag. "C'mon, please don't cry."

"Okay," I said, but still had to stifle sobs.

"All right, look," said poor, confused Arch. "You want to know about Todd's shoulder because it has something to do with Uncle Jack?"

"Yes. It's a long story."

Arch grunted. "That's what you always say." When I didn't go on, he took a deep breath, and I realized for the first time that I hadn't managed to cushion Arch from grief.

"Sweetheart?" I said. "Are you all right? I mean, I haven't even asked you how you're doing since Jack died."

"Mom, c'mon. I'm fine. Tom called me. I didn't know Jack as well as you did. And since I'm over with Gus, it's not like I'm looking at Jack's house every day, you know. I'm okay," he reassured me. "So." He yawned. "What was your question about Todd?"

"Tell me about the rotator cuff."

"Yeah, right. Todd was doing something in swimming that he wasn't supposed to. The guy at the doctor's told him to do exercises, but that just made his shoulder worse. A lot worse. His shoulder froze, at least, that's what the physical therapist told Todd when he couldn't make his arm move. So then Todd's mom took him to a specialist, and there was a long wait for an MRI, I think, but when they finally got one, it showed his rotator cuff was torn. So he had to have surgery." Arch stopped talking, exhausted and out of explanations.

"Is that it? Did somebody hurt Todd, or threaten him?"

"Threaten him?"

I rolled my eyes ceilingward and wished it were later, as in afternoon, which was when Arch got up in the summertime. "Arch," I pleaded, "please try to remember."

"Nobody tried to hurt or threaten him," my son said definitively. "Can I go back to bed now?"

"Just wait." I scanned the list. Every one of the conditions listed beside the names pertained to medical issues. "Didn't Todd start off at Spruce Medical? I mean, when he was first hurt?"

"I guess so. Why?"

"What doctor did he see there?"

"I don't know. Actually, I know he saw two people. Probably both doctors, I guess."

"Do you know who either doctor was, in case the police want to know?"

"No. Mom, please let me go back to sleep."

"Okay, sweetheart, thank you. Bye."

There was a pause on the line. "Did I help you?"

"Yes, Arch, thanks. You're great."

He groaned and signed off, and I went back to staring at the list. I don't know how long I'd been trying to make sense of it when Tom shuffled into the kitchen. He wore a blue terry cloth robe and white terry slippers, and his cider-colored hair was rumpled.

"Miss G." His arms encircled my waist. "You're starting to worry me."

"I'm okay."

"Yeah, right." Tom opened the walk-in, peered in, and removed eggs and vegetables.

"What are you doing?"

"Making breakfast?" he said. "It is morning, right?" He ran water over the vegetables. "So, I assume you've thrown in the towel on cooking at the spa?"

"No, Julian's doing breakfast. I'm going out there later. Don't worry, I called Boyd and told him about the change."

"Chop this onion for me, then, will you?" He handed me a red onion, cutting board, and sharp knife. "You're squinting at that piece of paper as if it could tell you all you need to know."

Was it the onion that was making my eyes water, or was it Tom's comment? "I just feel as if the person who attacked Jack attacked me, too."

"They did," Tom said simply. "That's the way it works, unfortunately." He eyed me. "You want me to get Victim Assistance over here for you?"

"No, I'm fine."

"Right." Tom began to slice broccoli. "You break into Jack's house—"

"I didn't break in! I had keys! That he had given me!"

"—then you decide to start working at a spa you dislike, forcing me to take one of my guys off of a security detail. After that, you sneak out of the house in the middle of the night—"

"I didn't sneak out! I was trying not to wake you up!"

"And then you focus on a list you found in a locker that could just as easily have been left there by the last duffer to use that space."

"No, Tom, that won't work. The locker key was on Jack's key ring, the key ring he had me take from him. That list refers to patients . . . maybe Doc Finn's patients? Maybe the handwriting is Doc Finn's?"

"We'll check on that, trust me."

"I already called Arch," I confessed, handing Tom the board with the onion, "to ask him why Todd's name is on the list."

Tom peered down at the list. "What did he say?"

"He clarified what Todd told us about it last week. Todd had a messed-up shoulder from swimming. The first person to see him at Spruce Medical told him to do some weight-lifting exercises, which only made it worse. Todd saw somebody else next. But then a physical therapist told Todd his shoulder was frozen and his mother took him to a specialist. He had an MRI and then surgery."

Tom slid a baking sheet with the vegetables into

the oven. Then he handed me a hunk of Havarti and asked me to grate a cup. Next, he broke eggs into a mixing bowl. He said, "You know that to make a straight line, you need two points? Investigation is like that. To make a straight line, you need two points, to get a context. Knowing about Todd gives you one point. You need one more."

I watched as he poured a cup of whipping cream into the beaten eggs. I suspected Tom was using Julian's recipe for Summertime Frittata. Oh, well.

"You see this, where he writes, 'All were told they were stressed out, should go back for a week or more'?" I asked. "And apparently three people had symptoms of addiction withdrawal?"

Tom gave me an inscrutable look. "Mmm."

"Well, that sounds as if Finn was maybe talking about clients of the spa. If you found a drug in a container in Doc Finn's trash, and a note that said he needed to get it analyzed, and you found a towel in his car from Gold Gulch, and you knew he'd been out there recently, couldn't you maybe make a leap that he suspected Victor Lane was feeding those Gold Gulch clients addictive drugs? I mean, without their knowledge? That would lead to symptoms of withdrawal."

"That's a big leap," Tom said. He plopped a chunk of butter into our sauté pan and turned the heat to low. "Listen, you can't mention this list to anyone."

I groaned, and told him I'd already told Julian about it.

Tom said, "Julian knows better than to talk about

it. Listen, Miss G., we know something is going on out there because Jack was attacked at Billie's wedding. But we're not completely sure what the issues, crimes, whatever, are. That's why I wanted Boyd to stick to you like epoxy while you were working in the kitchen, which I still think is a half-assed idea."

"I know you disapprove. I promise to keep being careful," I said, watching Tom pour the egg mixture into the pan. For my part, I pulled a loaf of Cuban Bread out of the freezer. Yolanda had taught me how to make it a dozen years earlier, and it had been one of our family's favorites ever since.

Tom shoveled the vegetables into the pan, sprinkled the Havarti on top, and slid his concoction into the oven. He watched me trying to cut the bread. "Here," he said, "let me slice that for you."

"Thanks." I watched him saw expertly at the frozen loaf. When he popped two pieces into the toaster, I asked, "Any word yet on Lucas's inheritance?"

"Sorry, I forgot to tell you what we found out about Jack's will. Lucas stands to inherit four million dollars from Jack. And, Lucas is the sole beneficiary of Jack's will, I'm sorry to say . . . or sorry, anyway, if *you* were expecting something."

I hugged Tom. "The memories Jack left me are more valuable than that. But listen. Wouldn't four million smackers be motive to kill someone? Especially if you were having money problems?"

"You bet it would be." He took out two plates, then slathered the toast with butter.

I shook my head. "That worthless Lucas—"

Tom shrugged as he took the frittata out of the oven. "You need two points to make a line, Miss G. Remember that."

As I was groaning, Tom's cell rang. He listened for a moment, then said, "You're sure?" When he heard that whoever had called was indeed certain, he signed off.

He picked up his fork to dig into the frittata, then put it down. Finally he said, "The traces in the vial in Finn's trash? Valium."

"Good Lord. But not enough to make a line to Gold Gulch."

"Not yet."

I insisted Tom go to work. He took the paper I'd found in the golf club locker, and promised he would have his handwriting people on it ASAP. I gave him the main number of the switchboard out at Gold Gulch Spa, if he couldn't reach me on my cell. He promised to call if he had anything, he said, that was "earth shattering."

Speaking of calling, I still hadn't heard back from Hans Bogen, Aspen Meadow's premier jeweler and clock repairer. By the time I'd finished the dishes, it was nine o'clock, so I dialed the Bogen household.

Hanna answered on the first ring. She said, "I know he's working on your clock, Goldy, and that he has the machinery spread out all over his workstation at the store. But so far, he hasn't found anything."

I gave her, too, the numbers of both my cell and the main switchboard out at Gold Gulch. I told her the clock situation was one of some urgency.

"Why don't you just buy a new travel clock?" she asked.

"It's not a gift for someone. It just . . . is of great importance to me."

"Let me tell you," said Hanna. "Clock repair is like marriage. There will always be vexations."

Omigod, more Jane Austen. I gritted my teeth, but thanked Hanna and told her I hoped to hear from Hans soon.

Next on the list was O'Neal. If this was the O'Neal I knew, then finding the answer to the dehydration question should be fairly easy. But Dodie had left a message on her voice mail saying she and her granddaughter would be out of the country for the next week. Great. Norman O'Neal was not in the office, a receptionist crisply told me, but she would certainly put my name on his desk for when he came back.

"Sorry," I said, "this is a very pressing matter. It's quite urgent." Actually, the only urgency was mine, in that I didn't want to face a lot more emotional emptiness, the kind bred from grief. Better to keep moving, I told myself, and to get others to move along with me, if possible.

"All matters that Mr. O'Neal deals with are of some urgency," she said, as if I were speaking about the need to go to the bathroom.

"Oh, yeah?" I replied. Ordinarily I am not rude, but the combination of lack of sleep and this woman's hostility was breaking down my hold on civility. "This is Goldy Schulz, and Norman himself called me from the hospital a few nights ago. He was desperate for me to help him be reconciled with his daughter. I am able to do that now," I lied. "So, why don't we skip the baloney here, and you just tell me where he is right now, okay?"

"One moment, please," was her chilly response. Within twenty seconds she was back on the line. "He's at the Grizzly," she said, a faint, very faint, whiff of apology in her tone. "He's having an early breakfast. Do you know where the Grizzly is?"

"Yes, thanks." I hung up, and reflected that the only kind of breakfast they served at the Grizzly was the liquid variety. And I didn't mean smoothies.

Inside the Grizzly Saloon, it was fairly easy to pick out Norman O'Neal. He was the only one at the bar not wearing a cowboy hat. In front of him were a shot and a beer chaser. So much for deciding to go to rehab.

"Gee, Norman," I said cheerfully, "thought I'd never find you."

"Who're you?" He narrowed his watery eyes at me.

"I'm Goldy? The caterer from Ceci's wedding? The wedding you ruined by getting plastered and then coming in and knocking out the priest?"

His facial muscles quirked. "I did that? I don't remember."

"You called me from the hospital and asked if I could help you become reconciled with Ceci."

Norman's unshaven jaw dropped slightly. "Yeah. I want that."

I lifted my chin in the direction of the booze. "Why

don't you leave that, and come up to our house for some coffee? We only live half a block away."

"I'm coming," he said, before downing the shot and taking a long pull on the beer. Great.

When I had Norman O'Neal in my kitchen, I brewed a pot of coffee. I also toasted him a couple of pieces of Yolanda's Cuban Bread, which I liberally slathered with butter.

"You got any peanuts?" Norman asked.

We did, of course, but I said, "No." I didn't want to give Norman anything that would make him thirsty. With his haggard, gray cheeks and skin hanging loosely on his bones, he looked as if he'd been existing on peanuts for the last six months.

"So," said Norman, "how are you going to help me with Ceci? I thought she was on her honeymoon."

This negotiation was going to be delicate, and it would have helped if Norman O'Neal were not already a couple of sheets to the wind . . . not long after nine o'clock in the morning.

"Ceci is on her honeymoon," I said, "and Dodie has taken your granddaughter out of the country."

"She can't do that!" Norman protested, weaving a bit on his kitchen chair. "That's my granddaughter, too!"

"You told me you'd never seen her. Your adopted granddaughter, that is. You also told me she almost died."

Norman's rheumy eyes regarded me warily. "What does this have to do with my . . . being reconciled with Ceci?"

"It has everything to do with it, Norman," I said coolly, "because I need to know what your granddaughter almost died of. I need to know all the details you can remember. And after I hear them, I promise I'm going to call Ceci, and leave a message on her voice mail telling her I must talk to her about her father. And when I do talk to her in person, I'm going to tell her how much you want to see her and be a part of her life. I'm also going to tell her what a great idea being reconciled to you is, especially if you decide to go into rehab, which is where you belong."

Norman O'Neal sucked in one side of his mouth. "That sounds like an awful lot of conditions."

"You want this deal, or not?"

There was a long silence in the kitchen.

Norman said warily, "Why do you want to know what was wrong with my granddaughter?"

"What difference does it make why I want to know?"

Norman reared back. "Because there are privacy laws concerning health information these days, missy."

"Oh, yeah? Well, when you called me from the hospital after ruining Ceci's wedding, you didn't care about privacy laws. You were too busy crying about being reconciled with your daughter and being a grandfather to her adopted daughter. That was before you puked your guts out, though."

Norman winced, then slammed down some coffee. "The baby almost died of dehydration."

"Dehydration?"

"Yeah." He took a long pull of coffee, then went on, "Ceci wanted to adopt a baby so badly. So she went through some Eastern European adoption agency." He smirked at me. "Dodie isn't the only one with spies, you know." When I said nothing, he said, "The baby got over here, and supposedly she'd been checked out by doctors at the orphanage she came from, but for whatever reason, Ceci couldn't get her to take a bottle of formula. So Ceci took her to Spruce Medical, and some physician's assistant there told her she might be allergic to formula, try her on soy. So she tried her on soy, no luck."

"Wait. A physician's assistant? Who? Lucas Carmichael?"

"I don't know who they are there." Norman weaved a bit more, as if he were trying to figure out where in the story he was.

"On soy, no luck," I prompted.

"Okay," Norman said, with effort. "So then Ceci went back to Spruce Medical, and said she wasn't leaving until somebody helped her. A doctor saw her, and told her to give the baby a bottle of water. But the baby wouldn't take a bottle of water."

"What doctor?"

Norman shrugged. "The water didn't work either." He closed his eyes.

"Norman! Is there more to this story?"

"Yeah. My spies tell me Ceci finally called Doc Finn, even though he was officially retired. But he'd been her doctor when she was little, and she trusted him. He recognized that the baby was severely dehydrated. Finn convinced her to take the baby down to Southwest Hospital, where they put her on an IV. They said down there that in another twelve hours, the baby would have been dead. That's the rest of the story."

"That's all of it?"

"Ceci was eternally grateful to Doc Finn. That's why she wanted him to give her away at her wedding." Norman's eyes filled with self-pitying tears, which he brushed away. "Instead of me."

"I understand," I said, and Norman finally seemed more chipper, as if he'd just been let out of class. "Uh, Norman? Is there something else, something you're not telling me?"

Norman squirmed. "Well, this next part, I'm not supposed to know."

"Seems to me you shouldn't be knowing any of this."

"Well," said Norman bitterly, "aren't you the soul of compassion." I stood and refilled his coffee, hoping that would make me seem more . . . compassionate. Alcoholics are always saying no one understands them, Tom had told me often enough. "Dodie began malpractice proceedings against Spruce Medical."

"Against a physician's assistant or doctor in particular?"

Norman shook his head. "Don't know that. All I do know is that somebody came along claiming to represent the practice, and told Dodie if she dropped her suit, he'd give her three hundred thousand dollars. That's a huge amount, given that the doctors in Romania or wherever it was had given the little girl a clean bill of health. I don't think anyone in the entire country of Romania has three hundred grand. Dodie must have known she was on slippery ground with the suit, so she took the money. It paid for Ceci's wedding and a down payment on a large house for Ceci and her husband."

"Wow." It seemed to me that Norman O'Neal might be estranged from his ex-wife and daughter, but that he was doing a pretty good job of keeping up with their doings.

"So will you help me with Ceci?" he asked, his voice pathetic with desire.

"Absolutely," I replied. "I'm sure you'll be a great grandfather."

"I'm a drunk," he said, with doleful insight.

"That's why there's rehab," I told him. And then I drove him home. Afterward, I called Norman's office and said somebody would have to deliver his car to his house, as he was now indisposed. And, I hoped but did not say, Norman's on the phone right now with rehab centers.

Chapter 24

It was half past ten. I was already feeling guilty about leaving Julian with all the work out at Gold Gulch. So I jumped into my catering uniform, phoned Boyd to ask if he could still meet me at the spa, and hopped into my van. On the way out on Upper Cottonwood Creek Road, I called Tom and told him all I'd learned from Norman O'Neal.

"I'm not seeing a straight line yet," I said.

"A dotted one, maybe." Tom was uncharacteristically silent.

Wait a minute.

"Charlotte's blackboard," I said. "The name O'Neal had been written down, and then erased. Maybe Billie wrote it down when she was looking for me last Friday morning, and blasted into Ceci's wedding. But maybe it had to do with Dodie's lawsuit."

Tom said only, "Okay, go on."

"Look, Tom, you said for me to look at the relationships among these people. And of all the people connected to this case, the Attenboroughs are the only ones I know who have three hundred grand just lying around. They also would have the motivation to try to save Spruce Medical, because they didn't want anything to sully the name and reputation of their dear Craig Miller."

Tom said, "Big leap."

"What about the piece of paper I got at the golf club? Did you analyze the handwriting?"

There was more silence. In a low voice, Tom said, "It looks like it's Doc Finn's writing. I'm sorry, Goldy."

"You're sorry?" Once more my brain wasn't functioning quite properly. "Sorry about what?"

"Well . . . we always suspected these two cases were linked, and now we know it for sure."

Okay, maybe my brain wasn't firing on all cylinders, but my emotions were picking up signals from Tom that made me anxious. "So the two cases *are* linked," I repeated. "What else?"

"I've sent guys out to try to find the right people to match the names on the list. Unfortunately, most people won't admit to having symptoms of addiction," he added. Still, this was good, I thought, as the sheriff's department had much better resources for finding people than yours truly with a phone book. Tom paused again.

"Tom, what is it?"

"Okay, Miss G. We got the preliminary results back from the autopsy on Jack. He did die of a heart attack. But the attack was induced."

"Induced? How?"

"He was taking verapamil for his heart. We talked to his cardiologist, and she insists Jack was very faithful about his medicine. The only problems she had with him were his smoking and drinking." Tom took a deep breath. "I wish I could be with you to tell you this. Jack had a very excessive amount of verapamil in his system. Our guess at this point is that a liquid form of verapamil was put into his IV . . . at the hospital."

I pulled over to the side of the road.

"So Jack was killed at Southwest Hospital," I said flatly.

"I'm sorry, Goldy. Yes. They don't have surveillance cameras pointed at the patients' rooms, so we have no idea who could have gone in or out. Liquid verapamil? We asked ourselves, who with a motive to kill Jack would have access to that? At first, we just came down to Craig and/or Lucas. But then we thought, wait a sec, wasn't his girlfriend Charlotte a nurse, back in the day? Maybe she would have a way to get hold of it. Plus, Billie the Bitch Bride hated Jack, and she has money, so she could probably get whatever she wanted on a black market somewhere. And finally, we have Victor Lane. You said he videotaped Jack hunting around in the Smoothie Cabin. Maybe Victor got real nervous about what Jack was up to, and decided to get rid of him. He knows how to make smoothies, maybe he knows how to put stuff in an IV."

"But . . . did all those people know Jack took verapamil?"

"We don't know. Listen, Miss G., I'm aware that Marla's out at Gold Gulch. Is Julian still there, too?"

"Yes. In fact, I'm on my way to help him. Boyd's going to meet me, then we'll drive in together." Tom said nothing. "I'll be fine. I'll see you tonight."

"Wait. Where's Boyd meeting you?"

"On the dirt shoulder beside the turnoff from Upper Cottonwood Creek Road that leads to the spa. Please don't worry, Tom." I made my tone reassuring, because I'd kept my poor husband up most of the night with the country club key caper, and as long as I was feeling miserable anyway, I might as well feel guilty about that, too.

We signed off with assurances of mutual love. This helped.

As I waited for Boyd, I glanced across the street at the old Spruce Medical Group building, now virtually empty. Two trucks with the logo FRONT RANGE DRAINS were parked on the side, but I didn't know if they were the last or even the only remaining tenants of the building.

I took a sip of the coffee I'd remembered to bring and averted my eyes from the former medical building.

I couldn't help feeling that I had failed Jack, not to mention Doc Finn. Doc Finn had tended so lovingly to Arch, it made my heart ache now. And Jack had come through for me, over and over. He had showered me with many things, but what I'd most appreciated was his steadfast love.

Outside, the weather was sunny and cool. The plethora of rain we'd had in the past month had left everything freshly green and refulgent, not at all like a normal Colorado August. Still, the tall, swaying grasses and the thick bunches of wild asters did nothing to brighten my mood.

Boyd signaled me with his lights when he was a hundred feet from the turnoff. When we rolled into Gold Gulch Spa, my watch said it was almost eleven. The clients must still be in classes, because I didn't see anyone around except staff people. They were rolling their laundry carts from door to door, depositing soiled towels in one side of the cart and pulling fresh towels out of the other.

Julian greeted us at the kitchen door. In answer to my question, he said nothing unusual or weird or crazy had happened that morning, except the women had loved the vegetable frittata. Victor had shown up as usual with his vat of fruit cocktail, and he'd even had a bite of the frittata.

Julian's face broke into a wide grin. "He didn't ask how many calories were in it, or even what I'd used. He just offered me a job, 'to replace Yolanda,' he said. I told Victor if he wanted to hire me, he was going to have to hire you, too. He just walked away with the empty vat of fruit cocktail."

I shook my head and thanked him. "What are we fixing for lunch?"

"Chicken salad with fat-free mayo. I doctored it up with fresh sliced scallions and really crisp celery. I also alternated thick slices of farmers' market tomatoes with slices of buffalo mozzarella and leaves of fresh basil. Then I poured a bit of pesto over that."

I rolled my eyes. "Victor's going to kill us."

"Nah," said Julian. "Hey, Boyd, you want to taste this Tomato Napoleon? It's great, and it's vegetarian."

"Yeah," said Boyd, as he followed Julian into the kitchen, "but I'll bet dollars to doughnuts that Napoleon never ate it."

We got through lunch, which the clients raved about. Lucas nodded to me, but didn't speak. Maybe he was softening toward me, I didn't know. Charlotte and Billie came in together, deep in conversation. Either they didn't see me or they ignored me, but in any event, we didn't speak, and I didn't have a chance to ask if either of them had bailed out Spruce Medical to the tune of three hundred thou. Marla winked at me and murmured that she could tell Julian and I had been working on the food, because it was suddenly scrumptious.

"Give Julian the credit," I said.

Marla smiled at Julian. "I'm always willing to do that."

Soon all the other clients shuffled off for their smoothies. Today's flavor was mango-strawberry. I hoped that was all that was in them. Once we'd cleaned the dining room and kitchen, I was ready for a break. Boyd and I went outside and sat on the deserted lawn furniture. Scraps of yellow police ribbon still fluttered in the light breeze, and the sulfuric smell of the hot spring floated down to the spa's main grounds. I wondered if anyone had ever cleaned up the hot pool.

As usual at this point in the day, the spa looked as

quiet as a Mexican town square at siesta time. Boyd and I sat in silence, while I tried to think. I scolded myself for not finding out which of the dormitories Marla was housed in, because I surely would have liked her company.

As it turned out, she had sneaked back into the kitchen with Julian. She was asking if there was going to be anything decent to eat for dinner.

"Pork tenderloin, cauliflower mash, and steamed broccoli," Julian replied. "I'm going to lightly sauté the broccoli with garlic, and I'm making a stuffing for the pork that features figs. The cauliflower mash will have whipping cream—"

Marla burst out laughing. "So is this spa where you come to lose weight, or gain it?"

"For dessert, let's see," Julian continued, unfazed. He eyed the computer screen. "Canned plums with diet nondairy topping. I can't make something else, because I don't have the butter and eggs I'd need."

"Canned plums for dessert?" Marla cried. "That's it?"

I turned to Boyd and asked if he'd bring in the cooler that was in the back of my van. A moment later, when Boyd hauled the cooler into the kitchen, Julian cried out.

"I've got a feeling Goldy's got something better for dessert in that cooler!"

Ten minutes later, the four of us, plus Yolanda's two helpers and the two servers who'd just finished setting the tables for dinner, were enjoying the chocolate cookies filled with frosting.

"This is the flakiest, most buttery chocolate cookie I've ever had in my life," Marla said to me. "You're a genius."

"Thanks. I wish I'd been enough of a genius to keep my godfather alive."

Julian, Marla, and Boyd made sympathetic murmurs in my direction. Yolanda's helpers and the servers, all of whom had finished their cookies, looked awkward, and quickly excused themselves. They said if Victor caught them eating, they'd lose their jobs.

"That guy Victor is a maniac," said Marla, her voice lowered. "We all cringe when he goes by."

I exhaled. I'd been cringing in Victor's presence for many a year.

Boyd asked Marla, "Where is everybody? You'd think you'd see the guests walking around or something. The place looks as deserted as a beach after a hurricane."

Marla looked furtively around, then drew a plastic shampoo bottle out of her pocket. It didn't look as if it was full of shampoo, though, as the liquid had separated.

"I had to improvise," she said. "Yesterday we had strawberry, but today it's mango-strawberry. I thought you might want to test it, too. I dumped out my shampoo, and saved my smoothie. Have to say, Victor watches us pretty carefully to make sure we're finishing them. But when I saw him sucking up to Charlotte Attenborough, I put my smoothie cup in my pocket and held on to it all the way back to my room. Listen," Marla said confidently, as she reached for a second cookie, "I know my drugs, or, what I should say," she amended, batting her eyes at Boyd, "is, I know the effects of drugs. I know I shouldn't have tasted the smoothie, but I did. This is not just fruit and whatever else they say is in it. Something else is in this drink." She handed it across to Boyd. "Yesterday, even a little taste zoned me out. And I'm not talking chamomile either. My best guess is that it's a prescription tranquilizer."

Once again, I couldn't affirm her report, but I knew in my heart that it was true. I just prayed that the samples we'd taken yesterday would show what we suspected. Everyone else at Gold Gulch took a nap in the afternoon, but Marla had been wary, and with good reason.

"Can you arrest Victor Lane?" I asked Boyd.

"Not yet," he said. "We took samples of the fruit cocktail and smoothies, which are being analyzed. But the analysis has to come back before we can get a warrant for the Smoothie Cabin, Victor's office and house, and anyplace else. Then our guys can look for the drugs themselves."

I closed my eyes and tilted my head back, thinking of the list that Doc Finn had compiled, and that Jack had put in a locker at Aspen Meadow Country Club. "What if you had a bunch of people who had withdrawal symptoms when they got home from here? And the only way for them to feel better would be to come back to the spa?"

"You're asking me?" said Boyd. "I'm telling you, we can't arrest somebody unless we have evidence that will make the arrest stick. Sorry," he added.

"Maybe we should get going on dinner," said Julian. "I've already ladled the plums into little bowls, but we need to make the fig filling for the pork, and pound the tenderloins so we can put them together with the filling in the middle."

Marla said, "I'd better get back to my bed and pretend to be asleep." But before she left, she came over and gave me a warm hug. "You look like hell," she whispered in my ear. "Why don't you get Yolanda back here? What can you do that the police can't?"

I thought of Tom, and his insistence on having dots that connected. I thought of his request that I look at relationships. And I thought impatiently of the tests that Boyd said he would have rushed through the lab.

"I don't know," I said truthfully. Marla hugged me and took off.

Maybe I didn't know what I could do that the cops couldn't, but I did know, had known, my godfather. If I hadn't, then I never would have discovered the last puzzles he'd left for me: the key ring that had opened the way to the golf clubs, the country club locker, and the nonfunctioning travel clock.

But what difference did it all make? I wondered as I seared the stuffed pork tenderloins while Julian steamed and mashed the cauliflower and Boyd trimmed the broccoli. Jack was still dead, murdered. Doc Finn was dead, murdered. There were lots of suspects, but no clear lines.

"I think I'm going to go over to the office and make a phone call," I announced to Boyd. "I'll be fine."

"If you don't want Victor popping up and overhearing you," Boyd replied, "you can use your cell over in the trees up by the pathways. I could come with you. When Jack was hit, we found we could get more reliable reception over there."

"I forgot my cell. Plus, I think it might look suspicious if I took yours and went up the path for just a quick call. Look." I pointed at the path to the log cabin office. "The door to a regular telephone is just twenty yards away. You can watch me all the way there and back."

"Nope," said Boyd resolutely. "I'm going with you."

I sighed hugely, but it made no difference.

Isabelle was on the phone ordering supplies for the following week. When she saw me, she quickly finished her business, then handed the phone over to me.

"Thanks," I said.

"Don't mention it," she replied. "Just . . . if Victor fires me at some point, would you think about hiring me?"

"Of course. Thing is, I don't really have regular staff. But if he does let you go, I'll see if I can find someone who needs a staff person with your particular gifts."

"You mean, like breaking and entering?"

"Well," I said, "we didn't do any breaking. We just entered."

Isabelle giggled and took off. I sat down and dialed Aspen Meadow Jewelers. To my surprise, Hans

Bogen answered the phone himself. He said Hanna was on her way out to the spa, to give me what he had found inside the clock.

"Inside the workings?"

"No, Goldy. I didn't need to take it apart, after all. When there was nothing wrong with the mechanism, I began to take apart the clock case. I think I've found what you might have been looking for underneath the fabric of the case. It is a thin piece of paper, along with a small key."

My shoulders slumped. More keys. Terrific. I thanked Hans, and said I would pay him for his efforts.

The first bell for dinner rang, so Boyd and I hustled back to the spa kitchen, where Julian had filled all the hot tables with boiling water. Despite the fact that we'd departed from the spa's recipes a bit—well, a lot—we had to pile each client's plate to identical measurements. As every caterer worth her hand-harvested sea salt knew, a buffet was an invitation to disastrous overeating. The two extra kitchen helpers were in charge of keeping a cold buffet filled with nonfattening salad ingredients, so they bustled around doing that. I sliced the filled, sautéed, and roasted pork. Boyd, bless his heart, was bending seriously over the bubbling pots that he was using as a base for steaming the broccoli.

Victor Lane came into the kitchen while we were hustling back and forth with trays of loaded plates. He said nothing, but cast a judgmental eye around everywhere. I didn't know whether he suspected the big cardboard box on the kitchen island was filled with chocolate cookies and vanilla frosting, and I determinedly ignored both the box and Victor. On one of my return trips to the kitchen, he had left, but Hanna Bogen was waiting at the back door.

"Here you are, Goldy." She handed me a small key, much smaller than the ones that had been on Jack's key ring. "I must get back. There was a small, thin piece of paper in there, too." She put the paper in my hand. "It looks like a note." She paused as I stared at the two items in the palm of my hand. "Are you all right?"

"No, but please thank Hans for me."

I opened the note first. It was in Jack's handwriting.

> *Gertie Girl,*
> *If you're reading this, then I'm gone. Finn left me this key, he said, as an insurance policy, in case something happened to him. But I don't know what it goes to, and I couldn't figure it out. Maybe you can. I've had a good run, and you were a big part of it. Wherever God sends me, I want you to know that I'll be thinking of you.*
> *Love,*
> *Jack*

Hanna was still standing at the back door. "Goldy?"

At first I couldn't speak. Finally, I said, "I don't know what this is a key to."

Hanna shook her head. "It didn't have anything to do with the clock, Hans said."

No kidding. I thanked Hanna, and she left. I slipped Jack's note and the key into my pocket.

Somehow, we got through dinner and the many complaints that canned plums were not enough for dessert. While the servers were clearing the tables, a small line of women appeared at the back door.

"We heard you were bringing sweets," the first one, a brunette, said.

"Where's Victor?" I asked.

"On the phone in his office," the second one, who had long, auburn hair and a protruding jaw, replied. "Hurry! How much are you charging?"

"I'm not," I said. I asked Julian to help me form an assembly line. First he slathered the flat side of one cookie with the creamy vanilla frosting, then I topped the frosting with another cookie. I placed the cookie sandwiches on paper towels and began handing them, one per client, to the women. "Just enjoy them quickly, don't tell Victor where you got them, and don't blame me if you don't lose weight."

When all the sandwiches were gone, I began to wonder how well Yolanda was able to supplement the meager salary she got from Victor. At five dollars a pop, I could have made over a hundred bucks tonight. Not bad.

But how many of those women were addicted to Valium, and who knew what other drugs, that Victor was giving them? Really, it was a miracle that "all" they had shown was signs of withdrawal . . . someone could have died. If Valium was in the smoothies, what else was Victor using? No wonder this place cost so much. But people always returned, because the addiction monster was eating them alive. What a sorry state of affairs.

While we washed and dried dishes, I thought fiercely that when the time came, I certainly hoped that the sheriff's department closed this place down . . . and sent arrogant, scheming Victor Lane away for a very long time.

When we were done, I felt bone tired, and sat down on one of the two chairs in the kitchen. I missed Tom. I missed Arch. And, like a deep ache, I missed Jack.

"You want to go home?" Boyd asked. "It looks as if we're done here for the night."

"Not yet," I replied. I was thinking that Jack had probably tried that little key in every locked drawer of the Smoothie Cabin . . . to no avail. But he'd seemed to have been convinced that the key went to something out here. And I'd be damned if I was going to leave this place until I'd figured out what lock the little key opened.

"Goldy," said Boyd. "What's the matter?"

I cleared my throat. "Just miss Jack, that's all."

He nodded. Like Tom, Boyd had spent enough time with the relatives of victims of crime that he knew their despair could be unfathomable. Wordlessly, he moved to the big walk-in and retrieved a . . . jar?

"This is from Tom," Boyd said. "It's your Summertime Special, kept chilled in my cooler. He figured you'd need caffeine after we finished tonight, and that you'd be tired enough that you would sleep anyway, when you got home."

"Thanks." I unscrewed the jar and took a small sip. Wonderful. While Boyd fixed himself a large ice water, then sat patiently on the other side of the kitchen, I slipped my free hand into my apron pocket. I felt the note from Jack and Finn's small key that Jack had hidden inside the clock.

Oh, Jack, I thought, what did you get yourself into?

He'd been on to something, he and Doc Finn. It involved the spa, and it involved a number of people with medical conditions, none of whom I could reach. Jack had given me a bunch of keys that had helped me get into his house, where I'd seen a bag of golf clubs he never used, and an inoperative travel clock hiding a key and a note.

I took another swallow of the coffee and thought back to when Jack had first arrived here from New Jersey, how he'd been so happy to reveal he'd bought the dilapidated place across the street from us. I'd been equally delighted to have him there, and our time together had been joyful.

When Jack had brought us some trout one night, he'd regaled us with the faux pas he'd made concerning the cultural and governmental differences between New Jersey and Colorado. He'd made us laugh over his every mistake.

A waiter had given Jack a blank look when he'd ordered a salad with "Roquefort" dressing. He'd learned to ask for "blue cheese." Jack had piled up a month's worth of trash waiting for municipal trash collection, until I told him waste services were privately contracted. Most of all, he'd been stymied by our postal service. Everyone in Aspen Meadow was on a rural route, we'd finally informed him. Either you maintained one of a row of boxes near your residence, or, if you were very lucky, the mailman put your correspondence in a single box near your house. Otherwise, you were stuck with renting a receptacle at the post office. Jack's days of waiting for the mail to be delivered through a slot in his front door were over. Jack had just shaken his head and installed a box at the end of his driveway, like the rest of us on our street.

And then Jack had become friends with dear, kind Doc Finn, whose sharp intellect and compassionate heart, as well as his affinity for fishing and drinking, made him the perfect companion for my godfather.

But something had gone very wrong. Doc Finn had saved little Lissa O'Neal, that much I'd learned from her grandfather Norman, who I sincerely hoped was in rehab at this very moment. Perhaps the Druckmans had told Finn about Todd's rotator cuff. And then . . . had some patients suffering from withdrawal come to Finn, too?

At that point, Doc Finn had gone digging. Was this a big assumption, or not? Had Doc Finn known he was in danger? He must have, or he wouldn't have given Jack the piece of paper with the list of names, the one I'd found in the golf club locker. But the last part of the puzzle, this damnable small key, was something Jack had not been able to figure out. So he'd left it for me.

I drank some more of my coffee and ran everything I knew about the case through my mind once more. And then I had an idea. It was crazy. Or was it? Jack hadn't known what the key went to because he wasn't used to having this kind of service.

But I did.

What I had in my apron pocket was the key to a mailbox. And not one at Aspen Meadow's main post office, because I knew what those looked like. But where? Doc Finn had given Jack the key, or maybe Doc Finn had left the key where Jack could find it . . .

And then I knew.

"I need to drive somewhere," I announced suddenly to Boyd. "I'll be back in less than fifteen minutes."

"I'm coming with you," he protested. But before he could insist further, an absolutely horrible sound came through the screen door to the kitchen. It was the sound of people vomiting.

Vomiting and screaming and puking some more.

"What the hell . . . ?" asked Julian as he raced in from the dining room, where he'd been setting up for breakfast. He ran out the door ahead of Boyd and me.

The women I had given cookie sandwiches to were holding on to their stomachs and throwing up. The remains of some of the food were on the grass. There wasn't a person out there who had not received a dessert from me. I thought I was going to be sick.

"What have you done?" Victor Lane, who had suddenly appeared, shouted in my face. "Why are these women sick?"

"I don't know!" I said.

"Leave her alone," Boyd said, interposing himself between Lane and me.

"This isn't anything from our menu!" Victor cried, looking at the remains on the grass.

"Somebody call for help," I commanded Julian.

But Boyd said, "It'll be faster if it comes from me. Stay with her," he said to Julian, and then he rushed in the direction of the trees, where, up high, he had said, he could get a cell phone signal.

With Boyd gone, Victor Lane could walk right up to me again, too close. His skeletal face loomed next to mine. "You are fired from here forever and ever, do you understand?" And then he smiled at me, and turned away.

Julian and I tried to help the women on the lawn, who were quite ill. Whatever had happened to them? And had Victor gone to call for help?

"Goldy?" said Isabelle from beside me. "What's going on?"

"I don't know," I said truthfully. "Could you help me get these women some ginger ale? Do you have any? I think that would help them. Do you keep any antinausea medication around here?"

"No," said Isabelle, "but we have diet ginger ale. I'll get it for them."

I looked at the women holding their stomachs, at Julian talking to several of them, trying to determine what had made them sick, and at Isabelle, who'd just banged into the kitchen to pour glasses of ginger ale. I knew I was not being paranoid when I reached the painful conclusion they'd been given something to make them sick. And I hadn't done it. But I now had a pretty good idea who had.

"Let me help you," I said to one of the women as I knelt beside her.

"Leave me alone," she said. "What did you put in those cookies? Why did you try to poison us?"

"I didn't!"

"Go away," she said fiercely. "Leave us alone until a doctor can help us." Then she rolled away from me.

All right, whatever you want, I thought. Julian was talking to a woman who was lying on the grass. Boyd had disappeared into the trees.

So I walked quickly back into the kitchen, grabbed my keys, revved up my van, and accelerated out of there.

Chapter 25

The office space for lease sign in front of the old Spruce Medical Group building was creaking as it swung in the mild breeze. I ignored both the wind and the sign, and hopped up to the entrance, which, as I recalled, had a row of locked mailboxes out front. Jack hadn't thought to look here when Doc Finn had given him the small key, because Jack didn't connect the key with rural mail delivery. But I had that knowledge, and I prayed it was going to help me.

I certainly hoped I wasn't chasing a wild hare. But I had to know.

Only two of the mailboxes seemed to be in use: Front Range Drains and a lawyer's office. Still, there was an old, battered sign over the boxes that read, THIEVES WANT YOUR MAIL! REMOVE EVERYTHING EVERY NIGHT! Well, I certainly hoped a killer—I still had only an inkling of who it could be—would not have thought to come out here to try to steal mail . . . or whatever.

It suddenly occurred to me that in my haste, I had not checked to see if I had been followed. I peered into the parking lot, but saw only my van and the ones belonging to Front Range Drains.

I took the key out of my apron pocket and gingerly began trying it in the locked boxes. There were a dozen of them, most of which were unmarked. The little key went into the first seven just fine, it just didn't *move*. And then on the eighth, success.

A pile of wet circulars fell at my feet when the door creaked open, proving that retirement, and even death, couldn't keep the junk mail away. Who was still paying rent for this box, a year after Doc Finn had retired from Spruce Medical? Maybe Doc Finn had been paying it.

I went through every ad for roof repair, every credit card offer, every discount card for oil changes. Nothing. I sighed.

But something had made Finn give Jack this key, as a kind of insurance policy, in case something happened to him. What? I felt inside the mailbox: the top, the bottom, and then the sides . . . wait.

There was something small and rectangular taped on one side of the mailbox. With infinite care, I peeled the sticky stuff away, and then stared, with only dawning comprehension, at a . . . flash drive? Doc Finn, Tech Boy? I groaned.

I was twenty-five minutes away from home, and I had a load of women getting sick from food I had given them—but had not put anything bad into— back at Gold Gulch Spa. I'd left Julian wrestling with the problem, and Boyd in the woods, trying to get a cell signal. Once the cops and ambulances arrived, I was going to be at the spa all night, answering questions and allowing food to be packed up and taken for analysis. I couldn't abandon Julian and Boyd; I had to go back.

After all, I told myself, Yolanda kept a computer in the spa kitchen, and I could plug the flash drive in there. Plenty of people were milling around, like rubberneckers trying to get a look at an accident. And then the cops would be here again.

And so I went back. The scene had not changed much. Victor Lane was yelling at Julian, who was ignoring him as he passed out glasses of ginger ale. When Julian saw me, he stood up and handed the tray of glasses to Isabelle. Victor was still hollering at Julian, who walked away.

"What do you think made them sick?" Julian asked me, once he was close to the kitchen doors.

Of course, I had been thinking about this ever since I'd driven out of the spa. "My guess?" I said. "Ipecac. Stirred into the frosting while we were busy serving dinner."

Julian screwed his face into incomprehension. "But who would do that?"

"My money's on Victor," I said. "He wanted an excuse to get me out of the spa, and maybe to discredit me with the police. But it could have been someone else."

"One of the women here brought antinausea medication," Julian said. "She has to take it when she gets a migraine, and when she heard about the crisis, she came racing out here with her bottle. She and Isabelle and Marla are giving it to the sick women." Julian shook his head. "I don't think there's anything more we can do to help them until the ambulance arrives."

Boyd wasn't back from the woods yet, so Julian told me he was going to wash up, then pour out some more ginger ale. He sternly warned me not to leave the kitchen, and I agreed that I would stay put.

As soon as he was gone, I booted up Yolanda's computer, on the far side of the sink. While the machine was humming and dinging, I added some more ice cubes to my Summertime Special. It was going to be a long night, and I figured I'd need extra caffeine.

After a few moments of tapping my foot, slugging down the creamy coffee, and cursing technology, I was able to bring up the contents of the flash drive. I sat down on one of the stools Yolanda's people used when they weren't rushing around, and tried to figure out what Doc Finn had left on his flash drive.

There were five files.

The first was text. It said "Medical University of Trinidad—top student. He died in a climbing accident—Peru, where he'd gone with Tim Anderson, a close friend who had flunked out of MUT. Residency—Grady Memorial, Atlanta. Terminated, stealing drugs. Record sealed."

But who was this person? The file gave no clue. Next came the second file, also text.

"Victor Landheugel, became Lane—former pharmacy tech. Terminated, fraudulent billing to Medicare. Prosecutor: woman, whom he'd vowed to get back at. She later had fatal car accident."

I took another swig of coffee. Huh, Victor Lane. It had been my experience that if a person acted like a jerk, he had stuff to hide. And sure enough, Victor Lane had all kinds of stuff to hide.

The third, fourth, and fifth files were photographs. The first photograph I did not recognize. The caption said, "Craig Miller, Medical University of Trinidad." He was much younger then. But as I stared at the photo, I thought, *No.* This guy, this Craig Miller in the photograph, had a chubby, unattractive face; freckles; and okay, dark, wavy hair. The Craig Miller I knew had a full mop of dark curls, and was much better looking than the homely fellow in the photograph.

The second photo's caption also read "Craig Miller." It had the subtitle "Atlanta." Here was the handsome, easygoing doctor who had just married Billie Attenborough.

The fifth and final file was a photograph with the caption, "Tim Anderson, Medical University of Trinidad." And although he'd been much younger then, this was the person I knew as Craig Miller.

So. Right here—this was that final point, the one that would make a straight line.

The Craig Miller I knew was not Craig Miller; he was Tim Anderson. The real Craig Miller had died— or been pushed?—off a mountain in Peru.

Passing himself off as the deceased doctor—the

real Craig Miller who'd actually gotten a degree—
Tim Anderson had been able to secure a residency in
Atlanta. But he hadn't proven himself to be very com-
petent, had been involved with drugs and gotten fired.
He'd come to Aspen Meadow, probably disguising his
background once again, and taken a position at Spruce
Medical Group, where his track record with patients
had attracted Doc Finn's attention. He'd found a partner in crime in Victor Lane, and, it was my new theory, they'd conspired to use the spa to get clients
hooked on drugs. It never ceased to amaze me how
bad people tended to find each other. Tim Anderson/
Craig Miller had also been able to parlay his looks and
his fake doctorhood into a handsome payout from
Charlotte Attenborough, who was desperate to get her
daughter married off, and if the husband-to-be was a
doctor, so much the better. Charlotte had even paid off
Dodie O'Neal, so that Craig could avoid a lawsuit.

I got up so quickly my head swam. I had to find
Boyd. I had to tell him what I had found out. Then I
needed to get Julian, Marla, and myself out of here.

I blinked and tried to get my bearings. I walked out
the kitchen's back door, awkwardly skirted the omni-
present laundry cart, and headed for the various trails
where Boyd had gone.

As I rounded the main building, I could see that the
poisoned women were still on the ground, but at least
they weren't moaning anymore. Julian and Isabelle
continued to move rapidly from person to person,
making sure the women were as comfortable as possible.

I looked up into the trees, trying to make out exactly where Boyd had gone. I felt a sudden wave of confusion. Had he scuttled up the path toward the hot springs pool, or had he headed straight up the mountain? I decided on the path to the hot springs pool.

I gave the sick women and all the onlookers a wide berth, then began to stumble up the path to the hot springs pool. I blinked. Was it getting dark really quickly, or was I just moving slowly? Or both?

Once I was partway up the path, I stopped, confused. Which way had I thought Boyd had gone?

Why wasn't my mind working? I looked down. Where had the path gone?

My shoulder was tapped from behind, and I turned, thinking someone was there to help me. But it was Craig Miller, or the person I thought was Craig Miller, pushing one of the spa's ubiquitous laundry carts.

"How's that drug working for you?" he asked with such coolness that my skin prickled with gooseflesh. "That's the problem with Valium, you know? Especially in large quantities, stirred into your iced coffee. You never know how it's going to affect the patient."

"You," I said, "you—" But now my mouth wasn't working, either. I also didn't seem to have much control over my limbs, so when Craig/Tim pushed me into the cart, I fell into it with a painful awkwardness. "Don't," was all I managed to say before he threw a pile of dirty towels on top of me and began to push the cart up the hill.

"Just in case you're wondering," he said, "I took that flash drive that Doc Finn left." His voice sounded muffled. "Oh, yes, here we go, up to death," he said merrily as the cart rattled and bumped over the trail.

I tried to say, "Stop," tried to struggle, but an overwhelming lethargy was making that impossible. I clawed at the sides of the cart, and managed only to knock the towels off my face. I was being pushed . . . somewhere. And no one was noticing.

"Want to talk?" Tim/Craig asked merrily. "Oh, wait, you can't talk. Or not much."

I groaned. I had enough presence of mind, though, to know that I had to try to make myself puke, to get rid of as much of the heavy-duty dose of tranquilizer as I possibly could. The person pushing the cart had killed both Doc Finn and Jack, and since I'd become an obstacle, I was sure to be next.

When the cart went over a bump, I allowed myself to fall on my side. Even that was an effort, as was the attempt to put fingers down my throat.

"You'll be my fourth victim," said Craig. "I did too much partying in Trinidad, too many drugs, didn't get my medical degree. But old Craig Miller, the real Craig Miller, he didn't care. That nerd was so happy to have a cool, popular friend! So when we were in Peru, it was easy enough to push him off a cliff. By the time I'd hiked out, then returned with help, Craig's body was swollen, darkened, unrecognizable. I said it was my dear friend, Tim Anderson. All I had to do was fix his ID to look more like me, steal his diploma, and I was on my way."

I stuck my fingers down my throat and pushed.

Nothing. At least I made a retching sound, which fake Craig found funny.

"Everything was going just. fine until Doc Finn came sniffing around," he continued jovially. "He just couldn't leave well enough alone. Couldn't stay in retirement. Couldn't keep his trap shut. Yeah, that was the worst part. He told my dear fiancée that she shouldn't marry me. Lucky for me, he didn't give her a reason."

The argument out at the spa. Isabelle had been partially right. Doc Finn and Billie had been fighting not about the wedding, but about the marriage, period.

"But Billie," fake Craig went on, "felt duty bound to tell me all about it. Billie likes having someone take care of her; someone who isn't her mother. And I liked the idea of having all of Charlotte's money sooner rather than later. So I stole a pair of Charlotte's shoes to plant in Finn's car to attract the police's attention. Charlotte hated Doc Finn, too, because he was always taking Jack away on expeditions that didn't include her. I put the shoes in Finn's car once I ran him off the road, after I managed to get Finn called down to Southwest Hospital. And by the way! That was your first mistake. You had Yolanda lie to that greedy bastard, Victor Lane, and say she was in Southwest Hospital with appendicitis. Guess how hard it was for me to check that she wasn't there at all? Not hard in the slightest."

I groaned as he pushed the cart over a large rock.

"Your second mistake, Miss Caterer, was not doing

research on what brings people back to a place that serves food! I bet you think you knew all about that. Well, see, in China there was a restaurant that was really popular. Really, *really* popular, with lines of customers stretching down the street. Everyone said the food made them feel so good. No wonder, either. The food was laced with opium, and that's what gave Victor Lane the idea to make a killing here, if you'll pardon the expression, doing the same thing, but with different drugs."

A rotten-egg scent reached my nostrils. We were close to the hot springs pool, the same one that had been closed since Sunday, when I'd dropped the load holding Craig and Billie's dishes and glasses. Finally, finally, the sulfurous odor, plus my own attempts made me throw up.

"All out!" fake Craig said joyfully. He bumped the laundry cart to a stop, and once again I retched. "Girl, what are you doing?" he cried. "Don't tell me I'm making you sick! A doctor's not supposed to make folks sick!" He dumped the cart on its side, and I rolled out. "You know," he said, "I've never drowned anyone before. Push, bump, poison. This is a first. All right, in you go."

Just having a chance to breathe outside of the cart made me feel a tad better. Plus—was it wishful thinking or reality?—I was feeling stronger since I'd managed to clear out my gut a bit.

But I didn't act strong. I remained limp while the man I'd known as Craig Miller grunted and groaned as he dragged me to the edge of the pool. But I would *not* allow him to hold my head underwater until I drowned.

When I felt the relatively smooth concrete flooring under my behind, I took the deepest breath I could manage and rolled myself into the scalding water, which woke me up even further, thank God.

I allowed myself to go down like deadweight. As Craig's hands thrashed about trying to get purchase on my hair, I went completely under. Darkness had fallen, and the pool was unlit. So there was no way, or at least I hoped there was no way, he would be able to tell where I was.

I pushed off from the side and was able to come above the water for a moment, to take another deep breath. Craig cursed, stretching his arm out to grab me.

But I knew how to dive . . . downward. I was aware that I would have only one chance. My hands groped the bottom of the pool for a shard, a piece of that blasted china, a chunk of glass . . . and then my right hand closed around a large piece of broken dish. I felt for the sharp side even as Craig's hands splashed furiously to try to get me.

It felt as if my lungs were bursting. But I found the very bottom of the pool and crouched on it, because I knew I would need all my strength to push up, and have good aim.

I thought of Arch; of Tom; of dear Doc Finn; of my sweet godfather, Jack, and pushed hard, up, up, up to the surface, where Craig was so startled to see me that he didn't think to protect his face. In the fading light, I aimed straight for his eyes.

I missed them. But the broken dish sank deeply into his cheek. I pushed the sharp piece in as hard as I could, while Craig screamed in agony. He stopped trying to grab me, and brought both hands up to his face, which was streaming with blood.

I pushed myself clumsily out of the pool and called for help. My voice came out as a squawk. Drenched, scalded, and furious, I struggled with the gate to the pool and tumbled on to the walkway. My right hand with the broken dish was covered in blood. Boyd was already racing up the path toward me, shaking his head.

Behind him, to my surprise, came Billie Attenborough. "Have you seen Craig? Is he in there? This cop would only look for *you,* instead of helping *me.*" She muscled past me into the pool area and saw Craig, bleeding, on the ground. He was shrieking unintelligibly. "Goldy!" cried Billie. "What have you done to my husband?" She eyed me furiously.

I tried to say, "Nothing he didn't deserve," but I was still having trouble talking.

Two weeks later, we packed a reunion picnic lunch for Norman O'Neal, Ceci, and Lissa at the Mountainside Rehabilitation Center. Marla, who had "missed all the action at the spa," as she put it, had insisted on bringing a basket of fresh farmers' market fruit.

"Alcoholics love sugar," she confided to me. "In

fact, they need it." She frowned at the nectarines and peaches. "Maybe I should have brought something chocolate."

"I already did that," I said. In our cooler I'd packed a dessert made with vanilla ice-cream sandwiched between layers of a chocolate Bundt cake, which I'd glazed with more chocolate, then frozen hard. I was calling the confection Black-and-White Cake.

Black and white. A description of this case? Yes, if you thought only of the greed that had led Craig Miller/Tim Anderson to kill and kill and kill again. Billie had been greedy to be married to a doctor, and she'd been sufficiently flaky, temperamental, and spoiled not to notice that her groom didn't really love her. She'd already filed for divorce, and the last I heard, she had signed up for an Internet dating service.

After the memorial service for Doc Finn, Father Pete told me when the service for Jack would be. I had thought my grieving was over, but I cried anyway. When my godfather died, I'd believed that staying home and doing nothing but cry was not the way to mourn. I'd gotten out there in the world to figure out what had happened.

Craig Miller wasn't a real doctor, and he'd been incorrect in his diagnoses of patients, some of whom had gone straight to old, reliable Doc Finn for help. They'd brought tales of other patients being misdiagnosed, friends who were exhibiting signs of drug withdrawal after visiting Gold Gulch Spa. Doc Finn had decided to investigate, and that had put him on a collision course with Craig Miller and Victor Lane.

Of course, it was easy enough for Craig Miller to make that anonymous "emergency" call from Southwest Hospital to Doc Finn, then hightail it up the canyon until he saw Finn's Cayenne coming in the opposite direction. He'd made a U-turn and hit Finn's car so hard from behind that it had catapulted into a ravine. The cops found Craig's banged-up vehicle where he'd hidden it away. Once Miller had bashed in the doctor's head with a rock, he'd taken the shoes he'd swiped from Charlotte's voluminous closet and planted them in Finn's Cayenne . . . to point the cops toward her, and away from him, as part of his plan to get her sent to prison, leaving her new son-in-law free to take her money.

Of course, getting Craig Miller indicted for murder, and Victor Lane, his partner in crime, indicted for the illegal distribution of Valium and cocaine had provided some satisfaction for me. Yes, cocaine, the lab determined! That was what Victor had used to get the spa clients moving in their morning exercise classes! That was what was in the fruit cocktail that he had insisted on cleaning up all by himself! The Furman County Sheriff's Department had discovered the drugs in the Smoothie Cabin, once they'd finally gotten the analysis back on the drugs Isabelle and I swiped. Armed with a search warrant, they'd found what they needed zipped into those packets that read chamomile (for the crushed Valium) and protein powder (for the cocaine). Blech!

In the spa trash, investigators found the bottle of

ipecac that Victor Lane had mixed into my lovely butter icing when he was alone in the kitchen. He'd
caught me not once, but twice, trying to figure out
what he kept hidden in the Smoothie Cabin. Victor
Lane had been willing to make his own clients sick
just because he sensed I was getting close to figuring
out what he was up to. Brother.

"Gold. Fin. Key." Those were the words Jack had
written for me in the hospital, shortly before he was
killed. He had wanted me to go to Gold Gulch Spa.
He'd hoped I'd find out what Finn had discovered.
And that was why he'd left the key Finn had given
him inside his house, to which he'd also given me the
key. My godfather had been addled and sick, but he'd
been determined to give me enough to go on that I
could figure out his last puzzle.

The spa was closed by order of the county health
department. Last I heard, Lucas Carmichael was trying to buy it. He put Jack's unfinished Victorian up
for sale.

A teary-eyed Charlotte Attenborough gave me a
wordless embrace before Jack's memorial service.
What was there to say? I had no idea.

But I was quite surprised when Lucas Carmichael
gave me a strong hug briefly before the service began.

"I'm sorry about everything," I said.

"It's okay," he said, then leaned into my shoulder
and sobbed. "Oh, God, I feel so awful." I gave his
back a gentle pat, but he tore away and rushed into the
church.

As we processed slowly into St. Luke's, Tom murmured to me that we were on our way to getting justice for Jack and Doc Finn. Yes, okay.

As Father Pete led the prayers, my thoughts returned to Jack's last note to me: "Finn left me this key, he said, as an insurance policy, in case something happened to him. But I don't know what it goes to, and I couldn't figure it out. Maybe you can." And I had.

But despite my reconciliation with Lucas, I didn't yet feel a sense of comfort regarding the death of his father. No, not by a long shot. Once again, Jack's words came to mind: "I've had a good run, and you were a big part of it."

He'd given me puzzles and games, and love. And I'd always worked on solving his puzzles, including the last one. And I'd loved him right back.

We prayed, and Arch, bless his heart, got up in front of the congregation and talked about how much fun Jack had been. I hadn't been up to it; nor had Lucas. Tom squeezed my hand.

Finally, at the end of the service, I thought of the last words in his note: "Wherever God sends me, I want you to know that I'll be thinking of you."

Now, when I miss my godfather, that's what I remember.

Acknowledgments

The author would like to acknowledge the help of the following people: Jim Davidson, Jeff, Rosa, Ryan, and Nicholas Davidson, with particular thanks to Rosa for help with the Spanish in the text; J. Z. Davidson; Joey Davidson; Linda, David, and Becca Ranz, with thanks for giving me a place to work in Nashville; Sandra Dijkstra, my extraordinarily hardworking agent, along with her excellent team; Carolyn Marino, my superb and kind editor; Brian Murray, Jane Friedman, and Michael Morrison, all of whom have been very supportive of Goldy; Lisa Gallagher, for the tremendous job she has done at Morrow; Dee Dee DeBartlo, Joseph Papa, Wendy Lee, and the rest of the fabulous team at Morrow/HarperCollins; Kathy Saideman, for her remarkably insightful readings of the text; Richard Staller, D.O., who always patiently answers my many medical questions; Carol Alexander, for patiently and lovingly testing all the recipes; the following writers friends, who are always willing to be supportive: Julie Kaewert, Jasmine Cresswell, Emilie Richards, Connie Laux, Karen Young Stone, and Leslie O'Kane; Ed Neiman, the wonderful chef and chief caterer of Sage Creek Foods in Evergreen; Ed's phenomenal sous-chef, the tremendously talented Dave Pruett, who patiently instructed me for hours as he allowed me to work a wedding and reception with his team; Triena Harper, who, even though she is retired from being deputy coroner of the Jefferson County Sheriff's Department, still helps me enormously; and as always, my amazingly helpful source on police procedure, Sergeant Richard Millsapps, now also retired from the Jefferson County Sheriff's Department, Golden, Colorado.

Recipes in *Fatally Flaky*

Julian's Summer Frittata

Nutcase Cranberry-Apricot Bread

Totally Unorthodox Coeur à la Crème

Heirloom Tomato Salad

Arch's Flapjacks

Figgy Piggy

Yolanda's Cuban Bread

Chilled Curried Chicken Salad

Fatally Flaky Cookies

Black-and-White Cake

Julian's Summer Frittata

8 ounces fresh broccoli
6 tablespoons best-quality extra-virgin olive oil,
    divided
1 red onion, sliced
8 ounces fresh baby spinach
8 ounces fresh mushrooms
1 bunch green onions
2 tablespoons unsalted butter
12 large eggs
1 cup heavy whipping cream
1 teaspoon kosher salt
1/2 teaspoon freshly ground black pepper
1/2 cup freshly grated Parmesan (preferred type:
    genuine Parmigiano-Reggiano), divided
1/2 cup finely chopped or grated Havarti cheese

Preheat the oven to 350°F.

Rinse the broccoli and remove the stems. On a large cutting board, chop it into bite-size morsels. Measure out 2 cups and reserve the remainder for another use.

Line a rimmed baking sheet with foil; place the broccoli on the foil and mix with 1 tablespoon of the olive oil, then put the onion on top of the broccoli and pour 2 tablespoons of oil on top. Bake for 10 minutes, stir, then return to the oven for 15 minutes, or until the broccoli is tender. Remove from oven and allow to cool slightly. (Leave the oven on.)

While the broccoli and onion are cooling, wash the spinach and steam until wilted, allowing only the water that clings to the leaves in the pot. Watch carefully; do not scorch. This only takes a couple of minutes. Drain and allow the spinach to cool. When the spinach is cool enough to handle, use paper towels to carefully wring out all liquid. Remove the spinach to a cutting board and chop it.

Clean and finely chop the mushrooms. Using a clean cloth towel that can be stained, or paper towels, wring all liquid out of the mushrooms. Clean and finely slice the green onions. Measure out ½ cup and reserve the remainder for another use.

In a large, ovenproof sauté pan, melt the butter over medium-low heat and sauté the ½ cup green onions and mushroom pieces until the mushrooms begin to separate. Remove from the heat, place in a bowl, and wipe out the pan.

In a large mixing bowl, beat the eggs until they are well blended, then blend in the cream, seasonings, ¼ cup of the Parmesan, and Havarti. Mix the cooled spinach, broccoli, onion, and green onion–mushroom mixture into the egg-cheese mixture. Over medium heat, heat the remaining 3 tablespoons of oil in the ovenproof sauté pan just until it ripples. Carefully pour the egg-cheese-vegetable mixture into the pan. Sprinkle the remaining Parmesan on top.

Place the pan in the oven and bake for approximately 25 minutes, or until the center is set.

MAKES 8 SERVINGS

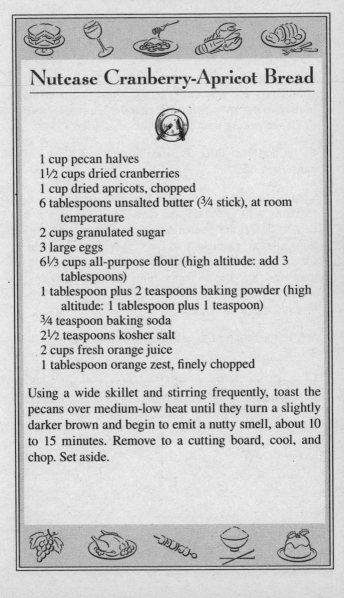

Nutcase Cranberry-Apricot Bread

1 cup pecan halves
1½ cups dried cranberries
1 cup dried apricots, chopped
6 tablespoons unsalted butter (¾ stick), at room
   temperature
2 cups granulated sugar
3 large eggs
6⅓ cups all-purpose flour (high altitude: add 3
   tablespoons)
1 tablespoon plus 2 teaspoons baking powder (high
   altitude: 1 tablespoon plus 1 teaspoon)
¾ teaspoon baking soda
2½ teaspoons kosher salt
2 cups fresh orange juice
1 tablespoon orange zest, finely chopped

Using a wide skillet and stirring frequently, toast the
pecans over medium-low heat until they turn a slightly
darker brown and begin to emit a nutty smell, about 10
to 15 minutes. Remove to a cutting board, cool, and
chop. Set aside.

Bring 3 cups of spring or tap water to a boil. Place the cranberries and apricots in a large bowl and pour the boiling water over them. Let stand 15 minutes, then drain and pat dry with paper towels. Set aside.

Butter and flour three 8½-inch by 4½-inch glass loaf pans. Set aside.

Cream the butter with the sugar until well blended. (Mixture will look like wet sand.) Add the eggs and beat well. Sift the remaining dry ingredients. Add the flour mixture alternately to the creamed mixture with the orange juice, beginning and ending with the dry ingredients. Stir in the fruits, nuts, and zest, blending well. Divide the mixture evenly among the pans. Allow to stand for 20 minutes.

While the mixture is standing, preheat the oven to 350°F.

Bake the breads for 45 to 55 minutes, or until toothpicks inserted in the loaves come out clean. Cool in the pans 10 minutes, then allow to cool completely on racks.

MAKES 3 LOAVES

Totally Unorthodox
Coeur à la Crème

2½ cups heavy whipping cream, chilled
8 ounces mascarpone cheese
1 cup confectioners' sugar, sifted
2 teaspoons pure vanilla extract
Pecan Crust (recipe follows)
1 pound fresh strawberries, rinsed, patted dry,
    hulled, and halved
1 pound fresh blueberries, rinsed and patted dry
1 cup apricot preserves*
½ cup spring water*

In a large mixing bowl, beat the cream until stiff peaks
form, about 2 to 3 minutes.

In another large mixing bowl, beat the mascarpone on
low speed just until blended. Add the sugar and vanilla
and beat only until well blended.

Using a rubber spatula, fold the whipped cream into the
cheese mixture.

Cut a piece of 2-ply cheesecloth large enough to line a large strainer or large coeur à la crème mold (the kind made with holes in the bottom, so the mixture can drain), with enough cheesecloth left over to fold up over the combined mixture.

Wet the cheesecloth and wring it out. Line the strainer or mold with the cheesecloth.

Gently spoon the mixture into the lined strainer or mold. Fold the ends of the cheesecloth up over the mixture. Suspend the strainer or mold over a bowl and put into the refrigerator. Allow to drain overnight.

To assemble the coeur, make the Pecan Crust and allow to cool completely. Spoon the chilled and drained mascarpone mixture into the cooled crust. (You may cover the coeur with plastic wrap at this point and chill up to four hours.)

Just before serving time, arrange the strawberries and blueberries in rows on top of the mascarpone mixture.* Place any leftover berries in a bowl to pass.

MAKES 12 SERVINGS

*In a small pan, heat the preserves and water and cook over medium-low heat, stirring. Remove from heat and

cool slightly. Using a pastry brush, brush this syrup over the berries, covering them completely.

Pecan Crust

   1½ cups pecan halves
   2 cups all-purpose flour
   3 tablespoons confections' sugar
   1 cup (2 sticks) unsalted butter, melted

In a large sauté pan, toast the pecans over medium-low heat, stirring constantly, until they emit a nutty scent, about 10 to 15 minutes. Place the nuts on paper towels to cool. As soon as they are cool enough to touch, place the nuts on a cutting board and roughly chop.

Preheat the oven to 350°F. Butter the bottom of a 9-by-13-inch glass pan well.

Sift the flour with the confectioners' sugar into a large bowl. Using a wooden spoon, mix in the melted butter and pecans. Pat the mixture into the bottom of the prepared pan.

Bake for 10 to 15 minutes, or until the edges of the crust begin to brown. Place on a rack to cool completely before filling.

Heirloom Tomato Salad

1 pound (16 ounces) fresh heirloom or vine-ripened
 tomatoes
12 large fresh basil leaves
2 to 3 fresh garlic cloves
8 ounces Camembert cheese
1/2 cup red wine pear vinegar or red wine vinegar
1 tablespoon smooth Dijon mustard
1/2 teaspoon granulated sugar
Sea salt and freshly ground black pepper
1 cup best-quality extra-virgin olive oil

Cut the stems out of the tomatoes. If they are large, halve them horizontally. Holding them, one at a time and cut-side down, over the sink, gently squeeze until most of the seeds come out. Place them on a cutting board and cut them in fourths if they are small, or eighths if they are large. Place in a large glass bowl.

Finely chop 8 leaves of basil and measure it. You should have 2 tablespoons. Sprinkle the chopped basil on top of the tomatoes. Push the garlic through a press and measure it. You should have 2 teaspoons. Sprinkle the garlic on top of the basil. Using a sharp serrated knife,

trim most of the rind from the cheese. Slice it into 16 equal segments, and place them on top of the garlic.

In a medium-size glass jar with a lid, combine the vinegar, mustard, sugar, and salt and pepper to taste. Using a narrow whisk or a spoon, stir well. Screw the lid onto the jar and shake well. Remove the lid, add the olive oil to the vinegar mixture, screw the lid back on, and shake vigorously, or until the dressing is completely emulsified.

Pour the dressing over the ingredients in the bowl and gently toss the salad. Cover the bowl with plastic wrap and chill the salad at least 4 hours, or up to 24 hours, before you serve it.

When you are ready to serve the salad, place it in a pretty bowl, sprinkle lightly with a bit more salt and a grating of black pepper, and arrange the remaining whole basil leaves on top, as a garnish.

MAKES 8 SERVINGS

Arch's Flapjacks

¼ cup small-curd cottage cheese
1 large egg
1 cup buttermilk
2 tablespoons vegetable oil (preferably safflower or
   canola)
1½ cups all-purpose flour
2 teaspoons baking powder
½ teaspoon baking soda
½ teaspoon salt
1 tablespoon granulated sugar (optional)
Additional vegetable oil or clarified butter
Butter, maple syrup, and/or fruit preserves

Whirl cottage cheese in blender. In a large bowl, beat
together the egg, buttermilk, and oil. Stir in the cottage
cheese and set aside.

Sift together the flour, baking powder, baking soda, salt,
and sugar, if using. Add to egg mixture and stir with a
large wooden spoon just until combined. If mixture is
too thick, add 2 to 3 tablespoons more buttermilk.

Heat a tablespoon of oil or clarified butter on a griddle or in a skillet over medium heat until the oil ripples. For each flapjack, pour in a bit less than ¼ cup batter. Cook flapjack until it is covered with bubbles and dry around the edges. Turn and cook the other side until it is golden brown.

Serve immediately with butter and toppings.

MAKES 9 FOUR-INCH FLAPJACKS

Figgy Piggy

Two 1-pound pork tenderloins, marinated overnight
    in Dijon Marinade (see below)
Figgy Stuffing (see page 399)
2 teaspoons kosher salt
2 teaspoons freshly ground black pepper
⅓ pound prosciutto, cut in strips
2 tablespoons best-quality extra-virgin olive oil
½ cup dry white wine

Dijon Marinade

½ cup smooth Dijon mustard
2 tablespoons pressed or minced garlic
½ cup dry red wine
2 tablespoons dried thyme leaves, crushed
1 teaspoon freshly ground black pepper
1 teaspoon granulated sugar
½ cup best-quality extra-virgin olive oil
1 bay leaf

For Dijon marinade: Using a wire whisk, mix together
the mustard, garlic, wine, thyme, pepper, and sugar in a

9-by-13-inch glass pan. Whisking constantly, mix in the olive oil until the mixture emulsifies. Slip the bay leaf under the surface of the mixture.

Using a sharp knife, remove the silver skin and fat from the tenderloins. Pat them dry, then place them in the marinade. Turn them to make sure they are evenly coated. Cover the pan tightly with plastic wrap and place in the refrigerator to marinate overnight.

Figgy Stuffing

  2 shallots, peeled, trimmed, and chopped
  1 tablespoon best-quality extra-virgin olive oil
  ½ pound dried figs, stems removed, chopped
  ¼ cup homemade or canned chicken stock
  2 tablespoons chopped fresh sage

For Figgy Stuffing: Using a large, ovenproof skillet, sauté the shallots in the olive oil for about 5 minutes over medium-low heat, or until they are limp and translucent. Add the figs, stock, and sage, raise the heat, and bring the mixture to a boil. Reduce the heat to low, cover the pan, and simmer until the figs are tender and the liquid is absorbed, about 5 to 10 minutes. Set the

mixture aside in a bowl to cool slightly while you prepare the tenderloins.

When you are ready to prepare the dish, preheat the
oven to 375°F. Place one of the oven racks in the middle
of the oven.

Remove the tenderloins from the marinade, wipe them
dry with paper towels, and place them side by side on a
cutting board, with the thick end of one next to the thin
end of the other. Using the flat side of a mallet or the
palm of your hand, pound the tenderloins until they are
an even 1-inch thickness. (This will make them able to
hold the stuffing.) Sprinkle them with the salt and pepper.

Spread the Figgy Stuffing mixture down the length of
one of the tenderloins. Carefully place the other tenderloin on top. Place the proscuitto strips crosswise down
the length of the tenderloin "sandwich."

Cut 4 feet of kitchen twine into four 12-inch lengths.
Carefully slide the pieces of kitchen twine crosswise, at
even widths, _underneath_ the tenderloin "sandwich." Tie
the pieces of twine and cut off any excess.

Wipe out the ovenproof sauté pan and heat 2 tablespoons of olive oil over medium-high heat, just until the

oil ripples. Add the tenderloin "sandwich," curving it to fit the pan. Sauté for three minutes. Then, using tongs, very carefully turn the tenderloin "sandwich" over to sauté for another three minutes.

Remove the skillet from the stove and add the wine to the skillet. Insert a digital meat thermometer into the pork and place it in the oven. Roast the pork until the thermometer indicates the internal temperature has reached 140°F (about 15 minutes).

Carefully remove the tenderloin "sandwich" to a platter and cover it with aluminum foil. Allow the pork to rest for 10 minutes.

Remove the foil and the pieces of twine, slice crosswise in ¾-inch slices, and serve. (You can pass a bowl with the pan drippings, if there are any.)

MAKES ABOUT 8 SERVINGS

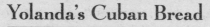

Yolanda's Cuban Bread

2 cups spring water
2 tablespoons dark brown sugar
4½ teaspoons active dry yeast (contents of two
   ¼-ounce packages)
2 tablespoons Bread Dough Enhancer (recipe
   follows)
5½ cups bread flour
¼ cup soy flour
¼ cup nonfat dry milk
2 tablespoons wheat germ
1 tablespoon sea salt
2 tablespoons (or more) poppy seeds

In a small pan, heat the spring water until an instant-read thermometer reads 110 to 115°F. Pour the water into a warm bowl and stir in the sugar and yeast. Place in a warm spot to proof, about 15 minutes. If yeast is active, the mixture will be foamy and covered with bubbles. (If it is not foamy and bubbly, toss the mixture and start over, using new yeast.)

While the yeast is proofing, mix together the Bread Dough Enhancer, flours, dry milk, wheat germ, and

salt. Place this mixture into the large bowl of a mixer with a dough hook. Add the proofed yeast mixture and stir until well combined. Insert the dough hook into the mixer and knead 10 minutes.

While the mixture is kneading, butter a large bowl. Place the mixture into the bowl, cover with buttered plastic wrap, and set aside to rise until doubled (about 30 minutes).

Remove the plastic wrap, punch the dough down, and divide it into 2 equal pieces. Shape the pieces into 2 round loaves and place them on a baking sheet lined with a silicone baking mat. Using a sharp knife, cut a 1-inch-deep cross into the loaves. Brush the loaves with water and sprinkle the poppy seeds on top.

Note: Do not preheat the oven.

Place a cake pan filled with hot water on the bottom rack of the _cold_ oven. Place the baking sheet with the loaves on the middle rack of the oven. Close the oven door and turn the oven to 400°F. Bake 30 to 40 minutes, or until the loaves are golden brown. (They will open up and look like flowers; this is normal.) Serve warm or cool.

Note: This bread does not keep well. If you are not going to serve both loaves immediately, allow the second loaf to cool completely, then freeze it in a zipped plastic freezer bag.

MAKES 2 LOAVES

Bread Dough Enhancer

1 cup wheat gluten
2 tablespoons lecithin
1 teaspoon powdered pectin
1 teaspoon ground ginger
2 tablespoons gelatin powder
½ cup nonfat dry milk

In a large bowl, mix all ingredients. Place mixture in a heavy-duty zipped plastic bag and keep in refrigerator. Mixture will last 6 months; use 1 to 2 tablespoons in all yeast bread recipes.

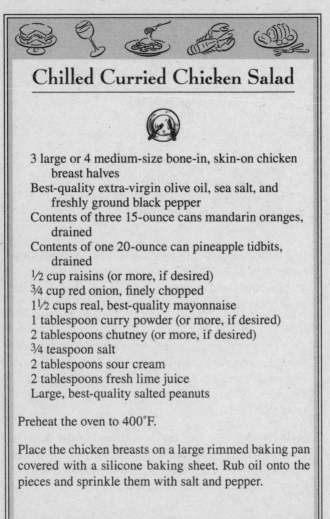

Chilled Curried Chicken Salad

3 large or 4 medium-size bone-in, skin-on chicken
   breast halves
Best-quality extra-virgin olive oil, sea salt, and
   freshly ground black pepper
Contents of three 15-ounce cans mandarin oranges,
   drained
Contents of one 20-ounce can pineapple tidbits,
   drained
½ cup raisins (or more, if desired)
¾ cup red onion, finely chopped
1½ cups real, best-quality mayonnaise
1 tablespoon curry powder (or more, if desired)
2 tablespoons chutney (or more, if desired)
¾ teaspoon salt
2 tablespoons sour cream
2 tablespoons fresh lime juice
Large, best-quality salted peanuts

Preheat the oven to 400°F.

Place the chicken breasts on a large rimmed baking pan covered with a silicone baking sheet. Rub oil onto the pieces and sprinkle them with salt and pepper.

Bake the chicken 25 to 40 minutes, or until thoroughly cooked. Check by slicing into one of the pieces, all the way to the bone. All the meat should have turned completely white, with no trace of pink. Remove the pan from the oven and allow the chicken to cool completely.

When the chicken is cool, remove the skin and bones and tear the meat into bite-size pieces. Measure it; you should have 4 cups. Reserve any remainder for another use.

In a large glass serving bowl, place the chicken, drained oranges, pineapple, raisins, and red onion.

To make the dressing: Place the mayonnaise, curry powder, chutney, salt, sour cream, and lime juice in the bowl of a food processor fitted with the steel blade. Blend all the ingredients on high, or until almost completely smooth. You may have to turn the processor off and remove the top one or two times, to scrape down the sides with a rubber spatula. This should not take more than 2 minutes.

Pour the dressing over the ingredients in the serving bowl and stir carefully but well, until all the ingredients are evenly distributed. Cover the bowl with plastic wrap and chill the salad for at least 24 hours.

Serve with a large bowl of peanuts to sprinkle on top of each serving.

MAKES 4 TO 6 SERVINGS

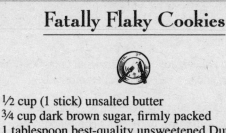

Fatally Flaky Cookies

½ cup (1 stick) unsalted butter
¾ cup dark brown sugar, firmly packed
1 tablespoon best-quality unsweetened Dutch-
   process cocoa powder (recommended brand:
   Hershey's dark European style)
1½ cups quick-cooking oats
1 tablespoon all-purpose flour (high altitude: 2 tablespoons)
1 teaspoon baking powder
¼ teaspoon sea salt
1 large egg
2 teaspoons pure vanilla extract
Filling: Either 1 quart best-quality vanilla ice cream
   (recommended brand: Häagen-Dazs)
Or Vanilla Buttercream Frosting (recipe follows)

Preheat the oven to 350°F. Line 2 rimmed cookie sheets
with silicone baking sheets.

In a large, heavy-bottomed pan, melt the butter over low
heat. Add the sugar and raise the heat to medium. Using
a wooden spoon, stir until the mixture bubbles, about 3
to 5 minutes. Remove from heat, pour into a heatproof

bowl, and set aside to cool while you prepare the rest of the ingredients.

In a large bowl, stir together the cocoa, oats, flour, baking powder, and sea salt until well combined.

In another bowl, beat together the egg and vanilla. Stir into the oat mixture until well combined. Add the cooled butter mixture and stir well.

Using a 1-tablespoon ice-cream scoop, measure out the batter onto cookie sheets, allowing at least 2 inches between cookies (they spread, and you need all the cookies to be a uniform size).

Bake the cookies, one sheet at a time, 10 to 12 minutes, or until the cookies are completely cooked. Allow to cool on the sheets for 5 minutes, then, using a wide, rubber-tipped spatula, carefully transfer the cookies to cooling racks. Allow to cool completely.

When you are ready to serve, spread 2 tablespoons of either the ice cream or the Vanilla Buttercream Frosting on the flat side of one cookie, then top with the flat side of a second cookie. Serve immediately, or freeze.

MAKES ABOUT A DOZEN SANDWICH COOKIES

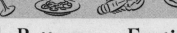

Vanilla Buttercream Frosting

½ cup (1 stick) unsalted butter, softened
2 cups confectioners' sugar, sifted
Whipping cream or milk
1 teaspoon pure vanilla extract

In a large mixing bowl, beat the butter on medium speed until it is very creamy. Slowly add the sugar, a quarter cup at a time, beating each time until the sugar is completely blended into the butter. If the frosting begins to get too stiff, add a tablespoon of cream or milk. Beat in the vanilla, and if the frosting is still too stiff, add another tablespoon of cream or milk. You want the frosting to be fairly stiff so the sandwich cookies stay together. Cover and refrigerate any unused frosting.

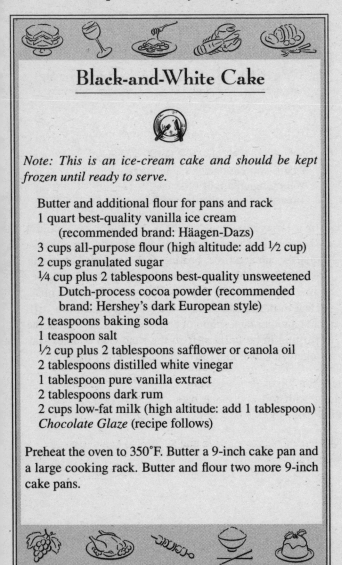

Black-and-White Cake

Note: This is an ice-cream cake and should be kept frozen until ready to serve.

Butter and additional flour for pans and rack
1 quart best-quality vanilla ice cream
 (recommended brand: Häagen-Dazs)
3 cups all-purpose flour (high altitude: add ½ cup)
2 cups granulated sugar
¼ cup plus 2 tablespoons best-quality unsweetened
 Dutch-process cocoa powder (recommended
 brand: Hershey's dark European style)
2 teaspoons baking soda
1 teaspoon salt
½ cup plus 2 tablespoons safflower or canola oil
2 tablespoons distilled white vinegar
1 tablespoon pure vanilla extract
2 tablespoons dark rum
2 cups low-fat milk (high altitude: add 1 tablespoon)
Chocolate Glaze (recipe follows)

Preheat the oven to 350°F. Butter a 9-inch cake pan and a large cooking rack. Butter and flour two more 9-inch cake pans.

Soften the ice cream in a microwave oven, just until it is spreadable. Spread it evenly in the buttered pan and place it back in the freezer.

Sift together the flour, sugar cocoa, baking soda, and salt. Sift it again into a large mixing bowl. Add the oil, vinegar, vanilla, rum, and milk. Beat on low speed for 1 minute, then scrape bowl. Beat on medium speed for 1 to 2 minutes, or until batter is completely mixed.

Pour the batter into the buttered and floured pans and bake for 25 to 35 minutes, or until a toothpick inserted in the center of one of the layers comes out clean. Cool in the pans for 10 minutes, then turn out onto the buttered rack to cool completely.

When you are ready to assemble the cake, soften the ice-cream layer slightly and unmold it onto a plate. Place one cake layer on a serving dish. Place the ice-cream layer on top. Carefully place the second cake layer on top of the ice cream. Loosely cover the whole thing with foil and place back in the freezer. Freeze until firm, about 3 hours.

Make the Chocolate Glaze and allow it to come to room temperature.

When you are ready to serve the cake, remove the serving dish from the freezer. Slowly pour it over the cake, smoothing it over the top and sides. Using a serrated knife dipped in hot water and wiped dry, cut the cake. Refreeze any unused portions.

MAKES 12 LARGE SERVINGS

Chocolate Glaze

10 ounces best-quality bittersweet chocolate
(recommended brand: Godiva dark)
10 ounces (2½ sticks) unsalted butter
3 tablespoons light corn syrup

Using a sharp knife, chop the chocolate. Place it and the butter in the top of a double boiler. Bring 2 inches of water to a boil in the *bottom* of the double boiler, and place the pan with the chocolate and butter on top. Place the double boiler over high heat and stir occasionally until the butter and chocolate are melted. Remove the top pan from the heat and whisk in the corn syrup. Allow to come to room temperature before pouring on the cake.